As the fourth child in a busy household, Holly was often left to entertain herself. She wasn't cool enough to hang out with her oldest siblings, and she wasn't a good enough goalie to hang out with her younger sibling. Luckily, she quickly found the world of books and since then, she has never looked back. As a kid, Holly often went to sleep with at least four books underneath her pillow just in case she needed them. And she often did. Books have saved her time and time again.

After a stint working at a literary agency, then a stint working at a big-four publisher, and then a stint working as a book buyer, Holly made the terrible decision to become a management consultant. After four years, and still no idea what the job actually entailed, books saved her once again. She wrote her first novel *Just Friends* (published by Transworld in 2020) when she needed to escape. Her second novel, *The Mix-Up*, followed in 2021.

She is currently working as a freelance editor and writer, and lives in the outskirts of Oxford with her dog, who she lovingly named Schitthead (Ted) after the best TV programme known to man. She is fuelled by baked goods and a need to make people laugh.

If you want to get to know Holly (and Ted) better, follow her over on Instagram (@by.holly.mcculloch) where she mainly shares dog photos and curates memes.

Also by Holly McCulloch

Just Friends
The Mix-Up

THE ICK

HOLLY McCULLOCH

ЯENE
GADE

RENEGADE BOOKS

First published in Great Britain in 2025 by Renegade Books

1 3 5 7 9 10 8 6 4 2

Copyright © Holly McCulloch 2025

The moral right of the author has been asserted.

All characters and events in this publication, other than those clearly in the public domain, are fictitious and any resemblance to real persons, living or dead, is purely coincidental.

All rights reserved.
No part of this publication may be reproduced, stored in a retrieval system, or transmitted, in any form or by any means, without the prior permission in writing of the publisher, nor be otherwise circulated in any form of binding or cover other than that in which it is published and without a similar condition including this condition being imposed on the subsequent purchaser.

A CIP catalogue record for this book
is available from the British Library.

Paperback ISBN 978-1-408-74885-5

Typeset in Caslon by M Rules
Printed and bound in Great Britain by
Clays Ltd, Elcograf S.p.A

Papers used by Renegade Books are from well-managed forests
and other responsible sources.

Renegade Books
An imprint of
Dialogue
Carmelite House
50 Victoria Embankment
London EC4Y 0DZ

The authorised representative
in the EEA is
Hachette Ireland
8 Castlecourt Centre
Dublin 15, D15 XTP3, Ireland
(email: info@hbgi.ie)

www.dialoguebooks.co.uk

Dialogue, part of Little, Brown Book Group Limited,
an Hachette UK company.

To my steamboats,
for being absolute dreamboats x

Chapter 1

On her way here, walking to the pub along the bustling London streets, Gem had felt that something good was coming her way. She has always noted that spring and the joy it brings can have a halo effect on the rest of your life. People laugh more in spring. Your skin brightens. Your feet stop feeling so tired. Sandwich shops have your favourite lunch option available. Coffee tastes sweeter.

And, as Gem is in the midst of discovering, your love life thrives.

Finally, after all of the toads – calling them frogs is too generous – Gem has met her prince, and he comes in a six-foot-two-inch package, just like she has always hoped he would.

She has the perfect view of Atlas as he sits opposite her. Unlike Gem, who never quite knows what to wear, especially in the transitional months, Atlas has nailed office casual. He's wearing a lightweight, teal jumper and fashionably casual trousers in a tonally complimentary, yet darker colour. He has a dimple just underneath his right eye and strong-looking hands that wouldn't look out of place chopping wood for a campfire.

The door to the Dog and Duck opens and once again, he is bathed in glorious sunshine. If she were the sun, she would shine on him too. Gem has always believed that symmetry is a sign of beauty, but Atlas's face must be the exception to the rule. It is ever so slightly lopsided, but instead of detracting from his good looks, it adds to them. It makes him seem like a smile is only ever millimetres away. His hair is thick and luscious and deliciously dark brown, and Gem has to stop herself from pushing back the soft curl that keeps escaping at the front of his face. But by far her favourite feature is his eyes. The blue gets darker the closer you get to the iris, drawing you in.

'So, Gem, tell me . . .' His voice is the ideal mix of silky baritone and East End. He's masculine, but cheeky.

'Tell you what?' Gem's voice, meanwhile, is coming out a little too wispy for her liking. As though she might faint.

As he smiles, Gem notes that the left side of his mouth always ticks up first.

He is so perfect that he makes Gem wish she had made more of an effort – with both the choice of date location and her outfit. She is wearing one of precisely five work outfits that she owns – all of which are made suitable for the season via the appropriate dernier of tight and a simple change of shoe. Today's dress is fitted on the top and concertinaed in the skirt. She's let her hair down, out of its usual workday bun, but her red locks do little to jazz up the faded black dress.

She feels a little bit like the pub looks.

The Dog and Duck is a typical post-work City haunt, full of people who all look and dress the same. There are repro paintings of bucolic hunting scenes on the walls, not that anyone in here has smelt fresh air for years. Their lungs are so used to the fumes of Commercial Road that they would probably get the bends if they travelled outside the M25. Having lived in London her whole life, Gem wouldn't have it any other way.

Atlas's shrug is as cool as his whole exterior in general. 'Anything you like.'

Usually, Gem would find this kind of ridiculous request too vapid to answer. But Atlas is perfect, so instead she smiles her most flirtatious smile. Every woman has one. In Gem's case, her eyes go slightly to the side, and she half hides behind a shoulder.

'Anything?'

'Anything.' The intensity in his eyes is almost too much.

Her smile widens. 'I'd love another glass of wine.'

At Gem's cheeky misdirection, he laughs. It is deep and rumbling, and his whole body joins in. God, even his laugh has Gem praying.

'Well,' he winks at her before starting to stand up.

He moves his body with the ease of someone who is in complete control of all of his limbs. Gem imagines that he's one of those gifted humans who can draw a perfectly straight line without any help. 'That is wonderful timing.' He picks up his beer, which is still half full, and takes a sip. 'Because I need another drink too.' Now fully standing, he points at Gem's glass. 'You had the Tempranillo, I believe?'

Gem swoons. He remembers her wine preference. 'I did.'

'Same again? Large?' The second question is accompanied by a raise of the eyebrow. It's an unspoken rule that you only ever get a second drink, let alone a large second drink, if you are interested in the other person.

'Yes, please. To both.' Internally, Gem adds, *it's a yes to everything.*

'A large Tempranillo coming right up.' And with one more wink, Atlas and his perfectly in control limbs, walk to the bar.

As soon as he turns away, Gem relaxes. She is having a great time, but her body is on high alert and her neck is starting to tire from the effort. She needs to take a breath and get control of herself. She is about three hours and two glasses of wine away from asking Atlas what he thinks of a quickie marriage in Las Vegas. They could fly this evening.

But then, even before her neck has had a chance to get completely comfortable, Atlas turns back towards her. Luckily, Gem had been watching his butt as he walked away, meaning she had early warning of his change in direction.

'Do you want anything to eat? I'm gonna get a packet of crisps too. Only had soup for lunch and I'm starving.'

The smile that had formed on Gem's mouth, ready to come up with another witty response, goes stale. Her neck finally cricks, and not because she is too alert, but because her whole body has just spasmed.

It's impossible to say what might cause the ick. They are non-transferable and nonsensical. But once Gem gets hit with it, there is no going back. And this is one of those occasions.

At his mention of soup, Gem's insides go cold. She feels as though she is fourteen again, being forced to jump into her school's outdoor swimming pool. It only ever got filled when the weather was half decent because their school was far from being well-funded enough to both have a pool *and* to heat it. And because Gem herself wasn't well-funded enough to buy a new swimming costume every year, it meant that half the time she had to swim in her underwear.

To some, soup might seem like an acceptable lunch option. But the thought of it makes Gem's toes curl. She can't shake the image of him wearing a bib and gently blowing on a spoonful of tomato and basil soup, or even worse, *butternut squash*. A little bit of liquid dripping off the bottom of the spoon and landing on the table.

Despite the emotional and physical pain she's feeling, Gem still needs to answer Atlas. He is waiting patiently, and Gem knows from experience – a lot of experience – that the best way to deal with the ick, is to do so as efficiently and as quietly as possible. She shakes her head. 'No. No, thank you. No crisps for me.'

At her answer, Atlas saunters away, but this time, Gem doesn't watch his butt as he retreats. Instead, she gets out her phone and sends a quick message.

S.O.S.xx

'Oh no, that sounds bad. You all right?'

Atlas is just on his way back from the bar with their drinks and his packet of crisps. Gem gives him a tight smile as he sits down. She mouths a silent, but very pronounced, *I'm so sorry*, and then turns ever so slightly away, phone clutched to one ear, her finger over the other ear as if she is struggling to hear. Her body language tells everyone around her, *This is a private conversation, and I am trying my hardest to end it. My friend just won't let me go.* Yet, crucially, she doesn't turn quite far enough away to keep their supposedly private conversation, private.

'I can't. I'm on a date. I can't just leave.' Gem adds in a deliberate pause and tenses her shoulders. 'There has to be someone else you can ask.' She chews her bottom lip, and glances up, briefly, at Atlas. He gives her a very big, very easy smile, then opens his crisps.

The door to the pub opens, and a loud, jovial group of friends make their way inside. The sun momentarily blinds her. The sight of spring now sickens her. No good things are coming, Spring merely tricks you into thinking they are. She turns her focus onto Atlas.

She should have known that he was *too* attractive.

While being attractive is good, being too attractive is a big no-no. Beautiful people get away with (or simply just *get*) too many things. Preferential treatment in queues. Fewer fines. More promotions. Plus, there's an innate and uniquely aggravating arrogance that comes with being too good-looking.

Right on cue, he gives her a little chin nod, and winks.

Gem feels just as much revulsion towards the man in front of her as she does towards herself. To think that five minutes ago she would have found that wink attractive.

It gives her hives.

Although ostensibly perfect, Atlas is undeniably completely wrong for Gem. She collects icks the way other people collect loyalty card points, and five minutes ago, Atlas added another to her collection.

She barely manages to supress a shudder.

She has to get out of here.

On the other end of the phone, she can hear Shanti, her housemate, her friend and currently also her saviour, eating popcorn.

'Can I hang up now?' Shanti's voice is distracted, possibly even bored. Gem can hear the TV in the background. The first few times they'd acted out this scene, Shanti had come up with some pretty good emergencies and had been quite believable. Once she even broke a bowl, hoping the sound effects would travel through the phone, right into the ears of Gem's date. But now, having run through variations of this scene over a hundred times, her performance is a little stale.

Gem's, however, remains as animated as ever. It has to. She has a live audience. She lets her shoulders droop as if she's finally given up and releases a sigh.

'OK, OK. I'm coming.'

Her act is so convincing, she almost believes it herself. If she didn't need financial stability, Gem would consider being an actress. As it is, she's stuck in accounting. 'I'll be there in twenty minutes.' And with that, she hangs up and turns back fully to face Atlas.

'I'm so sorry. That's my housemate, Shanti. She's ...' Gem pauses. *Shit*. The need to escape has come on so suddenly she's forgotten to come up with an actual excuse. 'Had an emergency.' There's no time to think of anything better. She needs to leave quickly, otherwise she might scream.

'I could help. I'm really good in an emergency.' Atlas takes a sip of his second beer before putting it back down – as though being inebriated is a good idea when you need quick reactions, fake scenario or not. 'Let me come with you.'

'Oh, God, no.' Even with the din of the surroundings, Gem can tell that her answer came out a little too quickly, and far too forcefully. But what kind of person says they're good in an emergency? It's exactly the kind of weird brag that men think is attractive. Like boasting about being able to beatbox. Plus, what is a man who eats soup for lunch really going to contribute to an emergency? A spoon?

'That's not a good idea.'

'Why not?'

Gem is already halfway out of her seat. The audacity of this man! 'It's ... an embarrassing emergency.'

'Well, now you have to tell me what's happened.' The hint of humour in his voice is echoed by a hint of a smile on his lips, almost as though he wants to make this as uncomfortable as possible for her.

She narrows her eyes at him.

'No, I don't.'

'Yes, you do.' Apparently, he won't take no for an answer – another ick. 'If you're going to abandon me here, in this awful pub with no company and two-and-a-half drinks to get through, the least you can do is tell me what embarrassing thing has happened.' He pauses, a smile looking even closer to appearing now than it did before. He is definitely goading her.

But Gem can play his game, too.

'She's . . .' But as hard as she tries, Gem's brain is still coming up blank. She looks around the pub for inspiration. Unfortunately, the first thing she sees is a painting of a dog that is just about to jump over a hedge. 'She's gotten stuck in a bush.' And then, sensing this isn't quite enough, she looks back to the dog which isn't wearing a collar and adds, 'Naked.'

Even Gem wouldn't blame Atlas if he pulled her up on this.

Yet for some unknown reason, he just nods. Gem can't tell if she is relieved or a little disappointed.

Either way, she's finally released. She picks up her bag, reaches in for her wallet and takes out a tenner. She must be the only person who still carries around cash, but in severe cases of the ick, waiting for a card machine takes too much time.

'Here. This is for my drink.'

She slaps the money on the table and walks out of the pub as quickly as possible, without looking back.

Chapter 2

Standing in the middle of an overstuffed corner shop is one of Gem's favourite pastimes. It's the only time she doesn't feel overwhelmed by the amount of choice on offer, and instead relishes it. She could stand here for hours. Indeed, if you add up all the time she's spent in here, she *has* stood here for hours. Every time she sees the bright lights of its signage, she knows she is nearly home. They call out to her like a lighthouse, guiding her way. This shop is the only place where time stays still, and not only because the stock has a lackadaisical attitude towards expiry dates. The shop has looked the same for the last fifteen years, and unlike all of the other local supermarkets, there isn't a self-checkout in sight.

Unlike Atlas who she imagines loves a self-checkout, Gem isn't a vain person. She rarely looks at her reflection, especially late in the day. As soon as she leaves work, she starts shedding layers. This close to home, she knows that along with her hair, now starting to frizz, her cheeks will be wearing more mascara than her eyelashes, and she wouldn't be surprised if she found at least one ladder in her tights. It's like her body is trying to break free from the pretend skin she wears during the day.

A ping sounds from somewhere in her bag. She refuses to be the type of person who answers every phone call simply because a piece of technology is screaming at her, but she will happily check a text.

Hey. Hope your flatmate is OK.x

She's mildly surprised that Atlas has messaged her, especially after she ran away and used an extremely weak and obviously fake excuse, but not enough to reply. She puts her phone back in her bag. He'll get the message soon enough. He probably just wants to make her feel bad. But it's not her fault that she had a visceral reaction to his taste for soup.

Now, far from rushing home to Shanti after her fictional emergency of being stuck in a bush, she's been standing in the middle of what she assumes is the appetiser section for a solid fifteen minutes. The overhead too-bright lights are flickering, and she doesn't know what most of the food is, but that's part of the fun. The only thing she steers away from is the meat aisle.

The cardboard boxes that are stacked on the shop floor make it difficult to see everything on offer. It wouldn't be so bad if the boxes were just boxes, but they've slowly morphed into shelf units, and now not only keep food in them, but also display food on top of them. She finally decides on a jar of sauerkraut that she can just about reach. It's the least exciting option, and she knows that its novelty will wear off after a couple of servings, but she vaguely remembers reading an article about it being good for your gut. Something to do with fermentation. She can already imagine the jar lingering in the back of the cupboard along with her unused tins of jackfruit. But still, she picks it up.

'Just this, please.' She places the measly offering onto the counter.

Gem and Shanti have lived in the same flat for the last four years, and no matter what time they visit this shop, the same guy is always behind the counter. They are pretty sure they once heard someone call him Jay, but they have never been able to confirm this; he is yet to speak a single word to either of them. They have a competition going to see who can get him to talk first. Whoever wins gets control of the TV for a month. If you get him to smile, you get control of the TV *and* all of your laundry done (including putting it away, which is arguably the worst part). If you get him to laugh, the whole flat is yours for the rest of time, including their much-coveted novelty pig salt and pepper shakers.

With this in mind, Gem smiles at him and points towards the jar. 'I've heard it's really good for your digestion.'

No response.

She's not overly surprised. It isn't the strongest line.

He rings the price up on the machine.

The corner shop is the other reason Gem still carries physical money. You can pay on card, but rumour has it, Jay prefers cash. So, for the second time this evening, but under significantly more pleasant circumstances, she reaches into her bag for her wallet. The jar costs an illogical £3.87, so she gets out £4 and puts it on the counter.

'You can keep the change.' She says it in her happiest voice, but still gets absolutely no reaction.

But Gem doesn't let this rile her. Or at least she doesn't let the fact she is riled show. Instead, like every other semi-functioning adult she knows, she lets her feelings fester and picks up the jar without another word. Smiling as wide as she can.

Chapter 3

The last part of Gem's journey home always takes a little bit longer than it should. She blames it on the fact that it's slightly uphill. Her legs are protesting by the time she reaches the harsh concrete steps that lead up to the front door of their building. Today, the final leg of her journey is made better by the almost blooming blossoms, but by far Gem's favourite thing about this time of year is that feeling of walking into a room and not having to put a light on to see where she's going.

As usual, the key sticks slightly in the lock. She tries not to add it to her growing list of grievances, but sometimes it feels as if the universe is trying – in really small, really passive-aggressive, but *really* incessant ways – to keep her from getting home and being able to relax. But finally, with a shoulder to the door, she's inside.

No matter how much Sensual Sandalwood air freshener they use, the shared entranceway always smells of food, and not in a good, mouth-watering way. It's in the way that will cling on to your clothes and block your pores, leading to a post-pubescent breakout. The yellow tinge of the overhead light, the magnolia walls that were last painted in the nineties, and the bright red carpet, which she hopes was only chosen because it was heavily discounted, do nothing but add to the clogged feeling of the hall.

Even so, it's a welcome sight. Just one more door and she's home.

As soon as she's inside, her jaw relaxes – not all the way because there is still a lot to be anxious about and being permanently slightly tense is now a habit – but enough that her teeth no longer hurt. The combination of knowing she is about to see someone she loves, the smell from Shanti's oil diffuser and the knowledge that she can now take off her shoes makes Gem happy. She plonks the jar down on the table in the kitchen and looks through to the lounge.

Their kitchen is tiny. Their whole flat is pretty small, but it has a couple of fun features that make up for the lack of space. And a few that don't. It was cheaply converted from a lovely single-dwelling townhouse, so it comes with bubbling linoleum and walls so thin (despite the layers of embossed wallpaper that nobody is brave enough to take down in case half the plaster comes with it) that Gem knows exactly how much sex their next-door neighbour is having, and also when they're about to have it. They've made a playlist that starts with 'All of Me' by John Legend and ends with 'Cbat' by Hudson Mohawke.

She's never actually seen them, but at this point, it's probably a good thing. She knows far too much about their sex life to look them in the eye without blushing. In an act of friendly neighbourly hypocrisy, they sometimes even bang on the walls to let Gem and Shanti know when they're making too much noise. Not that either one of them has had sex in months, if not years. Gem is too picky, and Shanti far too busy.

By far the best feature of their flat is the hatch that Gem is now hanging through. It sits between the kitchen and the lounge, and everything passes through it. Food. Drinks. Phone chargers. Conversation. Even furniture. The hallway is so narrow that the hatch is the only way to get the dining table from the kitchen into the lounge. It's not something they do often, only when they have people over for a fancy dinner. Otherwise, it's usually just the two of them, sitting on the sofa and eating with teaspoons from bowls that are nestled on top of decorative cushions.

As she looks through, Gem can see her flatmate wrapped up like a caterpillar in her blanket, only her head visible.

When she first saw Shanti at the other end of a classroom more than twenty years ago, Gem knew they were going to be friends. First, because they had the same type of bag – two sports backpacks in a sea of shoulder bags – and second, because Gem needed to know what Shanti did to make her hair so glossy. Gem's hair, which has always been a little difficult to tame, is the polar opposite of Shanti's beautifully tamed locks. Her friend's hair only ever looks perfectly conditioned. Her wide eyes, heart-shaped lips and long limbs only add to her overall beauty. She's the kind of person who makes life look easy. Gem would hate her if she didn't love her so much.

'Did you get a smile?'

'Not even a grunt.'

At Gem's answer, Shanti doesn't look away from the TV, but Gem can see her face scrunch up in disappointment. The Jay Challenge has been going on for so long now that they just want one of them to break him. Of course, it would be difficult for either of them to prove they had actually managed to get any words out of him, but they don't lie. They may have secrets from other people, but never each other.

Gem leans further into the lounge, resting her elbows on the frame, the top half of her body in a completely different room to the rest of her. The lounge is the best room in the house, partly because it contains two sofas – one for each of them – but mainly because a lot of bonding has been done there.

'You want a toastie?'

Eyes still on the TV, Shanti shakes her head. 'No, thanks. I've already eaten.'

Shanti stopped joining in on the toastie action after a particularly questionable combination. Although Gem will admit that the banana and bacon pairing backfired, she is still a firm believer that every food item is made better by being sandwiched between two layers of carbs and turned slightly crunchy. It's an opinion that Shanti frequently disagrees with.

Feet still crying despite now being free, Gem gets to work, turning the toastie maker on before she's even decided what to put into it. It's a risky move, but it helps ensure she will eat within the next three hours, instead of just *thinking* about it. On tonight's menu, she will definitely be having sauerkraut, but she's unsure what it goes with. She grabs the jar on the way to the cupboard, whacking the lid hard against the counter, before twisting it open.

'Ugh.'

One whiff is all she needs to know that sauerkraut won't go with anything. The only way to describe it is *tangy*. Like an earthy vinegar. It smells like it has already gone bad. Gem gives it another strong, brave sniff, just in case it gets better. It doesn't. She immediately puts it down.

Is it really worth living to one hundred, if your days have to be full of fermented cabbage?

Perturbed, but stubborn, she opens up the cupboard, hoping for inspiration.

Obviously, she will be adding some cheese, as cheese fixes everything – even Gem's perpetual fear that she's going to be alone forever unless she eventually finds somewhere to rent that allows pets. While she could leave it there – *maybe* adding a bit of mustard for a kick – all of a sudden, she feels brave. She reaches into the cupboard and pulls out a tin of beans.

Too busy working out how to layer the ingredients so there's the least chance of them falling out straight away, Gem doesn't notice Shanti until she's right behind her.

'You've put beans into your toastie?'

Gem jumps.

'Fucking hell, Tee! *Don't* sneak up on me like that.'

'That must be one of your bravest combinations yet.'

Grimacing, Shanti retreats and sits down at the table, slightly shuffling as she goes, the blanket still wrapped around her body. She chooses the chair that is furthest away from the toastie maker.

'So ... how did the date go?' she asks, like Gem didn't just use one of her lifelines to phone a friend.

'You know it went badly. They're all the same.' Gem checks on the Cheddar. Although she experiments with the other ingredients in her toasties, she only ever uses Cheddar. It has the perfect melting style, although from the looks of things, it's not quite melty enough yet.

'Everyone seems fine on paper.' Although of course she mainly looks at them through a screen. 'But there is always something.'

'What was it this time?'

It's Gem's turn to grimace. 'His lunch of choice is *soup*.' From her tone, you'd think she'd just said he microwaves fish.

Shanti's perfectly shaped eyebrows draw closer together, like a loose thread being pulled in a knitted jumper. 'But you eat soup.'

Gem can't stop the full body shiver that comes over her. The issue with the ick, she has found, is that you either get it or you don't. Like marmite. Or the obsession with Harry Styles. And between the two of them, Shanti has always been the more logical one. But the ick isn't logical.

After one more quick cheese check, Gem sits down opposite her friend, giving her sandwich a bit more time. 'I know, and don't ask me to explain it, but the idea just really turns me off.'

'You are ridiculous.' There is a lack of amusement in Shanti's voice.

'You have to admit, it's weird.'

Shanti's silence says more than any words could. But it's her eyes that are doing even more of the talking; they narrow just a little bit.

Gem might've only just sat down, but she gets back up to check on her toastie so she can escape Shanti's stare.

'Listen, I know you don't get it, but my reaction to the soup is a sign. The ick is my intuition telling me that we're not compatible. It's a warning system. There is something deeply wrong with him. Probably even dangerous.' She's facing away but Shanti's eye roll is so pronounced, Gem can feel it.

If it had been ten seconds earlier, Gem would have at least considered fighting her corner a bit more enthusiastically, but her dinner is ready. She doesn't even need to check on the cheese. Much like her ick, her intuition is telling Gem that her toastie is now at the pinnacle of crunch and melt. She picks up the bendy spatula – the one that's reserved specifically for one purpose: to expertly move her toastie to the plate. Not even a single bean escapes during the transfer. She grins at the mini win.

Most people Gem's age are out chasing the Big Wins. A new job. A healthy relationship. A dog. A baby. A third Iron Man. A new, vegan restaurant that only serves coffee previously pooped out by an endangered species of cat.

But not Gem. She is just happy to be surviving. Although she would be happier still, if she could discover the perfect toastie. She turns off the machine and cleans up the small bits of spilt cheese. Melted cheese is delicious and fun, but burnt cheese is like a clingy, smelly guest that won't leave.

'So, have you chosen a topic for your paper yet?' Gem throws the question into the corner of the room, where Shanti is still cocooning.

Shanti is one of the ones after something *Big*. The Big Thing frequently changes, but at the moment she's in the final stages of training to become a Clinical Psychologist. She's explained it many times, but Gem still doesn't understand what the difference is between a psychologist, a clinical psychologist and a psychiatrist. All she knows is that becoming a clinical psychologist has made Shanti extra feisty, especially in the past month. It makes perfect sense: Gem already knows that humans are pretty horrible, so studying them in any kind of depth would make her tired and irritable too.

The lack of answer sends another prickle down Gem's spine. In all the years they have known each other, Shanti has never been without an answer. She is always the most prepared person in the room, even when she is faking it. Gem risks a step away from her dinner and looks at her friend.

As soon as she sees Shanti, she is instantly put on edge.

There is no scowl, no anger, no frustration to be seen. Instead, there is a wide smile. Most people would think this is a good sign. But Gem knows Shanti's facial expressions better than her own.

'What? What's happening? What's wrong?'

Shanti is still smiling. 'Nothing's wrong. In fact, I've come up with a great topic. It's a really good idea. Nobody else is doing it.'

'Oh, cool!' Although there's nothing overtly wrong with anything that Shanti is saying, Gem's hairs are still standing to attention. Her intuition is telling her to run, even more so than with the soup. And she would run if she could, but apart from the fact she doesn't really have anywhere to go, her feet are tired, and she is now really quite hungry.

So instead, she sits down opposite Shanti, loaded plate in front of her. 'So, what's the topic?'

The delay does nothing for Gem's nerves.

'Well, actually . . . *you* made me think of it.'

Gem picks up her toastie, keeping it level in a way that showcases her expertise.

'Oh, why, thank you. I can be quite inspirational.' She goes to take a bite, then pauses, as she slightly rewinds. 'Wait, how do you mean?' Gem's eyes are now glued to her friend, leaving her sandwich to tilt slightly. A bean takes the opportunity to escape.

'When I tell you, just bear in mind that we've been friends for years, and please believe me when I say that I kinda suggested the idea jokingly. I didn't think it would gain as much interest from my tutor, but she is *really* interested, and I don't think I could change the topic now even if I wanted to.'

Gem laughs. 'You're making me nervous, Tee. Just tell me what it is.'

Shanti's smile subtly changes, looking much more like a grimace. 'I need you to keep dating someone until you get past the ick. I want to test whether or not intuition is real.'

Chapter 4

'So what do you say?' There's hope in Shanti's voice.

'To what?'

Shanti squints at her friend. 'To the idea of me studying the ick for my final paper and you being one of the participants.'

Gem inhales, and the whole room inhales with her.

'You mean using me as a lab rat as though I'm something completely bizarre?'

'Yes?' The hope in Shanti's voice is weaker than it was a moment before. Like Gem's sanity, it is hanging on by a thread.

Gem shakes her head precisely once. 'Absolutely not. No.'

Shanti's face falls. 'Oh, come on! You have to admit, it would make a really interesting topic.'

'Well, I'm glad you find my love life so entertaining.'

Shanti's head tilts to one side. 'You know that's not what I mean. Yes, you are the inspiration behind the idea, which is why I think it would be really cool for you to take part in the study, but I'd also be observing other people's intuition too.'

Gem may not be learning about human behaviour or whatever it is Shanti's trying to do, but she can still read her best friend pretty well. 'Listen, Tee. I know that you think the idea of "the ick" is ridiculous, but *I* believe it. I believe that it's my body's way of telling me who I am or am not compatible with. When I should or shouldn't run.'

'But what if the ick isn't your intuition? What if it's something else?'

'Like what?' Another bean escapes the toastie.

Shanti shrugs, and Gem knows she is about to get a taster therapy session whether she wants one or not. 'People often have strong reactions to situations for deeper reasons than simply not liking something. The brain is an amazing, but complicated organ, and it frequently creates memory pathways between particular events and corresponding reactions.'

For the second time in two minutes, a silence falls over the kitchen.

But not for long. 'I don't know what any of that means,' she says finally, 'but I think it's bollocks.' Gem directs her attention back to her food. The only thing worse than non-melted cheese in a toastie, is cheese that has rehardened.

'Well, I guess that's what the study would try to find out.'

Gem should have known that something like this was coming her way. After all, they know everything about each other. Even their menstrual cycles are synced. So while Gem knows that she might be adventurous in terms of her sandwich fillings, she also knows that Shanti is the real challenger. It can be tiring for Gem to keep up.

A lot is now riding on the success of her gastronomic combination. Gem worries that not even the tastiest toastie will be able to salvage her day.

'You have to admit that for someone who claims to want to be in a relationship, you find a lot of excuses to stay single,' Shanti continues. 'All of your icks are completely ridiculous. Nobody stops dating someone because they eat soup. At this rate, you're going to be alone forever.'

Gem's scowl entrenches a little deeper, but luckily Shanti's next words follow quickly enough to take the sting out of the previous ones.

'Well, not *alone* alone, because you'll always have me.'

Gem's urge to kill her best friend lessens, just a little.

'I don't want to stay single. But I don't want to date just *any-one*. I want to date the right person. The person who I am meant to be with.' Before another bean escapes – and before Shanti says something else – Gem takes a bite of her toastie.

Unlike some people, Gem has learnt not to judge a toastie too quickly, but in this case, she's glad that she didn't take a bigger bite. A bigger bite would mean more sauerkraut, and from Gem's admittedly limited experience, this wouldn't be a good thing. If she's being kind, Gem would say that sauerkraut is an acquired taste. If she's being optimistic, she would say that it tastes *healthy*. If she's being honest, it tastes like something you find in the back of the fridge and should throw away. Somehow, it's still cold even though all the other ingredients around it have warmed up. It's as though it's not quite of this world.

The only good thing about the sauerkraut is that it takes quite a long time to chew, which also gives her more time to think.

Of course, Gem wants to be in a relationship. Being in a relationship makes sense.

Apart from anything, it is cheaper. Sure, in the short term you have a lot of outgoings, but in the medium- to long-term, being in a relationship is cost efficient. She's done the maths, and she has the spreadsheet to back up her workings.

And then there are all of the other benefits that have nothing to do with money. As a single woman you're at the bottom of the pavement hierarchy. You're the one who's expected to move out of the way of oncoming traffic as everybody else has priority. But once you're in a relationship, people will move around you. Excluding mothers, children and old people, of course. Plus, you no longer have to handle social situations alone. You have someone to share the boring chores with, like taking out the bins and changing the bedsheets. You have someone to share ideas with. To problem solve with. To laugh with. To blame when things go wrong.

But most importantly, you have someone who is contractually obliged to listen to even your most boring and ridiculous worries and thoughts.

'Think about it,' says Shanti. 'You go on dates all the time. It's just that this way, you'll be dating the same person for a while, instead of a new one each week.'

Gem's insides squirm.

At the sound of an incoming text, she could kiss her phone. A distraction from this conversation is very welcome. She looks over at it without putting down her toastie; it's not structurally sound enough to risk being moved too much. The message is from Atlas. Her relief disappears.

Let me know if you change your mind and need my help.x

Sending a second follow-up text when the first is still unanswered is such a turnoff, and a total validation of Gem's feelings towards Atlas and her whole philosophy in general.

'The very fact you would suggest this highlights the fact that you don't understand the ick,' replies Gem. 'I can't just repeatedly hang out with someone who makes my skin scrawl. If you had ever felt the ick, you'd know that this is an impossible task.'

Shanti's eyes go wide, and her right eyebrow hitches up. It's dangerous.

'You never know. You might even prove that the ick *is* your intuition. I might be wrong.'

The hint of challenge in Shanti's voice invokes a familiar reaction in Gem. She knows that Shanti is pushing her buttons, but like a moth to the flame, Gem would be lying if she said the idea of proving Shanti wrong isn't tempting. She would love to make Shanti admit that her intuition and the ick are real.

But ... 'Still, no.'

With nothing else to give, Shanti offers one final temptation. 'You'll get paid.'

At this, Gem's focus concentrates solely on her friend. Her sandwich collapses in the blink of an eye even though she is too shocked to blink.

Money has always been a bit of a delicate subject between the two of them. Namely because Shanti has a plethora of it, and Gem doesn't. It's a good reflection of her character that Shanti could easily afford to live somewhere much nicer but doesn't because she wants to live with Gem.

Despite Shanti's typically relaxed attitude towards money and where she lives (an attitude that Gem believes only people with money can afford), it's such a delicate subject that even Shanti is rarely brave – or desperate – enough to bring up.

And with good reason.

Mainly because it never ends well.

'My answer is no.'

Chapter 5

Gem has her key out, but the front door pushes open without it.

'Mum?'

Gem tries to dull the panic in her voice. There are many, really logical reasons for the door to be open, but Gem's mind instantly goes to her mum being kidnapped and held for ransom, in which case the best she can offer in return is an old Oyster card that may still have some money on it. And a partially used jar of sauerkraut.

'Hey, love. I'm in here.'

At the sound of her mum's voice, the sense of comfort that comes from being home falls over Gem, as well as the soothing balm of relief from knowing her mother hasn't actually been kidnapped.

Still, when she shuts the door, she makes sure it clicks closed.

Gem spends most of her time at work pretending to be someone a little different to who she actually is. A little quieter, a little less openly experimental with her food options. Basically, a little less Gem all around. Her mum is the one person in the world she never has to pretend with.

Unlike Gem's flat, which had a revolving door of uncaring

tenants before she and Shanti moved in, leading to a heavy amount of wear and tear, her mum's flat is extremely well looked after. It is also a bizarre mix of both extremely minimalist and extremely colourful.

Apart from a collection of photos of Gem and her awful school artwork that's hanging on the wall in the lounge, there are absolutely no trinkets anywhere. In contrast, almost every wall is a different colour. The hallway, with its glistening white tile floor, has bright yellow walls. Her mum says she wants anyone coming into her home to feel happy as soon as they walk in. Gem's sceptical, but she can't fault her mum's choices. She smiles every time she comes home.

There is a set of three hooks for jackets hanging on the wall. Her mum's winter jacket's already there, although soon it will be time for the biannual wardrobe swap, the winter clothes getting relegated to a box under the bed until next year. But not yet. Apparently, her mum thinks it's still soup weather, too.

Gem puts her bag down on the ground, takes off her own jacket and puts it on her hook. The last one is reserved for Uncle Mike.

Her phone pings, *again*. Atlas is still messaging her, even though she is yet to reply. She looks at her phone, quickly, sees the text is, indeed, from him, and puts her phone in her dress pocket. If she wasn't already completely turned off by him, his continual messaging would do the trick. He doesn't even say anything interesting. All he had to say this time was, *Happy Wednesday* with a picture of a whale underneath it.

She walks down the hall, past the storage cupboard which contains all of the cleaning equipment and is ironically the messiest place in the house, and into the kitchen. The olive green floor, canary yellow cabinets and red accents are another colour combination that Gem initially balked at, yet once again, her mum proved her wrong. It's weird to think that the craziness of the city is just outside when it is so peaceful in here.

The only slightly out of place item is the grabber that usually hangs on the side of the fridge. Today, it's sitting next to her mum who is at the circular table in the corner of the room. There is a book of sudokus open on the table next to the grabber and a bunch of flowers in a vase on the windowsill. Her mum only ever buys flowers from the Lidl around the corner. Her theory is that if they are strong enough to survive in Lidl, they are strong enough to survive here, in the Parker household.

The sun shines through the window, making the most of her mum's hair, which is a little more muted in colour and even less tamed in volume than Gem's. She's wearing an outfit that Gem will always associate with her mother. Dark blue leggings with white daisies printed on them and a striped T-shirt. Like the flat, her mum is an odd mix of being very utilitarian while also very colourful. She would never wear anything with frills, ties or anything unnecessary, but she rarely wears less than one pattern or three colours.

'Why was the front door open?'

There is the smallest pause before her mum answers. She looks up from the book in front of her. She doesn't wear glasses, but she peers at Gem as though a pair has slipped down her nose. 'Hello to you, too.'

At the gentle reprimand, Gem remembers to breathe. Her job can get stressful. Not necessarily because the work is hard, but because the people can be. Sometimes it takes her a while to transition from Work Gem to Home Gem.

Eventually, she does.

Then she steps towards her mum, bends down and gives her a kiss on the cheek. 'Hey, Mum.' She lasts two seconds before she asks again, 'So, why was the front door open?'

Gem notices her mum pause again.

'Oh, I just left it open for Mike. He should be here any minute.'

Gem's eyes narrow. 'But Uncle Mike has a key.' Her mum has never been a good liar: she's far too innocent. Something is going on. Gem just doesn't know what.

Fortunately for Gem, but Unfortunately for her mum, Uncle Mike chooses this exact moment to make his grand entrance.

He makes so much noise that if Gem hadn't heard him come into this flat a thousand times, therefore able to instantly recognise his heavy footsteps and general clatter, she would've thought that the kidnappers had finally arrived. He's so loud that she hears the exact moment he hangs his jacket – probably his fleece – on the final hook in the hallway.

'Let's take a look at it then.' Uncle Mike strolls into the kitchen with a confidence that most people only feel when they wear wellies in the rain, and slams his toolkit down on the kitchen counter, right next to Gem's work bag, still oblivious to her presence.

In stark contrast to Gem and her mum's surplus of hair, Uncle Mike is completely bald. His head is the only part of his body that shines, the rest of him is covered in a dusting of hair, or sometimes simply dust. Unlike her mum, Uncle Mike's clothing choices are slightly more muted in colour – navy is the most radical colour he wears. They are also significantly more dishevelled. He's a man who is always on the move and because he never carries a bag, all his trousers have substantial pockets.

Uncle Mike carrying a toolkit isn't anything out of the ordinary. A handyman by trade, he can repair anything and everything.

He's the kind of person who would survive an apocalypse without planning for one. He opens his kit, holds his hands up and wiggles his fingers as though he's a five-year-old at a birthday party where they've just brought out the slab cake. Once he's decided on the perfect tool, he dives one hand in and pulls out something that Gem thinks is a spanner.

'Don't worry, Georgie. I'll get this fixed before Gem comes home and finds out.' It's at this point that he turns around and finally notices his niece. His hand freezes, mid-air.

'Get what fixed?'

At Gem's question the blood drains from Uncle Mike's face, but his broken nose is proof that he's not one to back down from a tricky situation. He smiles, but Gem can tell that it is forced. 'You know,' he uses his spanner to point at the two women in front of him, 'you two look like sisters when you're both scowling like that.' Unfortunately, his broken nose is also proof of the fact that two against one is a bad situation to be in.

Gem's scowl deepens. 'What do you need to fix?' she asks again.

Her uncle's smile morphs until he looks more like a deer in headlights than a handyman. 'The er ...' He looks around for inspiration. 'The door!'

He points the spanner towards it, as though the door has just done something wrong. 'It's been making a weird squeak all week.' And with that, he walks away, stopping just before he reaches the hallway, and hits one of the hinges so hard with the spanner that it leaves a dent. 'That'll do it.' Unfortunately, when he swings the door to test his handy work, it squeaks. 'Well, that's a bit better, I think. Don't you, Georgie?'

Gem turns from her uncle to her mother. 'Mum. Save him. Tell me what's going on.'

Her mum sighs. It's very rare for her mum to look depleted, but she does. 'My chair just needs a bit of attention.'

'What kind of attention?'

'One of the wheels is sticking a bit.' Her mum's voice is dismissive. Too casual to be truthful.

'And it doesn't like turning any more.' Her uncle's voice, however, holds no hint of a lie.

Gem looks between the two of them. Unfortunately for her mum, Uncle Mike's eyes are trained on the floor, so he completely misses the pleading look that is aimed in his direction, a silent shout to stop him talking.

'She can only go forwards and backwards in a straight line. Very slowly.' He motions with the spanner just in case anyone needs to know what a straight line looks like.

Gem looks at her mum. She's mid-eye roll.

'Gem, be grateful that you're an only child. Younger brothers never get less annoying.'

'Hey!' Mike looks up, but he makes no move to defend himself. Not because he doesn't want to, but because he can't.

Apart from lying badly, her mum's other defence mechanism is making light of bad situations. Most of the time, Gem can see the benefits. Her childhood would have been a lot less magical if her mum had given into the darkness that followed her car crash and losing the use of both her legs. Or the struggles that came with single parenting. But she didn't. Instead, Gem's childhood was filled with magic and laughter. And, of course, Uncle Mike.

But her mum's wheelchair isn't something to be made light of. It isn't an accent chair that sits in the corner of a room and works double time as an overflow wardrobe. Her chair is the way she moves. It's how she is able to see the world and live in it. Without it, she can't move around the flat easily, let alone anywhere outside. Gem knows that the fact it *needs a bit of attention* means her mum won't have left her flat at all: she wouldn't want to get stranded somewhere.

Relying on the kindness of strangers doesn't usually end well, and her mum hates being a burden to her family. One time, she got a wheel caught in one of those metal grids in the pavement. The type that lets steam out of the underground, or possibly let's rain in. It ruined the wheel – just the rubber part, not even the metal spokes – but it meant she was stuck inside for a week until a replacement wheel came. Even in that short time, she lost weight, not to mention part of her sanity.

'Why didn't you tell me?'

Gem's mum reaches out a hand to her. 'Come on, love. Mike'll fix it. Let's just have a nice evening. There's no point borrowing tomorrow's problems today.'

Gem's face scrunches up. The chair not working properly sounds very much like a today problem. 'But what if he can't fix it?'

Mike gets in there first before Gem's mum can placate her. 'I know you didn't just question my ability to fix something.'

Gem sighs. 'No, bu—'

'There is nothing I can't fix.' Uncle Mike cuts her off. 'I'm *famous* for fixing things that can't be fixed. In 1998, I fixed that horrible flying toy you had, despite the fact it nearly blinded me.'

'Yes, bu—'

Uncle Mike cuts her off again. 'In 2001 I fixed your rollerblades.'

'I know, bu—'

'And then in 2004 I even fixed your bloody blow-up chair. I fixed that thing so well that it never deflated again.' He looks around the room, as if a crowd of supporters are waiting in the wings, ready to riot on his behalf. 'That is unheard of!'

Out of the corner of her eye, Gem can see her mum struggling not to laugh.

When he speaks again, some of the fight has gone out of him. 'Of course I can fix her chair.'

For someone who – objectively – looks quite intimidating, Uncle Mike is touchingly sensitive. He also isn't wrong. He is good at fixing things.

'Fine.' Gem backs down, even though her shoulders tense up a bit. 'So, can I make us dinner then?'

'Nope.' Mike puts his spanner away, and then turns to them both. 'I thought I'd make us my speciality.'

Gem has only ever known Uncle Mike to make one meal. 'Cooked breakfast?'

Mike nods. 'With mushrooms.' He winks at Gem. 'I know how you young people like your veg.'

Chapter 6

'So how come you came over for dinner?'

They may live in the same city, but when Gem moved out, she was careful to move far enough away that it was a little inconvenient to come home – otherwise the temptation to visit all the time would be too much. It means that dinner during the week is an unusual occurrence.

She should have known that her mum wouldn't let her escape without figuring out what was wrong. The last time she came over during the week, they'd just learnt a new actor was going to play Geralt in *The Witcher*.

She sits down on the couch, tucking her feet under her. There's something so odd about trying to relax in tights.

'I was working from a different office this afternoon. Closer to home.' She makes sure not to look at her mum as she answers. It's not just her mother's scowl that Gem has inherited. She's also pretty bad at lying. The only offices nearby are local estate agents and dodgy beauty salons. She had to travel fifty minutes in an illogical direction to get here. She will have to travel even longer before the night ends, but sometimes you just have to be surrounded by the comfortable and familiar.

She also didn't want to be with Shanti. Being close to someone can have its drawbacks. It means that when things are a little off, it feels as though the world's axis has flipped. So even though Gem managed to leave work on time today – a rare occurrence that would usually see the two friends at home watching a terrible movie or just hanging out in silence while carrying out some essential grooming – tonight, the idea didn't hold much appeal.

Because Gem is angry.

Shanti's total dismissal of the ick annoys Gem on two fronts. First, it annoys Gem that she hasn't found the right words to convince her friend of her beliefs. She doesn't necessarily need Shanti to believe in the ick, but it would be nice if Shanti could at least admit that the ick exists for Gem, and for the reasons that Gem gives. And second – and reluctantly – Gem's arguments are starting to weaken in her own mind.

Why can't she stand the idea of someone eating soup?

She finds Atlas physically attractive, and to start with they had a witty repartee going. In theory, she should at least be able to go on a second date with him, but the idea of it gives her the same feeling she gets when someone is eating coleslaw and gets mayonnaise stuck in the corner of their mouth.

The combination of Gem's anger, pride and general disgust are stopping her from returning home until she sorts herself out. She's coming to terms with the idea of accepting her fate, moving back home and never seeing Shanti again, but seeing as it has only been twenty-four hours, she might give it a bit longer to work everything out.

'Well, it's lovely to see you.' A slight shift in her mum's position is the only warning Gem gets before her sneak attack. 'So how is Shanti?'

Gem looks at her mum, trying to figure out where the source of her sixth sense is hidden.

'She's good.'

Unlike his sister, Mike isn't subtle. He squishes into the other side of the sofa, and even though there really isn't room for him, he seems to fit perfectly. 'So what's up? Why're you here? What's wrong?'

Gem glances at her mum who just shrugs. Nobody can change Mike. You just have to accept him as he comes.

'Nothing's wrong. Can't I just want to have dinner with you guys?'

Uncle Mike, whose face is normally moments away from smiling, looks fierce. 'I'm not a big fan of how easy that lie was to tell.'

'I'm not lying,' she whines. But Gem's rebuttal comes too fiercely to be true.

Uncle Mike stretches his feet out in front of him, using the same momentum to stretch his arm out at the same time, resting it on Gem's folded knee. 'Don't bother trying to lie to us again. It's a waste of energy. You're a terrible liar, just like your mum. Maybe worse.' The fingers of his other hand dance in the air. 'We also have that tracking thingy on your phone, so we know you weren't close by—'

'Oh, come on. Just the other week you were telling me how the weather must be wrong because your phone said it wasn't raining even though it clearly was. You can't honestly trust a location app,' she added, trying to wheedle out of it.

'Right, well, you got me there. But honestly, Gem, you must think we're stupid or something. What office could you possibly be visiting that's close by?'

It's almost like Uncle Mike knows exactly what buttons to push.

Backed into a corner, Gem gives up. She slumps. 'Things are just a bit weird between Shanti and me at the moment, so I'm avoiding the flat.'

Uncle Mike's casual posture disappears in an instant. He sits up so quickly that both Gem and her mum jump a little. 'Do you want me to go sort her out? Cause I will.'

Uncle Mike has been offering to 'go sort people out' since Gem first started going to the playground. It all started when an older kid pushed her down the slide before she was ready, but since then, there have been many people deserving of his special skills. The parent who told Gem that she needed to be braver and go into the ball pit. The teacher who told her off for colouring outside the lines. The colleague who forgot to include her in project emails. Yet, despite all of his promises, he's yet to do any sorting.

'Don't worry about it, Uncle Mike. I think it will all be OK.' Or at least Gem hopes so.

Mike's body still says he's ready to go, but a soft hand on Gem's other knee lowers the energy in the whole room.

'I'm sure it will, honey.' It's not particularly hard, but her mum always takes a more measured approach than Uncle Mike. 'You and Shanti have been through so much.'

Her mum is rarely wrong, and she certainly isn't wrong now. Gem and Shanti have been together for all of their formative life experiences. Growing boobs. Going on their first sleepover. Learning to drive. Getting their ears pierced. Cutting in a fringe. Growing out a fringe. The first sip of alcohol. The first sip of tequila. But more than that, Shanti was there for Gem when her mum broke her back and couldn't walk, and Gem was there for Shanti whenever her parents made her feel like she wasn't working hard enough despite her perfect grades. Gem can't look back on any of her childhood experiences without seeing Shanti by her side, and she can't imagine any future experience without her there either.

'If you can get over her using the last of your body spray before the Y2K dance, and she can get over you losing one of her favourite slipper socks, I know that you'll get through this too. Even if it takes a beat.'

Uncle Mike, whose body has relaxed, squeezes her knee once more. 'But you just let me know if you change your mind about me sorting her out. I like Shanti, but I love you more. Never forget it.'

For the first time all day, Gem smiles. 'Thanks, Uncle Mike.' She rests her hand on his. 'But I think you can stand down.'

'Fine. But remember, you only have to ask. I need to come clean out your gutters, oil your locks and check the batteries in your smoke alarms, so it's no hassle to add something else onto the list.'

'You don't need to do any of that either. I can—'

'I know you can, but have you?'

The feel of Uncle Mike's stare makes Gem squirm. 'No.'

'And will you?'

Gem squirms again. 'Also, no.'

'Exactly. So, as I said, I'll be round to see to it.'

'Thanks, Uncle Mike.'

'Right, well. That's my work done here then.' He heaves himself out of the sofa with far more noise than he needs to, and then gives Gem and her mum each a matching kiss on the forehead before leaving.

'Call me if you need anything!' He even taps the kitchen door frame on his way out – right where he hit it with the spanner – chuckling to himself as he goes.

They wait a few moments after he shuts the door to make sure he's not coming back. He's always welcome, but he's also always very loud.

'Have you got any new dances to show me?'

Gem reaches for her phone. 'Here. This was from Monday.'

With the week she's had, Monday feels like a long time ago, instead of a mere two days.

She scrolls back and finds the video in question, flipping her phone on its side and pressing play. Being the worst day of the week, Monday is reserved for street dance. Popping is as close as Gem (and Uncle Mike) would ever get to throwing a punch (not that Uncle Mike would admit this, and not that Uncle Mike knows what 'popping' is). This week they danced to a remixed mashup of some of Beyoncé's most iconic songs. The result made Gem feel both absolutely knackered and completely energised.

She hands the phone over to her mum and tries not to watch for her reaction. Even now, when she is technically an adult with a proper job and her own, separate phone insurance, the idea of her mum being proud of her is still such a motivator.

As the video starts, Gem watches. As usual, she and Shanti are dancing side by side. More than anything else, the thing that links Gem and Shanti together is their mutual love of dance. It's the one thing that Gem knows will always bring them together. The idea makes her heartbeat settle and, for the first time all day, she really does know that they are going to be OK.

About ten seconds into the video, a grin slowly spreads across her mum's face. Gem's mum had been their dance teacher right up until the accident. It still shocks Gem that her mum seems genuinely to enjoy watching her dance. She's never said as much, but Gem is pretty sure most of the grief her mum felt following the accident was assigned to the fact she would no longer be able to dance. All of the other changes – how to dress, how to shower, how to cook, how to navigate public transport – she could work around. But not this.

'Oh Gem, you are such a beautiful dancer.'

Even Gem has to admit that this bit of the dance is pretty cool. Having been in a V-shape formation, dancers appear as if out of nowhere, doubling their numbers and the power behind the co-ordinated fist pumps and leg stomps that make them look like they are part of something bigger, which in a way they are. They are all there to dance.

Still able to pick up moves as quickly as ever, her mum's upper body syncs in time with the music, the shadow of the dance playing through her. She can never hear music without moving.

'I'm not the dancer, Mum, you are.'

For the second time in one night, Gem's mum swats at her daughter. 'Oh, tosh.'

But, in Gem's mind, her mum will always be the better dancer.

Only after her mum has watched the video three more times does Gem get her phone back.

A heavy, but hugging silence fills the room. And although Gem doesn't want to break it, she does.

'Uncle Mike's tried to fix your chair before, hasn't he?'

Her mum doesn't say anything, which is answer enough.

'It didn't work, did it?'

Her mum sighs. 'No, it didn't.' She turns to face Gem. 'But don't talk to him about it. You know what he's like. Prouder than a peacock. Besides, it still does what I need it to do. I can get around the flat just fine, and it's not like I've been shopping in an actual supermarket for years. It's all delivered to the door now anyway.'

'You need a chair that works, Mum.' Now that Gem knows what's been going on, she can see the things that haven't been put back in their place, and the bags under her mum's eyes. A wave of guilt washes over her. Gem only asked her mum at the last minute if she could come over. She can picture her now, panicking about the state of the house, tidying up as much as possible before her arrival, trying to hide the truth.

'I know, love. I've already been in touch with the council, and a new one should be coming soon. Don't worry about it.'

But of course, this is all Gem does.

Chapter 7

When Gem was younger, she loved putting on plays. Her mum and Uncle Mike were very enthusiastic audience members. She would transform the lounge into a stage, and they would sit, obediently, in the stalls throughout the whole performance. Most often she played the role of a dancer, but she has also been an astronaut. A personal shopper. An artist. A teacher. A tennis player. A dog trainer.

Not once did she play an accountant.

And yet, despite the lack of practice, right now she is putting on the best performance of her life. If Uncle Mike could see her, he would be clapping louder than ever.

As a junior accountant, Gem's job is rarely glamorous. Most of the time she sits behind a computer, looking at various spreadsheets, trying to find the missing money, or more often than not, trying to explain when a company has too much of it, and *then* trying to hide it, or at least helping them keep as much of it as possible. Not, of course, that anyone at Gem's work would admit to doing this.

It's never been a job that thrilled Gem, but most of the time she can feign some interest. This afternoon, though, is a struggle.

She's been staring at the same spreadsheet for most of the day, so when her phone pings, she looks at it.

It's *another* message from Atlas. She made the mistake of finally replying to one of his texts. She made sure to avoid any kind of question or potential conversation opener, but apparently, he still hasn't been put off.

I'm off to a White Horse pub this evening. I'll let you know how it compares to the Dog and Duck.x

'Have they sent over the missing invoices?'

It is just Gem's luck that her manager should acknowledge her existence at the very moment she is looking at her phone.

Gem nods as keenly as possible while also putting the phone face down. 'Yes, they came in this morning. I'm just looking through them now, but it seems like everything is here.'

Martin smiles at Gem in a way that is so over-animated it can't be genuine. 'OK, great.' He is a man who tries to be nice, but frequently misses the mark. 'See. I told you. A quick reminder was all they needed.'

Gem nods again. She has sent their client daily 'quick reminders' for the last two weeks. What they really needed was an email that they would bother reading, sent by someone who they would bother to listen to, even though he would be saying exactly what Gem has been saying. But with an added typo or two.

Her mum always told her to dream big. It's understandable that she was a little surprised when Gem came home to say she'd accepted a job as an accountant. But her most enchanting dreams are the ones where she can buy a new pair of shoes without having to agonise over whether she can afford them. In Gem's world, new items are only bought if she can balance the equation in her head, if she can work out what else she can substitute or sell in order to afford a little indulgence. Of course, she'll never tell her mother any of this. In front of her mum, she's careful to insist that she loves her job. She loves it so much, in fact, that she frequently works late and at weekends.

'Well.' Martin closes his laptop. Unlike Gem who has genuinely been working all morning, except for her one minor transgression, he's kept himself busy all day by reading the news. If his face hadn't given him away, the reflection in his glasses would have. 'I think it's lunch time. I'm starving. haven't eaten anything since breakfast.' He looks at Gem. 'You want to come? I'm just going to grab a quick sandwich.'

Gem shakes her head. 'No, thank you though. I brought my lunch in with me today.' Just like she does every day, except for the first Friday of the month when she treats herself.

Martin shakes his head at her. 'I'm so impressed. I don't have time to make my food beforehand. I don't know how you do it.'

Gem just smiles, even though there is a not-so-subtle dig in there. If she has enough free time to make lunch, she isn't working hard enough. But the truth is, she makes her lunch because she has to. Unless she doesn't want to eat, which is sometimes an option. Today might be one of those days. She's doubled down on the sauerkraut, hoping to either get used to the taste, or work her way through the jar as quickly as possible, so she doesn't have to eat it again.

'Anyway, I'll see you in a bit.'

'Bye, Martin.' She gives him a little wave. 'Enjoy your lunch.'

She waits for him to leave the little cubicle room they work in. When he's gone, she exhales as deeply as her pencil skirt will let her and stretches her back. She still has five hours to go until tonight's dance class and her neck, back and soul are crying out for it.

Dance is the one thing that she doesn't ever want to give up. Depending on the month, she's had to cut out meat, new shoes, a new phone charger, a train ticket to see a friend. But cancelling dance has never been part of the equation – Gem would rather sell her soul. But today, she's coming to the realisation that she might just have to.

She's looking for a new chair for her mum.

Gem was a lot younger the last time her mum bought a new chair, and she can't really remember being involved, or, if she's being brutally honest, all that interested. Up until two hours ago, she had no idea just how many options there are. There are foldable chairs, lighter weight chairs, electric chairs. There are chairs made of aerospace-grade aluminium. And, most important of all, there are chairs that would allow her mother to dance again.

Unfortunately, they cost more than Gem's dance classes and monthly take-out lunch combined.

She opens up her bank account. Rather inconveniently, there have been no mysterious, large donations and, despite the fact that her job has made her very good at finding missing money, even Gem can't magic a few thousand pounds out of thin air. Yes, she could go for a less expensive model, but her mum always made sure Gem's childhood was filled with everything she needed, plus a little bit of magic. Now, it's Gem's turn to repay the favour. Her mum deserves the best. This is why Gem never allows herself to buy expensive cheese. If she ever found something better than Cheddar, Gem worries she won't be able to go back.

Shanti's offer replays in her ear. She doesn't know how much she could get paid, but right now, any extra money would be welcome. She's not exactly one to buy stuff on credit.

Gem's phone lights up with a message from Shanti.

Hey. You coming to dance this evening?x

She turns the phone face down again on the desk. It would take her less than ten seconds to reply, but it's not a lack of time that delays her response. It's the thought train that she is currently on.

Her reasons for rejecting people are completely valid. There was the guy who walked funny. The guy who slouched so much that he looked like one of those illustrated people in a book, whose bodies have been morphed to form a letter. There was the guy who breathed too loud. The guy who shaved his arms and legs all in the name of triathlons. There was the one who never laughed, but just smiled and said, 'That's funny.' The one who wanted to hold her hand across the table. Then there was the guy who texted back too quickly and had an addiction to using ellipses. The guy who asked her what her star sign was. The guy who took her cycling on their first date, but then spent the whole time cycling on too low a gear, treading water with each pedal. And the guy who pronounced David Bowie's name wrong.

Yes, the list of icks is long. And yes, the common denominator is Gem. But that is purely a coincidence.

Shanti doesn't know what she is talking about. Gem's ick is her body's way of warning her; either about a general incompatibility or something deeper.

Gem once read about the Frequency Illusion; the theory that once you start learning about something, it becomes all you see and think about. For example, Gem once listened to a podcast about how to get a healthy gut. After that, she told everyone she could that all of their problems originated from a lack of natural yogurt in their diet. (Of course, this was pre-sauerkraut, which – right up until the moment Gem tried it – she had been hoping might become a new obsession.) If someone's tired, they need natural yogurt because it enhances your gut and helps absorption of key vitamins and minerals. If someone keeps getting ill, they need natural yogurt because the zinc in it boosts your immune system. And if anyone complains about being tired after the gym, they need natural yogurt because of all the protein in it that helps replenish and repair muscles.

Basically, psychology (or possibly psychiatry?) is to Shanti what natural yogurt is to Gem. There is a Bigger Psychological Reason for everything that Shanti sees. That person who is yelling in the middle of the street isn't just angry. They are dealing with an unhealed trauma. That person who just threw their rubbish in someone's face isn't being rude, their boundaries have been crossed. Gem doesn't get the ick because she finds some characteristics instantly off-putting, taking it as a sign of their natural incompatibility. She has commitment issues thanks to an unresolved incident during her childhood.

Gem scoffs at the idea. She loves Shanti, and she will support her no matter what goal she's currently going after, but Gem has always had a strong sense of intuition, and she isn't interested in ignoring it. She looks at her computer screen, flicking between the fancy wheelchair and her empty bank balance. But that doesn't mean she can't make money off of it.

Chapter 8

'Hey.' Shanti moves her jacket and scarf onto her lap, making room for Gem, who squeezes in beside her. 'You're late.'

'I know. Sorry.'

As per usual, Martin returned from lunch just after 4, gave her about three hours of urgent work to do at 4.15, and then left at 5, saying he needed to be home on time for once. Obviously, he dropped enough hints to let Gem know that the work needed to be completed by the end of the day. The end of Gem's day. Not Martin's.

It meant she was late leaving the office and doubly anxious, in even more need of dancing now. She needs to let out the emotions somehow. The atmosphere between Gem and Shanti is still a little off. Not '*lumpy milk*' off, but rather '*these crisps have been open for a little too long*' off. But the fact Gem showed up and the fact that Shanti had saved her a space is enough for her to know they are going to be OK.

Gem's cheeks are flushed, and she's already a little sweaty, but only in the way that being late and travelling with a bunch of strangers makes you. It feels a little dirtier, sweat popping up in annoying places. Like Gem's upper lip. She wipes it off as subtly as she can.

'Here.'

Shanti reaches out, her top stretched out to cover her hand, and wipes an area just under Gem's eye, another area where commuter sweat likes to spring. It's an intimate act that Gem wouldn't let anyone but her friend get away with.

'Thanks.'

Gem has only ever seen Shanti rushed and sweaty once in all the years they've known each other. Even at the end of the class, despite having danced for an hour and a half, Gem knows that Shanti will still be well put-together. She's the only friend Gem really has, but even if she wasn't, she would still be the best dressed. Typically, the idea of wearing second-hand exercise clothes would make Gem's skin crawl, but anytime Shanti has a clear-out – which is quite often – Gem gets first pick. Everything else of Shanti's gets a slight refresh – a new embellishment, a bit of embroidery, a slash – and is then sold on.

Shanti's current outfit won't be going anywhere else but into Gem's eager hands. Her top is lime green and close fitting, made from a material that looks thicker than normal and apparently has no seams. From the looks of things, Shanti has added a few loops at the end of the sleeves, so they can hook around her middle finger and thumb, giving the outfit a little extra edge. Her trousers are those cool, slightly shiny, loose-fitting, black warm-up trousers, rolled over at the top and made famous (at least in Gem's world) by Julia Stiles in *Save the Last Dance*.

'Do you know what we're dancing to today?'

Shanti's eyes light up. 'It's a good one.'

It is Shanti who introduced Gem to the joys of Bollywood dancing. The only area where Gem willingly experiments is her toastie flavours. Without Shanti pushing her, she would miss out on so much.

For quite a few Bollywood classes, Gem was awful. She struggled to move her body in the right way. She has had to become significantly more flexible, particularly in her spine and hips. Bollywood dancing requires a level of coordination that Gem still finds a little tricky to master. She spent one particularly difficult class simply trying to get her hands right. She didn't succeed, yet she did improve.

And, as soon as she improved enough, Shanti pushed her some more. There is a growing, modern movement in the Bollywood dance scene. As soon as Gem mastered the basics – all except for her hands – Shanti furthered her education.

'It's fast, but you're ready,' Shanti says now. 'I wouldn't push you, if you weren't.'

There is a silent beat, and then the two friends smile at each other, the awkwardness of the last few days finally breaking.

'OK, I absolutely would push you even if you weren't quite ready. Speaking of which—'

The music cuts Shanti off.

For the next hour, all Gem wants to do is let go – and try to fix her hand placement. So, she stands up and drags Shanti up with her.

'Come on. Let's dance. We can talk about it later.'

Shanti was right – the song is fast, but for once, Gem's hands are complying with her brain.

The song – 'Yimmy Yimmy' – starts for the last time. Facing the floor-to-ceiling mirrors can sometimes feel intimidating, but it also means that Gem can sneak a glance at her friend. Shanti stills look perfectly coiffed, despite the song choice and matching choreography. A few pieces of hair have escaped, but they are so elegantly curled at the side of her neck that, far from detracting from Shanti's overall look, they add to it. But the thing that makes Gem smile more than anything, is that her friend is looking right back at her, a silent message passing between them.

This is fun, and I am so happy to be dancing with you by my side.

They're so distracted that they almost miss the intro beat, but they catch up almost instantly.

The song is fun, and the moves match it perfectly. Gem tries not to pick favourites, but the best part is where your hips snake forward. If you manage to make the move look how it should – your hand follows, half a beat behind, as though your hips really are leading you. It's magic.

The song ends sooner than Gem wants, even though her lungs disagree.

'That was really great!'

Shanti smiles. 'I told you it would be a good class.'

Now that there is nothing to distract her, Gem can once again feel the sweat on her upper lip. For the last hour she was been able to forget about everything, but the dance is over and her nervous system has kicked right back in, starting exactly where it left off. Remembering the conversation she needs to have with Shanti.

They sit off to the side. Gem has never considered herself to have an addictive personality. She doesn't need to eat something sweet after dinner. She's never been tempted to smoke. She doesn't even reach for ibuprofen when she has a headache. But if she could bottle the feeling she gets when she dances, she would reconsider her assessment. Dancing makes her feel alive and indestructible. It makes her believe she can do difficult things.

Things like apologise to her best friend.

She turns her body to stretch towards Shanti, only to find her friend mirroring the action back.

'I wan—'

'I'm—'

They both start and stop talking at the same time.

'You go,' Gem motions to Shanti.

Shanti waits half a second before shuffling towards her friend. 'I'm so sorry.'

As soon as the words are out, Shanti's shoulders relax even though dancing for an hour should have already seen to that.

'I knew it was a shitty thing to ask, and I shouldn't have put you on the spot. And then it was even shittier to try and bribe you.' She inches closer. 'Listen, I don't give a shit about the paper. I can still study intuition. Or I can pick a different topic. I still have time to come up with something else.' Her eyes and mouth both tighten in awkwardness. 'I mean, sure, only about a week.' She looks back at Gem. 'But it's fine. What I do give a shit about though is you. And these last few days have been really weird.'

Gem closes the distance between them. 'No, I'm sorry, Tee. I shouldn't have avoided you. I'm sorry I made things weird between us. All you did was ask a question.' She shrugs one shoulder. 'It shouldn't have bugged me so much.'

'I'm still sorry.'

'Don't be.'

Now it's Gem's turn to feel awkward. The other reason she was so late this evening was because she spent a fair amount of time trying to find a way – *any* other way – to make a fairly significant amount of money in a fairly insignificant amount of time. But the only option she could come up with is the one she didn't even come up with herself.

'See, well, the thing is . . . I've changed my mind. I'll do it.'

This time, Shanti takes her time speaking. 'You will?'

'Yes.' Gem nods.

'Why? What's changed?'

Gem knew that Shanti would ask this question; it's the one that Gem has been dreading answering. She's not ready to share the truth: that she needs the money for her mum. So instead, she decides to suggest another, very possible, reason. She can't fully commit to a lie – there really are no intentional lies between the two of them – but she can suggest it.

'You're right.' Gem points her chin up, taking on a very forced air of superiority. 'I want to prove you wrong.'

Shanti smiles, and Gem relaxes.

'You sure?' One of Shanti's perfectly shaped eyebrows arches up.

'I am.'

Shanti's body starts to vibrate, just a little. Gem can tell that she's holding back her excitement. Or at least trying to.

'Like, *really*, *really*, sure?'

Gem nods. 'Really, really sure.'

Unable to hold it in any longer, Shanti grabs both of Gem's hands, letting out a high-pitched scream. It's loud enough to make everyone still in the room, including Gem, jump.

'Sorry!' Shanti looks around. 'Sorry!'

But she doesn't sound it. In fact, Gem can't remember the last time she has seen such a big smile on her friend's face. Gem thought she was going to have to feign her happiness, but seeing Shanti so happy has put a genuine smile on her face.

It's so potent that it *almost* makes the niggle in the back of her mind disappear. The one that's telling Gem this is an absolutely terrible idea.

Chapter 9

'Listen, if we're going to do this, we have to do this right.'

Gem puts her phone away. For a change, the message she's just finished reading isn't from Atlas. It was from a spa she went to once after she found a voucher online. In fact, Gem realises, Atlas hasn't messaged her for at least twelve hours. Maybe, he's finally realised that they are never going to see each other again.

Unlike Gem and Shanti, who are currently looking at each other. They're standing in the corner shop, both aware of Jay's hooded eyes and resolutely unsmiling face following their movements throughout the aisles. Dancing always makes them hungry, but tonight's meal is going to be less of a meal, and more... 'Study Snacks?'

Shanti nods at Gem's informed guess. 'Works a treat every time.'

Of course, when the tradition of Study Snacks was born, Gem and Shanti were at school and had never even heard of Jay, let alone challenged each other to make him smile. But while their age, the shop and the available snacks have all slightly changed, their essence remains the same. Study Snacks are foodstuffs that are easy to eat and can help you achieve whatever task you have ahead of you, mainly through distraction, but also through sustenance. Both Gem and Shanti attribute the passing of their school and university exams to their careful curation of snacks.

Shanti puts in some fancy cheese as a celebration or bribery, some nuts for the brain power, popcorn for the volume, carrots and apples so they can feel somewhat healthy, some tangy sweets to wake them up if they start to lag and a large bag of chocolate-covered raisins, another nod to health.

Their food chosen, Shanti heads towards Jay who is standing behind the counter, making the register look more like a control room than a piece of outdated technology.

'Well, I think we have enough snacks here to see us through drawing up the contract.'

They've decided that if Gem is going to do this, they need to make it official.

Shanti plonks the basket on the counter with slightly less care than she would usually take. They do their best not to aggravate Jay.

Realising her mistake, Shanti flashes him her most powerful smile. 'Gosh. I'm so sorry about that. I'm just overexcited.' She nods towards the giant bag of popcorn that Jay is about to ring up, making her play for his smile. 'I hope you know that this store is the best thing about the whole neighbourhood.'

From her position, Gem has a clear view of Shanti's full wattage smile. By contrast, Jay's frown gets deeper with every item he puts in the bag. She just hopes that Shanti's study goes better than her attempts to woo Jay.

'OK, I think that's it.'

In the end, drawing up the contract only took half the bag of popcorn, all of the chocolate-covered raisins and triple the recommended daily allowance of nuts (per person), which is an upsettingly small amount.

It isn't exactly iron clad, especially as they don't have a printer and therefore have to write it out by hand on a pad of giant sticky notes that Gem once stole from work. But it does cover a lot – if, not yet, quite all – of the points.

The first stipulation is that Gem needs to go out with someone that does at least initially give her the ick. In Gem's experience, this is a given. But they have also come up with a number of other parameters. Shanti gets to approve who Gem dates. Gem will go on at least one date a week for six weeks, giving Shanti just enough time to finalise her write-up before her dissertation needs to be submitted. The study, after all, is only going to be supplementary to the main body of work, and six weeks should be long enough to unearth whatever secret incompatibility is lurking underneath the surface, or prove that there isn't one, suggesting that the source of the ick isn't in the date, but in the dater themselves. If Gem's date should be the one to end things with her, and not the other way around, then the whole experiment gets reset. The final stipulation is that he must never, ever know what is going on, at least until after the study is completed, otherwise the whole thing is null and void.

'What happens if, like, you end up falling in love?'

Shanti's question makes Gem pause. The two friends look at each other. Gem's deadpan face says it all. 'OK. No, you're right.' Shanti looks back at the list. 'That's not going to happen. Don't even know why I asked.'

While Gem might think she isn't going to fall in love because her intuition is going to alert her to a deeper lack of connection, Shanti thinks Gem isn't going to fall in love because she has significantly deeper issues going on, and her so-called 'intuition' is simply Gem refusing to deal with them. Gem may be able to get over someone eating soup, but she won't be able to get over her deeper problems with commitment. Especially if she can't even admit to them.

Shanti puts the pen down, but there is one more point that Gem needs to add. The issue of reparation.

Gem really doesn't want to be the one to mention it, but she will if she needs to. A lot is on the line, and she's agreed to plenty of rules and requirements without even knowing if it's going to be worth it. She hopes it will be, otherwise she will have to give up dancing. Even her pride will go before the dancing does. She needs four-and-a-half thousand pounds to buy the chair she wants for her mum. Another thing nobody mentions is that having a disability is expensive.

She looks at her friend, willing her to remember. 'Is there anything else that we need to discuss?'

Shanti's face scrunches up as she glances at the list.

'Oh, my God. I almost forgot!' She points at the top of the note. 'Your payment!'

'Oh. I'd forgotten about that.' Gem is a better dancer than actor, but luckily, Shanti isn't the kind of person to point this out. 'So do you know how much I might be getting?'

'Well, we've all had the same amount of funding approved, so you'll be getting five thousand pounds. Paid in three instalments. The first two instalments, paid at two-week intervals of £1,500, and the last, paid on completion, the remaining £2k.'

'Holy shit!' The words are out before Gem can stop them.

Shanti blinks widely at her friend's outburst. 'Does that sound OK to you?'

It takes all of Gem's self-control not to scream and dance around the room.

'Yes. Yep,' she says instead. 'That sounds great.' She will dance another day. More importantly, so will her mum.

'So,' Shanti holds out a pen for Gem to take, 'shall we make it official?'

Gem only hesitates for a moment before taking the pen.

'Where do I sign?'

Chapter 10

'Did you demand final approval of who I date purely for your own enjoyment?' Gem asks her question clearly and loudly, but it goes unanswered. Shanti's eyes are glued to Gem's phone. Online dating is only depressing for those doing it. For everyone else it is purely entertaining.

'Oh, God. Is this really what the online dating scene is like?' Shanti briefly looks up. Her eyes have taken on a slightly glazed expression. 'Maybe it's just the people you're attracting. They can't all be this bad.' Gem watches as Shanti's face scrunches into a frown. It's the same face she pulled when she first tried her hand at coding.

'What are you doing?' Gem's voice holds more than a drop of panic.

'I'm trying to find your profile.'

Gem flings herself off her own couch, and towards Shanti as quickly as possible. It's one thing to let Shanti look at other people's profiles, but it's a whole other thing to have your own profile judged.

Unfortunately, she's not quick enough.

Shanti holds up an arm. 'Got it!'

Accepting defeat, Gem perches on the coffee table. She watches Shanti's hands like a hunter, waiting for the first opportunity to snatch it back.

Slowly, an even deeper frown forms on Shanti's brow.

'What's wrong?'

'Nothing.'

'No. Tell me. I can see the frown.'

Shanti looks up at her. 'I mean, you look good, and you've picked OK prompts, although they are all quite cringe. But ...' Shanti flicks through Gem's profile again, double-checking. 'It's not really you, is it?'

'What do you mean?'

'Well, this just isn't how I see you. I see you as a dancer and a friend, and a soft person who is giving and kind and loyal.' She looks down at the phone again. 'But you've chosen a photo of you at after-work drinks, you on a bike – which is highly unusual behaviour – and then one where you aren't even looking at the camera, which is just a shame because you are beautiful. There is *one* photo where you look like yourself. The one I took of you at that potato market.'

'Well, who can't be happy around potatoes? The loaded fries! The gnocchi. The Giant Yorkshire Puds filled with roasted potatoes!'

Shanti nods her agreement. '*The homemade potato waffles.* I still think about them at least once a week.'

Shanti and Gem spend the next ten seconds thinking about the waffles.

'But apart from the potato, there's not much of you in here.' Shanti sounds confused, but for Gem, this summary is pretty perfect.

'Of course there isn't.'

It's clear Shanti doesn't understand, but Gem is about to educate her.

'Online dating is a completely different universe to real life. Trust me.' She pins Shanti with a stare. 'You have to admit that I get a lot of dates—'

Shanti's nod is reluctant but accepting.

'—The point of a profile isn't to show your *actual* self. The point of a profile is simply to get matches.'

Gem has been on enough dates to know that a profile is only ever as good as the person reading it. She has read too much into some profiles and not enough into others. And despite the hours and hours she has dedicated to online dating, she is yet to improve on being able to tell which profiles are good, which are bad.

Obviously, there are some clear red flags: you should never go on a date with someone who only uploads memes or photos of themselves that are too distant to make out any actual features, and you absolutely must avoid meeting up with someone who only has photos of themselves with their chest out. The former needs to be avoided for safety issues, and the latter needs to be avoided because ... well, everyone knows why. They are insufferable human beings. But there is a lot of space between these two ends of the spectrum, and the middle ground is almost more dangerous than the extremes. Everyone can look friendly and personable and functioning for the second it takes to pose for a photo. Even psychopaths.

No profile can be trusted, and the faster you learn this, the better.

Eventually, Shanti nods. 'Fine. You're the expert, I guess.'

'Does that mean I can have my phone back?' The hope in Gem's voice is palpable.

'Not yet.' Shanti's focus turns back to the screen. 'I still have to look at who you've matched with. We gotta pick you a good one.' Once again, Shanti looks confused.

'What's wrong now?'

Shanti isn't often speechless, but she opens her mouth and then closes it again a few times before finally finding words.

'Is *this* the guy who eats soup?'

For the first time since getting her hands on it, Shanti risks losing control of the phone, as she turns it around for Gem to see.

It's undeniable.

Atlas's face is shining across at her. It's slightly pixelated; Gem assumes he cut everyone else out of it or zoomed in on himself, but even so it is undeniably him.

She shivers. 'Rancid, isn't he?'

'This man is definitely *not* rancid.' Shanti turns the phone back so she can look at him again. 'Gem, I don't often like men who smile too much, too optimistic for me, but he is *really* attractive—'

'He's also arrogant in the wrong way, and his hair is just too floppy.' Once an ick is caught, it catches on real quick.

The perplexed look comes back, and Shanti does some more flicking on Gem's phone.

'His messages are funny. They don't exactly scream arrogant *in the wrong way*. Whatever that means.'

'It means I don't want to date him again.'

Shanti's face doesn't register that any words have been spoken.

Instead, she hands the phone back to Gem, and smiles. It's the same smile that she used to try to dazzle Jay. It has a similar level of success now as it did earlier in the evening.

Gem studies her phone, then her friend. If anything, she feels even more anxious than before. 'Tee. What's happening?'

Shanti's smile turns positively wicked.

'I know who I want you to date.'

Chapter 11

There is a lot of pressure when it comes to dating.

The mental prep.

Thinking of potential topics to talk about should the conversation go quiet. If the conversation dies, you need to figure out how to leave as quickly as possible.

You need to make sure you have a good day beforehand, so you aren't drained.

You need to eat well so your brain is properly fuelled to be sharp and witty.

You need to speak enough about yourself to not seem standoffish and give the other person some material to bounce off, but you need to also ask enough questions about the other person, so you don't seem selfish.

You need to get enough sleep so you aren't tired, but you also need to see people – good, mood-boosting people – in the run-up so you can remember that you are funny and know things and are not, in fact, a social pariah who has been left on the shelf by every other person you have ever dated.

And then there is the physical prep.

No part of your body should be overlooked.

Gem has never been a sex-on-the-first-night kinda gal, because quite frankly, meeting new people is awkward enough without having to handle a queef, but looking good makes you feel good.

For two nights before, you need to make sure you complete your full skincare regime, moisturise properly, maybe even add in a toner and a serum.

Wear underwear that doesn't sag, but also doesn't cut in.

Wear an outfit that makes you smile.

Wear shoes that you can walk in, but that also don't make you feel like a Victorian headmistress, even though it must be said that the ankle support is impressive.

Essentially, it's all an absolute load of bollocks.

Despite what Gem told Shanti, she does frequently think that it would be easier to show up as the most honest, unbarred version of yourself, and if they go running, then it wasn't meant to be, ick or no ick.

For Gem, this would mean turning up dishevelled from a dance class, wearing her oldest trainers, moulded to perfection through years of service, and her bobbly grey sweatpants that are so thin around the crotch area she has to be careful every time she puts them on in case she accidentally puts her leg through them. Of course, to truly be herself, Gem would have to show up with her mum, and probably Uncle Mike, too.

But Gem doesn't want to give herself away that easily.

Who she is, is all she is.

And not everybody – especially not anyone she has met through a dating app – deserves to know who she really is. That is something she reserves for a select, trusted group.

The truth is she was actually going to take a break from dating. The definition of madness is to keep doing the same action, over and over again, while expecting a different outcome. And although Gem doesn't think she is mad, she has been on a lot of *maddening* dates, finishing every single one with the same feeling of disappointment. So, what's the point?

Of course, it's that *maybe*.

Maybe, just *maybe* she might find someone who enhances her life, rather than takes away from it.

A colleague once told Gem that dating was simply a numbers game. That you have to date as many people as you can because most of them are awful, and you have to do a lot of searching and even more sifting to find the one that is right for you. She's now living on a barge, happily married with a kid and one of those pans that does everything.

But Gem has done a lot of sifting and even more searching, and, so far, the barge, the kid, the pan and, most obviously, the man all seem very far away.

And that's irrelevant now: the point has nothing to do with pots or pans, and instead has everything to do with paying for her mum's new wheelchair.

Gem looks at Atlas's profile again. Shanti is right. He *is* cute.

He has shaggy, luscious brown hair and a good smile. He has the obligatory photo of him with a dog (a golden retriever with whom he is sharing the exact same facial expression) and another of him with a group of people so it's clear he can make friends in real life, not just via the internet. He has listed 'sport' and 'running' as two of his interests which, in Gem's experience, can go one of three ways. **Option one:** he likes sport to a normal, and workable amount. (This is the least likely scenario.) **Option two:** he is obsessed with his sports team of choice and spends a ridiculous amount of money and time on them and their shirts, all of which look exactly the same. Or, **Option three:** he's put 'sport' as an interest because he is vain, but also smart enough to know that it's no longer acceptable for men to say they only want to date skinny, hot girls.

The idea of going on another date with Atlas forms a pit of nausea somewhere near Gem's lower ribs. The only benefit is that at least she already knows that he meets the requirements: he definitely gives her the ick. She can see him leaning over the bar, ordering a drink and giving the barmaid a well-oiled wink. She needs to practise a better resting face, otherwise her true feelings are going to show far too quickly.

Maybe she'll get lucky, and he won't want to see her.

As if he knows she's thinking about him, a message comes through from Atlas.

Only the fact she can't afford to buy a new one stops her from throwing her phone across the room.

Has your friend emerged from the bush yet? Have you gotten stuck too? Is that why you aren't texting me back?

Chapter 12

'Are you ready for this afternoon?'
 'This afternoon?'

Martin scowls at her, his glasses slipping down his nose.

'Yes. We have the monthly board meeting. Are you ready for it?'

The tension leaves Gem's body.

By, *Are you ready for it?*, what Martin really wants to know is: *Are the slides ready?*

Most people don't look forward to monthly board meetings, but the idea of standing in front of fifteen suits and talking through the progress they made on the accounts – specifically where to cut back costs, an area that Gem excels in – is considerably preferable to the only other event she has planned for this afternoon. Her second date with Atlas.

'Yes, everything is ready. I sent you the slides this morning.' Although of course he missed them. He's been too busy keeping his mind sharp with wordles and worldles and nerdles to do any actual work. 'They might have gotten lost in your inbox though.' Along with an increased understanding of numbers and all of the most boring parts of the financials that sit behind businesses, Gem has become an expert in the passive voice. 'Let me know if you want me to resend them.'

There are a series of clicks, and Gem can see a number of tabs getting minimised in the reflection of Martin's glasses. It's strange to think that someone who can't comprehend the idea of clicking on the one app that you need, rather than minimising a whole load of ones you don't, is in a management position. It really makes her wonder what job Uncle Mike might've had if he had been born into a family a few streets closer to the park.

Martin looks down his nose at the screen. 'If you could send it through again, that would be great.' Another few clicks follow. 'Honestly. My inbox is a nightmare today.'

'Of course, no worries. I'll do that right now.' Although Gem has perfected the passive tense, the other passive thing she has perfected is her aggression. She forwards the email she sent to him at 8.26 this morning.

She can hear it land in his inbox. Martin's one of those people who keeps the sound effects enabled.

'Ah yes, here it is.' As though he actually had to put a bit of effort in to find it, instead of simply waiting for it to drop into his inbox.

'Well, on that note, I'm going to pop out to get some lunch, and read this while eating. I hate taking a working lunch, but sometimes you just can't fit everything in, can you?' He closes his laptop and puts it into his bag. 'I'll be back before the meeting so we can go in together.' He says this as if he's doing Gem a favour, when, in reality, he needs Gem to show him where the room is.

'OK. Sounds good. See you in a bit.'

When she first started working, Gem found the idea of a corporate office intimidating. They were the tall buildings in the skyline. She would never dream of going into any of them. But she had to get over the feeling of being an imposter pretty quickly. From her research, an accountant was the best-paying and easiest profession to get into that didn't require any additional qualifications on entry. Probably because relatively few people want to become accountants, and those few that do are best avoided. Yet it meant Gem was thrown into the deep end – meaning grey-washed fishbowl offices.

The sheer amount of glass in the office makes it very difficult to hide, which is a particular shame today because Gem has something to do which she doesn't want anyone to see. She waits just long enough to know Martin must be out of the building before she makes her escape.

She takes the stairs so she doesn't waste any time queueing for the privilege of standing in a metal box literally designed to plummet to the ground. Also so she doesn't have to talk to anyone. Plus, taking the stairs is significantly more exciting than taking the lift. It's thoughts like this – even more than her growing appreciation of the power of Excel – that make Gem worry about her chosen career path. Monotonous office life can make things like taking the stairs instead of the lift feel like you're about to commit a crime. Anytime she meets someone in the stairwell, there is *always* an air of deception. It's mildly thrilling.

Not that she needs to be thrilled.

If anything, she needs to calm down.

She's done everything she can to make sure that she is both physically and mentally prepared for her date this evening. She's even cut out caffeine in the hope it will lessen her reaction to his icks. She looks good. She feels good. Or at least as good as she can without outside help. Because although she's been trying to keep calm, treating her date with Atlas like any other date with any other human, there is a lot riding on it.

Which is exactly why she is choosing to indulge in what she's about to do. Sometimes you need professional help.

She reaches the bottom of the stairwell without seeing anyone else on the way. Once outside, the fresh air is an elixir for her lungs. The door closes behind her a little louder than she expects it to, and she looks up to the right, towards the main entrance to the office. It is rammed with people coming and going. She quickly turns left, hoping to hide from any interested eyes. Getting caught now would ruin her whole escape plan, and the closer she gets to her appointment, the more giddy she's getting. After all, it's the kind of appointment that you need to build yourself up for.

Gem's insides do a little flip as she turns down a side alley. She rarely comes this way. It is a pocket of artisanal shops, including a bakery, a craft studio and a gaming shop and, therefore, holds limited appeal to the local clientele.

As she walks, Gem spies the sign she is after. She looks surreptitiously down both ends of the alley, just to make sure that nobody she knows is around.

With the coast clear, she pushes the door and goes in. The heat and bright lights of the outside world are immediately snuffed out and instead, Gem is transported into a room that has been transformed – at least partially – from a concrete and steel box into a softly furnished den. It takes a lot to completely rid a place of its corporate beginnings, but they've put in a good effort. There are no hard, shiny surfaces anywhere. Everything is covered in fabric. Even the door in the corner. There is also a total lack of natural light. Instead, muted red bulbs add to the ambiance. As the door closes, a little bell rings to let everyone know that she is here.

There is only one person – apart from Gem – in the shop.

Madame Sybil. A reader of fortunes.

'Ah. Gem.' She is standing behind the only blue light in the room. It makes her look like something out of a nineties children's programme. She spreads her hands, completing the look.

'Welcome. I've been expecting you.'

Chapter 13

Gem doesn't really believe in fortune tellers or tarot reading or star signs. At least not when she's feeling calm and centred. But as soon as anything gets stressful, she looks for signs that she is doing the right thing and that everything is going to be OK. Ahead of her GCSEs, she avoided walking over cracks in the pavement. Before her mum's last operation, she looked everywhere for two magpies and would close her eyes as quickly as possible if she could only see one. Before her job interview, she spent a good eight hours searching every patch of grass she could see for a four-leaf clover. She visited her first fortune teller just before she moved out with Shanti. She was guided well then, and she hopes she will be guided well now.

Looking around the room and specifically at the floor, which seems to be covered with the same carpet tiles as the office next door, it doesn't look as though Madame Sybil is doing all that well out of her profession. Then again, maybe she is here for a reason that isn't connected to money. *Maybe she is here for Gem.*

'I will ask you to clear your mind.'

Madame Sybil's voice is deeper now than it was when she opened the door, but at least she has moved away from the blue up-light. She is now sitting on the opposite side of the table to Gem. There are so many rings on her hands, Gem doesn't know how she manages to do anything. She certainly couldn't open a jar.

'My preferred method of divination is cleromancy.'

Madame Sybil places three little silk bags in front of Gem on the table, all with different patterns on the fabric.

'Please choose whichever bag speaks to you.'

Gem, a little unsure about what cleromancy involves, and regretting her lack of research, leans in slightly. Surprises have never really been her thing, mainly because more often than not they are bad, but she does as Madame Sybil asks and chooses a bag. It doesn't speak to her – luckily as otherwise she'd have run away – but the pattern of the fabric is the most appealing. It's covered with brightly coloured dinosaurs. She only notices the ominous shooting stars that appear to be flying towards the dinosaurs when it is too late. Surely that can't be a good sign? Can it?

As she leans forward to hand the bag over, Madame Sybil shakes her head. '*Oh, no.* The bag is for you. Only you should touch its contents.' She moves the other two bags away before sweeping her hand across the table. 'Please.'

She gestures at Gem. 'Open the bag and place the objects in your hands. They need to feel you.'

Gem knows that sometimes things are on sale for a reason – namely because nobody wants them. Yet, when she saw that Madame Sybil was offering sessions at a discount, she had chosen to take it as a sign; now, she is questioning this logic. She does as she is told, though.

'Once they are securely in your embrace, clear your mind, and then ask your question, making sure you direct your words towards the objects. Once you are confident they have listened, throw them onto the casting mat. I will then interpret them for you. Do not worry.'

At her words, Gem's heart – and hands – stop, instantly even more worried about what is in the bag. She really wishes she knew what cleromancy actually was.

'The mat and the objects have all been cleansed since their last use. They will only be channelling your energy and seeking to answer your question alone.'

'Great.' Gem nods. And then, with nothing else to do, and no more time available to waste – she really does need to get back to the office – she opens the bag and empties the contents into her hand.

There is a moment of silence and Gem's brain realises what she is looking at.

'Are these ... erasers?'

In her hand she can see five little animal erasers, the type that only kids who turn out to lack empathy have the heart to use. She had been fearing bones, but somehow these are more chilling.

'They are.' Madame Sybil's face remains pin straight. 'Now, please, your question.'

'Oh yes, right. My question.'

Gem holds the miniature animals in her hands and closes her eyes. Despite the, quite frankly, ridiculous scenario she finds herself in, Gem turns serious. She wouldn't be here if she didn't need to be. She has a question, and she needs it answered.

Is going on a date with Atlas the right thing to do?

She repeats the question until it is the only thing in her mind, no simple feat. And, again as she has been instructed, Gem opens her eyes and throws the objects onto the mat. She'd imagined them landing in a scattered way, some touching, some off to the side. One possibly even looking at her. What she doesn't imagine is all the little animals landing nowhere near the mat. The pig has travelled so far that she is on the floor, the cow and sheep are in a very compromising position in a dark corner and the duck, staying true to its nature, has somehow managed to fly away and has landed in Madame Sybil's hair.

Gem looks up. 'What does that mean?'

Madame Sybil's face has paled, and it has nothing to do with the strange choice of lighting. She looks at Gem and shakes her head once.

'Nothing good.'

Chapter 14

She almost cancelled. She still might. It's not too late, even though she's standing outside the pub she suggested meeting at. It's not quite as awful as the last one she chose, but it is a close cousin. The only marked difference is that this time the pub is on the riverbank, and so instead of reproduction hunting paintings, they have fish.

She could cancel and just tell Shanti that it didn't work out. Shanti would let her start this whole process with someone else. It's in their contract. Of course, what she can't do is tell Shanti that an ominous bunch of animal erasers is the thing that pushed her over the edge.

Gem gets out her phone so she can message Atlas. His smiling face fills her screen as she accidentally clicks onto his profile instead of their message thread, all thumbs as she fumbles around, trying to decide what to say.

Atlas, I'm sorry for the late notice, but I've had to work late.

She pauses, and then deletes. 'Terrible.'

After walking a bit further away, she tries again.

Atlas. I feel bad about cancelling on you, but I've come down with a terrible cold and I'd feel even worse if I made you sick.

Gem shakes her head. 'Nope. That's not it.'

She keeps walking.

Atlas. I'm sorry I can't come this evening. I went to a fortune teller at lunch time, and she told me that if we met, my whole life would fall apart.

She starts deleting before she's even finished typing. 'You sound insane.'

And although she does, it is also the Unfortunate truth. Madame Sybil told her that never in the history of cleromancy have *all* the erasers landed so far from the mat. She refused to let Gem redo the throw, and practically pushed her out of the door.

Gem tries again to find the right words, or at least the words that will get her off the hook without sounding like she's lost her mind.

Atlas... I'm going to have to—

She deletes once more and restarts.

Atlas—

Unfortunately, Gem is concentrating so hard on what to say that she doesn't have any concentration left to spare for where she is walking, and more specifically who she is walking into.

'Oh, God. Sorry!' She looks up and into the most beautifully sculpted face she has ever seen in real life, despite the fact it is a little uneven.

'Atlas.'

Once again, he appears to have magically dressed to suit the occasion and the temperature, which is a particularly difficult thing to do in London. The tube, the streets, the office, the parks and the Prets all have their own ecosystems, and you need a different outfit in all of them. But Atlas, wearing another pair of smart-casual trousers, a casual-looking shirt that he has once again left unbuttoned at the top, and a fleece to stave off the quickly cooling evening air, looks like he would be comfortable in whatever environment he finds himself in.

Gem, meanwhile, suddenly feels a little too warm.

Aware of the fact she has some making up to do, Gem wore her favourite trousers to work this morning – they are a very dark grey with a black stripe down the side – and a new top. (She picked it out from the box under Shanti's bed this morning, which holds all of the clothes that are due to be donated or done up.)

Atlas's right eyebrow hitches up and he smiles. 'Gem.'

Then he looks down to her phone.

'Oh.' She puts it away, almost dropping it in the process. 'I was just messaging to let you know I was here.'

His brow furrows. Gem isn't sure she has ever seen a *furrowed brow* unless it's been in a TV adaptation of a nineteenth-century romance. It could be attractive, if only it was on someone else's face.

'While walking away?'

'Erm . . .'

When she was younger, the fear of walking into quicksand kept her from walking anywhere even vaguely beachy, but in this particular moment in time, if she saw a sandpit, she'd likely sprint towards it.

'I was just . . . doing a circuit. I didn't want to look too keen.'

The one side of Atlas's mouth ticks up, preparing to smile. 'If there's one thing you don't need to worry about, it's looking too keen. How is your housemate by the way? Did she make it out of the bush?' The question is asked innocently enough, but Gem recognises it for what it is: a challenge.

'Eventually, yes. Thank you for asking.'

He points behind him, in the direction she was heading before his body stopped her. 'But honestly, you can leave if you like. I don't want you to stay if you don't want to be here.'

Gem blinks. Of all the things he could have said, this is not what she expected.

For a moment, her heart hopes that maybe this time the ick won't stick. Maybe she can forget the soup issue. Shanti is right. Soup is a completely acceptable lunch option. Sure, it *is* a little off-putting, but it shouldn't completely blind her. Hearts, after all, are slower to learn than heads. Maybe she just needs to let her heart lead her.

Maybe Madame Sybil is wrong.

She'd be sorry to risk the success of Shanti's dissertation, and she'd have to give up dance in order to pay for her mum's new chair (along with some other things), but any feelings of disappointment would quickly be outweighed by the overwhelming happiness she would feel at being with Atlas. She might even learn to love his name even though it sounds as pretentious as he looks wearing his expensive watch and smiling at her with perfectly straight teeth.

But then, he shifts.

It's not a big movement, but it is enough for Gem to see the giant backpack that has so far been hidden by all of his angles.

And once again, she is hit by the ick.

Gem has never been around someone long enough to discover that one person can have more than one ick.

A travel receptacle shouldn't be enough to turn someone off for life, but Atlas's bag is just so *big*. Unable to concentrate on anything else, Gem takes a closer look.

It makes him look like a snail.

She should take Atlas up on his offer and run away.

But, against her better judgement, her intuition and her feet, which have subconsciously angled themselves away, she hears herself saying, 'No. I want to be here.'

After all, this time, she wants to be hit by the ick.

The more, the merrier.

In retrospect, it would have been easier for Gem to stay if every move she made wasn't met with a shiver-inducing countermove from Atlas.

She sat down and he put his bag right next to her, so close that when it tipped over, her knee was the thing to catch it.

She ordered their drinks and he added on a packet of prawn cocktail crisps.

She went to take a sip of her wine and he did the same, lifting his glass in a way that made him look like a T-rex with tiny arms.

She moved her seat slightly away, so she could give herself a bit more distance from the bag, and he scooted in closer, so she now has very little space on either side.

With the exception of the T-rex arms, Gem wouldn't necessarily classify these grievances as an ick, per se. An ick carries a stronger, visceral reaction that can't be overcome. But an ick can sometimes also be merely the main part of a dish. At a restaurant you might simply order the 'chicken', but you don't just get chicken. You get carrots and peas and potatoes and a sauce.

Tonight, Atlas's bag is the chicken, and it comes with a lot of sides.

At least nothing catastrophic has happened, despite Madame Sybil's flying animals.

'Do you always carry such a large bag with you?'

She looks down. Like a drunk, dodgy man at a pub, the bag

keeps trying to touch her, no matter how many times she pushes it away.

'No.' Atlas's eyes flick a little, side to side. 'I actually forgot – just for a moment – that we had a date this evening. Otherwise, I would have left it at the office.'

The realisation that Atlas looks this good without even trying annoys Gem more than rationally it should.

'Speaking of dates, you left very quickly the other night. We never got to talk about the interesting stuff.' He winks at her as he picks up a fishy crisp.

She imagines that the original patrons of the Jolly Fisherman would be a lot less jolly if they knew how their favourite pastime and source of protein is now being synthesised and used to flavour little slices of potato.

'What do you do for work?'

Gem supresses her need to shudder as Atlas licks his fingers free of the remnants of orange-coloured flavouring.

'I'm an accountant.' It's only three words, but they are the three words Gem knows are sure to hasten the end of a conversation.

'Dang.'

Except, apparently not in Atlas's case.

'I was being sarcastic when I said we should talk about the interesting stuff, but this genuinely *is* interesting.' He moves even closer towards her. Gem has made the mistake of sitting on a chair, instead of the bench, meaning she can't shift as easily as Atlas can. All he has to do is slide along. Like a little slug.

'Nobody finds accounting interesting.' But then, a picture of Martin flashes before her eyes. He may rarely do any work, but he does bloody love talking about balance sheets and accounts payable.

'Then why do you do it?'

Usually when Gem tells people she is an accountant, that is it. The end of the conversation. Very rarely do people dig further, but for the first time, Gem wishes they would. That way she might have a pre-prepared answer that is as close to the truth as she can get, without actually giving anything away.

'See.' He wiggles his pointer finger towards her. '*Interesting.*'

'What's interesting?' It certainly can't be her job.

'You wiggled in your seat.'

'I did not.' But even as Gem denies it, she knows Atlas is right. Her shoulders have only just stopped moving.

'You did. You did this little ...' Atlas then replays her movements so Gem can see what she looked like. He sits up a bit straighter, the movement starts in his butt, travels to his lower back, up his spine and ends at his shoulders. 'Thing.'

The look he gives her when he is done is a little too intense for her liking. She is meant to be the one observing him, trying to find out why they are incompatible. She is not meant to be the one being observed.

Doing her best to feign nonchalance, she shrugs. 'It pays well.'

It's more truthful than she would have liked it to be, but she didn't have much time to come up with anything better. She just wishes she'd come up with something that didn't sound quite so vapid. Gem is only driven by money due to her circumstances, not her personality. She yearns for the day that her primary motivation can be something other than paying bills.

But all Atlas does is nod, accepting her answer at face value. Working in the City, Gem's answer is quite a typical one. She nods back at Atlas, who has one arm now sprawled across the back cushion as the other reaches for a crisp.

'So is your choice of crisp influenced by your surroundings?'

A crease forms in between his eyes. 'Huh?'

'We're at the Jolly Fisherman and you're eating prawn cocktail crisps. Last time we went to the Dog and Duck and you chose hoisin-flavoured crisps.'

Atlas's eyes pin her to her seat. 'You watching me?' A smile tugs at the side of his face, making it look even more lopsided.

Gem feels a slight blush creeping up, thankful that her top has a high neckline. 'No, but you have to admit they are quite ... unconventional flavour choices.'

Atlas's smile broadens and he looks down at the open bag of crisps on the table. Despite the fact Gem had insisted that she didn't want any, he'd opened the bag out completely, making the packet into a rudimentary sharing platter, just in case she changed her mind.

'I hadn't noticed that, but no, I just love prawn cocktail. Both the actual thing, and the flavouring. Besides, you picked another completely soulless pub for us. If you'd chosen somewhere nicer, I could have ordered actual fries.'

'Hey!' Gem's offence is only partially feigned. 'I purposely chose the Dog and Duck because I thought you'd like it. You have a photo of yourself with your dog in your profile.'

'My dog?' Confusion is written all over Atlas's face. His eyebrows draw together and his head tilts to the side.

Gem's nod is sharp. 'Yes. Your dog. The one in your profile photo.'

Realisation dawns on Atlas's face as his eyebrows relax. 'Oh! That's not my dog. I don't have a dog. If I did, you would know. I wouldn't be able to stop talking about her. I only put the photo up there because we have the same smile.'

Gem should have known that dog isn't his. She was right when she told Shanti that everyone lies on their profiles. It just goes to show that you can never judge a book by its cover.

But he's also right. Gem looks around. The pub is a bit soulless. Some pubs are great. They have good food and a welcoming atmosphere. A local dog who spends more time wandering around its tables than it does at home. Menus that change with the season and availability of local produce. Chairs that have been cleaned. Tables that don't threaten to rip off a layer of your skin if you lean on them too hard for too long. This pub is not one of those places, but it is also exactly the kind of place she picks for dates. Somewhere that is just a bit nasty, so you aren't tempted to stay too long.

'Well, next time I promise to pick somewhere better.'

'Next time, eh?' Atlas looks like he just won a bet. If only he knew the truth.

She needs more dates with him, but she can't let him think she is actually that keen. She doesn't want to know how insufferable he'll become if he thinks she is genuinely interested. His arrogance is already pretty healthy.

'I just mean *if* we see each other again, I'll pick somewhere that's a bit more exciting.'

'How come you always get to choose what we do?'

Because she hates not knowing what's about to happen.

Of course, she doesn't say that. In fact, she decides to skip answering at all.

'You make a fair point.' She sits up a little taller. It's not quite the uncomfortable wiggle from earlier, but it is close.

'One day, you'll let me choose what we do for a date.'

For the sake of the study, and her mum's chair, Gem should be happy that Atlas is talking about potential future dates. But for the first time, despite his T-rex arms, poor snail impersonation and terrible crisp choice, Gem has realised something. Atlas is human, and she is, essentially, using him.

Guilt lodges itself in her lower left rib cage. It makes her feel a little uncomfortable. Right up until Atlas winks at her.

'That's *if* you want to see me again.'

It's such a smarmy move.

He picks up another crisp and pops it into his mouth with relish. On a downward spiral, Gem watches on, unable to stop her nose from scrunching up in disgust. The crisp is gone in mere seconds.

'So,' Gem turns his earlier question back on him, needing to focus her energy on something that hopefully reduces her loathing of Atlas, 'what do you do for work?'

At this point, Atlas brings his hands together, dusting off the remnants of fake prawn, before resuming his position. 'I'm in cybercrime.'

It's a good job that Gem isn't eating, otherwise she would have choked.

'You're a criminal?' She leans forward, getting dangerously close to the crisps, and then starts to whisper. 'Don't you think that's something you should have shared with me earlier? And also ...' she looks around, luckily the pub is still quite empty, 'in a more secret place?'

While Gem is sure she's about to get arrested by a swarm of undercover police officers, Atlas looks like he's about ready to burst out laughing. Which is exactly what he then does.

'No.' The remnants of laughter can still be heard in his voice. 'I work *against* the criminals, not with them.' His head tilts to one side. 'Although we do also have a few ex-criminals on our team, and they are really good at the job.'

Gem doesn't know whether to dig a hole or run away. She hates the bag even more for trapping her.

'Despite this rather handsome exterior,' Atlas gestures to himself, 'I am just a computer geek at heart.'

He smiles, no doubt thinking his line is cute.

One of Gem's biggest pet peeves is when people ask you about your job first, only to come out with a corker of a response to the same question. It's like they're setting you up to fail. There's a unique sense of humiliation when you tell someone you're an accountant, only for them to turn around and tell you that they're a doctor or a personal shopper or a zookeeper. Or, in this specific case, a crime fighter.

Not for the first time, Gem wishes she had a secret reserve of money.

But she doesn't.

What she does have is five more weeks of Atlas.

Chapter 15

'He licked his lips? And that was unacceptable?'

Shanti and Gem have just reached a pivotal part in the table-moving process – the moment when the table legs are standing on the narrow ledge between the kitchen and the lounge.

'Yes. The idea of those shiny, slippery lips getting anywhere near me. *Ugh.*' The last of Gem's words is accompanied by a shiver.

'And he was eating crisps?'

'He was. *Prawn cocktail.*' At the memory, Gem almost drops the table.

'So surely licking his lips is something totally acceptable and normal under the circumstances?'

After the date with Atlas, Gem had come back too late for a debrief; Shanti was already in bed, and Gem was slightly suffering. By the end of the night, the wine had actually started to taste quite nice, which should have been warning enough to stop drinking. So, they're having a debrief now.

It might be Sunday, but Shanti has been up since six getting their apartment ready for guests, and Gem – who only woke up half an hour ago – is helping out before she escapes home for

Sunday lunch. Luckily, Shanti is too distracted by the logistics of the table move to be overly confused by Gem's lack of reasoning.

'You got it?' she shouts to Shanti, but she already knows the answer.

'Yep.'

Gem looks at the table once more, paying particular attention to the placement of its legs. One time she made the mistake of putting a leg on the little ridge in the middle of the hatch. The shock when it slipped was much bigger than the five millimetres it actually fell. But this time, they look good. She runs into the lounge, taking her place opposite Shanti on the other side of the table, holding the side of the table from the bottom, ready to move it into its final position.

'OK. I've got it. Lift?'

Their eyes lock under the table that is now being held above both of their heads, table legs still perching on the hatch. Shanti nods once. 'Lift.'

They are definitely not moving the table in the most logical way, but this is the way they lifted it the first time, and so this is now the way they always do it. They only move furniture, however, when nobody else is around. There are some things best kept between friends.

They lower the table to the floor, but it slips slightly and makes quite a loud bang, so loud that their neighbours – who they have *still* yet to see – bang loudly on the adjoining wall. Shanti hisses in their general direction, then shakes her head elegantly to clear the hair from her eyes. Gem just blows hers out of the way. Much good it does – it lands back in exactly the same position. With the table on the floor, Gem goes back into the kitchen, lifting one chair through at a time, passing them to Shanti.

'Remember that you need to keep seeing this guy. I hope you hid your feelings, however ridiculous they are.'

Shanti puts the chair down and walks back to the hatch.

Gem picks up another chair and angles it through.

'He messaged me this morning, actually.'

The shock on Shanti's face is almost comical. 'He did?'

'Yes, Tee, he did.' Gem sounds confident, but in reality, she wasn't sure he would. Shanti is right, she doesn't have a good poker face.

Shanti takes the chair from her. 'Well, I'm proud of you.' She smiles. 'Giving someone a chance.'

Gem rolls her eyes. 'I'm not *giving him a chance*. This is all for research purposes. Remember?'

Shanti nods. 'I remember.'

She puts the chair down and faces her friend. 'Hey, listen. Thanks for doing this. I can't imagine it's much fun hanging out with someone who you don't really want to spend time with. Even though I still think you are *ridiculously* picky.'

Gem holds out another chair. 'He said that *Die Hard* is his favourite Christmas movie.'

At this, Shanti grimaces. 'OK. You can have that one.'

'Right?' She lets go of the chair. 'Everyone knows it's the choice for people who are *trying* to be cool and alternative.' Gem's face looks like she just ate something really sour.

'At least he didn't say *Elf*.'

'Oh, God.' At the thought, Gem almost drops the chair she's just picked up.

'But you're going to see him again?'

Gem passes the final chair through, which Shanti takes. 'That's part of the deal, right?'

'It is, but I almost feel bad that I'm making you do this.' Shanti puts the chair down, then rearranges the other three so they're all evenly spaced.

'Don't feel bad.' Gem looks at her friend through the hatch. 'It's not like I'm doing it for free.'

'Would it help if we concentrated on some of the good things about him, as opposed to just listing the bad?' Shanti blows more hair out of her eyes. 'Might make the next date not so painful to get through?'

'I don't think any amount of positivity is going to make me forget the soup thing. Or the lip thing. Or the bag. It's too much. I'm only human.'

Shanti gives her a look, the one where Gem knows her friend is really unimpressed.

'Fine.' It's taking a moment, but Gem eventually comes up with something. 'He said I could leave if I didn't want to be there.' She shrugs. 'That was nice of him.'

'So, he's a good choice of candidate to study then?'

'He's perfect.'

Gem freezes and Shanti gives her a cheeky smile.

'For the study. He's perfect for the study.'

The cushion she throws misses any intended target, and luckily Shanti is better at catching than Gem is at throwing. She plucks the cushion out of the air before it does any lasting damage.

One crisis averted, it's time to move on to the next.

'So, when are your parents meant to be arriving?'

Shanti looks at her watch.

'Shit. I've got less than an hour.'

Shanti's parents are great. They want the best for their daughter, they brag about her to their friends – even though they are still disappointed that she didn't become a proper doctor. Shanti's dad is there whenever they need a ride to a station or an airport. He lifts their bags out of the boot and always puts them down with great care. He makes sure their condiment drawer is sufficiently stocked. Meanwhile, Shanti's mum has a habit of magically appearing with weeks' worth of meals whenever work gets too busy for either of them to cook, and she always comes over to clean the house whenever either one of them is ill. While Gem might be Shanti's best friend, Shanti's mum is the person who knows her the best.

But that doesn't mean that they always see eye to eye.

Shanti's mum is desperate for her only daughter to get married.

'Who is it this time?'

'I think he's an optometrist.'

Shanti has perfect eyesight.

'A solid choice. Why don't you just tell your mum that you aren't ready to get married yet?'

'Because I don't have enough spare time to listen to the lecture that would follow. You know what my parents are like. I'd have to carve out a good couple of hours every day for at least a month for their calls.

'You remember when I asked them – *asked* them – if I could take art instead of geography for GCSE? This would be so much worse. They've had my whole life planned out for me even before I was born. If I tell them I don't want to get married, they'll probably just send me off to Auntie Aapti's house and forget to buy me a return ticket until I agree to marry someone and give them grandbabies to spoil.' She puts the candle back down in exactly the same place she picked it up from.

As close as Gem and Shanti are, there are some things that Gem will never be able to fully appreciate.

'I can tidy away all of the clothes and you go get showered.'

They both look towards Shanti's corner. There are about five different projects on the go – three jackets, a skirt and a dress – all of which Shanti has gone some way to mending, updating and personalising. While Gem wears clothes as they come, Shanti is always adding her own flair. It's how she relaxes. But it is also a secret that she keeps from her parents. Of course they *know*, but they only know in the way that they pretend they don't, hoping that it will go away. They believe that any spare time should be used to further your goals, namely studying.

'Thanks. That would be really great. Just shove it in the box under my bed.'

Gem nods.

'And be careful of the pins. Especially in the white jacket. It's quite a thick material, so I had to use quite a few, and some of them are sticking out at funny angles.'

'Are you sure you don't want me to stay?'

'Oh, God no. Only one of us needs to suffer through this lunch.' Shanti finally stops faffing and stands up. 'Besides, don't you have something to do?'

Chapter 16

'Gem. You shouldn't have done this.' Her mum looks at her as though Gem's just told her that the world is about to end and she's managed to save it just in time by sacrificing her own future.

'I'm sorry that it's a bit clunkier than your last one.'

The dance wheelchair may be Gem's dream, and the council-provided chair may have been requested, but her mum needs to move now, not in six months. So after Gem finished prepping their flat for Shanti's parents, she travelled across town in the hope that her most recent online marketplace find would be a winner.

'It still fits in Mike's car though, and it uses the same wheels as your current one, so they won't go to waste.'

'It's great, Gem. Thank you.'

Despite the fact that the chair is a *little* clunkier than the old one, the smile on her mum's face is bigger than she's seen it in years. It makes Gem even more eager to see how happy her mum will be with her *new*, new chair. For now, this one will do. Plus, Gem hopes that buying her this interim chair might throw her off the scent of the new one. Her mum always ruins surprises.

She can smell a secret from a mile away.

'How much did this cost, Gem? Let me at least pay you for it.'

Gem moves her mum's broken chair out of the way, making room for the temporary upgrade.

'Don't worry about it, Mum. I promise it wasn't much.' She'd only had to sell her leather jacket, an old pair of Levi's that were already on their third life and a fancy candle she'd been given by work.

As soon as the brakes are on, her mum shifts so she can lift herself out of her place on the sofa and into her new chair, ready to test out her new wheels. When she moves forward and backward, to the left *and* to the right, without making any weird noises, her mum's resulting smile makes it all worth it. Gem would happily have sold more of her possessions just for that.

Not that she isn't selling part of her soul already.

An image of Atlas's face pops into Gem's mind. The feeling of guilt hasn't quite left her, and although ignoring it is partially working, Gem has decided that it is going to be vital to keep as much distance between them as possible. This could be difficult to do, seeing as the whole point of dating is to get to know someone better, but this is also why the choice of location for their next date is key.

Getting close, but not too close, is a fine balance, and one that Gem is going to need to strike.

'Thank you, Gem.'

Shaking herself out of her thoughts, she bends down to kiss her mum. 'It's my absolute pleasure.' She watches as her mum keeps moving about. 'The guy we picked it up from said it sometimes catches on the right wheel. Can you feel anything sticking?'

'Nope. It's absolutely perfect.' Her mum places a free hand over Gem's. 'You can stop worrying now.'

Of course this doesn't happen, but the slight weight of her

mum's hand does give Gem enough of a break – her lungs finally remember to breathe.

'If I'd known that I was going to be able to move enough to do the cooking, I would've bought something different for us to have for lunch.'

'Hey.' Uncle Mike pops his head into the lounge. He's really good at disappearing when things get emotional and reappearing to provide some light entertainment. 'You have chicken pie almost every Sunday of the year. You can have a cooked breakfast for dinner twice in a month every now and then.'

Gem holds up her hands. 'Don't look at me. I love breakfast, especially for dinner, and I was raised better than to complain about the food put in front of me.' She looks at her mum, realising a second too late that what was meant to be kind could be taken in completely the wrong way. 'Not that I had a reason to complain about the food put in front of me.'

Luckily, her mum has never been one to give her a hard time.

'You absolutely did, but we're not here to talk about my food. We're here to talk about your birthday.'

Gem isn't quite quick enough to stop the groan that escapes. 'We don't need to do anything big this year.' Gem is in her early thirties, young enough to fear getting older, but not old enough to know that ageing is a blessing.

She should have stayed silent. As a general rule, one her family learnt the hard way, it's better to celebrate whenever and whatever you can, and so birthdays – an event that even the unenlightened make a fuss of – are a big thing for the three of them.

Her mum goes over to the side table where all of the family photo albums are kept. Still getting used to the new dimensions of her chair, she knocks into a table leg on her way and has to rearrange herself and her chair. As usual, she doesn't say anything, but Gem notes everything. Her next chair will be lightweight enough to manoeuvre more easily and it should also be narrow enough that her mum won't have to be quite so self-conscious about her every move.

'Here, love, grab these, will you?' Her mum pulls out multiple albums full of photos and soon a kind of production line is formed. 'Thought we'd look back at some old photos for some inspiration.'

When all of the albums are out, her mum makes her way back over to the table. She opens one of the more worn albums first, the one with a bright turquoise cover. It creaks a bit as it opens, the plastic sheets sticking together.

'We could do a crafting party. I've seen a lot of people making their own candle holders. Or a pirate party?' She reaches for another album. 'My favourite was the bagel theme, but then I've always had a weakness for carbs—'

'Mum, you know I love you, and you know I love a party—'

'Why do I hear a "but" coming?' Her mum closes the album she's looking through with a snap.

'*But* we really don't need to have one this year.'

Gem's mum just stares at her. She stays so silent and so still for so long that Gem wonders if she's heard her.

'Are you and Shanti still arguing? Is that what's wrong?' she asks finally.

Uncle Mike pops his head back in, right on cue. 'Do I need to go teach her a lesson?'

'No. You don't.' Gem turns back to her mum, Uncle Mike still wielding a spatula. 'And no, everything is fine between us. It's not that.'

'What is it then?'

'Nothing. There is nothing wrong.' She glances at her uncle, then her mum, then back again. 'I promise. I'm really happy to celebrate my birthday. I just don't need a party.' She tries to say the next words with the gravitas required to highlight how truthful they are. 'I just want to be surrounded by the people I love. I don't need or want anything else.'

Both her mum, and now also Uncle Mike, fall quiet for an unusually long time.

Apparently, Gem succeeded in her goal. Her words really hit home.

When it all becomes too much, Uncle Mike escapes silently into the kitchen. He really doesn't do well with emotion. But her mum just looks at her.

'Well,' her eyes start to shine with unspent tears, 'when you put it that way.'

Chapter 17

'The cinema?'

Atlas is standing next to Gem, staring up at the old-fashioned signage, the type where the lettering needs to be manually changed and looks a little bloated, like it might pop out at any moment. She is annoyed to notice that the bright evening light is making his features even more pronounced. The angles of his jaw are even more stark, and his five o'clock shadow looks more like an eight o'clock silhouette. He looks down at her, pointing his thumb towards the entrance. It's surrounded by big movie lights, with old-fashioned red carpet leading up the wide staircase completing the retro feel of the place.

'This is what you consider to be a bit more exciting?'

'Yes.'

She had spent a lot of time thinking about what would be the perfect third date with Atlas. Concluding that what annoys her most about him are his looks, which are too beguiling, and the words that come out of his mouth, which are too annoying, the cinema seemed like the perfect place.

He looks back up at the sign and shakes his head. 'No.'

'What do you mean "no"? I've already bought the tickets.' Gem waves the little pieces of paper in front of him, *Lord of the Rings* printed on them in large lettering. She'd made sure to pick seats next to people so Atlas would be even less tempted to talk and hoped that the length of the movie would also mean Atlas wouldn't suggest going for a drink after.

It's the perfect plan.

But this time, he doesn't just look at Gem. He turns so he is positioned in front of her. At least tonight he left his shell at home.

He holds his hands out, palms upwards, as though he's checking for rain even though they are bathed in glorious sunshine. 'We are not wasting this beautiful evening being stuck inside.'

Gem hates to admit it, but the idea of spending the next three hours inside doesn't fill her with joy either. The only thing worse would be to spend it outside, with no buffer between her and Atlas.

'Again, I've already bought the tickets.' The excuse sounds even weaker now than it did ten seconds ago.

'I'll pay you back,' Atlas says firmly.

Gem glances at Atlas, squinting as the sun momentarily blinds her. She shuts her eyes, only opening them again when she can feel the clouds have shifted and she isn't going to risk damaging her corneas. Then she sees that it isn't the clouds that have come to her rescue – Atlas has moved to the right, acting as her own personal sunshade. At his quiet kindness, the retort she had planned dies on her tongue, and the words that come out of her mouth are not the ones she'd planned on saying.

'What would you suggest we do instead?'

The change in his demeanour is instant. He stays still, making sure the sun can't reach Gem, but his shoulders are no longer sunken, his smile reaches his eyes, crinkling the corners, and his feet dance a little on the spot, too excited to stay still.

'Thought you'd never ask.' The glint in his eye puts Gem on edge. 'I have the perfect idea.'

Eight minutes later, the two of them are once again standing side by side. But instead of a retro cinema, they are standing in front of a garden. It's one of those idyllic squares that are littered around London. They are usually only accessible to local residents, forcing everyone else to look in envy at what's inside, except on the rare occasion when they open their doors to the public for a fee. Today is one of those lucky days.

'This is your perfect idea?'

Atlas shoots Gem a side glance before looking back at the garden. His hands rest on his hips, and he's standing as though he's a landowner surveying his grounds.

'Yep.'

Gem surveys the scene in front of her. There is a little pergola surrounded by blossom trees, gentle slopes in the ground that have no doubt been added in, and a painfully well-manicured lawn on which they've laid out a bunch of different games — giant Jenga, a couple of twister mats, chess, as well as various bean bag throwing games that all look remarkably similar. There is also a rather tempting smell of barbeque coming from somewhere.

The event appears to be targeted towards children. Gem can only see one other pair of adults who appear to be taking part in the games themselves instead of acting as butlers to the crazed little dictators. In this case though, the kids look more appealing than the adults. The couple have come decked out in athleisure wear, and even have their own water bottles.

'So, what do you say?' Atlas turns to face Gem, wiggling his eyebrows.

At least it isn't a wink.

'Can I challenge you to a game of Jenga?'

Interactive games in the sunshine are about as far away from a dark cinema as you can get, but the harsh truth is they've missed the start of the movie, and Gem is contractually obliged to be here. So even though there is no oversized bag blocking her exit this time, Gem doesn't run away. Instead, she steps forward, leaving Atlas to follow a few steps behind.

'Fine. But only if you promise *not* to let me win.'

Against her better judgment, Gem is having quite a good time. It turns out that Giant Jenga is very enjoyable. The fear of the tower falling on you adds the perfect level of thrill that is just the right size to be genuinely scary while not actually being dangerous.

But the thing giving Gem an even bigger thrill is watching the other pair of adults – and, surprisingly, watching Atlas as he comes to exactly the same conclusion that she has.

'Fucking hell, they're annoying.'

Gem nods. 'I told you.'

Atlas and Gem have taken a quick break between games to catch their breath, eat some overpriced ice cream and judge people from behind the safety of their sunglasses.

'Look!' The excitement in Atlas's voice is in stark contrast to the straight face he is masterfully maintaining. 'They're limbering up!'

Gem turns. The pair are standing in front of the Twister mats. They are holding on to each other's shoulders, swinging a leg each back and forth, before twisting slightly side to side, and then going through exactly the same motions with the other leg. It looks extremely well-practised, and completely ridiculous.

Atlas scoffs. 'I reckon they go from park to park, destroying other people's fun and shaming the human race.'

It appears that Atlas and Gem aren't alone in their feelings. An invisible but undeniable halo has formed around the limbering pair. Whenever they transition to a different game, parents shoo their children away.

'How flexible are you?'

Atlas's question catches Gem slightly off guard. She turns back to face him, a little flustered.

'I'm sorry, what?'

But Atlas isn't looking at her. His eyes are still trained on the doubles partners behind her. He nods towards them.

'What do you think?'

'What do I think about what?' This time Gem's question – or her tone – makes Atlas shift his attention so it is now fully focused on her.

She hasn't realised until now how close they have got. So much so, she can see the individual smile lines that pepper his cheeks. She can also see that they are slightly deeper on the left side of his face, the same side that hitches up first when he smiles. Gem leans away, but Atlas is still staring at the couple.

'D'you reckon we can take them on?' There is a hint of barely supressed excitement in his voice.

Gem glances at them, using the move to gain a bit more distance. The pair are now stretching out their backs, but she's seen enough.

'You want to go up against them?'

Atlas nods. 'I do.' He is still wearing his sunglasses, but she swears she can see him wink through the dark lenses. 'But only if you do it with me.'

Gem pauses, a 'hell, no' freezing on her lips.

Maybe it's the heat, maybe it's the level of Gem's annoyance, maybe it's the couple's embarrassing, choreographed handshake, but for some reason, all of Gem's other feelings – her yearning for the safety of the cinema, her annoyance at Atlas's wink, her guilt over what she is doing – fade in comparison to the righteous competitive spirit coursing through her veins.

'Fine.' At her answer, Gem swears Atlas jumps, just a little. 'Let's do it.' In one movement, she throws away the remnants of her melted ice cream and starts to walk away, but a gentle hand on the crook of her elbow stops her. The combination of her forward momentum and Atlas's anchor has her spinning like a car racing around a hairpin turn. Only when she stops, it's Atlas she bumps into.

She's even closer to him now than she was before. She needs to breathe, but for some reason her lungs aren't working.

'Not so fast. I have a plan.' His hand drops from her arm.

'A plan?'

Atlas nods. 'Yes. We're going to hustle them.'

Gem squints at him even though both his body and her sunglasses are protecting her. He's been moving around her all evening, making sure she's out of direct sunlight. And as a red head, she's not exactly going to ask him to stop. Shade is her best friend. She can hear the – now very familiar – whoop that comes signifying the end of the couple's handshake. It's the final push she needs.

'OK. I'm listening. What do I need to do?'

'Right hand to red.'

Gem can only spare a quick peek from under her armpit as she follows the instructions. A small, but emotionally invested crowd has formed around the two Twister mats, the number of spectators increasing with every play. One of the mums has even volunteered to call out the moves, and two of the dads are refereeing, one for each team.

Gem's hand, by way of Atlas's knee, lands on red.

It's difficult to hustle someone over Twister, but Atlas was right when he said the pair – Juliet and Tom – looked like the kind of people who would be so competitive that they would be blind to anything except their need to win. So, after purposefully throwing a game and feigning stiffness, when Atlas suggested going two against two, each couple on their own mat, the colour-coordinated pair readily agreed.

Although Juliet and Tom are good, Gem can see a trickle of sweat running down the side of Tom's face, and Juliet has started grunting under the pressure. Atlas was also right when he said that their two bodies – Atlas's tall and Gem's short, his strong and hers more flexible – would complement each other well. If they worked together, Gem could go for the spots that were closer together and more awkward for Atlas to twist into, while Atlas could reach for the spots that were further away.

And it's all going to plan, except for the fact that Gem and Atlas keep finding themselves in awkwardly intimate positions. In her haste to agree, Gem had forgotten that Twister inevitably ends up with entangled limbs, or – as in Gem and Atlas's case – bodies piled on top of each other. The whole premise of Twister sounds like the kind of game someone made up on the spot, needing an excuse for being caught in a compromising position. But Atlas is apparently very strong and although he is effectively cocooning her, he is doing so while keeping the biggest distance between their bodies that he can, even if it isn't much.

It's not easy for Gem to admit, but his gentlemanly ways are having an effect on her.

'Left foot to blue.'

A grunt comes from the other team, and Gem and Atlas briefly lock eyes. A silent static of excitement travels between the two of them. They are winning.

It's only when Gem looks at her own body, and then where blue is, that she sympathises with the grunt. Whereas Atlas can reach the blue easily, Gem is going to have to either go under him and risk her right foot, or go over him, and test the limits of her muscles. She tries going under, but she can't quite make it work. She has to retreat at the last moment, risking life, limb and her ability to walk easily tomorrow to hold her left leg up in the air.

Seeing her dilemma, Atlas nudges her hip gently with his own; a move that forces Gem to look at him once more.

He nods purposefully towards her foot and then over his leg. 'Go on.'

Gem still doesn't move.

'Just trust me. I got you.' He says the words so casually, and with no hint of strain, as if he plays Twister every day. It would be the perfect line, if only he didn't wink straight afterwards.

Gem is too late, and her nerves are too wrecked, to stop her eyes from rolling.

She can feel the laughter coming from him even though no noise escapes.

'Sorry. The wink was too much. I promise I won't do anything dodgy, and if you want to stop, we can. I'm OK with losing.' The steadiness in his eyes suggests that he is telling the truth. 'But, if you want to hook your left leg over me, I wouldn't say no.'

Gem glares at him and his barely camouflaged sexual insinuation. But then his face turns serious, if now slightly shaky from the physical strain. 'I promise to help hold you up. It's your choice.'

Her right butt cheek is screaming for her to make a decision and so, without overthinking it, she does. It is interesting how a mutual dislike of others can bring two people closer together, in this case, literally. Luckily, Gem's left foot lands just in time, with the steady support of Atlas now supporting her from underneath.

'Thank you.' The relief in her words is nowhere near as palpable as the relief she feels physically.

'It's my pleasure.'

Although Gem can't see a wink, she can imagine it perfectly, but before she can think too much about it, the next instruction is called out.

'Left hand to green.'

This time, Gem gestures to Atlas to move first, his left hand straining slightly under pressure in its current position. It lands neatly. Gem feels his muscles relax when he's comfortably in place. When she is sure he is stable, she moves, her own hand having to skim past his, her shoulder and head now tucked under his own. They are so close that she can feel his breath against her ear. A lock of her hair tickles her neck and she quivers.

'Sorry.' Atlas's voice is closer than she has ever heard it. 'I'll try to breathe somewhere else.'

'No, don't.' Her answer comes out more quickly, and a lot more breathlessly, than she would like. His body is still on top of hers. A badly timed need to readjust her right shoulder brings them even closer together.

'I just mean you don't have to. It's OK.'

Up until now, despite all of the awkward moments, all of the compromising positions and all of the close passes, Gem has managed to maintain her cool. But now, she can feel a blush creeping up her neck. The only saving grace is that Atlas, for once, doesn't say a word. There are no cheeky winks or sexual innuendos.

Instead, the only thing she can hear is the sound of someone shouting.

'Out! Out! Foul! Fault!' Despite being enthusiastic referees, the dads evidently don't know what words to use. Nevertheless, the shouts have the desired effect.

Gem and Atlas both freeze, along with everyone else. Gem looks at all of their limbs, checking for any faults, fouls, or outs but she doesn't see any. Holding position, she then looks across at the other mat. Juliet's left leg, unsupported unlike her own, has collapsed.

It's difficult to know if the general uproar is because Gem and Atlas have won, or because the other team has lost, but either way, the mood is infectious. Gem can feel more than see the relief and happiness in Atlas. His body fully relaxes. It brings the two of them closer together.

'I'm gonna try to get out of this position as gracefully as I can.' His breath is still on her neck. 'But I warn you,' his knees bend and he tries to push his upper body up and away, Gem feeling every move, 'my body is pretty tired.'

Even if Atlas hadn't warned Gem, she would have known that he wasn't going to be able to right himself without taking them both down. Over the course of the game, her body couldn't help but pick up subtle clues from his. And so, despite his best efforts, they land in an ungraceful heap, their legs still tangled, staring into each other's eyes.

Twister is not exactly a game full of talking, but the silence that stretches out between the two of them makes Gem realise quite how intense it was. And it's impossible for her not to feel a slight kinship with Atlas – it's been a long time, years possibly, since anyone has seen Gem's body so closely, from so many different angles,

When Atlas speaks, he's still trying to catch his breath. 'Twister is more difficult to play than I realised.'

Relieved at the lightness that comes with Atlas's well-chosen words, Gem looks back at their opponents, sensing Atlas doing the same. They appear to be having a post-match discussion, arguing over where they failed, both of them gesticulating at the mat.

'We were wrong to make fun of them. I can see now why they limbered up.' She is watching the couple when the sun once again magically disappears. Atlas is somehow standing, holding out a hand to her.

Gem takes it, and he pulls her up. The power still left in Atlas's arms and Gem's own eagerness to stand propel her right into his arms. Although her butt has just been in his face for a solid twenty minutes, standing face-to-face as they now are feels a lot more intimate.

It would be the perfect moment to kiss him.

That thought alone is enough to make Gem cough and step away.

'Well...' Gem searches, unsuccessfully, for the words that will make the situation less awkward. 'Thank you for holding me up at the end. I would have fallen over without it.'

Atlas shakes his head. 'No thanks required. We make a good team.' For some reason, his words once again make Gem blush, and the look in his eyes makes it hard for her to move. 'What I do require though is a promise.'

Gem hesitates. 'What kind of promise?'

There is more than a hint of fear in her question, and more than a hint of cheek in Atlas's eyes when he answers.

'I get to choose what we do on our next date.'

Chapter 18

'Where are we going?' Gem's question comes out with a few more prickles than she means it to, but she's had quite a stressful day at work. Had her date been with anyone else, or without a bigger purpose, she would have cancelled. She's in the mood to quit everything. Her dating life. Shanti's study. Her job.

Especially her job.

Surely it wouldn't be so bad to move back in with her mum, work at the local pub, stop dancing, and instead just eat cheese? Once again, she had been the one to collate everything used to pitch for a new account, and once again Martin used it. She wouldn't mind so much if he at least credited her, but the only time Martin does that is if they get something wrong.

The fact she doesn't know what Atlas has planned is also adding to her frustration levels.

As is the fact that there are so many people around.

Gem rarely falls out of love with her home city. She knows that it smells, has a pigeon problem and that it attracts just as many slightly crazy people as it does good eggs, but usually the magic of the city outweighs everything else. Not today. Today there are too many people, slightly crazy or otherwise. The tube was too noisy, and the smells were, well, far, far too smelly. The warmer weather means there are even more people on her beloved streets, and therefore more fragrances. Plus, Atlas has made her come all the way to Greenwich. It's nice here, if a little *artisanal*. They've just walked past a pet shop where a coat – for a dog – costs more than her whole outfit.

'Well,' Atlas looks down at her, a smile tugging at the side of his mouth.

It would be cute, and Gem can imagine it working on a lot of people, but he's also doing this thing where he's clearly (but subtly) manoeuvring her around the pavement, pulling her a bit this way and pushing her a bit that way, so she doesn't hit people. She is more than capable of walking, and even if she does hit someone, she will probably survive. With the mood she's in, although she only stands at five foot two on a good day, it's the other person who should watch out. 'That depends on you.'

'On me?'

'Yep.'

'But it's your turn to pick.'

'Oh, I know. But I'm giving you a choice between two options. It seems only fair considering I influenced our last date.'

He takes hold of her hand, pulls her to the side and simultaneously steps slightly in front of her. She is so annoyed that she steps around him, or at least she tries to, but this time, the tug on her arm is less subtle, and more impossible to ignore or break free from, even though she tries.

'Hey—' But her words are cut short.

He tugs her back again, and not a moment too soon. One of the crazy people London attracts hurtles past them on an electric scooter, totally oblivious to the fact he should be on the road, and even less aware of how fast he's going and that his wheels are aimed at everyone's ankles. It would be bad enough in winter, but now people don't even have the extra protection of a boot to cushion the impact.

As soon as he is past, Atlas lets go of her hand, but their bodies are still close. His eyes widen, and his body stills. Neither of them moves away. They are so close that Gem can see a little scar marking Atlas's right eyebrow and count his heart beats. He licks his lips before he talks, but this time, the move doesn't repulse Gem.

She blames the near-death experience for her momentary weakness.

'Sorry I grabbed you without warning. I could see him coming and I didn't have time to explain *and* pull you out of the way.'

Gem, who had been ready to push Atlas away right into the path of the scooter, feels the last remnants of anger leave her body, her shoulders physically deflating from their absence. Atlas isn't the enemy here. Martin is. And anyone who uses a scooter.

'Well, thank you.' The words come out slightly stilted.

Atlas nods and coughs a little. 'You're welcome.' But when he moves again, Gem notices he does so stiffly. For someone who usually moves with such confidence and surety, it's as easy to spot, as it is mildly intriguing.

For the next portion of the walk, until the crowd thins out a bit more, allowing them to walk side by side, she lets Atlas guide her. After all, he is significantly taller than she is, and she doesn't want to get hit. He can see potential dangers coming from further away. Plus, Atlas does this thing where he straightens up, making himself look even bigger than he is. And when he does, people move out of his way leaving Gem to follow safely behind. It's the first time she has ever truly experienced being higher up the pavement hierarchy. She feels powerful. She feels less burdened. She has more space to catch her breath.

'Anyway, back to today.'

Atlas falls into step beside her, his physical ease seeming to have returned. 'You are zero for three on date activity. I might not know that much about you yet, but I can safely say that you have terrible taste when it comes to deciding what to do.'

Gem can't argue. After all, it is her strategy to go on slightly boring dates. 'Fair point. But if that's the case, why are you letting me have any say at all in what we do today?'

She's so out of her comfort zone that she doesn't really notice until it's too late that Atlas has led her off the main road and down an empty side street. One of the ones that has a vape shop that nobody ever seems to go in but somehow stays open, a taxi company and a phone repair shop. Gem can't imagine that the people who meticulously laid each pebble on this street would be happy with the shops currently occupying it.

'Is this where you murder me?'

Instead of answering her, Atlas simply stops walking.

'You have two options.'

Luckily for Atlas, he's earned himself some good grace with that scooter save, and so Gem plays along.

'OK. What are they?'

'Well, option number one is a little boring. There's a nice pizza place around the corner. We can have a thin crust margarita, and then go for a walk. Maybe pick up a hot chocolate or an ice cream for dessert, if we're feeling adventurous.'

'And option number two?' Even as she asks the question, the idea of eating circular carbs covered in cheese has her soul singing. The thought of pizza is so distracting that it takes Gem a moment to realise that Atlas looks like she has never seen him look before: a little unsure.

'Are you OK?'

He ignores her question. 'Option number two requires you to be all in.'

'All in?' Her whole body is a question. Her shoulders hitch and straighten. Her eyebrows knit together and her jaw clenches.

Atlas nods. 'All in,' he repeats. 'You don't know me. Beyond your awful pub preferences, I don't know you. Quite frankly I was a little surprised when you agreed to see me again after that first date. I genuinely thought the whole, "*my flatmate is stuck naked in a bush*" story was a lie.' He shrugs, and Gem tries to steel her face.

'But if you pick option number two, we'll be doing something much more personal to me. So, just for a couple of hours, I need you to be all in.'

He shifts on his feet and misreads Gem's facial expression. 'I'm not after a commitment here, so you can stop looking so scared. I don't need help paying my rent or someone to timeshare a dog with. But this is important to me. If you pick option number two, you will be part of something bigger. Bigger than pizza.

'You'll have the power to change the future.'

His words are eerily similar to Madame Sybil's.

'You know you aren't making any sense, right?'

His half smile appears.

'I am, you just don't know it yet.'

Once again, he's challenging her. Gem can see it in his eyes. He thinks she's going to pick the pizza. Part of her wants to pick the pizza. She loves pizza. She also knows what pizza is, and she doesn't know what's behind door number two.

But she also loves a challenge.

She stands up a bit straighter. 'Why would you trust me with this, if it's so important to you?'

Atlas shifts again. 'Honestly?'

Gem nods, relieved that the question isn't directed her way. 'Honestly.'

'Because I really want to go. And when I said yes to meeting up this evening, I kinda forgot that tonight was, well, *tonight*.' He shrugs. 'But separate to that I do actually think you'll have a great time.'

'Keeping your dates straight isn't your speciality, is it?' The memory of his snail bag is still burnt in her memory.

A shrug is his only reply, yet the challenge is still there in his eyes. It makes it hard for Gem to think straight, so she looks away. First, she glances at the street. Swathes of people are walking down the road, making their position seem even more intimate – and abandoned – than it is. Then she looks down. How has she only just noticed that his hand – the one he had been using to guide her – is still holding hers? She doesn't know, but she can't come up with a way to get out of it. At least not one that seems natural. So, she leaves it where it is. Her focus back on her original problem, she takes a final moment before deciding.

'Fine. I pick option two.'

Before she has even finished speaking, Atlas raises his eyes to the sky, thanking whoever or whatever he feels the need to. When he looks back down at Gem, his smile is bigger than ever.

'You won't regret this. I promise.'

Atlas might be a fully grown adult, but in this moment, looking as naively happy as he does, Gem can imagine him as a kid in school. Running, slightly high from the sugar in the school custard, limbs with space to grown into, his carefree happiness yet to be dampened. She doubts they would have been friends in school. She colour-coordinated all of her notes, whereas she doubts Atlas even took any.

'Will you tell me where we're going now?'

With a quick squeeze of her hand – which is *still* in his – Atlas leads her back towards the river of people.

'I'm taking you to your first football game.'

Chapter 19

As Atlas passes her a food parcel that he bought from a rusting van, Gem wishes she had pressed him a little more on whether he was going to murder her.

They walked for about ten minutes before stopping for food, more and more people joining them as they meander in the middle of the road, no cars in sight. Today, the road has been taken back by the people.

'If you're doing this, you're doing this properly, and that includes the snacks.'

She takes the parcel from him. 'I'm not sure a fully sized burger counts as a snack, but thank you.'

'You're welcome. I asked for extra onions and tomato ketchup. It compromises the structure, but it's delicious.'

She just hopes the sauerkraut has done its thing and made her gut healthy. She has a feeling she's going to need all the help she can get to digest this. 'Do we eat now or wait until we get inside?'

He looks at her as though she has just committed a crime.

'What? What did I do?'

He shakes his head. 'You should never eat and walk. It gives you indigestion. It's *very* bad for you.'

Her eyes roll all of their own accord. 'Right. Because it's the walking while eating that's unhealthy, not the actual burger itself and the amount of saturated fats.'

Now that they have their food, they rejoin all of the people heading towards the stadium. In an ironic twist of events considering his earlier behaviour, Atlas keeps bumping into her. It's annoying, but also kind of reassuring to have someone familiar around in this mad sea of people.

She has no idea who is playing, or which team Atlas is here to support, but even Gem can feel the sense of anticipation in the air. The last time she felt something similar was when she went to go see Beyoncé in concert. Although at least then she was able to join in on the excitement, whereas now she feels a lot like a voyeur. There was a very similar vibe though – a sense of community, selling of merch, some singing – not that she is about to admit this to Atlas.

'I have two words for you—'

He's walking them towards an entry gate. It's comically small in comparison to the large building it's guarding. Just a little turnstile. Gem reckons on a good day she could jump it. Just before they reach the booth, pushed forward by a slow-moving but powerful wave of people behind them, Atlas reaches inside his coat, pulling out two tickets. He hands one to her as he leans down, nudging her in front.

'All. In.'

She reaches for the ticket, and for a moment, time stops. When Gem's lungs eventually remember to work, they are brought back to life by his scent, an intoxicating mix of something spicy and something fresh.

'*Oi!* You goin' in, or what?'

This time, not even Atlas can protect her from being bumped into as the man shoves past, but he is there to catch her before she falls.

'Thanks.'

'Any time.'

She eventually pulls away.

It takes her longer than she'd like to admit to regain her balance.

'These seats, up here?'

She turns to Atlas who is following behind, having an easier time navigating his way over and around all of the legs and the bags.

The stadium is pretty big, but the team isn't one that Gem has heard of. Obviously, she doesn't admit this.

Everyone around her is wearing bright red. Some even have the little swords of Charlton FC drawn on their cheeks. More than one looks like a penis.

Again, Gem keeps quiet.

'Yep.' Atlas nods, and Gem keeps going, narrowly missing kicking over a full tumbler of beer.

It was a bit of a stupid question considering there are only two seats left in the row, but as they get closer, everyone starts staring at them. Gem feels the urge to confirm that she does, indeed, belong, even though she feels completely out of place.

As she picks her way over feet and bags and drinks and children, her steps get heavier as she goes. Unlike her soulless pub choices, being here means a lot to Atlas. This is a very personal date. And Gem is just using him to get money – Twister games and hand holding, apart. So, despite managing to reach her seat without injuring herself or anyone else, the pride she would usually feel is far outweighed by another, much more unsettling sensation that she's doing her best to ignore.

She slips into the seat – quite literally as it's made of very shiny, very cold, plastic – and smiles at the person next to her. It's not her natural smile, but he smiles back as though she's just sat down next to an extended-family member at dinner. The type of relative that knows exactly who you are, but the last time you saw them was when the memory part of your brain still hadn't developed.

'Hello.'

Her potential uncle-thrice-removed is still beaming at her, and when Gem feels Atlas sit down next to her, she is so relieved that it takes her a few seconds before she gets annoyed at quite how close he is sitting. She shifts away as subtly as she can, even though she would prefer to magically shrink, like a grape transitioning into a raisin.

He leans forward, reaching out a hand. There is a moment of potential awkwardness when Gem's reaction is to swat his hand away, but when it lands, it doesn't land anywhere near her. Instead, it lands on the knee of her faux thrice-removed uncle, and instead of hitting it away, as Gem nearly did, another hand lands on top, holding his in place. It is a little weathered by age, but Gem can tell it still holds a lot of strength in it.

'Hey, Howie,' she hears Atlas say.

'Good to see you, my boy.'

Another hand appears, this time from behind, and lands on Atlas's shoulder.

'We didn't know if you'd show. You've turned into a part-time supporter.'

Atlas turns to the man behind him, his hand slipping away from Howie, briefly kissing Gem's knees on the way. 'Hey, Johnny.'

Atlas hangs his head. 'I know. I'm sorry.' Despite the fact this is just a game, Atlas's apology sounds sincere.

The woman next to Johnny playfully hits him on the knee. 'Oh, stop it, Johnny. Just because our Atlas has other calls on his time and all you have is your dahlias.' Then she smiles at Atlas. It reminds Gem of how her mum smiles at her. But then, that same smile is turned on Gem.

'And who are you, love?'

Gem, who has already assumed the position of a spectator, takes a while to answer. 'I'm Georgina. Gem.' And then, embarrassingly, her hand – the one that is still holding the burger – waves. 'Hi.'

The kindness behind the smile in front of her doesn't fade. 'Well, Gem, it's lovely to meet any friend of Atlas. I'm Katie, and this,' she gestures to the man next to her, whose hand is still on Atlas's shoulder, 'is Johnny. We're all season regulars. Friends of Atlas. We keep his seat warm for him when he can't make it. And keep him in check when he can.'

A nod from Atlas is his only response.

Gem can imagine Katie being the kind of person who would tell you off for nicking food one minute, then the next, bring out a plate of brownies she made just for you.

The woman gestures to the people around their seats. 'That's Tayles.' Pointing to a man with no hair whose legs are jittering at a hundred miles an hour, clearly eager for the game to start.

'Harry.' Pointing to someone who has just taken a larger than advised bite of burger, that from the looks of things also contains onions and ketchup.

'Howie, you've already met.' Howie nods at her, and then Katie points at two more people who are huddled slightly together looking at something on a phone.

Everyone here – at least on this side of the pitch – is dressed relatively similarly, but something about these two suggests that they are dressed to complement each other. They look like they both order their clothes from the same catalogue. They're wearing jeans in the same colour wash, and their matching scarves are tied in the same way around their necks. 'And that's Saoirse and Chris.' They both look up at the same time. It's clear that they have no idea why their names have been called but have reacted purely on instinct. Clearly, it isn't just Atlas who Katie keeps in check.

Once again, Gem waves awkwardly.

'It's nice to meet you all.'

Howie nods towards her. 'You've come to a good game.'

'Hopefully.' From Johnny's tone, he is anything but hopeful.

Katie flips him again. She makes contact in exactly the same place, and Johnny doesn't even jump from the shock, her hand landing so softly that even a peach wouldn't bruise.

The welcome is undeniably warm, yet it makes Gem want to run. Unfortunately, her only escape route is blocked by numerous knees and a niggling desire to stay, just to see what might happen.

'It's actually my first football game.' At her confession, all eyes, including Saoirse's and Chris's, swivel to her. Gem has the feeling she's said something she shouldn't have.

'I'm sorry.'

The stares persist, everyone, except Atlas, looking at her with wide, disbelieving eyes. By contrast, his eyes crinkle up at the corners. He is enjoying her discomfort. She squints at him, the universal sign that she is going to exact revenge at the first opportunity, but all this does is cause his crinkles to become even more pronounced. He *really* is enjoying this.

'As in ... the first football game you've gone to in person?' Chris looks confused.

Gem shakes her head slowly, sticking to her promise of only lying when absolutely necessary. 'Erm, no. First football game ever. In-person or otherwise.'

'You didn't even watch the World Cup, or anything?' His voice has risen a pitch or two.

Gem shakes her head. 'No. It seemed a bit ... in-authentic to watch it just because everyone else was?'

She's not looking at him directly, but she can tell that her answer has made Atlas smile.

'Well,' Harry speaks between bites of burger, 'that is an attitude I can admire.'

Howie laughs. 'And, if this is your first one, you've definitely come to a good game. Might as well jump in at the deep end.'

'Why?' Gem has the same feeling she used to get whenever her classmates used to laugh at jokes she didn't find funny, or understand. They never had a TV licence growing up, making it a bit difficult to keep up with the latest cultural gossip. Or football.

Harry answers, a bit of burger visible as he explains, 'Grudge match. Crystal Palace are our local rivals.'

Finally, Atlas chips in. He leans in, just a little too close for Gem's liking, and puts an arm around her shoulders. He might just be trying to be friendly, but she's never been a fan of PDA. Although, his touch doesn't feel awful. 'We've won the last two times we've played against them, but our overall record is still, well, not in our favour.'

'But we're at home, and we've got no injuries, and our defenders have been looking really sharp this season.' Katie is clearly the optimist in the group.

'So maybe you're due a win?' Gem offers the question, not really knowing if it's the right thing to say, but she's aware that she means to be all in, while simultaneously trying to ignore the arm that is still draped across her shoulders.

'*We.*' This comes from Howie.

Gem shoots him a confused look, 'Huh?'

Howie nods. 'We. *We* are due a win.' He gestures around with his hand. 'You're part of this now.'

She doesn't know what to say, and this time she can't even wave away her lack of confidence.

Atlas squeezes her shoulder, a smile on his face. 'All in?' he repeas his words from earlier.

The increasing heaviness of guilt weighs on her, and Gem considers running. Instead, she shrugs, matching Atlas's smile. 'I guess so.'

Thankfully, as the silence between the two of them stretches out, the group conversation ends. Howie goes back to his drink, Harry goes back to his burger and Katie goes back to fussing about something Johnny is doing. But with Atlas's hand still in hers, it's almost like the two of them are back in the deserted alleyway.

She sees Atlas's eyes widen. Just a millimetre, but it is enough. And for some unknown reason, instead of letting go of his hand as she thought she would, she gives it a quick, reassuring squeeze.

'Maybe I shouldn't have confessed about this being my first game?'

But Atlas doesn't answer her question. Instead, he just looks at her. 'I didn't know your full name is Georgina. I just assumed it was Gemma or Gemima, or something like that.'

This is not an unusual conversation for Gem. But recalling her promise to only lie when absolutely necessary, Gem's answer is unusual. It's a truth she rarely shares. One of the pieces of information she keeps reserved for the special people in her life.

'My mum is Georgina, and she named me after her, but I couldn't pronounce Georgina, I could only say Gem, and it just stuck.'

'Well,' Atlas nudges her shoulder with his, 'it suits you.'

Needing to concentrate on something else, Gem pulls away and starts unwrapping her burger, even though her hunger is now non-existent. There's a huge surge in noise across the stadium. She waits for it to pass before trusting her voice.

'So how come everyone here knows you? Do you always buy the same seats, or something?'

'Kind of. We all have season tickets, so we sit in the same seats every game. I've known all of them for at least five years. But,' he nods towards Katie and Johnny, 'I've known them since I was eight.'

'I should have known these were season tickets.' Gem studies her burger. It is far too large for her jaw. This is not going to be pretty.

'No, you shouldn't have.' He nudges her again. She's going to have to find out the route source of her icks soon with Atlas, otherwise she can tell she's going to risk getting too far in. 'You got any more questions in that head of yours? I'll answer them all.'

She looks around, less for inspiration, and more because she needs to breathe. But there is something that she would really like to know. She leans in as close as she can without making it feel awkward, far enough away that she won't risk accidental contact, even if he turns to her. Still, she's close enough that she's glad she chewed some gum on her way over.

'Actually, yes. Just the one.'

She pauses, a hint of embarrassment sneaking in.

'We're supporting the team in red, right?'

Chapter 20

'So did you like it?'

Gem and Atlas are, once again, alone in an abandoned street. They seem to gravitate towards them. Atlas has insisted on taking her home, and for some reason she's decided to take the slightly different route from the station. The quieter one. The longer one.

'It wasn't quite what I expected.'

She can hear his question in the silence.

But she can't answer. At least not right away.

There is a *lot* to dislike at a football game. All the people. All the noise. All the leftover mess. The seats don't give you much room to move, and God help you if you want to go to the loo.

Gem has mentally added at least another three icks to her list, the biggest of which is the red football shirt that Atlas is still wearing. He pulled it out of his bag as soon as he finished eating his burger. Apparently, he doesn't wash it often to keep it looking as fresh as possible for as long as possible, so he only puts it on after he's finished eating in case he spills. As if this isn't ick-inducing enough, Gem can't understand why you would wear a football shirt if you're not *actually* going to be playing football.

Yet, reluctantly, if she's honest – and she's trying hard to be – there are also some things Gem could learn *not* to hate.

The burger wasn't terrible.

It was quite exciting when they scored a goal, and it was even more exciting when they won.

She also loved watching grown men cry.

Atlas wasn't one of them. He also wasn't one of the people who yelled at the referee – the poor guy was just doing his job. But Gem did have to take a moment to herself when Atlas started singing along with one of the chants. The only reason it didn't develop into a full-blown ick is because it turns out that Atlas has quite a good singing voice. If he'd chanted out of tune, that would have been one ick too far.

Wouldn't it?

Distracted, Gem almost walks into a tree, only waking up just in time to sidestep it.

'That song that you sang. What are the lyrics?'

Atlas inhales deeply, puffing out his chest. 'You just want to hear me sing again, huh?'

Before he can begin chanting, Gem grabs an arm. 'Don't actually sing them.'

He stops and turns towards her. His breath is still caught up in his lungs. He releases a little bit, smiling when he sees the wide panic that Gem knows is in her eyes. 'Why not?'

'It's late. Everyone's asleep.'

'We're not.' He shrugs. 'Besides, what's the worst that could happen?'

He inhales again and this time, channelling her inner Katie, she flips him on his arm.

'Ouch! OK, OK. I won't sing.'

Gem dodges another tree, this time cutting it too close and brushing up against Atlas.

'The lyrics go, "*Many miles have I travelled, many games have I seen, following Charlton my favourite team.*"'

'That's much more wholesome than I expected.'

A noise, somewhere between a scoff and a laugh escapes from Atlas. 'Don't get me wrong, there are some decidedly *un*wholesome songs too, but even I wouldn't shout those down a street.'

Despite the darkness that now surrounds them, Gem can feel Atlas watching her. 'You planning on learning the lyrics so you can join in next time?'

'God no. I have an awful singing voice.'

'Doesn't stop Howie.'

This time, Gem is the one to laugh. 'No, that it doesn't.' She rubs her ear for the comedy effect. 'I'm not sure my hearing is ever going to recover.'

'But you had a better time than you thought you would?'

Noting that this is the third time Atlas has asked, subtly or directly, and she hasn't replied, Gem finally admits, 'I did. I mean, obviously I recognised that it was good when they scored, but beyond that, I had no real idea what was going on, except a lot of running one way and then the other.'

They're nearing Gem's house. She's pretty sure that Atlas can already tell that she's taken him on a longer than necessary route. But the evening doesn't feel over yet. Another type of location needs to be created that isn't as public as a pub but isn't as private as a house.

'To be honest, I even kinda like it when they're losing. Sometimes it makes the game more interesting.' This time, they dodge a bin together, and when Atlas speaks again, he sounds closer than before. 'Just don't tell anyone I said that. Especially not Howie. But you're right, the football itself isn't the main reason why I go either.'

'So, why do you?'

Gem slows down. They've only got three houses to go until they reach her front door. It takes Gem two small steps to realise that Atlas has come to a complete stop. She doesn't make a habit of standing still in the dark, but she doesn't feel a huge urge to rush inside either.

'Definitely don't tell Howie this, but I go for the people. They've been good friends to me over the years. We never hang out beyond the pitch, but they're some of the best friends I've ever had. I know that if I needed help, they'd be the first to come running. It's a community. You feel a part of something bigger.'

He steps towards her, narrowing the distance between them. 'Speaking of which, I think the gang liked you. Katie is particularly discerning, but even she approves.'

Like a magpie to a compliment, Gem smiles. 'I hope so.' There is a pang of discomfort, but it's swallowed up by other feelings. 'I liked them.'

Atlas's grin is quite the sight, even in the darkness. Especially in the darkness. 'So, was it better than pizza?'

His question is innocent enough, but when Gem replies, the lightness that was in her tone mere moments before has disappeared. The atmosphere is now positively charged. 'I did.'

Aware of his closeness, Gem stands a little straighter. It feels as though there is a harness holding her, pulling her towards him. She tries not to breathe.

She really wishes he wasn't still wearing his football shirt. Not because she wants to see him naked. Although she is *mildly* intrigued about this. But more because it is hideous, and he doesn't wash it.

Luckily, he closes the remaining distance between them, making it impossible to see the football shirt in its entirety. Standing this close to him, she can feel the same heat coming from him that she felt sitting next to him all afternoon. It's as electrifying now as it was then, especially as the temperature has cooled. And it's strangely comforting.

It takes Atlas a while to reply, as though he too doesn't quite know what to do.

'Good.'

The word is small, yet weighted.

The world around them shrinks.

Then he lifts his hand, brushing away a completely non-existent piece of wayward hair, pausing a little too long for the touch to be accidental. Standing this near to him, Gem can see the streetlights reflected in his eyes.

She can't remember it happening, but her own hand has somehow moved, resting above Atlas's heart. She uses it to pull him towards her, grabbing on to his hideous, otherwise ick-inducing football shirt, finally finding a positive use for it.

Between Atlas's hand holding Gem close, and hers pulling him closer, it's obvious what's about to happen, but even so, as soon as his lips touch hers, a number of things happen.

First, despite the cool night air, Gem feels warm all the way through to her bones, as though she's just stepped off a plane and is finally on holiday.

Second, Gem can't remember the last time – if ever – a kiss has travelled from her lips all the way down to her toes, especially when Atlas's hands move up to cup the back of her head, somehow anchoring her, but also making her feel as though she is soaring.

And last, she realises she is in deep shit.

Chapter 21

'*You kissed him?*' Shanti pants next to her.

Tonight's class is another Bollywood session. Gem's hands feel a little clunky throughout the whole thing, but her lower back movement pops a lot better this week. It feels good.

'I did.'

Having a debrief at dance isn't exactly what they had planned – Shanti had suggested having dinner together on Thursday night so they could go over everything – but Gem's work got really busy and Shanti had already gone to bed by the time she returned home.

Of course, Gem also wanted to avoid the conversation for as long as possible.

It takes a moment, but at her confession, Shanti's face changes. She's perfectly put together tonight, wearing a pair of leggings in a very brave light stone colour that Gem would definitely spill tomato sauce on, a matching sports bra and an oversized T-shirt with a tiger on the front that's slashed at the top. It looks as though a tiger could have actually taken a swipe at her for turning their ancestor into a fashion statement.

Gem can see her friend struggling not to smile.

Her eyes widen very slightly, and her ears prick up. She raises a hand, and points vaguely in Shanti's direction. 'Don't do that.'

'Do what?' Shanti's voice takes on a light, teasing tone, a dramatic hand placed on her chest. '*I* haven't done anything.'

Gem is still pointing, but it's more defensive than offensive. 'Don't forget that I know you. I can tell what you're thinking. You're thinking that you're already on the way to proving that *the ick* doesn't exist. But let me tell you something, just because I kissed him doesn't mean that the ick I feel isn't also a completely valid feeling. I still know that, ultimately, we are incompatible. And I will find out why.'

This time, Shanti can't hide her smile. Gem, on the other hand, can't hide her scowl.

Gem knows the only way to get Shanti off her back will be to prove her point. To find the source of the ick. The thing about Atlas that the ick is trying to warn her about. Not the wink. Not the bag. The *real* cause of the ick. He may be cute, but her body is trying to keep him away from her. She can't get distracted by a kiss. It's only a matter of time before she discovers the source of the ick. Maybe they have incompatible political beliefs. Maybe he's a massive misogynist. Maybe they have absolutely no sexual chemistry.

Although Gem fears this last point is moot.

'I couldn't *not* kiss him,' she blurts out.

Part of her had considered not telling Shanti about the kiss. But apart from the fact she needs to – it is, after all, part of the agreement and having ordered her mum's chair, she now really needs the money – she also *wants* to speak to someone about it. And Shanti's her best mate.

'Wait.' Shanti pauses. She's stretching out one leg, her breathing finally coming back under control, but her face has now turned as fierce as the tiger on her T-shirt, 'You mean he *forced* himself on you?'

'Oh, God no. Nothing like that.' For once, Gem is relieved that she goes red when exercising; it makes the blush harder to see. Indeed, from memory, it was Atlas who had to end the kiss. If it had been up to Gem, they would still be kissing now.

'It just happened.'

Shanti's eyes narrow. 'It just happened?'

Gem nods, giving her friend one of those half smiles, the kind that gets caught on your teeth, and is usually reserved for random people on the street.

'Well, what was it like?' Shanti perseveres.

Confident.

Hard to forget.

So good it's wiped Gem's memory of all the kisses that came before it.

Memorable enough that she can still feel him on her lips.

She's caught herself daydreaming about it at work and before she falls asleep.

She's even daydreamed about it on the bus, and nobody can daydream on the bus. A bus's movement is too unpredictable and the bus itself is too full of crazy bus people, hitting into you with their crazy bus people bags that are about to fall apart and might just contain an animal that should not be kept as a pet.

But it isn't only the kiss that takes up her daydreams. They are also full of other, bigger, more complicated scenarios that haven't even happened – seeing him somewhere unexpected and getting swept into a quiet corner, laughing at him sitting in their lounge – as well as smaller details about the kiss that she hadn't even realised at the time.

His breathing after the act, that was almost as beguiling as the kiss itself.

The slightly wild look in his eyes.

The feeling of his chest rising and falling under her hand. His physical warmth.

The gentle kiss that followed less than a minute later as he said goodbye—

'*Hello?* Still here.'

Gem drags herself back into the present. 'Sorry. I was just trying to think how to answer that question.'

'Clearly,' the teasing in Shanti's voice evident.

Gem doesn't fight back. She deserves to be teased. 'It was better than I thought it was going to be,' she admits.

Silence. Then, 'Oh, my *God*.' Shanti's voice is loud enough that at least three other groups of stretchers look their way. 'I need a bit more than *that*.'

'You do not need more. There is no way your final paper needs details about his kissing technique.'

Shanti's eyebrows wiggle. 'Oh. So, he has a *technique*, huh? Pray tell? Don't forget, I am your friend first, and your Ick Doctor second.'

'Ick Doctor?'

'It was the best I could come up with under pressure.' Shanti holds out an imaginary microphone. 'So, are you willing to admit that the ick has nothing to do with an innate incompatibility with the other person?'

'No.' Gem's answer comes out quickly and confidently. 'I'm not weak enough to get distracted by a kiss.'

No matter how delicious it was.

She switches position, bringing her legs out to the front, folding forward. 'The kiss doesn't matter. Yes, it was good.'

Gem closes her eyes as she admits, 'It was better than good, *but* it doesn't mean that the ick has gone, or that it wasn't still a warning. It just means that I haven't found out what it's warning me against.'

She deepens the stretch as much as she can. 'Yet.'

Shanti's eyes narrow, and her mouth twists. 'OK. Fine. I'll allow it.' She stretches away from Gem. 'Doesn't mean that you had to kiss him though.'

'I can't exactly date the guy for six weeks and *not* kiss him.'

At this, Shanti does actually take a beat. 'I hadn't really thought about that.' Her face scrunches up, but only a little as her friend is keen to avoid frown lines.

'Neither had I.'

In fact, the more Gem thinks about the whole experiment, the more she realises that there are a lot of things they haven't thought about. The now familiar feeling of guilt intensifies in her lower stomach.

'Also, it hasn't been six weeks. It's only been like, what, two?' Shanti wiggles her eyebrows at Gem. 'At this rate, you'll be shagging him in four.'

They were both on the verge of laughing until Shanti says this. Instead, they fall into an uncomfortable silence. Because along with not thinking about kissing Atlas, Gem hasn't – until that kiss – thought about doing anything more with him.

And quite frankly, now that she is thinking about it, the thought makes her want to throw up, the reasons for her nausea nothing to do with Atlas himself. Or indeed any of his icks. The reason for her nausea, is guilt.

It has grown from a mild discomfort to a large, melon-sized lump wedged permanently in Gem's thoracic spine.

'Well, do you have any idea yet – even a small inkling – about what the ick could really be warning you against?'

Gem sits up and pulls her feet in, her knees falling out to the side, like she's reading the soles of her feet.

The truth is, she has absolutely nothing. But there's a growing part of her that doesn't really want to find out. When she thinks of Atlas, yes, the first thing her mind thinks of is the soup, and her heavy guilt turns into nauseous butterflies. Then the bag. And then his T-rex hands holding the wine glass. But then, as soon as the butterflies have flown away, the strangest thing happens.

Instead of the soup, she can see Atlas's face as clearly as if he were standing in front of her. Instead of the embarrassing bag, she can see his eyes that look as though he has just been laughing. Instead of the little T-rex hands, she can see the way he positions his body, subtly, in a way that is protecting her very slightly from everyone else who is walking by. She can see, and also feel, his hand as it lightly touches her elbow to avoid her getting hit by another passer-by. And for the first time, she's in the uncomfortable position of hoping her ick is something other than her intuition.

As much as she claims that she isn't going to be distracted by a kiss, she is.

'Hey.'

She looks up. It's another of the dance regulars. 'Hey, Taru.'

'Great class today, huh?' Taru's eyes are wide, and she's quite skittish. She reminds Gem of a rabbit.

'Yeah, although I kept messing up the same steps. It's like my body just couldn't figure out what my brain was trying to tell it to do.'

'Well, I didn't notice you mess up.' Taru pulls at the bag strap hanging over her shoulder, but Gem knows she is being generous. Taru has some of the cleanest moves Gem has ever seen.

'I've got your jacket.'

This comes from Shanti, who then leans a long limb behind her, grabs the pristine paper bag – the fancy kind that keep their shape and that you only ever see in movies or expensive shops – and hands it over to Taru. 'I hope you like it. It was fun to work on.' Along with customising her own clothes, Shanti has a growing number of customers at their dance classes.

Unable to wait, Taru takes the jacket out of the bag. When Gem last saw it, this time last week, it had been a plain denim jacket. Now, it's anything but. Shanti has embroidered flowers and vines along the sleeves and front panels, but the true beauty is on the back – a magical tree, complete with birds and blossoms. It is bright, and colourful, hints of metallic showing through.

'Tee, that's amazing.' And it is.

Taru is running her hands over the stitches in a kind of awe. 'I can't believe you did this. It's so much more beautiful than I thought it was going be.' She stops moving and looks Shanti in the eye. 'And I thought it was going to be really beautiful. Thank you.'

All Shanti does is give a one-shoulder shrug. 'You're welcome, but it's nothing.'

Gem and Taru share a look, both silently disagree.

'Well,' Taru takes out her phone, and in a few moments, a ping can be heard from somewhere near Shanti's butt. 'I've just paid you. A little more than you asked for, but you deserve it.' She puts the jacket on, a huge smile on her face, and practically dances out of the studio, more bounce in her step now than during the class.

Shanti continues stretching, but Gem is distracted by something other than the flexibility of her hamstrings.

'You know, you should be a clothes designer instead of a psychologist. You could set up your own company and sell customised, vintage items. Like upcycling, but for clothes. It'd be great.'

Shanti's face is still somewhere near the floor, but Gem has known her for long enough now to tell when she is rolling her eyes, even if she can't see them.

'You just want me to stop the study so you can go back to your old ways.'

'No. Seriously, have you thought about starting your own clothes company? You already do it casually anyway. Why don't you try doing it for real?' Shanti may be studying to be a psychiatrist, or something adjacent, but Gem knows clothes aren't just clothes to her friend. They are part of her being.

'Don't be ridiculous—'

'I don't think it's ridiculous.'

'Well, I do. Where would I get the time? I'm about to qualify as a clinical psychologist, remember? And even if I had the time, what am I meant to do, just give up my education for the life of a self-employed creative? My parents would kill me,' Shanti mutters. 'The fact I didn't choose to become a surgeon, or even a GP, is still a lot for them to handle. Telling them that I am going to start my own business, in the *fashion industry* of all places, would be even worse. If they didn't kill me for telling them the news, just hearing it would kill them. And I do love them. Remember?'

'I know you do. But couldn't you do both for a while?' Gem persists. 'See what happens?'

Shanti stops stretching. She studies Gem. 'Do you really think my clothes are that cool?'

Gem nods. 'I do.'

Although Shanti smiles, it's quickly followed by her body, led by her shoulders, slumping forward.

'Ugh, OK. Come on. Let's go home. I know you're just trying to distract me,' she adds.

'From what?'

'The fact you kissed Atlas and liked it.'

At the mere mention of the kiss, Gem's lips remember the feel of him, and start to tingle. She has to lick them to stop the feeling spreading.

She watches with mild envy as her friend manages to stand up without a hand touching the floor, unwinding her crossed legs as she goes. As soon as she's standing, she smacks Gem on the butt, which is unceremoniously pointed skyward, halfway to standing.

Gem straightens, feeling a little lightheaded and nauseous being vertical. 'I didn't like it.' She rubs her butt cheek. 'And I'm not trying to distract you.'

Shanti says nothing.

But then she doesn't need to.

Chapter 22

'Oh love, you look tired. Are you OK?'

This does not come across as quite the caring comment Gem's mum means it to be, but Gem tries to take it as such.

'I'm good, thanks, Mum.'

While Gem's answer isn't quite a lie, it is adjacent to one. When Gem was a kid, she could sleep through anything. Fire alarms. The noise of thirty sugar-high kids on a bus travelling to the zoo. The chorus from that Las Ketchup song being sung increasingly loudly and on repeat because it was the only part of the song anyone knew. But as she grows older, sleep has been increasingly difficult to come by, and when she does manage to nod off, she wakes up early with a really tired jaw. Usually, she blames her lack of sleep on money troubles or worrying about her mum, but both of these problems have recently been resolved – and yet her eye bags are flourishing.

Despite her mum's accidentally cutting remark, it is particularly good to see her outside the house and in a chair that, while not exactly high-end, does at least work. This evening has been a fixed date in Gem and her mum's diary for years: it would have been absolutely gutting to cancel it.

Before her accident, her mum was a completely different person, and not just physically. The physical changes were the least significant ones that they had to get used to. Of course, some of the changes were short term.

Before the accident, Gem had never really seen her mum cry. Oh, she would well up at the occasional sad advert on the TV that hit at just the wrong time, with just the right music to take her emotions on a rollercoaster ride, but Gem had never seen her properly cry. Sometimes Gem wonders if every person has a limited number of tears, and that her mum had been saving hers up for the years before the accident, as though her body instinctively knew they would be needed.

The biggest change, though, wasn't the short-term impact on tissue consumption and the resulting deforestation, or the long-term fact that mum's legs no longer worked. It was the fact she had to become a *planner*. Before the accident, Gem's mum never knew what they would be doing at the weekend, or what they would be eating for dinner more than an hour before they would be eating it. But carrying heavy shopping bags and travelling on a whim is a lot more difficult when you need your hands to move and can't just reserve them for carrying bags, and when you need to plan a trip around which stations have step-free access.

Gem's mum has a completely different view of the city to anyone who can simply hop on a bus or highlight their superiority by walking up the escalators. Every now and then, Gem sees people online claiming that they love to be spontaneous, touting it as some kind of enlightened state. They don't like to conform. They like to live life to the full and own an excess of Patagonia clothing. They look down on planners as though planners can't possibly be fun people.

But to Gem, spontaneity is another luxury neither she nor her mum can afford, financially or logistically.

'Are you happy with our usual Italian?'

Gem, having also become a planner on her mother's behalf, sorted out their first ballet trip a year after the accident, and it has become an annual tradition every year since. Of course, for the first few years, Gem hadn't been earning any money, meaning the tickets had to be bought by her mum, making the surprise not much of one. Now, even though the annual nature of the trip takes the spontaneity out of it, the tickets and the dinner are both on Gem.

But this time, her mum doesn't answer her question. At least with words. The look she gives Gem is answer enough.

'OK. Italian it is.'

There is a lot of unseen admin when going out in a wheelchair. Everything becomes a potential obstacle, no matter how determined you are to make sure your chair never gets in the way. By now, well past the tenth annual ballet trip, Gem and her mum have the evening down pat.

The two of them set off. They come to the same restaurant every year, but Gem always walks slightly ahead. Over the years, Gem has slowly but surely taken the roll of leader whenever they walk anywhere together. It's a method that works well, Gem can clear the path and double-check the way, and her mum follows seamlessly, now able to pick up on the subtlest of changes in Gem's pace, in the way her body is positioned, and even the way her arms move. Whenever Gem turns, her mum is already following.

So now, as Gem leads them down a street on the left, her mum is right behind her. Someone moves out of their way, doing one of those awkward half smiles, their eyes looking down just in time to see that they're about to get run over. Apart from her brief walk with Atlas, walking with her mum is the only time that Gem has experienced a higher place on the pavement hierarchy. The difference being that although people moved out of Atlas's way naturally, they move out of her mum's way slightly unnaturally.

People usually fall into one of three brackets when coming across someone in a wheelchair: the awkward ones, the bizarrely angry ones and the overly friendly ones. It's the latter that you need to look out for the most. About half of the time, the overly friendlies are completely oblivious to the fact that Gem and her mum might actually be on their way somewhere. It's almost as though they see speaking to Gem's mum as a charitable act, one she should be thankful for.

She briefly wonders which bracket Atlas would fall into.

It would be fascinating to see the two of them meet.

Of course, she wouldn't actually want them to meet.

That would be weird.

She wouldn't know what to introduce Atlas as, and she wouldn't even know if Atlas would want to be introduced. She would have to hide. Pretend she didn't know either of them. Fake a fainting fit. Anything to avoid it.

But if they did, Gem can imagine Atlas as being really good with mums.

She could totally imagine Mum liking him.

It's not one of her most admirable traits, and if you challenged her mum on it she would totally deny it, but she is extremely vain. And Atlas is extremely handsome. Usually, Gem has quite a difficult time recalling faces, but Atlas's is one face she can't get out of her mind.

There are little, unforgettable details that only seem to get sharper with time. The small scar just below his left eyebrow that looks a bit like a crescent moon. The dimple that appears near his right eye when he properly smiles. The laughter lines that remain even when he's looking serious, somehow making him look even more like a tragic hero, as though he is haunted by the memory of happiness.

But more than his handsome face, Atlas contains a certain boyish charm that she knows her mum would fall for. She can imagine him teasing her mum just as much as he teased Gem about Shanti's fake stuck-in-a-bush-naked incident. It's impossible not to appreciate someone who reaches for laughter over anger.

'Oh shit.'

Mum and daughter both stop, the former cutting it slightly finer than usual, but then Gem didn't give off any of her usual manoeuvring signals.

'Gem. *Language.*'

Under normal circumstances, Gem knows her mum doesn't care whether or not she swears, but these aren't normal circumstances. These are Be on Your Best Behaviour circumstances. They are in a posh area. There is a lack of rubbish on the ground. The buildings are a lighter colour and the front doors are wider. The small pockets of grass are well kept as opposed to being left to fend for themselves. And all of the cars are nice. Too large for London roads, but nice.

'Sorry, Mum, we must've gone too far.'

'That's all right, love.'

Her mum's words are kind, and on the surface they don't stand out, but both mother and child know that it's not like Gem to do this. She's rarely distracted, but today she is very much so, because she's been thinking about a particular, slightly lopsided face. Still, soon, they are back on track – after all she is a planner – and even more quickly they are outside the restaurant.

As soon as she opens the door, Gem can smell the truffle oil, cheese and general umami-goodness. Her mum, as independent as ever, uses her sheer will and incredible upper body strength to navigate the small, but not insignificant, step up. It is a small and almost insulting obstacle and one she will happily overcome for pasta. But what is an insurmountable, and totally devastating, obstacle is the newly refurbished seating options.

'Shit.' This time Gem's mum doesn't say anything about the swearing. 'They had normal height tables here just last week.'

Ever the planner, Gem had double-checked. But despite her best efforts, the old-fashioned, admittedly very worn wooden tables and red, tiled floors have been replaced with a new, trendy terrazzo flooring, gold hardware and tall bar tables with matching stools. It's not a big restaurant, and a very quick scan is all they need to see that there are no other seats available, occupied or not.

She feels the weight of her mum's hand reassuringly on her arm. 'Don't worry, love, let's just go somewhere else.'

Gem looks down at her mum. She and Atlas would definitely get on well together. They would both know how to make the most of this situation and take the disappointment in their stride.

But Gem is not her mum.

And she is definitely not Atlas.

She would love to be the kind of person who could argue her injustice in a clear and powerful way. She knows that later her brain will make up a different version of events where she fought their side eloquently, and in such a way that would conjure up a special table just for her mum. Unfortunately, there is a reason Gem went into accountancy as opposed to becoming a lawyer. She feels things too deeply to speak clearly when she's really upset.

'OK. We can do that.' Although obviously her nonchalance is totally and completely faked. Gem will never eat here again, and as soon as she is home, she will write them a negative review on every platform she can find.

'Let's just wing it, love. Go to the first nice place we see?'

'Sure, sounds good.'

Although it doesn't.

They aren't the type of family to spoil each other that much, and this evening has always been one of the nights when Gem does so for her mum. But now, thanks to some trendy, impractical tables, the memory of the night will always be slightly tainted with sadness, and a cruel, unnecessary reawakening that Gem's mum can't just hop up onto a barstool. Although, to be fair, sometimes neither can Gem. They really are very high, slippery when upholstered in pleather and particularly difficult to rearrange your bum on when they are upholstered in anything else.

They turn to leave, not even bothering to explain their exit. Gem had confirmed the booking less than four hours ago, but she won't be cancelling it. This minor inconvenience for them is a tiny bit of retribution. Gem might not be confrontational, but she's an expert in being passive-aggressive.

'Sorry, Mum.'

Her mum stops to look at her. 'It's not for you to apologise, Gem. And honestly, I don't mind.'

But Gem knows that a part of her mum does mind, because part of Gem minds too. She reaches over to open the door, and just as they go to leave the restaurant, Gem once again stops too quickly for her mum to follow. In the confusion, Gem's mum is outside, and all Gem can do is watch on as the scene in front of her unfolds. She blinks a few times just to make sure her lack of sleep isn't making her see things.

Because outside, in some kind of cosmic timing (yet another

reason to distrust the universe), Gem can see Atlas running across the road in a direct pathway towards them, dodging an angry taxi.

Of course, Gem knows she's going to see him again. They've almost finalised their next date. But she doesn't want to see him *now*. The fact she is now thinking about his tongue – and more specifically how his tongue feels against hers and how it sent a heavy, lust-filled weight right to her core – is enough to make her blush. Particularly as she is within a mile radius of her mother.

Although Gem doesn't fake a fainting fit, she does hide behind the overly large decorative plant that is just inside the doorway. Just before Atlas reaches her mum, she bets that he is going to be the type to awkwardly smile.

But when he reaches her mum, although he smiles, there is absolutely nothing awkward about it. There is no shifting of the eyes or lips stuck on teeth. It's one of his big smiles. Gem bets that if anyone were to look closely, they would even see the dimple near his right eye. The one she can't quite get out of her head and the one that's been plaguing her dreams.

She is powerless to do anything other than watch on as her mum, true to character and vain as ever, smiles back, still totally unaware that her daughter is hiding behind a large decorative plant, distracted as she is by a well-placed dimple and Atlas's perfectly skewed smile.

As quickly as he appeared, Atlas walks on down the street. Gem, although relieved, also feels a hint of something like sadness that he didn't see her or feel her presence, although admittedly it *would* have been a bit embarrassing if he saw her hiding behind the foliage.

'Can I help you?' The question comes from somewhere behind her.

Gem turns to see a waitress whose face doesn't even have a ghost of smile lines. The woman is giving off an air of being extremely displeased. She's wearing one of those small aprons that only covers about a foot of your outfit. It's there purely for decoration, just like the bar stools.

Gem's indignation refreshed, she straightens and remembers what it feels like to walk down the street with Atlas. The effect is instantaneous. Her confidence is so high that even the slightly creepy caress she gets from the plant doesn't distract her.

She looks at the woman in front of her and pretends that Atlas is standing by her side, silently pushing everyone else away.

'Yes, I'm fine. But your new tables are horrible.'

She turns to leave, the waitress staring after her, silent, but still completely line-free.

Before Gem steps down to the pavement, she turns back.

'Also, we have a table for two booked at 7 p.m. under Gem, but we won't be needing it any more. You have the new tables to blame for that. They are extremely inaccessible and were fashionable about ten years ago.'

Chapter 23

'I am really sorry about this.'

Atlas and his bag are standing in front of Gem. The only benefit to their combined size is the fact he is, yet again, blocking the sun from Gem's eyes. His head is tucked in, his bag once again looking more like a portable house than a receptacle made to ease the carrying of many – *many* – objects.

'I just don't understand how you can be so bad at remembering when you're already busy.'

Atlas's grimace widens. 'I don't either.'

'You realise that you were the one to suggest the day this time.' Gem halts. 'And, also, last time, come to think of it.'

He nods, sheepishly. 'I do.'

Luckily, Gem's recent lack of sleep has had her experimenting with a whole bunch of techniques to help her relax, and just this morning she tried meditation. At the time, she couldn't see how it could possibly work, especially as she realised about five minutes in that she had chosen a practice all about how to honour your womb. She thought yoni was just a new clothing brand. But right now, she leans heavily on the breathing techniques it taught her.

She inhales deeply through her nose for six seconds and holds her breath.

'Are you OK?'

Gem opens her eyes to see a very concerned-looking Atlas staring back at her. His hands are outstretched as though she might be about to pass out. It makes him look even more ridiculous, as though he's a turtle who has been caught running.

Gem releases the breath.

'I'm trying to centre myself.'

'Is it working?'

A large part of Gem wants to punch him. 'No. Let me concentrate.'

Luckily, Atlas steps back, out of range, and Gem once again closes her eyes.

It is very difficult to see the positive in this. It would be one thing to go watch another football game, but at least there she would have a place – a seat and some food. But today, Atlas hasn't even double-booked her with a football game that she can tag along to. He's double-booked her with his football coaching session. She exhales once more.

'You do a lot of football-related things.' Maybe her icky feelings towards him were warning her against his inability to plan and his unwillingness to build space for someone else into his life.

He nods again. Still looking like a snail. 'Yes. I do.'

She inhales one more time, still in search of something positive to take from this.

It's been a busy week at work, so she could go back home and do some chores. She could go for a run. She could pluck her eyebrows. However, as she thinks through the possibilities, none of them seem all that positive. Plus, if they can't fit in another date within the next few days, she's technically going to be in breach of contract. Although, if she does end up being in breach of contract, at least she can start over with someone else. Someone who doesn't hail from the order of the testudines. Someone who eats solid foods.

Someone who doesn't make her feel quite so guilty for taking part in the study. Someone who doesn't smile naturally at her mum. Someone who doesn't make it quite so easy to forget the ick.

And to think, on her way here she had been worrying about how to greet him, whether or not she should go in for a kiss. Their last goodbye had been a kiss, so did that mean all of their greetings and goodbyes will now be accompanied by some form of PDA? And what are the moral implications of a hello kiss in comparison to a night-time goodbye kiss? Somehow a goodbye kiss feels a lot more acceptable than a hello kiss. A daytime hello kiss, visible to a wider range of people and in sunlight hours, suggests something more purposeful and deliberate than a goodbye kiss. It's somehow a lot more intimate even though it's likely to be a lot less *involved*.

If it wasn't for the bag, she probably would have kissed him, and that would have been a mistake. She would have felt like a fool, greeting him with a kiss only to then learn she was being passed over for something that sounds suspiciously like work.

There would be no bag without the coaching session. At least the appearance of the bag reminded her of her goal – no football pun intended – and the icks.

She exhales, her positive angle finally found.

'It's OK. It could be so much worse.'

At least this way, the ick has been renewed. She had been beginning to wonder if she'd made the whole thing up. But no, it's still there peeking out from behind his shoulders. His own portable exoskeleton.

'That it could. I could be taking you to a pub that I knew was terrible all because I didn't want to spend that much time with you.' But then he smiles, a little bit of cheekiness behind the upturned corners of his mouth. 'Inviting you along to watch me coach a bunch of uncontrollable eight-year-olds is a much better way to spend our time together.'

Gem's face freezes, except her eyes, which widen just a little bit. She's invited? When Atlas picks up on her hesitation, the cheekiness disappears.

'Of course, you don't have to come.' He shakes his head. 'You probably have a thousand other more interesting things to do than watch me coach. Like ...' His eyes wander along with his thoughts, searching. 'Going food shopping or ...' His eyes wander about again, as if looking for inspiration. 'Doing your laundry—'

Gem narrows her eyes. 'There's a supermarket and a laundrette behind me, huh?'

'No.' The denial comes quickly; then his eyes flutter in faux offence. 'It's a dry-cleaners actually.'

She smiles, but the win doesn't mean anything to Gem. What makes her feel better is the swift return to joking with each other after she accidentally let her surprised face show.

'It's not that I don't want to come—'

Atlas tries to shake her off, but she doesn't let him speak.

'—It's that I didn't think you would want me to be there. I was surprised at being asked.'

Atlas searches her face and luckily he must be reassured by what he sees. 'Well, of course I want you to come. Will you?'

She tries to smile, but she's distracted. If she goes, at least she won't be in breach of contract.

'So, what do you say?'

She wants to say no. All of a sudden the idea of plucking her eyebrows seems so much more appealing than it did a minute ago. It might hurt, but at least her soul would be clean. But there is a light in his eyes, and she doesn't want to be the one to dim it. So instead of saying no, she says, 'I'd love to.'

'Great.' His eyes widen, and his lopsided smile is out in full force. 'I need all the help I can get.'

And with that, he starts to walk down the street, slipping his hand into hers as he goes, so Gem has no option but to go with him. He's held her hand before, guiding her through the crowd, but this time, the street is empty. He's holding her hand – and she's letting him – purely because she wants to.

'Hold on.' When she tugs lightly on his arm, he stops and turns to her, an unasked question on his face. 'I said I'd come with you, but I'm not going to help you. I don't know anything about coaching football.'

His responding smile starts in his eyes, his annoying little dimple appearing as if on cue. 'That's perfect, because neither do I.'

'Are you his girlfriend?'

As soon as Gem agreed to go with Atlas, he dragged her – although she went quite willingly – to a nearby sports ground. It turns out that today's eight-year-olds are built completely differently to yesterday's eight-year-olds. They are confident and sharp. They have learnt far more insults in their eight years than Gem has learnt in almost four times as long. And theirs are better. Or at least more painful.

And they certainly aren't shy.

Gem turns to the girl who asked the question. The girl in front of her seems to be the captain of the Goals Aloud team, otherwise known as the Goalies.

'Erm, no, I'm not.'

The look the girl gives back to Gem is one of severe distrust. Or possibly anger.

Luckily, Atlas comes to the rescue.

'OK, let's get started.'

Gem, along with everyone else, turns towards him, her appreciation of football skyrocketing. It turns out all she needs in order to appreciate a sports costume is for the right person to be wearing it.

Apparently, Gem has been too busy fending off questions to notice that Atlas has stripped down to shorts. He's also pulled up the sleeves on his top, giving her a view of his forearms. There is a tempting ripple of muscle, but she can also see the hint of a tattoo. She can't see the whole thing, but what she can see – a fine line of a circle – is intriguing. For the first time Gem can see why catching a glimpse of ankle could be considered scandalous. Before today – indeed before ten seconds ago – she had never really considered forearms to be particularly sexy. She hadn't really considered them at all. But then, before today she had never seen Atlas's forearms. She has a huge urge to grab hold of them and feel their strength underneath her fingertips, or better yet, to grab hold of them and pull them around her waist. All the feminism in her body has vanished in the blink of an eye.

'Today,' Atlas's voice cuts through her daydream, 'we're gonna concentrate on footwork.'

There is a general groan from everyone around, except from

Gem. She would happily go along with anything that Atlas says right now.

'I know, I know.' He shifts so he's holding the ball in front of his heart, pushing against it with both of his hands, causing Gem's ovaries to explode. 'But here's the thing. Solid footwork is the most important skill you can have in football.'

The silence suggests nobody is convinced.

'Can't we practise tackling again?' This question comes from the same girl who asked Gem if she is Atlas's girlfriend.

'No.'

Atlas's answer is unusually firm. It absolutely shouldn't, but it absolutely does make Gem's yoni stand to attention. All of her earlier calm from meditating completely disappears.

'We're going to start with some ladder drills.'

Gem exhales. The term 'ladder drill' has her reminiscing about a particularly steamy scene in the first season of *Bridgerton* – except two different people are involved. Namely herself and Atlas.

She prays for the return of the bag. Something – anything – to dampen the thoughts running through her mind. Not even the idea of him eating soup is making a difference. If anything, the idea of him blowing on something – even a spoon of butternut squash soup – has her melting.

Fortunately, considering the age group, this version of a ladder drill appears to be a lot more PG-rated. Gem watches on as Atlas lays what looks like a ladder down on the ground. Gem has to blink when he bends. There are children present. She needs to keep control of herself.

'Right. We're gonna be doing some slightly more complicated drills this time. We're gonna try the reverse crossover.' He moves to the left side of the ladder. 'Watch me as I work down the ladder, so you can see what I'm doing.'

As luck would have it, Gem is already watching him.

Atlas proceeds to work his way down the ladder, moving his feet up and down and across again and again until he reaches the end of the ladder. Then he turns back to them and does the move in reverse. This time, at a slower pace, so they can concentrate on his feet.

'See, one foot should come behind the standing leg, making sure you get a clean run so each time your foot lands, it lands within the square of the ladder.' When he reaches back to the beginning, he stops, and smiles. 'We'll go there and back for one. Got it?'

There is a general mumble of approval from the crowd, although it could be more like an acceptance of fate.

'OK.' Atlas nods. For a moment he looks a little unsure. But soon, his confident stance is back. 'I can see that we need some extra motivation here.' Then he walks towards his bag, dives his hand in and starts pulling out a selection of clothing, none of which seem to be what he is searching for. But finally, he stops, bringing out what appears to be a tinfoil brick.

While Gem is confused, everyone else appears to know what's coming – and they are excited. A current runs through the team.

Atlas holds the package up so everyone can see it. Nobody is moving, but they are bristling.

Gem leans down to the kid closest to her. 'What's happening?'

The kid whispers her answer, her eyes not leaving the prize. 'He's a really good baker.'

Having got her answer, although it wasn't the answer she expected and still doesn't explain what's going on, Gem turns her attention back to Atlas.

'Whoever gets the fastest time, wins the brownies.'

All of a sudden, all of the kids run to the start line. Gem has never seen a faster-moving group of humans.

'Ah, not *quite* so fast.'

As if a bucket of water has been thrown over them, everyone turns to face Atlas. He's placed the brownies on top of the bag, so they are still perfectly in view, and makes his way back over to the team.

'You're not just gonna be timed against each other. If you want my brownies, you're gonna have to beat me, too.' Then he takes something off from around his neck and gives it to Gem, who takes it without thinking. The sight of Atlas taking something off makes Gem catch her breath.

'Do you mind doing the honours?'

She looks down at her hands, and at what appears to be a stopwatch.

'What do you need me to do?'

She realises the stupidity of her question a millisecond too late, and when she glances up and sees the humour dancing in Atlas's eyes, she knows that he isn't going to let her get away with it.

He takes his whistle and places it in Gem's other hand. He then moves so they are standing side-by-side and places his hand directly over hers, so it is also holding the stopwatch. 'Tell me to go by blowing the whistle and hit start. And then when I come back again, hit stop as soon as I cross over the line.' He takes his hand away. 'Can you manage that?'

Gem tries her best to act indifferently to his touch, but she can still feel his hand around hers, even though it is no longer there.

'Of course I can.'

She just can't think straight with him so close.

'I just didn't realise I'd agreed to be your assistant.'

An eyebrow quirks up. 'My assistant, eh? I like the sound of that.' Luckily, he says it too softly for anyone else to hear, and he moves away before she can come up with anything witty in reply.

He stands at the start line, and Gem steps a bit closer so she can see clearly.

He turns back towards her and gives her the smallest of nods to let her know that he is ready.

She readies the stopwatch, double-checking she is going to hit the right button, and then brings the whistle to her mouth. She only has a moment to think about the fact she's placing her lips over the imprint of Atlas's, before she blows into it.

Atlas's feet move impressively quickly, but it isn't his feet she is mesmerised by. His butt looks excellent from Gem's angle.

She had thought he might knock a bit off his pace to make it fair, but he doesn't appear to. By the time he's finished, and Gem has hit stop, he is out of breath and panting hard.

'How'd I do?'

Gem looks down at the stopwatch. 'Ten point four-five seconds.'

At the reading, Atlas smiles, but it's joined by a chorus of groans.

'We are never going to be able to beat that.'

'Shoulda gone food shopping with my mum instead.'

'No point in even trying.'

'He never lets us have his brownies.'

'One of us has to beat him, just so he can stop being so smug.'

Despite dashing everyone's hopes, Atlas looks really pleased with himself. 'Come on. Don't be shy.' He plants his hands on his hips, still panting from the exertion. 'Who wants to go first?'

Nobody moves.

'OK. So we are shy today. That's fine.' Then, something very bad happens. He looks at Gem. 'Luckily, I have brought an *assistant* with me. Everyone, say hi to Gem.'

There is a *very* unenthusiastic chorus of 'Hi Gem', which Gem greets with an equally unenthusiastic wave.

'I'm assuming you were watching?'

'Oh-ho, yes. Yes, I was.' Gem answers like someone whose heart isn't quite beating at a regular pace. The look Atlas gives her – one of his cheeky grins that lets her know he knows exactly what she is thinking – only makes her heart beat more erratically.

'Great.' Still smiling, Atlas motions for Gem to head over to the one side of the ladder. 'In which case you can go first and try to beat my time.'

Gem gives him a quick shake of the head, but he only nods back, wide smile on his face.

There is a silent but strong standoff between them. Unfortunately, it is a standoff that Gem loses. With no visible way out, Gem walks over, meeting Atlas at the start of the ladder. He motions for her to pass him the stopwatch and whistle, and she complies reluctantly, a tight smile on her face.

'I'm going to make you pay for this.' She whispers to him so nobody else can hear, but when she looks at his face, and directly into his ocean blue eyes, her threat somehow turns to foreplay. It is not the effect she intended, but she isn't mad.

'I hope so.' He whispers it so quietly that if it wasn't for the heat in his eyes, Gem might almost have wondered if he'd said anything at all.

But then, he straightens and looks past her, reverting back to coach mode. It's difficult to know which she finds more intoxicating.

'OK, so it's pretty simple. All you need to do is get from one side of the ladder to the other and back again, as quickly as you can. The only thing that is more important than speed is accuracy. There's no point in doing anything fast if you can't do it right.' He looks at Gem.

Gem blinks.

Her mind really needs to clean itself up.

Atlas's focus narrows back to her, making her pledge a little hard to follow.

'And remember, if you get one step wrong, your time is discounted. You ready?'

Gem thinks she nods, but she can't be sure. At some point, he reaches out to hold her, his hands on her shoulders. It's a move that is likely meant to ground her, but the effect it has is quite the opposite. Despite the power that clearly sits behind them, the support he gives her is gentle. The contrast and inherent control sends a tingling sensation directly from his fingertips, right down to her toes.

Once again, his voice is solely for her. 'Don't worry if you were a bit preoccupied during my demo.' The slight cheekiness momentarily distracts her. 'It would actually be good if you could be a bit slow. Give the kids a bit of confidence.'

All Gem can do in response is nod. She has never been the type of person to be picked first in anything. So going first now is not something she is overly comfortable with.

Luckily, if there is one thing Gem can do, it's copy moves. She's been dancing for years, and this is no different. So instead of panicking, she walks to the start line and replays what Atlas did in her mind. She picks a song to play in her head, one with a quick, strong beat that matches the steps. And then, when Atlas whistles, she moves.

Her feet tap up and down, side to side, landing exactly in the middle of each step. The repetitiveness is a *little* boring, but it is also slightly meditative. Much more effective at calming her mind than simply breathing. In fact, she is so in the zone, that when she reaches the end of the ladder, she turns back without missing a single beat. She even keeps moving after Atlas has blown his whistle, letting her know that she has reached the end.

When her feet have finally stilled, she turns back to the group, really out of breath.

'So, how'd I do?'

And everyone, including Atlas, is looking at her with their mouth just slightly open.

When Atlas doesn't answer, one of the kids pulls his hand down so he can see the screen. Whatever he sees makes him smile and cry out.

'Oh, yes! Go, Miss!'

Gem has never been called 'Miss' before, but coming from a kid with a massive smile on his face, who's looking at her with a sense of awe, she doesn't mind it.

'You beat him. You got nine seconds.' Then he laughs as he looks up at Atlas who is still staring at Gem. 'FLAT!'

Chapter 24

'No, but seriously, where did you learn that? You must've done that before.'

After practice, Atlas insisted on taking Gem out for lunch. Or an early dinner. It doesn't matter. It doesn't even matter that they once again find themselves in a pub. Luckily, being a little bit further out of town, this one has a bit more of a unique character. There are boardgames that are actually being used, a dog that appears to have its own seat and, as soon as one of the regulars walks in, the barman changes the TV channel to a replay of a cooking show, so he can settle in and watch his favourite programme in peace. They even have chips. Much to Atlas's delight.

In fact, it has turned into one of those days when things just happen as they happen, and they're perfect anyway. Gem can't remember the last time she went with the flow. Especially someone else's. There's something liberating in it.

'I learnt it from you.' Gem takes a bite of chip. They are salty and delicious. The perfect mix of crunchy and soft. 'You're just a really good teacher.'

Atlas laughs, and Gem can't help but smile, despite the fact she can *still* see the bag. He's stopped trying to tuck it in under the table and people are having to step around it. She even quite likes the idea of kissing him – remarkably, the bag is doing nothing to counteract this desire.

'I am definitely *not* that good a teacher. How come your feet can move that fast? My dad used to make me do that ladder drill again and again and *again*. You were faster than me on your first try.'

Gem's red wine sits untouched in front of her, and the endorphins from exercise have long since left her body. The high she is feeling now is purely from being in Atlas's company. Unfortunately, the natural highs are the most potent. And so instead of fobbing him off with a half answer, she sticks to her promise to only lie when necessary.

'I like to dance.' Her words are accompanied by another bite of chip, and an anticipatory silence from Atlas.

'"I like to dance."' He tries his best to copy her mannerisms, with a bite of his own chip and a flutter of his eyelashes. The flutter he adds in himself. 'Footwork like that doesn't just come from *liking to dance*.'

She picks up another chip. The look in Atlas's eye is more potent than mere confidence.

'Fine. I like to dance, and quite frankly your little ladder exercise is nothing in comparison to the steps I usually have to follow.'

If his eyes are anything to go by, it would appear that Gem's challenge does nothing but intrigue Atlas even more.

He reaches over, coming a little closer than strictly necessary, and grabs a chip of his own.

'What kind of dance?'

'Anything really. But my housemate, Shanti, and I prefer either Bollywood or street dances.'

'And that's it?'

For the first time, Atlas's words make Gem prickle.

'Yes. *That's it.*'

Luckily for him, he picks up on the spiciness in her tone.

'Sorry, I didn't mean it like that. I'm just thinking of my own dancing, which is limited to basically walking but in a bit of a jazzy way. But if those fast feet came from dancing, I might have to take the kids to a dance class.'

'I've never heard anyone compare their dancing to jazzy walking.'

'Well, now you have.' He studies Gem. 'So dancing is your thing then?'

She is getting through her share of chips in record time, but she has to keep her hands busy with something innocent, otherwise who knows what trouble they might get into. 'My thing?'

'The thing that gets you out of bed.'

She takes another bite of chip. 'Yeah. I would say dancing is my thing. It's in my genes. My mum's a dancer. I get it all from her.'

A strange look passes over Atlas's face.

'What?'

'I mean, you tell me your mum is a good dancer, and I believe you, but you don't get it *all* from her.' Gem's instant reaction is to disagree, but Atlas keeps talking before she can get a word in. 'I saw you today. If you were twenty years younger and at all interested in playing football, I would try to recruit you into the Goalies.'

He looks at her feet, or where he imagines her feet might be, tucked as they are under the table. 'Those quick feet don't just come from good genes. They also come from a lot of practice.'

The silence that follows stretches out into awkwardness, but Gem doesn't quite know how to fill it.

'One day I would love to watch you dance.'

Atlas's request is completely innocent, but Gem hasn't let anyone watch her dance for years. At least nobody outside of those in the class themselves, and her mum, who demands to watch the videos.

Desperate to change the subject, Gem redirects. 'So how did you get into coaching a kids' football team? I kinda thought that was only something people got pressured into doing once they had kids.'

'Who's to say I don't have kids?'

Gem's stomach drops. Maybe *this* is what her ick is warning her against. Kids are fine but not yet. At least not for Gem. She isn't ready for them, and she certainly isn't ready to be an evil stepmother.

'Don't panic.' Atlas lays one of his hands on hers, and her stomach instantly stops dropping; it starts flipping instead. 'I'm only joking.'

Of course, Atlas hasn't abandoned a child. He's the kind of guy who would make a very present father.

'There was one *particularly* confident girl on the team.' Atlas's eyebrows hitch up, to ask who. 'The one who wanted to practise tackling.' And the one who asked if Gem and Atlas were dating.

'That's Shauna.' He picks up a spoon and looks at his reflection in the back of it, fixing a piece of hair that definitely isn't out of place. But Gem's too busy learning about the other parts of Atlas to care about the things she already knows, like his love of reflective surfaces.

'She's kinda petrifying.'

'That she is. Last week she tackled someone so hard that I had to explain to the boy's mum that the bruise really did just come from a tackle.'

'I don't know whether to be impressed or terrified.'

'A combination of both, I think. Her dad plays on the same team as me. He tackles like she does, except he's about five times the size.' His eyes widen. 'He's a good friend, and I'm glad he's on my side, but he still petrifies me. Not as much as she does, but still.'

The look in Atlas's eye is so earnest Gem's laughs. Instead of being upset, Atlas simply looks proud of the fact he made her laugh.

Gem bites down on her lip, tracking Atlas's eyes as she does. 'You're good with them.'

'I dunno about that.' Shyness suits him.

'I do.'

He hesitates before he answers, 'Well, thanks. My dad always said that the best teams were the ones that had the strongest youth groups, and the ones that paid most attention to the long game, rather than just signing fancy, expensive players.'

He shrugs. It's typically a casual move, but Atlas's is heavy, almost as heavy as his use of the past tense. 'I know that the likelihood of my little, scary group of footballers ever becoming professional players is slim to none, but it can't be hurting.' His eyes meet Gem's. 'And if a love of football helps even one of them in some small way – or at least if coming to practice keeps them out of trouble for a bit – I'll consider this whole thing a success.'

'So,' Gem's voice is quiet, gentle, 'your love of football comes from your dad?'

'It does,' he says, after a long moment. 'He was always the football fan. The season tickets were his, and when he died, I didn't like the idea of anyone else sitting in his seat. So, I took it over. Everyone there – well, except Chris and Saoirse – are really more his friends than mine, but it's nice to see people who remember him as well as I do. He died fifteen years ago in November.'

'So you were really young when he died?'

Atlas nods.

Gem shakes her head. 'Sorry, you really don't need to talk to me about this if you don't want to.'

She feels a gentle pressure on her hand. Atlas has moved his own so it isn't just covering hers but is holding it.

'No, I like talking about him.' His face does a funny little thing where it almost looks like he's about to sneeze. 'Or at least I think it's better to talk about him than never talk about him.'

Gem knows that if Shanti were here, even she would admit that Gem has no way out. So instead of pulling her hand away, she turns his hand over, so their palms are facing, and interlaces her fingers with his.

'What was he like?'

Atlas's eyes take on that faraway look, and Gem can tell that even though he appears to be looking at the weird, almost lifesized cow statue in the corner, he's seeing something completely different.

'He was loyal as anything. To his friends, his family. His football team, obviously. He always had stories. They were all total bullshit, but everyone would listen to them because he was so good at telling them. He always wore shorts, even when it was snowing outside. He loved brown sauce. He swore like a sailor but got away with everything because he also knew exactly what everyone wanted to hear. He could be a real sweet talker.'

'He sounds like a good dad.'

At some point, although Gem can't remember when, she must've started running her thumb along the back of his hand. Now that she knows what she's doing, she can't stop. Touching him is addictive.

'He wasn't as good as I remember him being though. He tried, but he was shit at doing anything he didn't want to do. He never remembered birthdays, I never got a birthday party. He rarely cooked. Every now and then he'd make us sandwiches, but that was kinda the limit of his culinary expertise.' Gem can see a boy version of the man sitting in front of her, with skinny legs and long arms, eating a sandwich with childlike wonder. But then Atlas frowns. 'He never helped with homework, or even really encouraged me to do it. He would disappear for days at a time, and my grandma would have to come look after me.

'He wouldn't always pay the electricity bill, so we'd live in the dark for weeks. It wasn't so bad when it happened in summer, but the winters were a different story. And he wasn't good at talking, not about serious things anyway. The only serious thing we ever really spoke about was the football. That's probably why I started watching it with him, so we'd have something to talk about. We always had football to fall back on.'

'What about your mum?'

Gem's question is met with a shrug. 'It's pretty much always been me and dad. She found out she was sick when she was pregnant with me and died a few months after I was born.'

'Oh, Atlas.' She can't stop the words that come out, but as soon as they do, she wishes she'd chosen some that were significantly less useless.

'I know it's a lot, but it's also OK.' His shoulder hitches up. 'At least for me. Obviously, I'd love to have known her, but I don't remember her. It's a weird kinda grief, I guess. It doesn't have anywhere to go. But my dad loved her. I never remember him dating anyone else. I think some of his worst behaviours were just a result of his sadness at losing her and not knowing how to live without her. It was always like he was looking for the thing that would make her death make sense, but I don't think he ever found it. Then when he died my grandma looked after me full time. She at least can cook better.'

'Well, anytime you want to talk about him, or her, I'm happy to listen.' Even if she has nothing comforting to say.

'Thanks.' He shakes his head, as if he's shaking the thoughts away. 'Anyway . . . what about your parents? What are they like?'

Despite the seriousness of Atlas's revelations, Gem smiles. 'It's just me and my mum.' She pauses. 'Well, and Uncle Mike.

'My mum used to tell me that my dad was a magician, which obviously when I was a kid, filled my mind with an idea that I might have some magic in me. For years I tried out card magic. Levitation. I even tried to read minds. But then one day I grew up and it finally dawned on me. He was a magician because he'd done a vanishing act.'

Atlas clearly doesn't know how to respond. Quite frankly, neither does Gem. He changes the subject instead.

'So, what are your mum and Mike like?'

'Well, you already know that my mum is a dancer.' Atlas nods. 'But she's also the total opposite to your dad in terms of birthday parties. She goes crazy for them. She plans them for months. Every year has a different theme. A different dress code. She even makes invitations, despite the fact that most of the time it's just the two of them, me and Shanti.'

'Shanti being your housemate?'

Gem nods.

'Does she still go big?'

'What?' Gem levels her eyes at him. 'Even though I'm older and don't really need to have a birthday party any more?'

'Well, yeah.'

'She goes *huge*.' Gem's eyes widen and draw the biggest circle that they can. 'I think she sees it as a challenge.'

'That's amazing.' The laughter in Atlas's voice lightens the moment, Gem's own heart following in kind.

'It is.'

'What kinda themes have you had?'

Gem thinks back to her mum's photo albums. 'Bagels, beagles, dancing – of course.' Atlas's nod is exaggerated in understanding. 'Cheese. Disney. We've had a pool party, even though we only have a shower above the bath—'

Atlas snorts.

'—Sheep. Cinema – although of course we didn't actually go to the cinema. One year I was obsessed with the dictionary, and so we had a word-themed party.' She blushes slightly at this. She'd gone as 'Puzzled' by glueing jigsaw pieces all over an old unitard and frowning. It was definitely an awkward time in Gem's adolescence. Shanti is the only friend remaining in her repertoire from that party.

'So what's the theme going to be this year?'

Gem's head shakes reflexively. 'Don't ask.'

Since saying that she didn't need a big party, her mum has been messaging her twice a week. With just less than two months to go, she knows the messages are only going to increase in frequency and potency. 'I've told her that all I want is to be surrounded by the people that I love.'

'How did that go down?'

'Not well.'

'So, what's your Uncle Mike like?'

Gem's eyes look up to the ceiling, thinking how to best to

describe her uncle. Despite spending a whole year obsessed with the dictionary, she's never managed to find a word that fits him.

'He's one of my favourite people in the world.' The grin that spreads across Gem's face is totally unconscious, even thinking about him makes her smile.

'He pretends that he's really laid back, but really he's a worrier. When I moved out of home, he came to the apartment and did a security check.'

She looks at Atlas, judging if she should stop. But his smile seems genuine, so she keeps on going, liking the look on him. It makes his eyes sparkle even more than they normally do, a welcome change to the sadness she saw in them when he was talking about his dad.

'He changed the locks, he put in new fire alarms in every room. He updated and moved the fuse box because he wanted it to be easier for us to access, saying if we blew a fuse and all the electricity went out, we'd be relieved not to have to climb up on a chair to flip the switch. He even swept it for cameras in case our landlord was watching us.'

'And was he?'

'No, but Uncle Mike still sweeps it every six months just in case.'

'Well, I reckon he's gonna love me when he meets me.' Atlas winks. It's a move that still makes Gem cringe, but this time, the cringe isn't accompanied by an insatiable need to run away. Instead, she feels a little protective over it. If someone were to mock him for it, she'd tell them that the wink is just part of him. An annoying part of him – but not *all* of him.

As Atlas's smile eventually fades, the noise from the rest of the pub starts to trickle back in. As does Gem's awareness of their hands. The magic of the moment is now slightly broken, and she has an overwhelming urge to free her hands, worrying that she might have said a little too much. She is meant to be finding out the source of her ick, after all. Unable to stand it any longer, she pulls her hand away from his, while smiling, trying to make both seem as natural as possible.

But before she can get away, Atlas moves. In a gesture that is somehow more powerful in its quiet casualness, he reaches up to gently tuck a piece of hair behind her ear, his hand coming to rest against her neck, his thumb skimming her jaw, her skin coming alive at his touch. Then, as if it is the most natural thing ever, he leans over and kisses her.

At first, Gem is shocked. She is kissing someone – *Atlas* – in a pub. In the daylight. Where everyone can see. And she is *enjoying it*.

She has a millisecond to worry about the health of her memory. She remembers the last kiss being good. But she doesn't remember it being *this* good.

It's an intoxicating mix between feeling new and exciting and feeling completely natural. The way they are moving together, his hand still reassuringly cupping her neck, his mouth moving in time with hers, makes her want more and more and more. He expertly uses his hand to dictate the speed, the angle, the pressure, so they are perfectly in sync. She is built for kissing him – and he is built for kissing her. His lips are soft, but confident, and when he gives her lower lip the smallest of nips, a fire is lit.

Never before has Gem understood why or how people get so caught up that they are charged with public indecency. But she is about two seconds from climbing onto Atlas's lap and ripping open his shirt. Her upper body strength has never been particularly impressive, but with so much adrenaline – not to mention other hormones – pumping through her body, Gem has no doubt she'd manage it.

Thankfully for her criminal record, after one more second, Atlas gently pulls away. His forehead stays resting against hers though, and his thumb is still busy caressing up and down her jawline. It is meant to be soothing, but all it does is make it impossible for Gem to stop wanting him.

'We should probably stop before we get kicked out. Or arrested.'

Embarrassingly, a noise escapes Gem that sounds suspiciously like a whimper.

But it looks like Gem isn't alone in her struggle. The look on Atlas's face suggests he is ravenous. And not for food that they are yet to order.

'You're gonna have to stop looking at me like that.'

'Like what?' Atlas feigns innocence.

'Like you are about to eat me.'

'I can't help myself.' His thumb goes back to work, and the pressure from his hand slightly increases. He draws her closer, so her ear is against his mouth. 'I think you're delicious,' he whispers.

Instead of kissing her lips, he kisses her gently just below her ear, sending a shiver down to the tips of her toes, before backing off, the only one strong enough to put some much-needed distance between them.

When his hand falls from her side, Gem instantly misses his touch. But it doesn't go far. It lands, perfectly, back on top of hers. And Gem doesn't even think of moving away.

Chapter 25

'Still no closer to finding the source of the ick?'

It's Sunday, which means Shanti and Gem are picking up supplies for brunch. It's their little ritual, helping them achieve balance in an otherwise crazy world. No matter what's happening, if they are together on a Sunday morning, they make their way to their favourite corner shop. It recalibrates them for the week ahead.

Currently, they are at the most vital step in the process. They are testing all of the avocados for the perfect ripeness, all while discussing Gem's most recent date with Atlas. Like any good local shop, the unwrapped fresh fruit and veg is displayed outside, getting coughed on by cars and passing pedestrians, while the packaged food stays extra safe inside. Gem knows there must be a reason for their illogical placement, but she's yet to discover it.

'Nope.'

'You still have some time.' Shanti squeezes an avocado, immediately putting it back when it doesn't give.

Gem is working her way through her own side of the box. She can feel their silent friend, Jay, watching them. She usually feels a bit guilty touching every single one of the avocados and the daggers in Jay's eyes would normally be enough to make Gem never want to even look at one of his avocados again, but no brunch is complete without them and there is nothing more sad than a crunchy avocado. Today, though, the practice is saving Gem from more than just a disappointing epicurious experience; it is also providing her with a distraction.

Her date with Atlas had morphed from being a potential disaster into being one of her favourite ever dates. The more time they spend together, a quiet but increasingly persistent voice keeps suggesting that maybe her ick isn't an intuition – maybe there's absolutely nothing wrong with Atlas. Maybe they are perfectly matched, and she can get over his excessively large bag, his overly good looks and his soup-eating. The idea makes her uncomfortable, and not only because she is worried about her ego. If whatever is happening between her and Atlas is real, she's going to need to tell him at some point about the real reason she started and has kept dating him. And there is no way Gem can come up with an angle that paints her in a good light.

Gem picks up another avocado. She gives the fruit a squeeze that's maybe a little harder than necessary. 'Oh! This one is perfect.' Despite effectively having just strangled it, she puts it into the basket with the utmost care, as if the basket might cause more damage than her own hands.

The two of them keep testing in loaded, but companionable silence.

'I think I should meet him.'

At Shanti's suggestion, Gem stops squeezing.

'Meet him.'

Shanti puts another avocado in the basket, looking at Gem as she does. 'Yep. When is your next date?'

'Not till next Saturday. He's away for the week with work and I said I'd go watch him play football and then get dinner with him after.'

'Great. I'll come too.' Shanti stops mid-test. 'Actually, not great. Do you guys do anything that isn't football-related?'

'It's the first time he could meet up, but he's promised to make it up to me. He said the next date won't have a football in sight.'

Gem is still squeezing avocados, so she misses the fact that Shanti has stopped and is instead just beaming at her. 'Plus, I would remind you of our contract. If I don't meet up with him on Saturday, I risk violating our terms. I'll have gone too long without seeing him.'

Gem doesn't actually know if this is true – she hasn't done the maths – but it sounds good. 'Besides, it's actually kinda fun.'

She pokes another avocado. Unlike the one immediately before it which felt like a rock, this one is far too soft. She tries not to grimace as she puts it back. Jay has spent so much time watching them that she knows he can read their every expression. She doesn't want him to know that she's just violated his fruit.

'*Interesting*.'

Gem briefly shifts her concentration to Shanti and instantly sympathises with the avocados. She too feels like she is being squeezed, tested for any hint of weakness.

'What's interesting?'

'It's rare to hear you defending someone.'

At Shanti's loaded statement, Gem has an overwhelming need to defend *herself*.

'I defend you.'

'Exactly. But I'm your best friend. What does this say about you and Atlas?'

Luckily, Shanti doesn't appear to require an answer, because Gem doesn't have one. It's undeniable that her thoughts on Atlas have changed, and not just because she is distracted by memories of his kiss. She is distracted by him in general.

His smile. His lips. His forearms.

His obvious love for his grandma.

His difficult relationship with his dad, but the way he also clearly loved him, despite his flaws.

The way the kids all listened to him.

The way he didn't want to let them win, but actually took his loss to her pretty well.

Even the way Shauna clearly loves him. Shauna scares Gem, but she can't deny that she has good taste in crush.

And Atlas is the perfect guy to have a crush on.

At this exact moment, even though she tries, Gem struggles to remember why the thought of him eating soup gave her the ick in the first place.

Shanti and she both add a (perfectly ripe) avocado each into the basket. Nobody comments that they now have one more avocado than necessary. When dealing with something as temperamental as an avocado, it's never a bad idea to have a backup.

By silent agreement they follow each other inside the store, Gem picking up some mushrooms on the way. The requirements mushrooms need to meet are significantly less difficult to reach, and therefore only requires one of them to choose.

'Why do you want to meet him?'

Gem knows that Shanti must be desperate to analyse them – Atlas and Gem – separately and together. She does a good job of hiding her therapist tendencies in front of Gem, but she doesn't always succeed.

'I just think that I might do a better job of hunting down a reason for his ick. Or your ick. The ick between you. You know what I mean. I can find out what's wrong with him.' Shanti walks a few steps more. 'And if there isn't in fact anything wrong with him, maybe we should look into a different reason for your commitment issues. I mean, *your* ick.'

Gem knows that Shanti's words aren't accidental.

And the casual shrug her friend now feigns isn't casual at all.

'Maybe you have a different reason to keep people away. Maybe you might even have some trust issues.'

Gem stops next to her friend in front of the bread display. 'I do not have trust issues, and I'm perfectly capable of finding Atlas's secrets out by myself.'

What Gem doesn't say is how easy it is to talk to Atlas. She genuinely liked finding out more about him. In fact, she enjoyed it so much, she hadn't thought about it in terms of Shanti's research. She'd even forgotten she was being paid.

This part she definitely doesn't admit to her friend.

Unfortunately, the silence that falls between them makes the quiet voice that's been following her seem even louder. Only this time, instead of making Gem question the existence of the ick, it's questioning her morals. Again. Was she really just having a conversation with Atlas? Or was she mining him for information? Any hunger Gem had completely disappears.

For the first time, she wants to call the whole thing off.

'The first payment should be hitting your bank account this week. Let me know if it doesn't come in by Friday.' Shanti's voice forces all of the others away. 'What are you going to do with the money anyway?'

And just like that, Gem's desire to call the whole thing off disappears. Her mum.

She shrugs, trying to convince everyone, including herself, that it's casual, even though she feels as if she is being torn in two. 'I haven't decided yet.'

Gem doesn't know why she hasn't told Shanti about her mum's new chair. It's not like Shanti isn't aware that Gem is financially challenged, but there is knowing something and fully understanding the repercussions of that thing. So, although Shanti might know Gem is strapped for cash, she doesn't always know what that means.

'Maybe you can finally go away on holiday.'

'Maybe.'

Even Gem isn't convinced by her answer, but before Shanti can push, there is something more pressing to decide on, and that is carbs.

'Shall we go fancy artisanal sourdough or bog-standard crumpets?'

At Shanti's question, the two friends look at each other. It's all Shanti needs before adding crumpets into the basket and walking to the front of the shop.

'Come on, let's go. Mum's taking me shopping for a sari to wear to my cousin's wedding and I need to prepare for her not-so-subtle suggestions that I should also be thinking of marriage.'

'They still pushing the optometrist on you?'

'Yes. Luckily he's as disinterested as I am.'

Gem looks at Shanti, silently asking why and how? Shanti is amazing. Everyone's interested in her.

'He's gay.' The joy in Shanti's voice is palpable.

'Ah.'

Shanti puts the basket up on the counter, smiling her biggest smile at Jay. As usual, she gets absolutely nothing back.

'Speaking of disappointing your parents, any more thoughts on quitting school and starting a clothing company instead?'

Shanti takes the last avocado out of the basket and puts it onto the side.

'Yes. And it's a no.'

For the first time, Jay's scowl isn't the deepest one in the room.

Gem hates seeing her friend upset, especially when she can't do anything about it. Although she realises there is a way to make Shanti smile again.

'Fine. You can meet Atlas.'

The squeal that comes out of Shanti is enough to make even Jay show some emotion. His glare deepens, and then craters when Shanti starts to jump around, grabbing on to Gem's arm.

'Yes! This is going to be great!'

But although Gem is happy to see her friend smile again, she can't ignore the pit in her stomach.

Chapter 26

Every now and then Gem is hit by the very surreal fact that she is hurtling through a thing called the universe, on a large rock that just happens to have contained all of the right elements required to support human life and is positioned just far enough away from a giant burning ball of gas so as not to burn up, but also close enough not to freeze. She's not even sure she really knows what the universe is. Sometimes she tries to understand it, if only so she can stop being so scared of it. But this can also backfire. Once – a glass or two of wine deeper than she should have been – she decided to bring the topic up with one of her colleagues. Unfortunately, he did know more about the whole thing, and so instead of simply being able to find companionship in going '*What the fuck?*', she came away completely petrified by the question that lodged itself in her brain: if the observable universe is expanding, what is it expanding into?

She freezes when she remembers that we don't know the answer.

Yet even when Gem is at the very height of her freak-out, she can still see the beauty of space, and the ever-expanding universe. It's just such a shame that instead of relishing in the magical serendipity of human life, we have instead decided to create silly little jobs for ourselves.

Of course, not everyone does a silly little job.

Gem looks around.

She is definitely not exempt.

The point of counting made-up coins that have very little literal value is sometimes more difficult to understand than the concept of space. Especially when most of the coins don't actually exist. It's all completely bonkers.

Gem's urge to run out of this grey-hued box has never been so strong, but Unfortunately she is stuck.

A few months ago, Martin was named as Retention Lead, and while Gem may dislike the majority of his character traits, she has to have some respect for the fact his confidence never waivers. She has been at the same company for five years, and in that time, Martin has been given a new internal role every six months. Instead of seeing this as a bad sign – that he is given each role as a placeholder until someone better becomes available – he believes it is because he is extremely well-rounded.

Naturally, Martin has attributed this new title to his innate leadership capabilities. After all, Gem has been with the company for five years, which is three more than the average, and for more than four of these she has been on projects with Martin. In Martin's mind, this must mean something, but, in reality, Gem's reasons for staying in her job have nothing to do with Martin and everything to do with her lack of an alternative, the regular pay cheque and the unlikelihood of her getting fired.

Plus, the idea of searching for a new job does very little for Gem. In many ways, it's similar to dating. Both require time and a bit of lying to make you look your best. Plus, both are soul-crushing. The only thing worse than openly making yourself so available is being turned down by someone you didn't even want in the first place.

Fortunately, this isn't a problem that Gem is currently experiencing.

Her phone is on silent, but she sees it light up. Again.

She doesn't have to look to know it's from Atlas.

I can't stop thinking about kissing you.x

Unfortunately, as with anything Martin does, this new role has quickly become Gem's problem as well as his, and so replying to Atlas's message will have to wait.

Looking around, it's difficult for Gem to see how Martin thinks a group made of two managers, five senior managers, two partners, two analysts (one of whom is only there to take notes) and Gem herself will be able to solve the issue. These aren't the people they need to speak to, a fact which is just about to be proven.

'Google have a great canteen and sleeping pods. We could get some sleeping pods.' Martin once attended a talk at their offices about the rise of AI. Gem had seen the invitation and the agenda. It genuinely looked interesting. Sadly, the only things Martin reported back on were the catering options and the sleeping pods.

'Personally, I don't think it's a problem with the company at all. It's a problem with the younger generation.' Someone who Gem has never seen before but could easily be confused for Martin's slightly older brother, laughs at his own apparent joke. 'I mean, they can even buy extra holiday days.' He chuckles again. 'When I first joined, I would have been laughed out the building if I'd asked for *more* holiday.'

A wave of quiet humour flows around the table, missing out three of the seats.

'But we have to buy back the days with our own salaries, so in a way it's another revenue stream for the company.' Luckily the analyst speaking – Danny – hasn't yet looked up from his shoes, otherwise he probably would have stopped talking. He hasn't yet learnt that his opinion isn't actually valued, at least not until it conforms with everyone else's. 'And each day costs the same amount for us to buy back as they do for you, yet your salary is significantly higher than ours. So, again, we aren't the ones to benefit most. You – meaning the more senior employees – are.'

As he looks up, there is a hint of naive hope in his eyes, as though his very valid point could be taken as being interesting. Maybe even something they could think about adjusting. Instead, everyone has taken it as an attack on the status quo, and what's worse is that it looks like Danny has just realised this too.

Luckily, Martin chooses this moment to talk. It could be because he wants to alleviate the general awkwardness, or it could be because it's simply been too long since he's spoken. Either way, it saves Danny.

'So, our main issue is women.'

At Martin's Unfortunate choice of words another generalised snigger travels around the room. Martin just smiles, pleased that his sense of humour – accidental or otherwise – is finally getting the recognition it deserves.

'So, with that in mind, I've come up with a few ideas of my own.'

Earlier in the day, Gem had seen him researching company perks. She also saw that the majority of his points seem to come from a website that was mocking them, instead of supporting them, but critical thinking has never been one of Martin's strengths.

'What about offering egg freezing? If women are leaving to have babies, why not relieve that pressure for them?'

From across the table, she can see Danny's eyes widen and his mouth open and close in shock, but Gem gives him the smallest of head shakes. His fight would be valiant, but it would also be completely pointless.

'Or money for beauty treatments?'

'Now this I could get behind.' The support comes from Martin's doppelgänger. 'There are a number of women who could really benefit from this on my projects alone. Maybe we should make it compulsory?'

It's at times like this that Gem needs to remind herself that she could be in any number of worse places.

She could be in a sewer clearing away a fatberg.

She could be working at a GP's reception in the height of flu season.

She could be watching darts.

She could be watching football.

Actually, the last one needs to be removed from the list. She'd vastly prefer to be at a football match, which is not something she ever thought she would say, or even think.

Of course, even more than a football match, she'd quite like to be with Atlas.

She looks longingly at her phone. Just knowing that he is somewhere in the universe makes the whole idea of it seem slightly less scary.

The knowledge that not all men are like the ones sitting in this room, is enough to make her feel a bit brighter.

A picture of him – as clear as the room in front of her – appears in her mind. His hair is slightly out of place with a little tendril escaping to tickle his eye, and he's smiling at her as if he doesn't want to be looking anywhere else.

Her phone lights up again. For the first time in her life, she has had to change her phone settings, so instead of seeing a preview of the incoming message, her phone only displays the name of the sender. His messages haven't been *outrageous* but they have been making Gem blush. Even just seeing his name is making her smile.

'Gemima?'

At the use of her incorrect full name, Gem is brutally brought out of her hypnosis.

From the looks of the faces staring back at her, this isn't the first time her name has been called.

'Yes?'

'Care to share what you were thinking about?'

No. No. She does not.

Sadly, Martin's question doesn't really appear to be rhetorical. The hypocrisy of his question makes Gem rile. But right now, Martin isn't the one who is under interrogation.

'Football.'

Her answer is as shocking to Martin and the rest of the room, as it is to Gem.

'You were thinking about football?' It's a good job that Martin's hairline is so far back. It gives his eyebrows more room to express their surprise.

Now that she's started down this road, she can't stop. 'Yes, football.'

Martin's eyebrows, if possible, go up a little higher. 'And how exactly does football relate to our employee retention issues?'

'Well...'

Gem has never been one to perform well under pressure. She sweats too much, she always picks the wrong line to queue in and occasionally, she even lets out a hint of fart. But despite the pressure building, she knows she needs to come up with something. Unfortunately, the only thing she can think of, is Atlas. Luckily, though, this time her mind manages to remain on the PG side of things, and instead of remembering the warmth of his hands on her, she remembers some of his more wholesome characteristics.

'I think if we really want to stop the more junior people from leaving, we need to concentrate on the long-term as opposed to concentrating on the short term.'

All eyes are still on her, and she can feel her sweat glands limbering up.

'If we look at the most successful football teams, for example, the ones that have really stood out and will be remembered for decades to come, aren't the ones who have hired the most expensive, impressive players. They are the ones who have nurtured their youth teams.'

Martin's eyebrows fall to a more acceptable and sustainable level, causing Gem's sweat glands to also calm down.

'I think there are a number of reasons for this, and I think that if you really want to improve the situation, you need to ask the people who are actually at risk of leaving what would have to change to encourage them to stay. And then I think you need to listen to the answers and do something about solving the issues they bring up.'

The silence in the room stretches out, and Gem has the overwhelming urge to fill it.

'But, going back to the football thing, the best teams are the ones who build and support their teams. At the moment, it feels like we support our leaders, but not our teams.'

At Gem's words, the minute-taker in the corner finally appears to be writing everything down, she herself coming from one of the youth divisions.

'Although I wouldn't want to make any assumptions, I would guess that if we did some research into how to keep the more junior staff, there would be a reparation aspect, especially in regard to salaries. And while sleeping pods and Botox injections might seem like good ideas, the money spent on gimmicks would be better spent on actual salaries.' She can see the doppelgänger's face turning increasingly puce. If she's pissing him off, she must be getting somewhere.

It takes about thirty seconds for the minute-taker to stop typing, the sound of her keys the only noise in the room.

At least until the original Martin adds his opinion.

'Right, well. What if we run a raffle for some football tickets instead?'

Chapter 27

'You look nice.' There is an element of surprise in Shanti's voice that Gem chooses to ignore.

The sun almost blinds her as her eyes adjust from the dim lighting of the underground which, like a casino, is devoid of all natural light.

'Thanks.'

They don't hug every time they meet at home – that would make their morning routine unbearably cheery – but when Shanti and Gem see each other outside the house, they hug. The rules are layered and complicated, but they must be followed.

They walk together down the street, falling easily into step with each other.

'Suspiciously nice. Are you transforming into a WAG? Are you on your way to a social media scandal? Do I need to start looking for lawyers?' Shanti's tone is teasing, but Gem can tell that she's going to need an explanation.

'Don't I always look nice?'

Having been busy doing separate things in the morning, they decided to meet at the station closest to where Atlas is playing football. Shanti's been shopping and Gem was at the flat. When Gem asked Atlas if she could bring a friend, she had been a little worried that he would think it was weird, or possibly a sneak attack – which, considering Shanti's sole reason for coming is to spy on him, isn't that far from the truth. But he'd just been enthusiastic.

Gem would have preferred him to be suspicious.

It would have given her a good excuse to tell her friend not to come. And she did consider it, but then Atlas's text had come in at the exact same time she was reading an email update on her mum's new set of wheels.

'Well, no, you don't,' Shanti says now. 'Remember that I live with you, and I was around when you went through that phase of wearing a sleeping bag that you cut feet holes into.' Gem nods, conceding. They narrowly avoid stepping in a dodgy puddle. (It hasn't rained for days.) 'I'm just saying that you seem to have made more of an effort than usual with your appearance.'

For the first time, Gem wonders if Shanti is here not just to observe Atlas, but to observe her, too.

'I had some extra time this morning. You know that sometimes it's just nice to play around with your clothes.' But while this is true, it isn't true in this particular circumstance. Gem has made an extra effort with her appearance on purpose, with Atlas in mind. They haven't seen each other since last weekend, and although all of his messages have been *very* positive, and very encouraging, all this has done is make Gem feel less confident about seeing him again. He must be building her up in his mind.

And she's encouraging it. She isn't usually a fun and light and occasionally flirty person, at least not for such a prolonged period. But all her replies have been just as fun and light and occasionally flirty as his.

Of course, she shouldn't care that she is deceiving him. She isn't really dating him. Going out with him is just a means to an end. A way to pay for her mum's chair. Besides, he still enjoys soup for lunch and he still owns an embarrassingly large bag.

But despite all that, she does care, and she doesn't want to disappoint him and his apparently flattering perception of her.

It is this fear that motivated her this morning.

It is this fear that even made her paint her toenails red. He's not going to see them, but she needs to feel as confident as possible, and painted toenails (along with styled hair, her favourite underwear, her most flattering jeans, her most expensive perfume and one of Shanti's most recently discarded tops) are helping.

In a convenient turn of events, Atlas is playing in the same place where last week's practice was held, meaning Gem knows that she has limited time with Shanti before reaching the pitch, and they have more important – or at least more pressing – things to discuss.

'We've got about two minutes before we reach the pitch, meaning we should get there a few minutes before kick-off.' It's crazy how quickly you can pick up lingo that until recently, you had absolutely no knowledge of. And even maybe a mild distaste for. It's almost uncomfortable how comfortable Gem feels.

'So, what's your plan of attack for today?'

'Well, I thought I would pretend to be an overprotective friend.'

'That won't be hard.' Gem says this with more than a hint of sentimentality.

'Exactly.' For a few steps Shanti's walk carries an extra level of sass. 'You know I always believe in playing to your strengths.'

'Just don't be too obvious about it. We don't want to give the game away. Be subtle.' And Gem doesn't want Shanti to go too hard on him. Atlas is an innocent player in a game he doesn't even know he is playing.

Despite knowing exactly where she is meant to be going, Gem is tempted to take a wrong turn. Unfortunately, any possible plans are ruined when she hears the angry voice in front of her. 'What are you doing here?'

Gem knows she's the one being spoken to. First, because she recognises the voice, and second, because the owner of the voice has stepped right in front of her, blocking her way. It's the girl who loves to tackle. The scary one who asked Gem if she was Atlas's girlfriend.

'Shauna?'

When the girl doesn't correct her, Gem assumes she's got her name right. Shauna doesn't give the impression of sparing anyone's feelings.

'*What are you doing here?*' This time the question is delivered with even more vitriol than before.

'I'm here to watch Atlas. What are you doing here?'

'I'm here to watch too. We always come watch the games.'

Slowly Gem realises that Shauna isn't alone; she recognises a few other faces. They're all members of Goals Aloud. She is totally outnumbered. 'You'd know that too if you ever bothered to come to one before.'

'Oh yeah, your dad and Atlas are on the same team, right? They play together?' Gem makes her voice so kind its saccharine, but Shauna looks indifferent.

'I'm *watching* you.'

'I like her.' Shanti's betrayal, whispered in Gem's ear, isn't a surprise; it also isn't helpful. It does, however, give Gem an idea.

'Shauna, this is my friend, Shanti. I think you two will like each other.'

The look Shauna gives Shanti is so unflinching that Gem can't help but be impressed. Shanti is her best friend, and even Gem can't look at her that directly.

'Are *you* Atlas's girlfriend?'

At the question, Gem feels rather than sees Shanti glance at her.

'No, I'm not.' Shanti only puts a slight intonation on the subject.

Shauna continues to stare at them for another few moments, but then Gem sees her visibly stand down. She takes a breath that she didn't realise she was in dire need of.

Then she has the exact opposite problem: she can't exhale.

Atlas is *striding* towards them.

Gem can feel her eyes widen at the sight of him, but it's like all the pathways inside her brain have knotted together. She keeps telling her eyes to go back to a normal amount of open, but no matter how loudly she tries to send the message, it's like she's shouting it underwater. Her eyes only get bigger as he gets closer, taking more and more and more of him in.

As frustrated as she is, she can't blame her eyes for their disloyalty. He is quite the sight. He has one of those tight undershirts on, once again pulled up at the sleeve, gathered so she can once again see a hint of the tattoo that adorns the outside of his arm.

It's strange to her that there's such a wide variance in the human form. It seems impossible that Atlas is the same species as some of the other men Gem has dated. The power in his legs alone, suggests that he is less human and more god. But all of these details are just that – details. Relegated to the footnotes. The main story is his face. His piercing eyes, focused in on her, his mouth, very slightly open as though he might be about to laugh or tell her something that he really needs her to know. But mostly, the happiness on his face. It's there for everyone to see. And it's there because he is happy to see her.

The realisation hits her, and it is more potent than any feeling that she has ever felt before.

'You came.'

There is a beat of silence.

'We come to every game.'

This, of course, comes from Shauna.

Gem is both relieved and completely devastated when Atlas's focus shifts. The slight change in his stance gives Gem a view of his side profile, which is almost as beguiling as the full frontal. He flexes his jaw. The sight makes her melt. Unfortunately, it also allows awareness of other things to creep in – namely Shanti, who is staring at Gem with an open mouth and a look in her eye that is alight with danger and knowledge. And realisation.

'My greatest supporter. Just don't tell your dad that I'm your favourite player.'

Shauna beams, and Gem can't blame her. Gem has always known that Atlas is an attractive guy. Not even the extra-large bag could detract from this, but there is an extra spring to his step today. An extra confidence that is making it impossible to look away.

At least until she feels a sharp elbow in her rib. Her head snaps towards Shanti who, from the looks of things, has been trying to get her attention for a while.

Luckily, Atlas's concentration is directed elsewhere, because Shanti isn't exactly subtle when she points at him. 'His photos don't do him justice.'

And then she mouths, 'He is *really* hot.'

Chapter 28

'Oh, my God.'
'*Ohmigod.*'

The subtleties of the game are definitely lost on Gem and Shanti. Every now and then Shauna has been kind enough to explain some things to them. Throw-ins. Corner kicks. Yellow cards. She even attempted to explain the offside rule. Broken down bit by bit from Shanti's charm and enviable aura, she has even smiled at them once or twice.

But right now, there are no smiles, and no need for Shauna to explain what's going on. Even Gem and Shanti know that it's a big deal for someone – Atlas – to be running with the ball towards the other goal, seemingly nobody able to stop him.

They might be at the edge of a field, held back by a wooden fence that is there more for decoration than use, but the excitement in the crowd is just as electrifying as it was in the professional football game. Somehow Gem, Shanti and Shauna have all become one, grabbing each other's hands partly for the emotional support and partly for the physical.

Others around them are shouting, but the three of them are too tense to do so. Plus, they aren't breathing deeply enough to support anything more than a whisper.

'I can't look.'

But contradictory to her words, Gem's eyes don't leave Atlas. They can't.

Watching him, she sees a delightful mix of power and finesse. His legs are all power. There is sweat running down his temple. His face is the picture of concentration. When he shouts, he sounds authoritative and everyone listens. And his clothes are plastered against him when he runs, so all she can see are fine lines of muscle. He looks unstoppable. But then, every few feet he taps the ball, directing it a bit this way, or a bit that way, making sure it keeps pace with him. How he can run with such strength, but then be so gentle with the ball impresses Gem more than she ever would have thought. And all of a sudden, she is transported to the bedroom, imagining his hands gently holding her down, his mouth trailing light kisses up her neck.

It's a good thing he is so beguiling. If Gem had looked away, she would have missed The Moment. Somehow, Atlas goes from running with the ball to kicking it and, although the goalie dives, the ball flies over his head, and straight into the back of the net.

The screams erupt, and even Shanti jumps – from excitement, not fright. Atlas, who is busy being hugged by all of his teammates as though he's just won them the championship, looks over to where they have been standing all game and grins.

And Gem is only slightly surprised when she realises the loudest shout of all is coming from herself.

'OK, I'll admit it. That wasn't the worst.'

Gem smiles at her friend. They're loitering outside the changing rooms. Every now and then the door opens, and Gem's heart skips a beat, but so far, Atlas is yet to appear. His goal had seen his team to victory, and Gem's pride is hard to hide. She might be in her early thirties, but at the moment, she feels more like she's back at school.

She turns to Shauna, who against all the odds, seems to now like her. Or at least she likes Shanti, and she's tolerating Gem. She is definitely petrifying.

'Does he normally take this long to come out? Is this where we wait for him? Should we be waiting for him? Or should we go somewhere else and tell him where we've gone?'

Gem thinks she's playing it cool, but when she sees the looks on both Shauna and Shanti's faces, it's clear that she is definitely not.

'He'll come. He's just showering. They always shower after, otherwise they smell really bad.'

'OK. So we stay here?'

This time, Shanti answers. 'Yes. We wait here.'

Instead of another, 'OK', Gem just nods. He's just showering.

He's just showering.

Instantly, Gem's mind is overrun with images of water cascading down his body, little rivers running over his broad back and shoulders, travelling everywhere that Gem is going to touch. Atlas, turning towards her, smiling when he sees her. Heated, when he looks at her.

As if she conjured him up herself, Atlas emerges from the room. She isn't sure which is more alluring, her vision of him, or the real thing. Gem beams when she sees him, all effort to be cool completely forgotten.

A few of the other freshly washed guys slap him on the back as they pass him. He says something to each of them, but his path never strays. Gem swears his gaze never leaves hers. Internally, she has never known such a struggle. Half of her wants to run up to him, the other can't move. The half of her that is shocked into stillness wins out.

As if Gem doesn't have enough temptation to resist, when Atlas finally reaches them, she makes the mistake of inhaling. She shouldn't have. He smells so very delicious. Kind of minty. Fresh. Spicy. Gem knows that if she were to hug him, he would feel just-out-the-shower warm, and the scent would be as comforting as the hug itself. The knowledge isn't helping Gem keep her cool.

Luckily, for the first time in her life, she is standing next to two people who do know how to act appropriately in public.

'You must be Atlas.'

Atlas smiles, and despite knowing that Shanti wouldn't do anything to risk their friendship, Gem worries that the two of them will kick it off too well. She is, after all, a lot cooler than Gem.

'You must be Shanti.' Despite Gem's worries, she senses nothing but friendship coming from him. 'The bush friend.'

What Gem hadn't foreseen was *Atlas* doing something to risk their friendship. She's never got round to telling Shanti the excuse she made up to get away from Atlas on their first date. It sounded ridiculous then, even more so now.

'Huh?' It's very rare for Shanti to look confused. She never lets any kind of weakness show, but she looks baffled now. 'The bush friend? I'm not a lesbian—'

'No! That's not what he means. He's talking about the time you got stuck in a bush. Naked. An actual bush. A short tree kinda bush.' Gem's eyes are wide, pleading. 'And I came to rescue you. Remember? I'd been on a date with Atlas.'

Shanti, unimpressed, just stares at Gem, making this infinitely more difficult than it needs to be. 'No. I don't.'

Changing tack, Gem turns back to Atlas. 'I told you it was embarrassing. She does remember, she just doesn't want to talk about it. She's probably repressing the memory. It was really embarrassing. I would repress it too.'

'Well,' Atlas says gamely, 'thanks for coming out all this way to watch us. I think this was our best attended game yet.'

There is real pride in his voice, even though the number of spectators was capped at forty.

'You played pretty well, Coach.'

At this, Atlas's head dips and he looks a little shy, completely unlike the confident, back-slapping guy who emerged from the changing rooms a mere minute ago. Somehow, this quieter version of him is even more desirable, and Gem's shower-image-induced-lust is joined by a feeling that's a little quieter, but no less intense.

'Thanks, Shaunie.'

'It was a really good goal. *But* you play defence, and you shouldn't have been that far forward.'

A man who is significantly larger than Atlas appears, giving Shauna a hug that she seems to both merely tolerate, and also relish in. With a quick, 'Hi, Dad,' she pushes him off, but doesn't step away. Instead, she stands close enough for him to rest a hand on her shoulder. Nobody looking at them would doubt their shared genetics. They even stand in the same way.

'Anything else I need to work on?' The question carries a smile that suggests Atlas isn't going to forget her cheek all that quickly.

The big guy looks down at Shauna. 'You giving him more pointers, Shauna?'

She just shrugs. 'You always give me pointers, and you always say that you only give them to me to make me better.'

Shauna's dad looks from his daughter to Atlas. Both men share a look that says they've just been bettered by an eight-year-old.

'Can't argue with that, Shaunie. I'll make sure to stay in my position next time.'

'Or maybe you should move from defence to attack.'

The hand on her shoulder squeezes. 'OK, now that's too far. I'm at the front, and you've got another thing coming if you think I'm gonna give up my position for this tw—' Luckily, he looks down at Shauna, registering her smile and the cheek behind her eyes before he can finish talking. The outrage in his eyes turns to pride. 'Come on, you. Let's go home before you go too far with that sense of humour of yours.'

But then, something happens that nobody could have predicted.

'Before we go ...' Shauna's voice morphs from being cheeky, to pleading. She points to Shanti. 'Shanti – who is Atlas's girlfriend's friend, so she's perfectly safe – said she'd show me some more footwork exercises. She promises they're more exciting than the ladders. Can we do that before we go?'

Everyone's eyes widen but nobody's eyes are wider than Gem's.

Luckily for Shauna, the situation – and more importantly the awkwardness – makes her proposal too tempting to turn down.

'Yeah.' Her dad's voice booms out. 'That sounds great.' He looks up, his eyes sweeping between Atlas, Shanti and Gem. 'Let's be anywhere but here.' He gives Atlas a final look. 'Nice game today, buddy.'

The only adult who doesn't look awkward is Shanti. She looks in her element, throwing Gem a grin before following Shauna, far enough ahead to give Gem and Atlas some privacy.

Unfortunately, privacy doesn't immediately equate to less awkwardness. In fact, somehow it seems to have added to it. Atlas's eyes are still looking anywhere but at Gem. It would be impressive, especially as she's standing in his direct line of sight, if only it wasn't also exponentially adding to Gem's discomfort.

As she stands there, the main thing she's thinking about is where her discomfort is coming from. And bizarrely it doesn't come from being called Atlas's girlfriend and wanting to run away. Instead it comes from being called his girlfriend and liking the sound of it, but knowing it's a lie. She feels like she did when she was twelve and her mum caught her making out with a Legolas poster.

Finally, Atlas's eyes land on her, and as soon as they do, Gem wishes they would go back to looking at anything else. There is nowhere to hide.

'So . . .'

When no more words appear, Gem nods. 'So.'

Although Gem initially avoided his gaze, for the second time today, she can't look away.

Which is good. Otherwise, she might've missed the smile that slowly takes over Atlas's face. The one that makes even the most awkward of Gem's feelings disappear.

Chapter 29

'This place is great.'

Somehow, although nobody could really tell you how, the three of them – Atlas, Shanti and Gem – have ended up heading back towards Gem and Shanti's flat and are now hunting and gathering for supplies in their favourite store.

Unlike Shanti and Gem who view each and every item with a distanced intrigue, Atlas has collected so many things that he has had to turn the front of his hoodie into a faux pouch – and he hasn't even made it to the snack aisle. By contrast, Gem has only picked up a tube of off-brand crisps with aggressive packaging, and Shanti has a bag of sweets that have so much sugar in them it shouldn't matter when they were created.

Atlas's backpack has reappeared, in fact it's been around all afternoon, but even though it's now joined by an embarrassing pouch of food that should be equally off-putting, Gem's feet aren't itching to go anywhere. Instead, they're pointing directly at Atlas. She may even be smiling.

'Now, don't take this question personally ...'

Shanti's voice rings out as clearly as the overhead fluorescent lighting. Gem turns to her, anxious as to what her best friend might be about to say, confident only in the fact it will be personal. When the three of them left the game together – footwork demonstration over – and then walked back to the station via a quick drink in the pub followed by a longer drink in the pub, and then, somehow, made their way back here, Gem had been a ball of nerves. Nerves that became even more fried when Atlas reached out and took a gentle hold of her hand. She knew Shanti would pick up on the physical contact. It would almost be impossible not to. But then he gave her a quick squeeze and a cheeky smile on the sly, and her nerves were replaced with butterflies.

But Gem knows that Shanti is about to make her move. After all, questions are the whole reason why Shanti came to Atlas's game. But Gem doesn't want Shanti to make Atlas feel uncomfortable, especially not today when he is still on a high from scoring the winning goal. Even more than this, she doesn't want to know why her ick appeared. She doesn't want to find out what – if anything – her body was warning her against.

She tries to use their secret best friend connection to communicate all – or at least most – of this to Shanti, but she isn't looking at Gem. Her eyes are fixed on Atlas. Gem can't stop herself from stepping in front of him. Shanti smirks.

'. . . Don't you think you have enough snacks?'

Gem exhales and sends a silent thank you up to whoever is watching.

Atlas, who is currently holding not one, but two different kinds of noodles in his hands, looks offended. In a move that tests the laws of physics, he grabs another packet of noodles and tosses them into his pouch. And then, with a little cock of his head, grabs another and repeats the action.

'These aren't snacks,' he states. 'They're sustenance.'

'OK, in that case, don't you want to be doing something, well, more fun to celebrate?'

At the question, Atlas's mouth hangs open in mock shock.

'Don't let my youthful skin and general healthy appearance fool you. Inside, I'm very old, and food shopping is genuinely one of my favourite pastimes. Plus, it's so expensive these days, if you count it as a hobby, it feels less like a chore, and more like you're doing something fun.' His eyes catch on to something interesting in the background, packaged, pre-fried carbs now safely added to his pouch. 'Oh! *Spices!*'

With Atlas now a safe distance away, the two friends look at each other. Gem's smile fades just as Shanti's grows.

'What?'

But Shanti doesn't answer.

'*What?*' Gem asks again, with a little more bite. And a little more fear.

'I know why you can't find anything wrong with him.' There is a glint in Shanti's eye. 'It's because there *is* nothing wrong with him.'

The one item the shop doesn't stock is soft furnishings, making a secret conversation impossible to have. Shanti walks away, making it even less possible for Gem to argue back. Not that she would. Not that she *could*. So instead, they follow Atlas to the end of the aisle. A family-sized bag of turmeric has been added to his haul.

'It's meant to be an amazing anti-inflammatory.' He looks at the bag, turning it over. 'Not really too sure if I'm inflamed, or if I am, where the flame might be, but it can't hurt to be prepared, can it?'

Gem instantly thinks of the sauerkraut over-fermenting in her cupboard but stays quiet.

It takes Atlas seven more minutes of perusing before he is ready to pay.

'Here,' as they reach the checkout, he plucks both Gem and Shanti's purchases from their hands, 'let me get these.'

Gem tries to grab back her Prongles, but Atlas is faster. 'You don't need to do that.'

'Consider it an early thank you for the footwork dance session you two are gonna run.'

Shauna had run over to Atlas after Shanti's little dance demo, and practically begged him to organise a crossover lesson.

'So that's definitely happening then?' Gem had hoped that it might be forgotten.

Atlas places both items on top of his teetering pile of goods.

'Yes. Unless you want to be the one to tell Shauna it's not.'

Gem and Shanti share a look, and then both answer at the same time, 'No!'

'We'll do the session,' adds Shanti.

'I thought so.'

Atlas turns back to Jay who is, as usual, unsmiling behind the counter. In a world where change comes at an increasingly fast pace, it is quite nice that some things never do.

The elbow bump that Gem gives Shanti is subtle, but Shanti knows exactly what Gem is telling her. It's Shanti's turn to try and make Jay smile.

With a final, slight purse of the lips and twitch of an eyebrow, Shanti steps forward, her pursed lips morphing into a smile.

'I would just like to thank you.'

Jay turns his attention to her before ringing through some chewy ginger sweets, his eyes remaining hooded.

'I imagine you'd like to be at home, but I don't know what we'd do without our emergency late night snacks.'

Steady in the face of change, Jay's face doesn't move. Instead, he simply keeps tapping in the prices of each item, half of which don't have prices on them, and passing them to Atlas, who has removed his bag from his back and is shoving each item in.

Eventually admitting defeat, Shanti silently moves back so she's standing next to Gem, taking the loss as well as she can. The two share a small conciliatory smile, and an even smaller shoulder shrug.

But then, the thin silence is interrupted.

'Nah,' this comes from Atlas, whose grin hasn't left his face since he stepped in the shop. 'Mate, don't go outside.' He then turns and waves his arm like he's drawing a rainbow from one side of the shop to the other. 'You have everything you could possibly need in here. The outside world is horrible. I do not recommend it.'

And then, as if the day hasn't been exciting enough, Gem and Shanti witness a miracle.

Jay laughs.

Typically, Gem is grateful for Shanti's company, but right now, she couldn't be happier that Shanti is by her side. There is no way Gem could have told her what just happened without Shanti accusing her of lying. Even having seen it first hand, Gem can't quite believe it.

In a state of shock, they look at each other, open mouthed, wondering if Atlas could actually be a god. He must at least have some kind of magic running through his veins.

'Young man, I couldn't agree more.' Jay shakes his head, a move that Gem and Shanti are familiar with, but this time, instead of being partnered with a tsk, it's paired with a smile. He picks up the final item in Atlas's basket, a jar of amchoor powder.

'This is very, very good on chicken. Make a marinade with this and some honey.'

He makes a kissing action with his hand.

'Delicious.'

He then puts the bag of spice on the other side of the cash machine, ready for Atlas to put in his bag. *And doesn't ring it up.*

Chapter 30

'I'm actually gonna head back to my parents' house. I've got lunch at theirs tomorrow, and it would be easier to wake up there.'

They are heading up the hill towards their house. It's late, and the street is one way, so they've decided to walk in the middle of the road, parked cars lining either side. But at Shanti's announcement, Gem stops short. Eventually, Shanti and Atlas do too.

Shanti's announcement comes as a surprise for a number of reasons.

First, they are almost home and although it's not a long walk back to the station, Shanti isn't known for being inefficient. If she had planned on going back to her parents', she wouldn't have wasted time in the shop. She wouldn't have even got off the tube; she would have travelled a further five stops, changed lines and then travelled the extra three needed to get to her parents'.

Second, Shanti never stays overnight at her parents' house. Since moving out, she worries that her mum will lock the doors and never let her out again.

'Are you sure?' Even Gem can hear the mix of emotions in her voice. There's disbelief, relief, hesitancy, even a hint of nerves. Shanti can't leave. She's meant to be here as a buffer. She's meant to remind Gem that this isn't real. That her thing with Atlas is merely a means to an end. If Shanti leaves, Gem will be more tempted than ever to forget the whole reason they're dating.

In the moment, the distance between the two friends seems much bigger than the mere three feet between them. For the second time in ten minutes, they have a whole conversation without a single word being spoken.

Shanti says she is sure, she is going to her parents'.

Gem says she doesn't want Shanti to leave. That their home is *their* home, and nobody, not even a stupid boy with a great arse and magical powers, is worth risking their haven. She will tell Atlas to go home. She doesn't mind.

Shanti tells her not to be so silly. It's still their home, and no boy – stupid or otherwise – will ever risk it. She's just giving Gem some alone time with the stupid boy with a great arse and magical powers.

This time, Shanti wins.

'I'll be back tomorrow.' And with a small skip and a wave to Atlas, Shanti leaves, her sweets still in his bag.

Gem watches her friend for longer than she needs to, all of a sudden very aware about how much of a security blanket Shanti has been. At some point (probably earlier than Gem is comfortable admitting, and probably around the time she started fantasising about Atlas in the shower), the day stopped being a game or a study or a discovery exercise. Instead, it just started being a nice day. A day where she stopped searching Atlas for his downfalls and simply started being with Atlas. It all felt very natural and fun and light.

But now that Gem is *with* Atlas, and *only* Atlas, all of the fun and light and naturalness has disappeared. The air around them, and certainly the air inside her lungs, is heavy. Of course, Shanti was casual with her departure. It isn't like she ran down the road yelling, 'Now you can have sex with him, or at least get your tits out if the mood arises. Whatever you want!' But Unfortunately, as cool as Shanti is, Gem is the opposite.

She turns back to Atlas, something adjacent to a smile on her face. She wouldn't be at all surprised if he ran away too. Unlike the feeling of distance that Gem just felt with Shanti, Atlas now feels much, *much* closer than he actually is.

'Did we take a different route this time? I swear last time I walked you home, it took a lot longer.'

Grateful for the dark that is hopefully hiding her blush, Gem feigns ignorance and starts walking again, needing movement to help regulate her heartbeat. 'Oh, I don't remember.'

Of course she remembers. She remembers everything about that night. The idea of creating future memories with Atlas finally makes her a little bit – not calm, if anything less so – happier.

'I like Shanti.'

The Gem of this morning would have applied an irrational layer of distrust to this confession, but nothing about Atlas himself is making her worry right now. Her anxiety is coming from a completely different source.

Did she put away all of her potentially embarrassing things? Her underwear? Her hair ties that still contain a healthy amount of hair? Did she take the hair off the shower wall? What if he lives in a really nice apartment and thinks their shoddily converted two-bed is unliveable? Will he hate the hatch?

'So, did I pass the test?'

At Atlas's question, Gem's heartbeat stops.

Did she put away anything relating to Shanti's dissertation? 'The test?'

A laugh leaves Atlas.

'Yeah, I mean it's clear that neither of you are football fans. I don't think Shanti came to watch the match, so I assume she came to make sure I'm worthy of you. Or – if not worthy – at least acceptable.'

When Gem first met Atlas, he gave the impression of being a little overconfident in the way he leaned on the bar to order their drinks, his habit of winking and his easy and loud laugh that made everyone look at them. But Gem gets the distinct feeling that this is the real Atlas.

Someone who is just a little unsure.

It kind of breaks her heart, but also makes it feel fuller than it has for a long time.

She stops walking and reaches out a hand to catch Atlas at his elbow, forcing him to stop alongside her. Needing to make sure he hears her.

'You are more than worthy.'

For the first time, Atlas doesn't look like he is going to smile. At least not with his lips. If Gem isn't mistaken, it looks like he is biting his lip to stop the smile from coming.

'Well. Good.'

Gem nods, a little awkwardly.

'Sorry about her checking up on you.'

'It's totally fine. She's your best friend. I would have been more worried if she didn't want to check up on me.'

If he knew the truth, he wouldn't be nearly as understanding. The familiar feeling of guilt lodges itself in her chest.

'And she's probably right. I probably should be celebrating in a cooler way. Maybe I should go.'

Having just been too scared to be left alone with him, Gem's heart now flips and goes in the exact opposite direction.

Is he going to leave? The thought crushes her. She can't let him leave. At least not without letting him know that's not what she wants.

'No. Don't go.'

The words are out before she can double-check herself. But despite a hint of embarrassment getting sprinkled into the mix of emotions she already feels, she doesn't regret saying them.

Especially when she catches the look on Atlas's face. He's looking pleased – maybe with himself, but definitely with the situation in general.

'Well, just like I don't mind that Shanti was around for the match, I also kinda don't mind that she left.' He steps a little bit closer. 'And, just to be clear, I don't want to go, and I don't want to celebrate with anyone else.'

Gem is pretty sure her face is stuck in an open and speechless position. But she is powerless to change it. And luckily she doesn't need to speak, especially when Atlas closes the distance between them and tilts his head down towards hers.

It's an invitation that she is happy to accept.

She almost meets him halfway; he is a little too tall for the split to be even, and the kiss is even better than she remembers.

He is always better than she remembers.

His lips are soft, his tongue is oddly addictive, and there is still a hint of spice when she inhales, but the thing that really gets her is his hands and the strength behind them. At some point, probably when her body reacted purely on instinct, she stretched up on her tiptoes. Her balance – although pretty good, thanks to dance – currently feels unusually weak. But it doesn't matter. Because he has her. Or more specifically – his hands have her. She can feel them, firm, safe, warm, reassuring on her back. They aren't roaming. Their primary use at this moment in time isn't focused on his pleasure; they are focused on her. On keeping her safe.

Eventually they break apart, but not far enough to breathe separate air, which is excellent news as Gem still needs the help of Atlas's hands to keep standing. Maybe even more so now than during the kiss.

'So . . .' Atlas is no longer trying to hide his smile. 'Are we going to keep moving, or do you want to stay outside all night? I don't mind. I've come to quite like it here. This street is turning into my favourite street in the whole city. Maybe the whole world.'

There's a cheekiness in his smile that Gem wants to remember forever.

'And I've always kinda wanted to try camping. Ideally glamping. But I can be flexible.'

'We're not staying outside.'

Gem then grabs Atlas by the bag strap and leads him the rest of the way to her apartment.

Chapter 31

'I really love your apartment.'

'Thanks.'

Atlas is in the lounge, concentrating on the wall art that Shanti bought one weekend at a supposedly affordable art fair, instead of the little pig salt and pepper shakers that Gem is currently hiding behind the travel mugs. She bought them on the same day from a charity shop on the way home. The salt has an added umami taste to it which is convenient and also a little off-putting if you think about it too much, which is why Gem doesn't think about it too much.

Luckily, the pigs are the worst thing she can see.

'Can I help?'

With a jump, Gem realises that Atlas has now found the hatch between the two rooms. From the smile on his face, it looks like he's a fan.

She turns to face him. It's difficult to know which of his faces is the most attractive. Earlier today, he spent most of the game looking determined, and full of concentration. He didn't smile, and his jaw occasionally clenched in that way that makes it ripple. Then in the pub he seemed laid back and happy, his shoulders relaxed. He looked like a man who spent most of his day chasing a laugh. Then in the shop, his eyes spent most of the time wide open with childlike wonder. Outside in the street they were like embers. But now, they're like little sparklers, alight with humour. Gem has always been the kind of person to stay silent when someone claims something ridiculous like 'eyes are windows into the soul'. But right now, she is considering changing her opinion. It appears that Atlas has an uncanny ability to make Gem reconsider a lot of things.

'You can take these.'

She grabs two glasses from the cupboard and passes them to him through the hatch. As he takes them from her, their hands linger. The nervous part of her screams to move away and pretend that there is something really urgent going on at the back of a cupboard on the other side of the kitchen. But a bigger part of her wants to lean down and taste him. The bigger part wins. His hands are otherwise occupied, but as hers aren't, she makes the most of his helplessness and kisses him in exactly the way she wants. And he tastes delicious. She only stops because the damn hatch – at once a window and a wall – is in the way.

'I really like kissing you.' As Atlas speaks, his eyes flick back down to Gem's lips, and an addictive swell of confidence bubbles up inside her.

'I thought I just kissed you.'

His half smile makes an appearance. Another one of Gem's favourite faces on him.

'It's a team game.'

She gives him an eye roll, but it's very half-arsed. 'Take the glasses. I'll just get the Champagne.'

'Champagne?'

'We're celebrating your goal. You deserve more than just shop-bought snacks.'

He takes the glasses. Gem sees a hint of a nod as he steps away. 'OK.'

The Champagne has been sitting in the fridge for about six months. Not being a frequent Champagne drinker, Gem recites a silent prayer that it's still OK, having no idea if it has an expiry date. She was given it at the end of a work event. The person organising the event had either been extremely bad with numbers or an alcoholic. Possibly both. Whichever way, at the end of the night, they went around giving out all of the leftover bottles, prioritising the people who looked like they would be grateful to receive such a heavy and cumbersome gift to carry home, instead of the people who include Champagne as a staple within their weekly online shop. Gem was given two bottles. The first she drank with Shanti on a random Sunday when they were both feeling a little fancy but couldn't really afford to *be* fancy. She swore to only open the second bottle on a special occasion.

And tonight feels special.

'Here, you can open it.' She passes him the bottle before settling on the sofa. Unsure how to sit on it with someone next to her, she eventually opts to tuck her feet under her, facing him, arm resting on the back.

By contrast, Atlas seems perfectly relaxed. But instead of feeling annoyed that he's invading her space and making it his own simply by being the biggest person around, she's happy that he seems comfortable.

She's also happy because although there's no sign or name tag on either of the sofas denoting whose is whose, Atlas is sitting on hers.

He leans forward, readying to open the bottle. Before he does, he gives a pointed look to the corner, where Shanti's half-dressed mannequin is standing, both a little dishevelled and simultaneously more fashionable than Gem will ever look. She's wearing a black leotard that Shanti has cut panels out of and covered with bright blue fishnet material.

He gestures with the bottle, 'What is all that about?'

'Ah ...' Gem settles into the sofa, finally feeling comfortable. 'That is Shanti's passion. She's studying to be a psychologist, or a psychiatrist, one of those, but really, I think she should scrap it all and become a clothes designer. She does it on the side anyway.'

'So why doesn't she?'

Gem releases a deep inhale.

'It's complicated.' She doesn't say any more, as the conversation is Shanti's to have, and Atlas doesn't push it.

'Well, for what it's worth, I hope it happens. I can see it now,' he twists open the Champagne cage and pops the cork without a hint of hesitation, as if it's second nature, 'the two of you sitting in this lounge, starting a fashion empire that will take over the world.'

Gem doesn't disagree, but she also knows that Shanti will need more than Atlas's well wishes before jumping ship into such a risky business venture. Especially with her family's expectations. Instead, she nods towards the glasses, which Atlas is currently filling.

'You're a pro.'

He even pours like a pro. Gem idly wonders how far his skills extend.

'I used to work as a waiter at fancy events.'

'So you *are* a pro.'

He puts down the bottle and picks up both of their glasses before leaning back and handing Gem one.

'Cheers.'

His free hand comes to rest on Gem's knee, and it takes everything she has not to completely overreact to what is essentially a very casual touch.

She taps her glass against his. 'To your successful football career.'

But before she can drink, Atlas's hand, the one she had been trying not to overreact to, shifts so its gentle strength rests on her arm, stopping her from moving.

'I think we should drink to something else. Something bigger. More important.'

Gem assumes a teasingly shocked look at his tone. 'Something bigger than football? Wasn't it you who told me that football was bigger than pizza? That simply by watching a football match I could change the future?'

'OK. OK. Yes, I did say that. But I really didn't feel like eating pizza that day.'

'Lies. Everyone always feels like eating pizza.' She's playing with him, but she can't help but feel he's right. Somehow, watching him today *has* changed her life.

'I can't remember if I said it before, but thank you for coming. I know it's just a silly local league full of guys with questionable footwork, but it felt really nice to have someone there to watch me play.' His voice quietens and Gem is forced to listen harder to hear him. 'It's been a while since anyone watching has been there just for me.'

At this confession, Gem's breath hitches. She has an overwhelming urge to tell him about Shanti's study, to confess all – and a simultaneous need to keep it from him forever. Instead she pushes her discomfort as far away as possible. It doesn't go very far.

'OK, well, I guess we don't have to toast to it, but your goal was impressive.'

'Good.' His eyes briefly lock onto hers before once again moving away. 'That's exactly what I was going for.'

'Well, then I'd say you succeeded. Shauna was particularly impressed, despite what she said about you not playing in the right place, or whatever. In fact, all of the Goalies were impressed.'

But when she glances across at Atlas, his hand once again resting on her knee, the humour immediately falls from her voice.

He's studying her as though she's an equation that he is trying to solve. His head tilts to the side, and a slight frown momentarily appears, disappearing quickly enough to call its whole existence into doubt.

He squeezes her knee lightly and gives a slight shake of his head, but his eyes never leave Gem's.

'It wasn't them I was trying to impress.'

When the meaning of his words sinks in, Gem's swallow gets stuck part way down her throat.

Someone with more experience of being in this situation would be able to handle it well. They would probably have the perfect response to the world's most perfect line. But Unfortunately, Gem is not that girl. Instead, she is the girl who has spent years vigorously avoiding any kind of emotional intimacy. Her list of icks has done a good job of keeping people away. So instead, all she can think to say is, 'Fuck me.'

Of course, she doesn't say it in the flirty, suggestive, way. She says it in the way that's only meant to be heard by her own internal audience.

Luckily, Atlas is a little smoother than Gem.

'I don't think that was an invitation.'

When Gem's brain catches up with her, she can feel the blush blooming on her cheeks. 'No.' This comes out quicker than it should, especially as having sex with him is *exactly* what she would like to be doing. 'No, it wasn't.'

He waits a moment, his hand still. 'Not gonna lie. That's a bit of a shame.'

Despite still not having decided on a suitable reason to cheer, Gem takes a mouthful of her drink. She needs it both for the liquid because her mouth is now dry as a desert, and for the courage, because she only has one life, and she knows that if she – her shyness, her fear, her hesitation, her worries, her anxieties, the voices in her head telling her to run – gets in the way of whatever this is, she will always regret it.

Determined not to stand in her own way, she leans forward and reaches for his drink, placing both their glasses on the coffee table. Then she keeps moving. She climbs on top of him, a knee on either side so she's straddling him. Despite being the one on top, there's no doubt that if he wants to Atlas could physically overpower her. But there's also no doubt that, right now, Gem is the one in control.

His eyes are wide with wonder as Gem's hands explore him. They trail up his arms, a finger slipping under the sleeve of his T-shirt, feeling the strength in his shoulders that she already knows is there. They work up to his neck where she can feel his quickening pulse. They come to rest just below his jaw. She wants to move more, but she also doesn't want to rush this.

When she stills, needing to breathe, it's Atlas's turn. Unlike how he held her outside, this time, although his hands remain a constant, reassuring pressure on her body, they also roam. And she lets them. They burn a path up her legs, around her waist and up her back, before they separate. One hand continues travelling up, into her hair, the other making its way to settle just above her heart. Her heart that she fears might genuinely be about to explode.

Then Atlas freezes. But the wait doesn't give either of them a chance to catch their breath. Instead, it just makes it even harder to breathe.

'Kiss me.'

His eyebrow kinks up. 'Is that an invitation?'

She leans forward, coming close enough to him so that when her lips move, he can feel her answer.

'Yes.'

As soon as the word is spoken, her world flips. Literally. Instead of her being on top, she is pinned beneath him. He takes her hands and stretches them above her head. She has never felt so wanted. So alive. So sexy. Once her hands are safely encased in one of his, Gem is powerless to stop his roaming. Not that she would want him to.

For the first time ever, she has no problem being put in her place.

Atlas's free hand travels down her body, leaving a scorched trail in its wake. But while his hand is moving, his mouth remains almost glued to the side of her neck. Her body is fighting to move and simultaneously wants to stay pinned. Distracted as she is by his mouth, edging closer to her ear, she doesn't notice his hand until it has already – magically – undone her jeans.

His mouth momentarily stops, and Gem is pretty sure she cries out at the lack, but her cries change to ecstasy when he starts talking. The feel of his breath along her neck and against her ear make her shiver, goosebumps springing up all along her arms.

'Your butt in these jeans drove me nuts all day. But now I really fucking want them off.'

His hand pushes its way under the denim and past her favourite underwear. For a moment she stills, worried that she won't live up to his fantasies, but when his hand cups her, and a finger – and then another – slides inside her, her worries vanish. He lets out a noise similar in meaning to Gem's cry, but much deeper. The muscles along his jaw clench.

'These need to come off. Now.'

With more agility than she would have guessed he possesses, Atlas moves so he is no longer pinning her arms. Instead, he is now on his knees in front of her, moving Gem at the same time so he can drink her in as she sits.

His hands reach out, lifting her top over her head and flinging it to the side in one swift movement. Unable to resist, he helps himself to her breasts, massaging one with his hand, and kissing the other exactly where her nipple is straining against the lace. A moan escapes. She would be embarrassed, but the noise only encourages Atlas, so she moans again.

Just as she thinks she might be about to explode, he creates some distance between the two of them, but only so his hands can grab the top of her jeans. With one swift tug and a well-timed lift of her hips, they are off.

He flings them across the room, but even in his lust, Gem notes that his aim is on point. They land in the middle of the floor, without hitting anything. Right next to her discarded top.

And then, he turns back to her. Looks at her.

The moment of stillness that follows does nothing to still the blood rushing through Gem's veins. Atlas looks like he might be about to growl.

Without breaking eye contact, he moves his hands, teasing them softly from her knees up her thighs. When they reach Gem's underwear, he hooks his fingers over the elastic and then gently slips off her knickers. The last of her defences.

His eyes briefly break contact as he studies her. When his eyes return to Gem's, he licks his lips and she melts.

And then he begins to worship her.

Chapter 32

Every now and then Shanti lets Gem use her weighted blanket. As Gem begins to wake up now, her body feels similarly content. The reassuring weight is calming her heartbeat and prolonging that luxurious window between being asleep and being awake. Her whole body feels like it's being cocooned.

But then, the weirdest thing happens. The blanket starts to move.

Her heart, which had been beating so steadily, suddenly goes into overdrive. Her mind immediately goes to the most obvious explanation: the world has been taken over by a semi-conscious fungus and it has invaded her bedroom.

Then it swings to the least likely explanation.

Atlas stayed all night.

Only when his hands begin to move, as though he can instinctively tell that she is awake, does she begin to remember. His hands are just the prompt her mind needs. She isn't sure she's ever going to be able to forget them. Or that she's ever going to want to. She remembers them trailing up and down her. Inside her. Making sure she was ready for him.

She should think about what this means.

For her.
For the study.
For her intuition.
For Atlas.
But she can't think of much right now.
Except for his hands.
And his mouth.
And *everything else*.

Atlas runs his nose up the side of Gem's neck, stopping at her ear. He kisses her just underneath it, so gently that the memory of it is already stronger than the kiss itself. Then, just as quietly, he whispers, 'Good morning.'

When his hands then continue to roam, her body melts some more. They can't have fallen asleep that long ago. Every time they lay down, they ended up finding new ways to touch each other. New areas that needed exploring. Logic suggests she should be feeling tired, but she's energised. She hates running, but if someone burst into her room right now and asked if she could run a marathon, she would leap out of bed and grab her trainers.

Or she would, if Atlas's mouth wasn't currently making its way very slowly down her neck. She's never before yearned to be a giraffe, but the idea of having a really long neck is currently very appealing.

Even the sound of his breathing is hot. She once abandoned a date during the interval at the theatre because she couldn't stand the sound of how he inhaled. But the sound of Atlas breathing is sending her wild.

Eventually, when she can't stay still any longer, she reaches behind, trying to grab any part of him that she can, just so she can pull him closer. Her hand pulls his hip closer, her leg tangling with his. The heat of his body under her fingertips lights her own on fire. He feels so strong against her hands.

Some kind of noise involuntarily escapes her. She would feel embarrassed, but it's clear that Atlas doesn't mind the noise. Indeed, even though they've only spent one busy night together, he already seems to be reading her cues as though they're written all over her body. It makes her wonder what the sex would be like if they knew each other even better. Can it be any better than this? Is that even possible?

There's another noise. It takes Gem a moment to realise that it's coming from outside. Someone is trying to enter into the flat. It can't be Shanti. Shanti is quiet. Shanti knows you have to turn the lock with the key still in, in order to open it properly, otherwise it gets stuck. Both Atlas and Gem freeze.

Something heavy drops on the floor. It sounds suspiciously close.

'Shanti?' Atlas whispers, and when she shakes her head no, he follows with another question. 'Are you expecting anyone else?'

Gem's heart is beating fast. Too fast to speak. Once again, her mind goes to the most obvious explanation. *They're being burgled.*

Gem is sure that she read an article that said most burglaries happen early in the morning. Night-time is too obvious and people assume that burglars are too lazy to wake up early. Especially at the weekend. It's why nobody calls in the unusual activity and how burglars get away with stealing all of your possessions while you sleep in on a Sunday morning.

Gem keeps her voice to a whisper. 'No.'

As if he can read her body's clues even when they aren't related to sex, Atlas rests a hand on her shoulder. 'You stay here. I'll go look.'

'OK.' And then because she is genuinely quite worried that they are being burgled, she sits up and adds, 'Be careful.' She watches him leave the room, dressed in only his sweater and boxers, making as little noise as possible. His back really is a thing of beauty. Gem can see the muscles moving as he walks away, making her almost happy that all of their possessions are about to be stolen.

Left alone, Gem's mind continues to race.

Should she swallow the necklace her mum gave her for her birthday so they can't steal it?

Should she give them her work laptop as a peace offering in return for them leaving quietly?

Should she get her phone out and ring someone so they can be witness to the whole thing should they get kidnapped?

However, instead of doing any of these things, she decides that the most important thing is to get dressed. She can't be naked when she confronts them. It's not like her boobs are big enough to be a distraction. If they were, she might be tempted to leave them free.

Her choice ends up being the right one.

Because as soon as her top is on, she hears a noise that makes all of her previous fears pale in comparison.

There's a whistle, followed by a high-pitched scream that she won't tell anyone about, especially her mum, and then there is a deeper shout of, 'Who the fuck are you?'

Followed by, 'I'm Atlas, who are you?'

She should feel relief. After all, they aren't being burgled. Not unless you count Uncle Mike eating all of their biscuits as thievery. But all she can feel is an overwhelming surge of embarrassment. Suddenly dressing becomes all the more important. Unfortunately, every single pair of leggings Gem reaches for is inside out. And her legs are having some trouble distinguishing between a leg hole and a side pocket.

'What kind of name is Atlas?'

Finally, she manages it.

'And why were you coming out of Gem's room?'

Luckily, Gem makes it to the kitchen before Atlas can answer, using the doorframe to help her take the corner as quickly as possible.

'Uncle Mike.' She isn't sure what he was about to do, but as soon as Gem appears, he stops moving.

It's impossible to say whether her quick breathing comes from the dash between her bedroom and the kitchen, or from nerves.

She turns from one man to the other.

Where Uncle Mike's face is still stuck in a snarl, Atlas's face transitions from hesitant intimidation to the dawn of realisation, before landing on pure joy.

Then Atlas turns away from her and back towards the 'intruder', this time holding out his hand. She can tell from the way his shoulders are sitting – a little higher, as though he is having to hold back from jumping – that he is excited.

'You're Uncle Mike. I've heard so much about you.'

The face she can see – Uncle Mike's – is still frowning.

'Why? Have you been looking into me?'

Apparently, it isn't just Gem who jumps to the least likely conclusions. It's a family thing.

'No.' Gem steps in between them. 'Uncle Mike, I told him about you.' Gem looks back at Atlas, who despite Mike's angry exterior, is still smiling. Clearly, he can see through the bravado.

'Atlas is my ...' As she hesitates, she can feel both sets of eyes on her. It was only yesterday that they had had to live through Shauna calling her Atlas's girlfriend. Sometimes, labels are helpful. In the case of foodstuffs and listing allergies, they are even imperative. But now? How can she label him as something when she doesn't know what they are? She answers as best she can. 'Atlas is my guest?'

Gem really isn't making any of the right choices this morning. However, her poor choice of word does at least add a much welcomed element of humour to the situation.

'*Guest?*'

The question comes from all sides. Both incredulous for different reasons. She doesn't know who to deal with first. Making the first correct decision of the day, she turns to Atlas and mouths a silent, 'Sorry.'

He doesn't look impressed. If Gem were to put a name on it, she would say – heart-wrenchingly – that he looks hurt.

Unfortunately, she doesn't have the luxury of time – or privacy – to explain that she doesn't know what to call him. She's never had sex with someone who she initially started dating in order to be eligible to participate in a study that was going to pay her enough money so she could afford to buy an outrageously expensive wheelchair for her mother.

She focuses on Uncle Mike, asking instead, 'What are you doing here?'

'What does it look like?'

She looks at him. He's wearing a pair of well-worn cargo pants that have so many holes in them they're almost indecent, especially considering all of the pockets appear to be full, putting the risk of them falling down at an all-time high. He's paired them with a shirt and a smart V-neck jumper that Gem recognises. Her mum bought it for him last Christmas. He's dressed up. At least on the top half.

'You kinda look like you've got a Zoom call in fifteen minutes.'

'I'm here to check the batteries in your smoke alarms and oil your locks. Then I thought I'd reseal your bathroom. Last time I was in there it looked like it needed redoing. You spend so long in there,' Mike twiddles his screwdriver dangerously close to his ear, and therefore his eye, 'doing your hair and stuff.'

Before she can tell Mike that none of this is necessary, especially as they only rent the place and all of this should technically fall to their landlord, Atlas manoeuvres himself so he is standing next to her. His arms are on his hips, making him look like a cross between a superhero and, well, Uncle Mike.

'I can help if you like.'

Mike's face, which had relaxed, returns to glaring, although, Gem notes, not as deeply as before. She can see him scanning Atlas from head to toe.

'You don't look *helpful*.'

Atlas laughs. 'All right, you got me there. You should probably only let me hold things. But then next time, I could maybe help.' Uncle Mike's glare deepens, and Gem hears Atlas's swallow. 'If you, erm, say that I can?'

Uncle Mike grunts. Or possibly snarls. He looks less like her uncle, and more like a lion in the wild. Sizing up an opponent and wondering if he can be bothered to attack, or just let him walk on his way.

Eventually her uncle breathes. So does Gem.

'Fine.'

Atlas relaxes next to her, but before he can get too excited, Uncle

Mike is once again dangerously wielding the screwdriver, and this time the pointy end is pointing towards Atlas.

'Here's what's going to happen. First, you're gonna go get some actual clothes on.' A quiet *for fuck's sake* is whispered, along with a disbelieving shake of his head. 'Then you are going to help me.'

Atlas makes a small sound next to her, but quickly – and wisely – shuts up before he can form any words.

'You will do *exactly* what I tell you to do, understand?'

Gem nods, even though the question isn't directed at her.

Then Uncle Mike's body relaxes, and he turns to her, smiling sweetly. 'And then, we're all gonna go back and have Sunday lunch together.'

Gem opens her mouth, but she can't think of a single thing to say.

'Sound good?'

'Sounds great.' This comes from Atlas. Gem is still mute.

Uncle Mike nods. 'Good.' Then he looks back at Atlas. 'Now go get some clothes on, *for fuck's sake*.'

Chapter 33

'I've got a surprise for you.'

Uncle Mike shouts down the hall to Gem's mum before he's even fully opened the door. Gem notes that her mum's hallway, usually pristine, is marred by tyre marks on the floor. More evidence that you can never trust an online purchase. But she doesn't have too much time to dwell. Not with Atlas right behind her.

For about the hundredth time today, Gem turns to him and mouths another silent 'Sorry'.

By contrast, Atlas looks delighted. In fact, he did so well with Uncle Mike back at her apartment that he was even treated to a rundown of Mike's bulb fixture preferences. Mike doesn't share these controversial insights with everyone. Atlas has promised to go home and check that his are all Bayonet 22s, and get in touch if they aren't.

'We're meant to be talking about Gem's birthday, not a surprise for me.' Her mum follows quickly after her voice, but both stop short when she sees an unexpected guest. Her eyes alight with questions.

For the whole of the journey over, Gem had been trying to come up with a subtle way to tell Atlas that her mum is in a wheelchair.

But not only was there barely a free moment to talk – the conversation being taken over by Uncle Mike, who it turns out, follows football a lot more closely than Gem realised – but it's quite a difficult thing to say, especially when from her perspective it isn't something that should need to be said. But it still kinda does, and in all the time that her mum has been in a wheelchair, Gem has never come up with the right words to say. What definitely does matter – at least to Gem – is that moment you see someone in a wheelchair and what happens next. Atlas is a good guy, so she knows he won't say anything horrible. But it's not the words: it's that fraction of a moment. That flicker of the eyes that sometimes follows. It isn't necessarily mean, or negative. But it is a flicker. It's a reaction that says her mum isn't what's expected. It's a flicker that hurts her mum, Gem knows. It hurts Gem, too.

Now, though, Gem's panic is twofold. She is also panicking for herself. She doesn't want to have to break up with Atlas because she can't get the flicker out of her mind.

She turns back to the front door, which Atlas has just manoeuvred through. Due to the lack of space, and the ridiculous size of his bag, which looks even more ridiculous taking up the whole width of the hallway, he's had to take it off while facing the door. It means he hasn't yet seen her mum.

It also means Gem has a front row seat, so she can see the moment the flicker comes. Only this time, it doesn't.

Instead, all she sees is his smile. And it's one of his best. The same one he gave her mum in the street when he didn't know who she was.

Gem's whole body is flooded with the same feeling she gets when she stands in the sun for the first time after a long and wet winter. She should have had more faith in him.

Of course he wouldn't flicker.

'Atlas, this is my mum, Georgie.'

Gem then turns back to her mum. 'Mum, this is ...'

Gem pauses.

She's not in her house. She can't call him a 'guest'.

Finally, after an awkward pause that is made even worse by Uncle Mike's giggle from the corner, she lands on the simplest answer.

'This is Atlas.'

As soon as his name is called, Atlas comes to life even more.

'Georgie! May I call you Georgie? It's so great to meet you.'

He pushes past both Gem and Uncle Mike, bending his whole frame down to engulf her mum in a hug. It should look awkward, but somehow it just looks friendly. And maybe a little over-enthusiastic. Her mum's eyes bulge out, and Gem doesn't think it's because of the emotional shock.

He steps away, and, strangely, Gem's enjoying this. She can't remember the last time her mum was speechless.

'Sorry.' He looks like he could be blushing. 'I'm a hugger.'

'You didn't hug me.' Uncle Mike sounds a little hurt.

'I thought you were a burglar. And I wasn't wearing clothes.' Atlas says this in such a casual way that he *almost* gets away with it.

Mike and her mum share a look.

'The little prick isn't lying. My eyes will never recover.'

'Well.' Her mum smiles, and Gem knows she is in trouble. 'Thank you for getting dressed and joining us for lunch. I've made chicken pie.'

'Perfect.' Atlas glances back at Gem briefly before making his way down the hallway. 'I love chicken pie.'

*

'So, Atlas—'

'This is delicious. I can see why it's Gem's favourite.'

Everyone around the table seems to be having a great time except for Gem. Atlas is halfway through his second plate, from the looks of things her mum is about to start researching wedding venues and Uncle Mike keeps bringing up old, embarrassing stories about Gem, like he's trying out material for his new stand-up routine.

She should be happy and yet the longer Atlas sits here, and the more comfortable everyone around her becomes, Gem's discomfort just increases. She shouldn't have let him come. It's complicated everything. Now she's going to have to explain his sudden departure from her life. After all, isn't that what's going to happen? When the study is done, there will be no need for her to keep seeing him.

The thought makes her even less comfortable.

'Atlas. That's an interesting name.' Uncle Mike's eyes narrow, but Gem has already noted that this comment is worded a lot more kindly than the shout from this morning. Gem really is in trouble if Atlas has even worked his way into Uncle Mike's heart. He saw them both half-dressed. That in itself would typically be quite the obstacle to overcome.

'Yeah. It was my dad's choice actually. My mum always wanted to travel. She said she wanted to see the world.'

Atlas's eyes flick to Gem. Not liking what she sees in his eyes, the vulnerability, her hand instinctively reaches out, coming to rest on his knee. It's not enough, and she almost feels like she's doing it more for herself than for him, but she needs to touch him.

'She never got the chance though, so my dad figured that by calling me Atlas, two of her wishes kinda came true at once.' He smiles. 'Of course, for it to really be true, they should have called me World, but even my dad thought that sounded a bit silly.'

At Atlas's attempt at humour, everyone smiles. But Gem can see the humour for what it is. A way to lighten the mood. An apology for being serious, when no apology is required.

'Well, Gem's also named after her mum, aren't you, Gem?'

Atlas looks at her. At some point his hand had come to cover hers on his knee. It's feels right. 'Oh yeah. I remember you saying.' He gives her hand a squeeze, as though he is thinking the same thing she is. It's a thought she can't give much space to. It's too addictive. Too dangerous. Too tempting.

'You couldn't pronounce Georgina, right? That's how it got shortened to Gem?'

Gem nods. 'Yep. I couldn't pronounce a whole bunch of words properly—'

'That's not it at all.'

At this news, Gem looks at her mum.

'What?'

'I mean the first part is true, but that's not why we call you Gem.'

Uncle Mike, of course, chooses now to let Atlas in on another family joke. 'It's why we call broccoli "rocky", but that's not why we call you Gem.' He looks at Atlas. 'For months we thought she was just a young film buff.'

Gem doesn't try to defend herself.

'Then why do you call me Gem?'

Her mum meets her eyes, mildly confused, as though she is surprised that she needs to explain herself. 'Because it suits you. When you were born, you were the most precious thing I had ever seen. My little gem.' A gentle smile appears on her mum's face. 'You still are. I couldn't imagine calling you anything else.'

The room goes so quiet it's almost as if all of the atoms have been sucked out of it. The only thing that stops Gem from crying is the now vice-like grip she has on Atlas's knee, and the comforting hand she can feel on top of it.

It's not that she's against crying as a concept. She just doesn't want to cry herself. But the lack of sleep, combined with this totally unexpected, emotional revelation is making her personal thoughts on the matter a little difficult to stick to.

'I never knew that.'

The news about her nickname is one thing, but the fact she's also glad to have Atlas here with her as support is a whole other revelation that is – if possible – making her even more emotional. She doesn't know what to say or do. About either.

'Speaking of your birth—'

At the interruption, Gem looks at Uncle Mike with a thankful smile. Less than a minute ago she had been over his comedic interruptions, but now she is grateful for the rescue. Even though she knows what's coming, it is still preferable to her crying.

'—what's the theme for your birthday? You don't have long to decide, so it can't be anything too big, but if you want, I know someone who says he could get us a tiger. I know you like cats.'

This time, Atlas's hand and hers both squeeze in sync.

'No. *No tigers.*' But she knows if she wants it, Uncle Mike would make it happen.

'OK, so what do you want?'

'I've already told you this.'

Please, please do not make her repeat it.

'You can't just have a birthday party where you are,' Uncle Mike puts down his knife and fork so he can make quotation marks, "'*surrounded by the people you love.*'" He picks them back up and stabs a piece of rocky. 'That's not a theme.'

'Well, that's all I want.'

'Oh, stop being so noble.' Uncle Mike looks like he could throw his napkin on the table, if only they used napkins. 'What if we finally had that food fight you always used to bang on about?'

'No!' This time the objection comes from her mum. '*No* food fights. It's such a waste. And normal parties that don't involve throwing food take long enough to clean up anyway.'

Uncle Mike's displeasure visibly deepens.

'So, what about you, Atlas? Did your dad ever go big on your birthday?'

'Oh, no. Birthdays were always quite a quiet thing for us.'

This time, it's Atlas who needs someone to step in and rescue him. And although he isn't part of the family, her mum does anyway.

'Well, then that's decided. You'll have to come, and we're gonna have to think of a much better, bigger theme.' She winks at him. 'Show you how it's done.'

Chapter 34

'Your family is great.'
'They are *bonkers*.'
Atlas nods. 'Yes. That is also true.'
'They like you.'

Gem had assumed that Atlas would need to go back to his house for clothes and to have a break from her, but it turns out the former is unnecessary (the bag, although still large, clearly has its uses) and the latter isn't what he – or even she – wants. So, they are standing in her kitchen, making one of Gem's questionable toasties. And she is guarding them closely. This is the first time he will be having one of her concoctions and she is conscious of toasting them too much. She doesn't typically eat on Sunday evening following lunch at her mum's, but all the sex has made her hungry.

She's making three rounds of sweet potato, hummus and beetroot sandwiches in case one isn't enough to satiate Atlas's hunger. His appetite appears to be endless. And yet, she has the strong impression, the only thing he wants to devour more frequently than food is her.

When they came back to find an apartment still empty of Shanti, Gem had briefly worried that her friend's mum had genuinely locked her in. But then a well-timed text from Tee had told her that she had decided to stay at her parents for one more night. Her mum had made lamb biryani and homemade aloo samosas, two of her favourites, bribery to make her stay.

Gem is jealous of the food, but, looking at Atlas, she wouldn't be anywhere else.

Especially when Atlas's arms cage her in against the counter, her back to his front. He briefly uses a hand to move her hair out of the way. Her head instinctively tilts to the side and he makes the most of the opportunity to kiss her in the crook where her neck and shoulder meet. Tingles travel all the way from her fingertips, intensifying just below her ear.

'Well, I like them back.'

The electricity she's feeling from his kiss is fighting for space with the sense of relief and pride Gem feels when she hears this. She knew they would all like each other. Or at least she really hoped they would. The issue is, although part of her is overjoyed, the other part is screaming at her like a siren. Gem doesn't know which part of herself to listen to.

'You never mentioned that your mum's in a wheelchair.'

Gem's heart skips a little beat. He's going to say something like *I obviously don't mind* or *That's cool*, which is infinitely worse.

But once again, she is underestimating him.

'It must be weird to know whether that's something you need to tell people about or not. It's a difficult conversation to have.'

'Yeah. It is. It's kinda why I stopped having people over. Shanti is the only person that gets invited these days.'

'Really?'

'Really.' Except, of course, now for Atlas. 'You know you saw her in the street once.'

'Huh? Who?'

'My mum.' She can feel the question in his touch as he gently squeezes her hips. 'It was about a week ago, actually. Mum and I were out and you passed by her in the street.'

'I don't remember seeing you, and I would definitely remember seeing you.' He kisses her neck once more, taking his time. The tingles come back, but she is a little too tense to pay them too much attention, waiting for what he says next.

'Are you sure it was me?'

Gem nods, but only a little. She might be tense, but she doesn't want to force his lips further away from her than they need to be.

'It was definitely you. But you wouldn't have seen me.' The next part of her answer is directed towards the toastie machine. 'We were near Soho. I was hiding behind a decorative plant inside a restaurant.'

At this point, the pressure on her hips increases, and Atlas spins her around so she is facing him.

'*Georgina Parker*. You did not hide from me?'

She's still looking at the machine as she nods, admitting, 'I did.'

A slight pressure on the underside of her chin forces her to look up into his baby blues.

'Why?'

Gem shrugs. She can't really remember. Or at least, her reasoning no longer makes any sense, his eyes mesmerising. 'I was worried about introducing you to my mum—'

'You're ashamed of me?' His question is asked lightly, but there is a heaviness in his eyes.

'No, not at all.' She hopes the squeeze on his arm and her embarrassingly desperate tone helps to convince him. 'I just didn't know what we were, and I . . . I don't often introduce new people to my mum.'

The hurt instantly disappears from his eyes. Instead they start flitting all over her. She can tell that he is trying to understand, collecting any small clues he can find to help. His hands, which are back gently holding her hips, keep her steady.

'I'm assuming the reason why you hid is connected to the reason why you don't have people over to your house any more?' It turns out that Atlas is very astute.

Gem nods. She turns so she is facing away from him, her back to him once more. Of course, her toastie check, her excuse for turning, is redundant. She knows from vast experience that they are nowhere near being ready, but she has to do something other than look into Atlas's eyes. If she keeps looking, she will stop talking. And she wants to talk.

'I've never exactly been very outgoing,' she tells the toastie maker. 'My birthday parties were really the only time I had people over, and then for my tenth birthday, all I wanted was a dance party.

'Mum used to be a dance teacher before her accident, and so I asked her to teach us a dance. After the accident she had to stop teaching professionally, but once she got better at moving in her chair, we would still dance together a bit in the kitchen, and she would teach me new steps. Even though she was in a chair, she was still a great teacher.'

There must be something about Atlas's hands. In addition to being capable of completely undoing her, they must be giving her some kind of comfort and strength. This isn't a conversation – or even a thought – that she often allows herself to indulge in. In fact, she has never talked to anyone about this, not even Shanti.

She risks the toasties and turns in his arms, so they are facing each other again. The comforting smell of him – warm spice with a hint of mint – engulfs her, making her feel even safer.

'I was on the cusp of the age where you start to be aware of things, you know? I remember my mum triple-checking with me that a dance party was what I wanted to do. I just put it down to her making sure I hadn't changed my mind. But looking back, maybe she knew there was a chance that it was gonna go in a direction I didn't think it would go in.'

The memory of her last big birthday party replays in her head. It's a vision that usually appears at about two in the morning, and although this time the hour is a lot more friendly, the replay is just as harsh.

'What happened?' he prompts.

'Eh,' she closes her eyes, momentarily unable to handle the potential emotions in Atlas's eyes. They are very expressive, and Gem is learning to read them very quickly.

'It wasn't that bad. It was just kids being kids, I guess. But at the time it felt *huge*.' She opens her eyes. 'I'd transformed the lounge. It took the whole week. I didn't let Mum or Uncle Mike go in there in case they ruined anything. And by transformed, I mean *transformed*.

'I'd moved all the furniture to the back, flipping the table on its side, using it as a kind of feature wall. I even bought a stupid, in hindsight pretty hideous tablecloth for it. I thought it would make a great background to dance in front of.'

As Gem speaks, Atlas gently takes her hands in his, raising one to his mouth to kiss it softly. While it is sexy, it isn't a kiss that is asking for more. It's merely a kiss to remind Gem that he is there. Not that she could easily forget.

'I'd set the camera up on a chair and everything. We were gonna make our own music video. When everyone left I rewatched the tape as soon as I could. I'd had a great time and I thought everyone else had too. But then when I watched the video back, I realised how stupid I'd been. I thought everyone was laughing because they were having a good time. But I'd been at the front. I hadn't seen that everyone was laughing at my mum. I don't know how I hadn't realised.

'I felt so embarrassed. Not because my mum's in a chair, but because I'd been so naive. How did I not see what was going on? I felt so stupid, and I felt so angry at them for laughing at my mum.' His kisses halt. She can feel him breathing steadily. It comforts her enough to keep going.

'The only person who didn't laugh was Shanti. So, after that, my birthday parties got a lot smaller. And my mum has never tried to teach me another dance step since.'

'Shanti is a really good friend.'

Gem nods, looking through the hatch to her friend's abandoned mannequin. 'That she is. I owe her a lot.'

Not least for giving her and Atlas some more space, especially when Gem sees the half-finished jacket. Sunday evening is usually peak design time for Shanti. Giving it up for Gem is a big deal. She makes a mental note to figure out a way to pay Tee back.

'I do not miss being a kid.' Atlas briefly rests his chin on the top of Gem's head. Cocooning her.

'No. Neither do I.' Although Gem would kinda still like the lower back of a ten-year-old. She didn't appreciate it then like she should have.

She checks back in with the toasties, inspecting the side that is facing down, assessing the browning as she talks. 'So yeah, it's a conversation that I don't know if I should have, but it's also a conversation that I didn't realise I might need to have, and I kinda wish I could still be that naive kid who didn't realise that people might judge you for things that you shouldn't be judged for.'

At these words, a weight that Gem didn't know she'd been carrying lifts.

And yet, there is another conversation that Gem knows she needs to have. And soon.

She needs to tell Atlas what's been going on.

It's in the rules that Gem can't tell him, but when they started on this journey, she'd never considered that maybe, for once, things might work out, or that she might actually end up liking the guy that she initially couldn't stand.

And she does. She really likes him.

Not just because he happens to be great in bed.

Because he fits.

He fits into her family. Her life. He makes her feel good about herself.

He makes her want to get out of bed in the morning (and get back into it at night).

With him by her side, Gem feels as though she could accomplish anything. Instead of jumping to the Worst Possible Conclusion, Atlas makes Gem feel like things might just turn out OK.

She should never have agreed to do this. She should have found a different way to pay for her mum's chair.

If only Atlas had turned out to be a dickhead, none of this would be happening. In a way, all of this is Atlas's fault. He's too great.

What a prick.

Not even her need to prove Shanti wrong about the ick is enough to persuade her to give up Atlas. Yes, it will be disappointing to admit this. And she isn't looking forward to seeing Tee's face, and more importantly having to live with her smugness, but she is going to have to. It would be pretty impossible to argue – let alone prove – that the ick was real in every case except for Atlas, but right now, she doesn't care. Let Shanti be smug.

Because Gem is smug too. She has Atlas.

She doesn't even see the bag any more. At least metaphorically. (It really is quite large, so the only way she could never not see it would be if she went blind.) But it's no longer big enough, or a big enough issue, to stop her from seeing all of the good things about him.

She plates the toasties and then turns once more, looking up at Atlas, studying him.

How could she not want to be with him?

She is absolutely knackered from her weekend, but she has never felt more awake. She's never been more aware of another person.

He moves and she looks to see where he's moving to. He laughs, and if he's laughing at something she has said, she smiles. If he's laughing at something else, she laughs with him.

She wants to try the food he likes and know what movies he hates.

She wants to know what he thinks of her favourite books, and his thoughts on anchovies in Caesar salad dressing.

If he prefers crunchy peanut butter or smooth.

She wants to know answers to all of these questions now, but she also doesn't want to rush getting to know him. She *loves* getting to know him.

'I mean, I get it.'

Her thoughts are so rambling that she has forgotten they are in the middle of a conversation.

'—There are some situations, and conversations that are more difficult to face.'

It's impossible to know why, but Gem knows that the mood

in the room has shifted. She instantly feels a little on edge, and when she looks at Atlas for reassurance, he does nothing but stoke her anxiety. His eyes almost seem like they are purposefully not looking at her. Her intuition – the same one that had a visceral reaction to him eating soup – is on high alert.

Part of her doesn't want to know any more about him. Part of her – the same part that agreed to Shanti's offer – wants him to stop talking. She doesn't want her ick to be validated. Not now.

Yet the other part of her wants to know everything there is to know about him. It wants Atlas to share his worries with her, not only because she wants to be one of the privileged few who he trusts, but because she wants to halve those worries. It's this latter part of her that wins through. The allure of him is too strong to deny.

'So, what's your difficult conversation?'

He inhales sharply, yet his eyes are soft. Even a little apologetic. 'The real reason I coach football.'

A tingle breaks out on the back of Gem's neck and not the kind from when he was kissing her.

'I mean, don't get me wrong, I love football. But that's not why I started getting involved—'

'You don't have to tell me.'

In fact, she kind of doesn't want him to, but he carries on.

'After my dad died, I went a little bit off the rails. I stopped going to school, I got mad at everyone. I was angry and lost and living with my grandma who I loved, but she smelt old, and all of my clothes started smelling old too. Everyone made fun of me for it. I'd go out with my friends and drink more than I should've. I stole stupid shit that I didn't need. I crashed my dad's car. I guess I was just being young and being a dick—'

There is no doubt in Gem's mind that they would've run in very different circles at school. The worst thing she ever did back then was cut in the lunch line when she had an early afternoon lesson.

'That doesn't sound so bad,' she says, but both of them know it's premature. He isn't done yet.

'I was dating this girl, Becky. She was in my year, it wasn't serious. I mean, I guess it was as serious as any relationship could be when you're sixteen, but then one day I found out she was cheating on me with my best friend. I caught them having sex in her bedroom.' His eyes look somewhere else, back to a different time maybe. 'It is *so* clichéd. I shouldn't have been as mad as I was, I guess. But I was. I was really fucking mad. And I wasn't even that mad about the fact they were making out. It was the lying. I thought they were my friends. I thought I could trust them. But I couldn't. The betrayal was the part that killed me.'

'So, what happened?' Gem worries that what's coming next is the thing that her ick was warning her against, and her guilt is growing right alongside the tingles from her intuition. She is betraying him too.

'I punched him in the face.'

'Ouch.' Gem's reaction is instant.

'Yeah. And I would have kept going.' He closes his eyes as though he doesn't want to remember. It's a feeling that Gem knows only too well. 'But then Becky tried to pull me off. She didn't really manage, but I accidentally elbowed her in the face pretty hard.'

'Shit.'

Gem's heart is beating heavily.

Atlas nods. 'Yeah,' but his tone says it all.

'What happened then?' Gem forces herself to ask the question even if she's not sure she wants to know the answer.

'I ran away. I felt awful. I don't even remember if I said sorry. I just ran.' His head shakes.

'I thought my life was over at that point. And I know it doesn't make sense, but I just needed to hit more things. So I found the first empty-looking building I could, and I smashed it up. I hit everything that looked breakable, and even some stuff that didn't. The only reason I stopped was because someone called the police.' But then, Atlas's shoulders relax. 'And then, for the first time in a long time, I got some good luck.'

He laughs derisively. 'Becky didn't press charges, and neither did Jack. And the guys who owned the building I smashed up didn't come after me. Instead, Becky and Jack just stayed away, and the guys made me pay back the damage by doing a bunch of community service stuff.'

Despite the seriousness of his confession, Gem smiles when she puts a few things together, making a few jumps forward. 'So that's how you got into coaching.'

He nods. 'Yeah. Well, kinda. Eventually. The building I smashed up is the same changing room we still use. For about four years pretty much all I did was clean the toilets, but I dunno.' He shrugs. 'Sometimes I think smashing that building up might've been the best thing I ever did.'

He brings both of Gem's hands up to his chest. 'At least until I said yes to going out with a random girl on a random Thursday night.'

He squeezes her hands, his tone quickly returning to being serious. 'The routine of going to practice every week stopped me getting into trouble. And then the people and the community saved me.'

Gem lets her hands rest where they are even though, logically, she knows that she should pull away. Grievous bodily harm is not something to be taken lightly. This is just the kind of secret that Shanti – and indeed Gem – had been after. It's just the kind of thing that her ick would warn her against.

She should be ecstatic that her intuition has just been proved right. She should have run the first time they met. And she should run now.

'I've spent every day since then trying to make up for my actions.' His head hangs as he confesses. 'I don't think I ever will.' He looks up at Gem, his eyes haunted.

This is more complicated than any situation she has been in before, but surely there is a difference between a genuine mistake – a young kid who has just lost his father, his girlfriend and his best friend – and someone who has a pattern of turning to violence.

Nothing about the Atlas sitting in front of her feels like the Atlas that he is clearly worried about being. The shaky breath he draws in makes Gem move.

Mirroring his own actions from a few minutes earlier, she pulls his hands towards her, and kisses them.

'Bigger than pizza, huh?'

He smiles, his relief obvious at their own mini in-joke, and nods. There's a sadness sitting behind his eyes.

'Yeah. Bigger than pizza.'

Chapter 35

'So what's so urgent that you made me leave the library early?' Shanti appears behind Gem.

The corner shop is busier than usual today, partly because it's earlier than they normally come, and partly because the weather is amazing which means that everyone has crawled out of their little holes for a bit of sunshine. The sunshine is welcome, but it always slightly annoys Gem when her favourite spots – spots that she visits just as much in the rain – get overtaken by others. She is no Fairweather Supporter, unlike the others taking up the limited space in the snack aisle. Jay's frown is angrier than ever, his eyes vigilant, even though Gem thinks he rather likes to watch out for thieves. One day he is going to catch one, and his whole personality will be validated.

Shanti looks at the food in Gem's basket.

'Study snacks?'

She's experienced enough to recognise the usual suspects straight away. Or Gem is just predictable. Although Gem has gone all out and added two types of cheese instead of the tradition one, and two fancy kinds instead of her traditional Cheddar. She hopes that their celebrations will be worthy of the cranberry Wensleydale and the Gouda. 'What are we prepping for? What have I missed? Are we planning the dance session for the Goalies?'

Gem grabs a bag of miscellaneous Italian crisp bread things, just to mix it up a bit. 'No, but we do need to think about that.'

Apparently Shauna hasn't stopped bugging her dad about it and, in turn, her dad hasn't stopped bugging Atlas about it.

Shanti inhales sharply and then puts on a mocking tone. 'Is it something else Atlas-related? Did you finally find out the non-existent source for your ick?'

'No. Atlas is fine. Atlas is great.'

Even Gem can tell that her answer comes out a little forced. She hasn't told Shanti about the whole 'breaking someone's nose' thing, and the snacks are definitely not to aid a psychology discussion. That said, Atlas has inadvertently contributed to Gem's plans. He has made Gem feel better about herself than three years' worth of social media motivational quotes. All of this positive energy needs to go somewhere, otherwise she is going to explode.

Her mum's chair is closer than ever to being ready, she has even been given a shipping date, so that is taken care of. Atlas is already receiving a significant portion of Gem's good mood, which then further increases Gem's positive energy, in some kind of never-ending circle of life. She isn't going to waste all of this positivity and energy on her actual job, and so the only other possible outlet is Shanti.

But more than just giving Gem the confidence boost she needs, Atlas also gave her the words.

'We're going to start a fashion empire that's going to take over the world.'

*

'Gem, I love you. And I love that you're doing this, but this is just not going to happen.'

'Tee, I love you too. And you're right. This might not happen, but that isn't the point of today.'

It's a strange role reversal – Shanti is usually the one to do the pushing in their friendship, but right now it's all coming from Gem.

'Listen, you and I both know that the vintage clothes market is growing,' Gem carries on. 'And you are the best person I know at taking old vintage clothes and making them into something even more amazing. I think it's a really good business idea, and I think it's worth thinking about. Yes, we could stay in our lanes, but who wants to do that when they could do something different? All we're doing today is starting to think about what we need to think about. It's a planning session. Or even a pre-planning session. To see if maybe one day, we could make this work.'

Shanti's face scrunches up. Gem ignores her.

She moves towards the pad of flipchart paper that she's borrowed from work and unceremoniously nailed into the wall. She did contemplate taking the actual stand too, but it was heavier than it looked and significantly more awkward to get out of the building. She'd visions of trying to manoeuvre it onto the tube at rush hour, and immediately decided against it. Her life is worth more. She glances at the wall that is now adorned with little nail holes – plus, Uncle Mike will love nothing more than having a proper job to do, instead of having to make one up.

'What are the things we need to start thinking about?' There's a hint of begrudging interest in Shanti's voice.

Gem draws a big question mark on the first sheet of paper. The smell of the pen ink is just as alluring now as it was in school.

Unfortunately, her handwriting is pretty much the same as it was in school. Why is writing on a board so different to writing on a piece of paper? Not that she is very good at either.

Then, just because writing up there is addictive, as are the fumes, she opens two more pens, writing *GEM* in green, and *SHANTI* in purple, so all of the different tasks can be assigned to whoever is best suited. Somehow, Gem can already tell that all of the more boring tasks will be hers. But even that knowledge isn't enough to wipe the smile off her face. Not today.

Then when she turns back to Shanti, she realises her friend is close to tears. It's not a sight that Gem is overly familiar with. It either means that she has done something very, very bad. Or something very, very good.

'You'll do it with me?'

Relief spreads through Gem.

'Tee. Yes. Of course. How could I let you rule the world without me?'

Chapter 36

'Where are you taking me?'

When Atlas had said he would be in charge of their next date – he still didn't trust Gem to choose – Gem hadn't really thought much about it. But now that they are walking down a dingy back alley in central London's Covent Garden, she wonders if she should have. The pubs she chose for their first two dates might have been devoid of character, but right now, being devoid of character is looking pretty good. Or at least better than the mysterious puddles, questionable smells and lack of natural light, despite the fact the sun had been shining before they'd turned into the alley. But, with her hand in his, Atlas could lead Gem pretty much anywhere, at this moment in time, and she would follow.

Atlas, conveniently, doesn't answer her question.

For the first time ever, she has taken a change of clothes with her in preparation for their date. The heady mix of sunnier days, making progress with Shanti's fashion venture, and the prospect of seeing Atlas, meant that she had chosen a happy, colourful outfit – a brightly patterned mid-length skirt and a tightly knitted bandeau top. She even took her hair out of its usual bun about halfway through the afternoon, so the kinks could all fall out. It is very rare for her to let her hair down at work, both literally and figuratively. Martin did a double take when he saw her. Not in an ogling way, but just because he didn't recognise her.

To be fair, Gem hardly recognises herself at the moment either.

'Can you at least tell me that I'm dressed appropriately?'

Atlas must sense the trepidation in her voice, because he stops immediately and turns to her. He is looking at her with puppy eyes. Gem has never before understood the idea of a 'Golden Retriever' boyfriend, but she does now. Atlas is the picture of enthusiastic, earnest, innocence.

'You look absolutely beautiful.' He steps towards Gem. The stillness is such a stark contrast to how quickly they had been moving before, first through the busy streets of London, and then dodging all of the dodgy paraphernalia in the hidden backstreets. She hadn't noticed how noisy and busy the whole experience was, until it all stopped. And now, it is just Gem and Atlas. She much prefers it this way. 'You always do,' he adds.

Using their hands, which are still connected, Atlas pulls her the rest of the way towards him, and she goes, willingly.

Their kisses have always been addictive, but they are now in the magical position of knowing what each other is about to do. The anticipation of what they have got to look forward to is almost – *almost* – better than the kiss itself.

It's crazy to think that there was a time when Gem didn't know how kissing Atlas felt. She never wants to go back to that period of history. And now, when they stop kissing, at least Gem knows there will be more to come. It makes the stopping a little easier.

'I mean, I would happily keep kissing you, but if we don't keep going, we're gonna be too late.'

'Where are you taking me?' This time, even though Atlas still doesn't answer, she can at least see his smile. She has never seen him look so proud.

'Fine. Don't tell me. I'm happy for it to be a surprise.'

Atlas's smile morphs into a laugh. 'You're not, but you'll find out soon.'

And with that, he guides her the rest of the way down the alley. When he reaches the end, he stops at a rusty door, raises his free hand and knocks three times.

It opens so suddenly it makes Gem jump.

But that isn't where the surprise stops.

'Harry?' Gem's recall of Atlas's football friends is limited, but the man is still wearing red this evening, which jogs her memory. But this time, instead of football red, he is wearing theatre red. He is dressed as an usher. He beams at her.

'Good to see ya again, Gem.' He nods towards her, but Atlas he hugs. Somehow it is all managed without Atlas dropping Gem's hand.

Then Harry steps aside, gesturing for them to come in.

Atlas glances at Gem.

'You ready?'

'I guess.'

Atlas doesn't move, instead nudging Gem ahead of him. All she can see is a long, grey corridor, dotted with boxes, as she moves forward. The door behind them shuts, making it even darker. It must be the only place left in London that is still cool.

'You know where to go, then?' Gem can just make out Harry who looks a mix of time-pressured and conspiratorially happy.

Atlas nods. 'I do.'

'And once it starts, remember you gotta keep quiet.'

'I promise.'

Harry points a finger at him. 'No funny business.'

Atlas opens his arms out. 'When have I ever made a joke?'

Unfortunately, Harry doesn't find Atlas as charming as he clearly finds himself.

Harry turns his attention to Gem. 'I'm trusting you to keep him honest, Gem. As soon as you see the performers get in position, you *have to keep quiet*.' Gem nods. This point is clearly very important. 'And for heaven's sake, don't touch anything.'

Still not quite sure what's going on, Gem gives him her word. More satisfied with Gem's answer than Atlas's, Harry grunts, and then heads away down the corridor.

Once again alone with Atlas, she hesitates, unsure what to do. 'Should we follow him?'

'Nope. We have somewhere else to be.' And he opens the door to his left. 'You going in?'

She peers inside but can only see a set of very narrow stairs. Unfortunately, it is so dark that she needs to step in even to see that properly, which gives Atlas enough room to close the door behind them. They are immediately encased in darkness. It is as exciting as it is mildly petrifying. She cautiously reaches out a hand, feeling around, trying to orientate herself, but when she eventually finds the wall, she only feels more confused. Carpet? On the wall?

'Oh, shit.'

Already heeding Harry's request, Atlas's voice is a whisper.

He finally lets go of Gem's hand and reaches for his phone. Using the torch, they can see again.

She looks at where her hand lies, what it is touching. The whole area, not just the wall, is covered in carpet. Even the ceiling. And apart from a very small landing, all Gem can see is stairs leading up.

'You want me to go up there?'

Atlas nods. 'I want you to go up there.'

Gem inhales; it is shakier than she would like to admit. But, still, she climbs.

And as soon as she reaches the top, she is glad that she did.

They are standing in a tiny room, not unlike one of those bird-watching sheds you see on daytime nature channels. The one with a narrow slit on one side, perfect for twitchers. It is still dark in the room, but there is light flooding in from the outside. She can see two chairs, and a bunch of old, dusty equipment. Gem steps closer to the gap and peers in, and then down.

'Where have you brought me?'

Again, even though she can feel Atlas behind her, he stays quiet, letting Gem figure it out for herself.

She is looking down on a stage. The orchestra is right in front of them, and the stage is hard to the right. She can hear people. She looks to her left and there are people starting to take their scattered seats. The audience.

Gem returns her gaze to the stage, but this time she looks straight ahead of her. Behind and between the curtains, she can see elongated limbs, refined by years of dancing.

'Are we at the Royal Opera House?'

She turns back to Atlas, her eyes finding him immediately, not because the space is small, but because she can feel exactly where he is.

'We are.'

She runs through her knowledge.

'Oh my God.' She can picture the posters now, littered throughout the tube. 'Are we watching *Frankenstein*?'

Atlas nods. 'Yep.'

All of the suave brought by her outfit is counteracted by the totally guileless look she is giving Atlas. But she can't help herself. She is speechless. 'I mean, I don't know anything about ballet, but this one looked pretty cool.'

Gem nods, and the moment helps her jaw to close. 'Really cool.'

She missed out on tickets the first time it came to London: she couldn't justify the expense. She still can't. She feels a little bit bad that her mum isn't with them. Their own ballet date had been perfect at the time, despite the run-in with the decorative plant and stupid seating arrangements. But the magic of this evening is already something else.

'Shall we sit?'

Gem nods, her ability to speak still a little hindered. She sits down as quietly as possible. There are a lot of empty seats still, so she knows that it'll be a while until the performance begins, but now that she is here, there is absolutely no way that Gem's going to risk getting kicked out. Harry has nothing to worry about.

Once she feels safe in her seat, comfortable that she isn't going to accidentally alert someone to her presence, she looks around some more. The only thing – apart from the chairs – that isn't covered in dust is what looks like a lunchbox in the corner. But it isn't only the lack of dust that makes it stick out. It is also Spider-Man-themed. She points at it, and whispers:

'What's in there?'

Atlas, clearly more comfortable in their surroundings than Gem, and also really quite proud of himself, leans towards her, talking softly in her ear, 'Ice cream. For the interval.'

When Gem turns to face him, she can't help but lean forward and kiss him. She needs to know that he is real. She's too excited for what's coming to kiss him for long, but Atlas doesn't seem to mind. He is ready, meeting her tongue with his, even for just a fleeting moment.

'Can I ask you a question?' His voice is still soft, and the lights of the stage are reflected in his eyes, making them sparkle.

'Anything.' It's not the kind of thing Gem would usually say, but sitting here isn't the kind of thing that Gem would usually be doing either.

'Did Shanti really get stuck in a hedge?'

At the question, the sparkles in his eyes light up even more, and Gem instantly regrets being so accommodating. She doesn't want to lie to him. Ever. She can't undo her lies right now – indeed, she can't really tell him about the study until after Shanti has finished. Not if she is going to get paid. But she doesn't have to add to her deceit.

So, she doesn't.

'No. I just wanted to get away.'

Luckily, the sparkle in his eyes doesn't dim. Instead, he is looking at Gem as though she is a present. One that only he gets to open. 'Can I ask you another question?' The sparkle is joined by a challenge.

Gem doesn't wilt. Instead, she tries to mirror his cheek.

'Anything.'

His smile really is perfect. His chin hitches, just a bit.

'If the first date was that bad, why did you agree to go on another one?'

This time, Gem takes a moment. In any other place, at any other time, now would be the perfect moment to confess. But, beyond even the contract and her mum's chair and Shanti's study, selfishly, she doesn't want to ruin the magic. Either for herself or for Atlas.

The Ick 263

As she searches for an answer that could be both true and also not incriminating, Gem notes there is a stillness falling around the theatre as the audience take their seats and the dancers begin to take their places. The answer comes to her just in time.

She leans forward, turning Atlas's head, so this time it is her lips against his ear. He goes as still as the dancers. Waiting, anticipating.

'Intuition, I guess.'

'Did you have fun tonight?'

'Atlas,' Gem turns towards him. 'I had the most amazing time. You have to thank Harry for sneaking us in.'

Gem has never taken a ballet dance class, mainly because the idea of the shoes really puts her off, and her mum always said ballet looked too magical to learn, but watching the performance this evening has made her reconsider. There was one moment when the lead dancer leapt through the air, and Gem could have sworn that his body froze midway into the jump.

'Ah, well, he gets first dibs on my seats any time I can't make a game, so he kinda owed me one.'

In a slightly odd change of events, one that Gem cautiously prepared herself for, they are now on their way to Atlas's flat. She's even packed a backpack in anticipation. Of course, it isn't as big as Atlas's bag, but it does contain a change of clothes. Her make-up. Her make-up remover. A toothbrush. She's even taken a spare pair of shoes, although she doesn't quite know why. It is quite a lot of stuff to carry.

Or at least it *was*, until Atlas took the bag from her. Ironically, this bag looks really small on him.

For the second time that day, she doesn't know where she's

going. It's a state that she seems to be getting more comfortable with, especially – or possibly only – when she is with Atlas.

They are walking down a slight hill, along what looks like a new road, even though Gem can't see how any new roads can fit into London. But it's very new. Very clean. Very quiet. It even smells quite nice, which is unusual for London.

There is a new apartment building in front of them. It's clearly only recently been completed, so much so there's still a skip outside, filled with bits of concrete and insulation. But it isn't a boring newbuild, with no character and a lazily minimalist design. Instead, the brickwork is actually quite intricate, and the building is set a little bit away from the road, giving it a bit more privacy. It looks like each apartment has access to a balcony. For a city where outside space is a luxury, balconies are the stuff dreams are made of.

'This is me.'

Atlas gestures towards the building.

'It looks new.' Gem's aware she's stating the obvious.

'It is.'

'*Very* fancy.'

They make their way inside, where there is a desk for a concierge and a wall of post boxes.

'I warn you now though,' he opens a heavy glass door for her and ushers her through, 'I don't have a hatch in the kitchen, so there's room for improvement, but I still like it.'

Atlas's apartment is on the top floor, but luckily there is a lift. There is a large mirror on one side of it, no doubt to help claustrophobic people feel a little more comfortable, and for everyone else to make sure they aren't leaving their apartment with spinach in their teeth. But tonight the mirror has an additional purpose.

She watches Atlas as he follows her into the lift. He presses the button, but as soon as that task is dealt with, his eyes lock with hers in the mirror.

'You are so beautiful.'

Thanks to the mirror, Gem can both feel *and* see the blush that is blooming up her neck. Stepping towards her he's so close Gem can breathe in his spicy scent, Atlas wraps his arms around her from behind and she watches as he slowly runs one of his hands down the side of neck, her arm, the crook of her waist. His other hand starts to lightly caress the skin left bare, thanks to her choice of outfit. She is mesmerised as he runs his fingers along her collarbone, her jaw, her neck. Everywhere that her blush has spread.

Wherever his fingers touch, Gem's skin is left tingling in their wake. She has never been more aware of another person. Her body is interpreting his every move, or maybe he can read her so well that he can tell where she wants to be touched. Either way, he is touching her in all the right places. Her heart has never beat so fast.

The lift doors open, but before he lets her go, Atlas kisses her just below the ear and then, using only a light pressure on her waist, makes her move. She follows him, blindly, down the corridor, all her senses on fire. She's going to need a reminder on how to get out of here. There is no way she'll be able to retrace her steps.

He pauses to unlock the last door in the corridor and leads Gem inside.

The space immediately feels like Atlas, although it needs more furniture. The floors are a dark, natural wood. The windows run all the way along the far wall and the view is beautiful. She can just about make out the lights of the City flashing in the distance. She steps towards them, wanting a closer look.

But an arm around her waist stops her, and Atlas pulls her against his chest.

'You can look around later, but now we have more important things to do.'

'We do?' She kinks an eyebrow, feigning innocence, not very well. 'Like what?'

'Well,' he spins her around, hunger in his eyes, 'I just moved in about a month ago, and I've been too busy to test out the kitchen.'

'We're making food?'

For a beat, Gem worries that she has completely misread the situation. But then he slowly walks her backwards, until her butt hits what feels like a ledge.

'Not in the traditional sense of the word. But I can't think of a better way to christen my kitchen counters.'

At the suggestion, her pulse quickens.

He moves his hands so they are gripping either side of her waist and lifts her up so she is sitting on the breakfast bar. Her legs open up on instinct, and Atlas steps between.

It's impossible to know who moves first, but all Gem can feel is Atlas's hands on her. One hand is still on her hip, while the other travels quickly up, pulling her mouth towards his with an urgency that takes her breath away. But Gem matches his need with her own. She needs to feel him. She grabs at his shirt, undoing the buttons as quickly as she can, working against her shaking hands. And apparently it isn't only Gem who needs nothing between them. As soon as his shirt is loose, Atlas takes it off. The break in contact is only momentary, his hands returning to her as quickly as possible. She needs to work on his trousers, but she also needs to feel his arms and shoulders; they are too tempting to resist. As soon as her hands start travelling, Atlas moves his mouth from hers, to her neck. The warmth of his tongue against her skin makes her want to scream, but also takes her breath away. The change makes the need to get his trousers off even more urgent. Luckily, Atlas senses her need. Their hands meet at his belt. Gem pulls it off, which gives him a few milliseconds' head start to undo his trousers. He pushes them down but doesn't step out of them. Gem almost wants him to stop, so she can drink in the sight of his strong legs, looking like they might be able to flex free of his boxers. But he moves quickly, as if he can't bear the separation, or the delay. His hands return to Gem's upper thighs, taking the skirt with them, gathering it as he goes, lighting a fire. He doesn't want to waste time taking this off either. But when his hands reach her sex, they freeze.

His whole body follows.

The electricity in the air suggests a thunderstorm is just moments away from breaking.

'You're not wearing any underwear?' His voice is strained. Barely controlled.

Gem shakes her head. 'No.'

'Thank fuck I didn't know this earlier. Harry would definitely be out of a job.'

Atlas once again begins to move. His mouth finds hers, as one hand moves to her back, pulling her towards the edge. The other he uses to help guide himself inside her, inch by delectable inch. Gem moves her legs so they are circling his hips, pulling him closer, her heels digging into his lower back, an insistent invitation. She whimpers as he enters.

When he is fully inside her, he takes a moment to breathe. Then he starts to move. He starts off slowly, stretching Gem out, so she can feel and adjust to every inch of him. And she is grateful that he does. Because then, when he starts moving faster, she is ready for him. And finally, the thunderstorm breaks.

Chapter 37

'Oh. Being naughty today, I see.'

For once Gem is the last one back from lunch.

It is warm outside today, well above the temperature at which Martin and his penchant for cashmere can cope. At times like this, he can only really function in air-conditioned environments. It's the only reason he's back before Gem.

And for (another) once, Martin's naively pervy and quite frankly ridiculous comments don't bug Gem. She can even acknowledge the fact that working for Martin isn't always *that* bad. Sure, she does occasionally see him in Lycra, but this only happens after he gets the monthly reminder that he's paying money to be part of the cycle-to-work scheme. He *is* useless at his job, but at least this means she is learning a lot. And yes, he might be misogynistic to his core, but in a way, it isn't his fault. His brain cells are too busy figuring out how to do everyday tasks to think critically, but even if he did recognise any of the injustices he sees, or even contributes to, he is too lazy to do anything about them. And too comfortable benefitting from them to try and change them. But, today, she just doesn't feel like fighting him, even passive-aggressively. So instead, she simply answers him.

'I am.'

She sits down at her desk, but not before placing a giant, ludicrously expensive Halloumi and avocado wrap on the desk in front of her. It might only be a Thursday, and it is nowhere near pay day, but she decided to treat herself and even bought herself a San Pellegrino Limonata, the fanciest of overpriced drinks.

'Well, I'm proud of you. You deserve it.'

'Thanks, Martin.'

And for once, she thinks he means it. Although he isn't technically wrong, today, indeed this whole week, has been a little unusual. But another good thing about Martin being as useless as he is, is that he has no idea how long certain things take. Part of her wonders if he would be even *more* proud of her knowing that she is following his lead and abusing company time.

Because for the first time, Gem has decided to make the most of Martin's weaknesses. So, when he asked her on Monday to create a video illustrating the findings from his first session as Retention Lead, she happily agreed. She finished the video within four hours and has spent the rest of the time working on her tasks for Shanti's fashion line – Gem was correct in thinking that she would be given all of the boring stuff, like options for funding and tax implications – and planning the practice dance session they will be running with Goals Aloud this evening.

Shanti and Gem will teach the Goalies a quick and fun dance, which will hopefully disguise the fact they are really teaching them how to move their feet quickly. She's planned a simple but repetitive set of steps that will improve their timing, their ability to change direction and, quite frankly, simply the enjoyment they take from moving their little bodies. Shanti has even made T-shirts.

Any free time outside of these two tasks has been spent daydreaming about Atlas.

Last night was one of the most memorable evenings she has ever had. She woke up deliciously sore and feeling extremely refreshed even though they barely slept. But although the sex was great, the thing that made her feel the warmest was when he'd hugged her to sleep. Her favourite place to be is in an Atlas cocoon.

Gem rang her mum and told her all about the ballet as soon as she could. Of course, leaving out details on the latter part of their evening. It's difficult to know which one of them was more excited about the earlier part of the date.

Gem's phone screen lights up with Atlas's name. It's a text.

She looks at it straight away.

Looking forward to seeing you later. I can't wait to finally see you dance.xx

Trying to maintain the appearance of professionalism, she reads Atlas's message, looking as though she's just received a note from her doctor informing her of her upcoming smear test. Then she turns the phone over so she can pretend to concentrate. Not that it does her much good. Even if she'd been doing something other than meticulously planning her next meeting with Atlas, she'd have been thinking about him.

She gets another message. Despite the fact she's put her phone face down, the light of the screen is reflecting off the table.

Unable to resist, she peeks at the message.

Only this time, it isn't Atlas's name that has flashed up.

It's the name of the wheelchair company.

They are upholstering her mum's seat and sewing the detachable travel bag.

All of a sudden, the idea of eating lunch does absolutely nothing good to Gem's insides.

It is getting more and more difficult to lie to Atlas. Or at least to keep the truth from him.

She wants to tell him.

She needs to tell him.

Surely, he is going to understand?

She is doing all of this for her mum.

He likes her mum.

He *has* to understand.

Gem looks at her calendar and counts six weeks from their first – technically second – date. She only has one-and-a-half weeks left before Shanti will start writing up her results. Ten-and-a-half days more of lying to him. But although the end is in sight, her guilt isn't lessening. If anything, the closer she gets to the finish line – and the better she knows Atlas – the worse Gem feels.

But she can do it.

She has to.

They are upholstering her mum's seat cushion. She can't imagine that she'll be able to get her money back now, even if she wants to. And she doesn't want to. It's her mum. In addition to the black, Gem's opted for a second cushion made with bespoke grey fabric and a pink trim.

Her mum will love it. Yet it doesn't solve the problem. What is Atlas going to do when he finds out why Gem started dating him? That it's because Shanti is paying her? How will he feel? How would *she* feel?

Gem looks at her giant, ludicrously expensive lunch, and suddenly feels nauseous.

She remembers the look in Atlas's eye when he told her about his first girlfriend betraying him. She's not sleeping with his best friend, so surely this situation isn't anywhere near as bad, right?

And then there's Shanti. She still hasn't told Tee about Atlas's confession. His history. If she did, it would at least prove that Gem's ick is her intuition, but if she'd listened to her intuition, she wouldn't have Atlas in her life, and that is not what she wants. He was young. He was hurt and sad and angry and his actions have not led to a pattern. If they had, the situation would be very different.

So no, she won't tell Shanti about Atlas's past.

She felt bad about lying to him before Atlas confessed to her about his ex, and knowing about his history, she feels even worse about it now.

She should tell him what's been going on. She has to.

But if she tells him, then he will know that she has been deceiving him, and Gem can't see Atlas forgiving her.

Maybe Gem should simply keep him in the dark? Forever?

She's never been married, but Gem imagines that even married people keep secrets from each other. Like their thoughts on new haircuts or what they really think about their partner's favourite book. And, in addition to the active lies, there are also lies of omission. You can't share literally *everything* with your other half, can you?

She really likes Atlas, but she doesn't want to know everything he is thinking. She can recognise that some things are too boring to share, but even more importantly she can see that some secrets need to be kept secret for a happy life. Maybe she can simply pretend that she's forgotten about Shanti's study?

She concentrates her thoughts on her friend. Gem has kept loads of secrets for Shanti over the years. Like the boyfriend she had in middle school who smoked and listened to rock music, and the fact it was Shanti who stole her mum's GHD hair straighteners only to accidentally burn a hole in the carpet. So keeping the study secret from Atlas is surely just making the whole situation a little more even?

Her mind made up, Gem pulls her wrap out of its packaging.

She is going to need the energy for dancing later.

And she isn't going to tell him.

Chapter 38

'Is he here? Can you see him yet?' Gem asks, looking around the very obviously empty dance hall, as though Shanti can see through walls.

'No.'

Gem can tell from Shanti's tone that she's trying to calm Gem down. It's the same voice that Shanti uses when she goes into therapy mode on her.

'But I'm sure he's coming. Don't forget that he's got to make it part way across town with a bunch of children.'

Dancing usually makes Gem relax. It makes her mind go quiet and her body stretch. But their own dance class finished ten minutes ago and neither Atlas nor any of the Goalies have arrived yet. Her phone rings, and she jumps. But it isn't Atlas, it's her mum. She doesn't pick up. But if her mum were here, she would understand. Her mind is already being pulled in a lot of different directions – Atlas, dancing, the guilt over Atlas – she can't add a conversation about her mum's sprouting garlic bulbs to the list.

'So,' Gem turns at Shanti's voice so quickly that her neck nearly cricks, 'are you finally ready to concede defeat and admit that you really like Atlas, that your ick is baseless?'

Shanti's tone has gone from therapist to light-hearted friend, but the question catches Gem off-guard and, in the moment, it takes everything for Gem to control her face. But Shanti has already seen too much.

'Oh!' Her eyes open up in shock. 'You mean ... your ick was actually warning you against something?'

'No. I didn't say that.'

Shanti's eyes focus in on Gem. 'Yes, you did. Don't you know that over half of communication is non-verbal?'

She didn't, but this new knowledge does make Gem turn away from her friend when she speaks next. 'Well, I haven't found anything out.'

She can feel Shanti's stare boring into her.

'So,' she hears Shanti say, 'does that then mean you're ready to admit that the ick isn't your intuition?'

Gem has feared this moment would come, that she would be tested, forced to choose between her sixth sense – a sense that has been her constant companion for years – and Atlas.

'Yes.'

Admitting defeat comes easier to Gem than she's imagined it would.

After giving the room another quick scan for Atlas, she finally turns back to her friend. She can tell from Shanti's open mouth that she is shocked. After all, apparently over half of all communication is non-verbal.

'So, wait. Does that mean ... like ... you and Atlas are actually a *thing* now? I mean I know you've had sex, but that doesn't always mean a relationship.'

The further down this road Gem goes, the more she realises she has absolutely no idea what she's doing.

'I actually don't know. I haven't really spoken to him about it.' Gem feels like a fool when the words are out. It's been so long since she's been in a relationship. She just knows that she wants Atlas in her life.

'Well, you should. And while you're at it, you need to tell him why you started dating him in the first place.'

The friends stare at each other.

'You *are* going to tell him, right?'

'Well ...'

'Gem.' Shanti's tone says it all. If she weren't training to become a therapist, she would make a great teacher. She's got that disapproving tone down pat.

She glances around the room, checking. Atlas still hasn't arrived, and for the first time his tardiness may be working in her favour.

'Well, I'm definitely not going to tell him before the study is over.'

'Screw the study. You can't need the money that badly.'

If only she knew. Part of Gem thinks she should just share her money woes with Shanti, but it's not an easy thing for her to confess.

'We've come this far. Another week won't make any difference.' Not that Gem plans to tell him then either. She can't risk it. 'Just, please don't say anything.' Besides, if she is ever forced to tell Atlas, she wants to make sure she tells him in the best way possible, to avoid hurting him as much as possible.

Shanti looks unconvinced, but after a few long seconds, she nods. 'Fine. But only because I can tell from here that you are as tense as fuck.'

Back on safer footing, Gem exhales.

'I am. I just want everything to go well. I don't want to look like a fool in front of him. Or Shauna. She still scares me.'

The confession is only partly a distraction technique.

And it also only partly works.

'Well, Shauna is going to love the tops I made them, so you can forget about her.'

But not Atlas.

She can't forget about Atlas.

'What if it all goes really wrong, everyone hates the dance we've planned, the kids cry, and Atlas can never look at me again without remembering what a failure I am?'

'Listen,' Shanti grabs both of Gem's shoulders, giving her a little shake, trying and failing to release the tension she can feel there, 'you need to relax. Just put a song on and have a dance.'

Gem's smile is genuine. 'When in doubt, dance it out?'

Shanti nods. 'Exactly. It's the best therapy. I should know.' She gets her phone out which is already connected to the speakers. 'Here, I'll pick the music so all you have to do is move.'

'You're too good to me, Tee.'

Much like deciding what to eat at the end of a long day, sometimes deciding what song to dance to can be just as difficult.

Shanti's shoulder hitches up. 'I know.'

She presses play. 'I've picked a good one.'

She slaps Gem's butt in the way only a best friend can, before walking away, the song already starting to blast out of the speakers. 'I'm gonna go make sure the T-shirts are organised. It's on repeat, so feel free to just keep going.'

And then Gem is left alone. Just her and the music.

*

Sometimes it's difficult to lose yourself in a dance. Sometimes the outside world creeps in and you can't help but fumble the steps or move a little stiffly. Sometimes you just have an off-day.

And when Gem stands up, the studio empty except for Shanti in the corner, she feels that today is not going to be her day. Her back and arms and neck will all feel rigid and slow. Her feet won't be able to follow what her brain is telling them to do.

But that isn't what happens.

Instead, she finds the beat almost instantly. It's not a song that she and Shanti have ever danced to before – at least not in a choreographed, formal way – but she knows the music. It's from one of their favourite movies, *Malang*.

She starts off slowly. Her eyes closed.

One of the most difficult things as a dancer is to make even your stillness purposeful. No good dancer ever just stands. They place themselves in exactly the right position.

Gem starts moving, leading with her hips. For the first few beats, she feels more like she is stretching and warming up than dancing. Then seamlessly, she is mixing together all of her favourite moves, her hands and hips in sync with the beat.

Shanti's picked quite a romantic song, and so Gem's mind instinctively begins to picture Atlas. Not only what he looks like, but how he makes her feel. How his touch makes her body feel alive. How his eyes light up when he sees her. How he makes her feel like she can do big things. It's all reflected in the dance she is building, and soon she forgets about everything around her. It's just her and the music.

It's only when she is part way through the third play of the song that she feels she's being watched. She has an audience. She doesn't know how long they have been there, but she can't stop now. She doesn't want to. She is reaching the best bit of the song – and incidentally the best bit of the dance. Stopping now would be like deciding not to finish a book that you can't put down. Or deciding not to eat the last bite of your meal, despite saving the best bits till last.

So she keeps going. Just a little more aware of the people watching her.

Shanti is standing just inside the doorway. Arms crossed, watching Gem with a smile on her face that Gem only usually sees on her friend when she herself is dancing. And standing inside the doorway is Atlas.

Her next move turns her away from him, but thanks to the wall of floor-length mirrors, she can watch his reactions.

Unlike the last time Gem saw him, Atlas is now casually dressed. He's wearing a pair of dark grey trousers and he's already commandeered one of the T-shirts that Shanti made for them. It's a little tight around the shoulders and arms, but Gem is definitely not complaining.

Yet it isn't the outfit that is making Gem smile. It's the look on his face.

His eyes are tracking her every move. She can tell that he can't figure out which part of her to watch, but it's obvious he likes what he sees. She should stop, but she likes the feeling of him watching her too much, so she keeps going, even as she hears more voices coming into the studio, falling quiet as soon as they see Gem dancing.

Only when the song ends, and Gem is breathing heavily, her hands slowly travelling down from her hair as her final pose breaks, does her audience once again make a noise. Even then, there are a few beats of silence before anyone moves.

'There's no fuckin' way I'm ever gonna be able to dance like that.'

'Oi!' This comes from Shanti who has broken away from the audience to walk towards Gem. With a quick look back to Shauna, she admonishes, 'You're too young to swear.'

But when she reaches Gem, her voice is, once again, quiet. 'Well, Gem,' the two friends aren't looking at each other directly, instead sneaking glances at each other via the mirror, 'I'm not sure that dance has exactly *relaxed* you, but, the good news is, Atlas definitely doesn't think you're a failure.'

And then, in a move that highlights just how good a friend she is, she shouts to the rest of the group, making them follow her to the table at the side of the room. 'OK, Goalies. Show's over. Time for your new uniform. Trust me, it's nicer than that rancid sweat-wicking stuff you've got on at the moment.'

Gem walks over to Atlas, still a little out of breath, though the dancing isn't completely to blame. 'Hey.' She smiles at him, but he doesn't smile back. 'I was starting to worry that you weren't coming.'

He just stares at Gem.

'That was ... I mean, I know you said you liked to dance, but I really didn't know ... That was ... *impressive*. Really impressive.' She can see his Adam's apple bob up and down, almost as though he is struggling to swallow. 'The kids ...' He looks at them briefly, eyes searching as though trying to remember where he is. 'They're all really impressed.'

At this, Gem can't help herself. She cocks her head to the side and does her best impression of a flirtatious Atlas.

'Well, that's nice to know,' she kicks her hip out and gives Atlas the most suggestive smile she can, 'but it wasn't them I was trying to impress.'

Chapter 39

'See you soon, Jay.'

Atlas has managed to achieve in two short visits what Gem and Shanti have been failing to achieve for years. Jay even waves him goodbye as they leave the grey shop with its luminescent lighting for the warm evening air and muted evening sun outside.

Luckily, Atlas isn't in on the competition. Neither Shanti nor Gem has any intention of letting him have control of the TV for a month nor want to do his laundry. The amount of sports he plays, not to mention the size of his bag, suggests he has an insane amount of clothes to wash.

This time, Atlas did at least show some control in the shop. He walks out with only three things, one of which is a small bag of crisps that made him squeal when he saw them.

'That shop is amazing. I haven't had a packet of these for *years*. I didn't even think they made 'em any more.' He opens them up, and offers them to Gem and Shanti, who both wisely turn down the offer to try the fish-flavoured snacks, that might not be made any more. It's not outside the realm of possibility that Jay found them in a back corner of his storeroom, where they've spent years lying in wait.

Atlas merely shrugs off the rejection. 'Your loss.'

The dance training session went well. Better than Gem had been hoping it would. The kids actually seemed to enjoy themselves, and Shauna only rolled her eyes once when Gem promised the song they'd chosen was a banger. But by far her best part of the evening is right now – walking down the street with her best friend and her, well ... Atlas.

She still has to come up with a word that fits what Atlas is to her. To do this, she is probably going to have to have The Conversation with him. Not the one where she confesses everything and risks him hating her forever and feeling irreparably betrayed, but the one where she gets him to tell her exactly what he is feeling, so she can potentially confess what she is feeling. As long as his feelings match – or exceed – hers.

Similarly to walking down the street with someone she might maybe, potentially, possibly want to call her boyfriend, having The Conversation is something she has never ever done. Atlas is so busy being gastronomically transported to his childhood that he doesn't notice Gem looking up at him, her eyes studying him just a little too intently. The only thing that shakes her out of her reverie, is her phone ringing. It's her mum. Again.

'You can get that if you want?'

She looks between the screen and Atlas who is finishing off his crisps.

'Oh, no, it's OK. I'll call her tomorrow.'

Truthfully, she would love to talk to her mum. But she doesn't want to talk to her mum in front of Atlas. She's probably ringing to see how the dance session went, and she doesn't want to have that conversation within Atlas's earshot. It would expose all of her neuroses and how nervous she had been in the run-up. It would also expose how happy she is that it all went well. Her mum is the one person who will know how much this evening meant, and the one person who would be *almost* as happy as Gem herself that it went well.

As though he can actually read her mind, Atlas, as soon as he has finished eating, slips his hand into Gem's, and Gem doesn't even blink when he does it. It's as though her hand has always been waiting for his.

'No, but seriously, you both did an amazing job. Thank you. I haven't seen the team have such a good time at practice for, well, maybe ever. Kinda put my coaching efforts to shame. Pretty sure they're all gonna be extra critical now when I show up only pretending to have a plan.'

'Well, we had a lot more fun dancing with them than we usually have at class.' The fact that Shanti feels happy enough to jump into the conversation almost makes Gem want to sing. If only she could hold a tune.

'It was nice to remember what it feels like just to have fun, as opposed to concentrating too much on the choreography.'

'Yeah.' Atlas, his hand still in Gem's, does a few of the steps that they had run through. He'd joined in on the session, having even more fun than the kids. 'I'm pretty grateful for that.' He only narrowly avoids tripping over the side of the pavement, mainly because Gem's hand drags him back onto safer ground.

'Well, for what it's worth, you moved better than I thought you would.' Shanti's choice of words is very clever, even though her tone is begrudging.

Only Gem knows that Shanti had assumed Atlas would be arrhythmic. Her prediction wasn't far from the truth. His skills do not lie in dance. Somehow, he looked like he was line dancing, which is worrying as the steps and music were both more like a modern street dance. It should have put her off, but Gem just found his total lack of skill kind of endearing. As if she needs another sign that she is in trouble. Plus, his moves in the bedroom are better than any dance Gem has ever seen.

'Well, I'll take that as a compliment, even though I'm pretty sure it's a little backhanded. Speaking of which, although there is no backhand to this at all, the T-shirts you made are great, Shanti. You should sell them.'

Gem can feel Shanti's glower. 'Did you tell him to say that?'

The two friends lean forward, so they can see each other around Atlas.

'No, I promise.' Mainly because Gem hasn't had a chance to fill Atlas in on their recent and *very* potential plans.

'Well, I think you should.' Atlas's voice remains decidedly chipper, totally unaware of the glower.

'Hmm.' Shanti continues to give Gem some powerful side-eye. 'You're not the only one.'

Without his snacks to distract him, Atlas looks from one to the other. Aware that he's done something, but totally unaware what that something might be.

Gem gives Atlas's hand a little squeeze. 'Shanti and I are starting to look into what we would need to do in order to start building a fashion revamp business.'

'Really?' Atlas's voice contains so much admiration.

'No.' Shanti stands taller. 'I'm studying to become a clinical psychologist.' They all walk a few more steps.

Anticipating.

Finally, Shanti breaks line. 'But we're looking into it.'

Atlas passes a small squeeze back.

'Well,' he mimics Shanti's earlier tone, '*for what it's worth*, I think that's a great idea.' But as quickly as Atlas's enthusiasm arrives, it leaves. 'Hold on, going back to that earlier bit though. Does that mean that you're like ... studying everyone around you?' His grip on Gem's hand tightens, and her stomach drops. This is exactly why she's been avoiding the subject. 'Wait. Does that mean you're studying *me*?'

Once more, the two friends lean forward, sharing the quickest of silent conversations.

Please don't tell him.

I won't. Mainly because it isn't my conversation to have, but he's uncomfortably close to the truth. And you need to tell him. Soon.

'No. I'm not studying you,' Shanti's voice comes out confidently.

Relief floods Gem at Shanti's careful choice of words. Technically, she isn't studying Atlas. She is studying Gem, and Atlas is simply collateral damage.

Atlas's grip loosens. 'Thank God for that. Although personally I think I'd make a fascinating study.'

Chapter 40

'It was fun to watch you two together. It's obvious that you're really close.'

'Who, me and Shanti?'

'Yeah, who else would I be talking about?'

Almost as soon as the three of them made it inside, the high of the evening dwindled and everyone – by mutual agreement – was as efficient as possible in getting to bed.

But now that they are here in her room, Gem, who was on the brink of falling asleep while brushing her teeth, has inexplicably woken up. Although, as inexplicable as her change in status is, it could possibly be due to Atlas's hands. They are slowly and lightly, but persistently, mapping every inch of Gem's body while his breath teases the back of her neck and his lips tease her ear. Her heart beats faster and faster every time his lips make contact.

'Well, we've been friends for years.'

One of his hands moves lower, and Gem, who has been soft and relaxed, instantly switches to being on high alert.

'I couldn't stop watching you dance.' The words, and also the feel of the words against her neck, make Gem's body hum. She shifts to get closer to Atlas, but even though almost every inch of her is touching him, it still isn't enough.

'Wait.'

Her mind's interruption couldn't have come at a more inconvenient time.

As soon as the word is out, Atlas's hands stop roaming, and instead of feeling their heat, all she can feel is their absence.

'Is everything OK?'

As much as she doesn't want to, Gem forces herself to face him. It means there is even more space between them. But this is a conversation that she needs to not only hear but see. She needs to be aware of what he's really feeling. She looks at Atlas in the dim light of her room, placing a hand on one side of his face. She can't see him completely clearly, but she can see enough to fill in the gaps. She knows his face better than she knows her own.

'What are you?'

A couple of beats pass before Atlas answers. 'Right now?'

Gem nods.

'A sexually starved man?' She can feel him smile.

'No, I mean, to me. What are you to me? What am I to you?'

A small crease forms between his beautiful eyes.

'I mean, are we seeing each other? Only each other, or are we seeing anyone else?'

The crease deepens and this time any humour disappears from Atlas's face. 'Do you want to see anyone else?'

'No. God, no. Sorry.' Gem closes her eyes against the inevitable moving on of time, hoping against hope (and physics) to rewind the clock. When she opens her eyes again, his crease is gone and his hands have returned to stroking her.

'What's up?'

'This isn't going to come out right, so bear with me.'

All he does is give the smallest of nods. She can't imagine having this conversation anywhere else but in bed. It really is an intimate conversation, only suitable for the most intimate of environments.

'I don't know what to introduce you as. It was super awkward when Shauna asked if I was your girlfriend, and then it was even more awkward when I introduced you as my guest to Uncle Mike.'

'I almost forgot about that.' She can hear the smile in his voice.

'But I don't know what to call you.' Of course, this isn't just a labelling issue. In fact, it isn't a labelling issue at all. It's a confidence issue.

'I don't know what we are. I don't want to be thinking that we're something when you think we're something else.'

'Well, what do you want us to be?'

It could be Gem's imagination, but is there a hint of caution in his question?

If only she knew where it might be coming from, she'd know how to answer without potentially looking like an idiot.

It could come from a total dislike of the question.

A need to avoid the seriousness of it.

A total aversion to any kind of commitment.

Or his caution could come from a better place. The same place where Gem's comes from. A need to not show your hand too early. To protect what little part of you is still left to be protected.

Earlier this evening, when dancing and then again when walking home with Atlas by her side, Gem had felt almost invincible. Perhaps even more shocking, she had felt optimistic. She tries to reimagine herself in that moment, dancing, feeling the confidence of the moves and the power of the music. And instead of catastrophising, she decides to tell him the truth.

'I only want to see you. And I only want you to see me. I want to introduce you as my boyfriend. And I don't want to feel weird about it.'

There is a beat of silence. Just long enough for Gem to slightly wither inside. Then Atlas smiles. He closes his eyes and rests his forehead against hers.

'OK. OK. Thank God.'

The air in the room seems to settle.

'You mean you want the same thing?'

At this, Atlas once again creates room between the two of them.

'Again, I don't know how old – or young – you think I am, but I don't have the energy to be dating more than one person at a time.' He kisses her gently on the nose before giving her the best smile she has seen on him yet. 'But even if I did, I wouldn't want to.'

'You wouldn't?'

'No.' He leans towards her again, removing the space between them. 'I wouldn't.'

He kisses Gem, taking his time. His lips are soft, and his tongue is teasing. He nips at her lower lip, as she hitches one of her legs over his and tugs him towards her, still wanting to get as close as possible. He starts to shift, pulling her on top of him. Seeing him beneath her, she trails her hands over his chest. She doesn't know which she prefers, being touched by him, or touching him. She traces her hands up from his waist, over his abs, his heart, his shoulders, and then down his arms. She takes his hands and places them where she wants them, right on her hips, and then runs her hands back up his arms so she can feel his biceps flexing underneath her fingertips.

When they are perfectly in position, him at her total mercy, she pauses.

'What are you doing on the 25th of May?'

Atlas's hands, which are still on her hips, freeze. She can see his face transition from his sex face to a more serious one. It takes him a moment. To be fair, the question did come from nowhere.

'As in the 25th of May that is just over two weeks away?' he asks, and Gem nods. 'I don't think I have any plans.'

She leans forward, placing a hand to either side of his head.

'Will you come to my birthday party?'

A smile returns to his lips. It gets her every time.

'You're inviting me to your birthday party?'

She nods again. 'I am.'

He moves underneath her, subtly altering the position of his hips, and hers. When he settles, they somehow feel even closer. 'I thought for your birthday this year you only wanted to be with people you love?'

'I do.' She closes the distance between the two of them.

'Which is exactly why I want you there.'

Chapter 41

'You need to tell him.'

'Tee, it's too early.' For a change, instead of being awake all night rehashing all of her most embarrassing conversations, she had been awake all night for significantly better reasons. Many of which involved Atlas's magnificent hands. Hands that she no longer associates with little T-rex arms.

'I don't think so. I think you should have told him the moment you even thought you might actually like him.'

'That's not what I mean.' Both of their voices are hushed whispers, the kind that can be heard very clearly and practically beg for people to strain their ears to listen to. 'I mean it's too early in the morning to be having this conversation.'

Gem puts the kettle on and gets out three mugs.

'Well, I'm taking you out of the study.'

For the first time since her mum's last missed call, Gem thinks of her. And her new wheelchair, which is due to be both completed and fully paid for by the end of next week. 'No. You need to keep me in.'

'Gem.'

'Tee, there's only one week left. And then I'll tell him, I

promise. I'm being serious. You have to keep me in, and you can use me as proof that the ick is totally ridiculous. I was wrong. It has nothing to do with intuition.'

'Well, no shit.'

Although Gem preps the mugs she got out for her and Atlas with coffee, Shanti is a tea drinker with a discerning taste that changes with her mood. This morning, she reaches past Gem for the ginseng.

Luckily the part of Gem that is chomping at the bit to tell Shanti that, in reality, she was right – that her intuition, her ick, was valid and that Atlas does have a red flag against him – is silenced by the bigger part of her that is telling her that Atlas was young, that he was going through an awful time, that he feels genuine remorse and regret and has learnt from his mistakes.

More importantly, it's silenced by the part that loves him.

'If I take you out of the study, at least the lie is minimised.'

'Technically I haven't lied to him,' Gem argues.

As the sound of the kettle boiling gets louder, so do their voices.

'What?'

At Shanti's pointed look, Gem feigns ignorance. 'I haven't. He even asked me why I went on a second date with him and I told him the truth.'

'What did you say?'

'I told him it was my intuition—'

'Gem.' Shanti's voice is as angry as she has ever heard it. 'Atlas is a really nice guy. He deserves the truth – the whole truth – from you. And soon. As in now. This morning. Along with his coffee.'

The kettle clicks off, but Unfortunately Gem's morning brain doesn't adjust the volume of her voice.

'It's not like I can just blurt out, "Hey Atlas, just so you know, I only started dating you because my best friend was paying me to as part of a project."'

She pours steaming water into all three of the mugs in front of her.

'What did you just say?'

At the sound of Atlas's voice, the friends freeze. Gem's heart feels as though it is both beating far too fast and far too strongly. She can't tell if she is going to faint or throw up.

She puts the kettle down carefully before she drops it and looks at Shanti for a report. For the first time ever, Tee looks completely and utterly uncomfortable. Gem's heart plummets.

She searches for a lie. Any lie that could make this better. Idealistically she is against lying, but she will gladly sacrifice her ideals to make the situation better.

But as soon as she turns and sees Atlas, she knows that no lie will do.

It is Atlas but he doesn't look like the person she knows. There is no cheeky hint of a smile, no familiar light in his eyes. Instead, his facial features look frozen, as though he is trying not to show an emotion at all.

'Atlas, I can explain. Please. It's not at all what you think—'

'I think you've been lying to me.'

'No. Well, yes, I have, bu—'

'You must think I'm an idiot. I bet you've been laughing about this behind my back. Having a good old time at my expense.'

'No. You're not an idiot.' *Gem* is the idiot. 'Please, Atlas.'

She steps towards him, but he steps away, rebounding off the doorframe with his shoulder as he turns. He walks out into the hallway, still wearing his dance top from yesterday, the loud print totally at odds with the situation they are now in.

Only an hour ago their limbs were so intwined, Gem had woken up not knowing quite where her body stopped and his began. Now the space between them might as well be miles.

'Please stop. Just wait. Please. Let me explain.'

He turns then. His eyes huge with unshed tears.

It's obvious he is waiting for her to speak, but she can't. Because he is right, she *has* been lying to him. No matter her reasons, no matter her motivation, no matter how wrong she knows she has been.

'Fuck.' This comes from Atlas. It's loud enough to make Gem jump.

A single tear falls down his face. She watches it, heartbroken, helpless as he leaves, taking his bag with him.

Gem is frozen in place. For someone who is usually so good at fearing the worst is going to happen, Gem didn't see this happening.

Shanti appears by her side.

She looks at her best friend. 'He is never going to forgive me, is he? How can he ever forgive me?' This latter question sounds more like a plea.

'I don't know.' Shanti has never been great at a motivational speech. 'But you have to try.'

'Shit.' Gem's heart continues to malfunction and she looks around, not knowing what she needs. '*Shit*. I'm gonna go after him.'

Shanti says nothing, instead shoving Gem's keys and her phone into her hand.

'Call me if you need me.'

It must have taken Gem a long time to slip on her most worn-in trainers, because by the time she leaves the house, Atlas is already at the end of the street.

'Atlas!'

She shouts his name loud enough in the quiet street that she knows he can hear her. Everyone can. It's only just gone seven in the morning. Nobody in their right mind is out of their house. A runner passes her, just to prove her point.

'Atlas! Please. Stop. Let me explain.'

As if they are both in some kind of flipped scary movie reality, the faster she runs, the further away he seems to get. For the first time, she hates his height and the long legs that enable it. An oblivious dog walker gets in her way, and she loses sight of Atlas between the trees and the cars and the rubbish and the stupid runner.

When she finally reaches the main road, despite the fact she knows he is still carrying his massive bag, she can't see him. She'd assumed he was heading towards the tube, but the pavement is clear. It's more empty than she has ever seen it, in fact, almost as though the whole universe wants her to know just how alone she is. The only person she can see is Jay.

He's standing outside his shop, watching Gem with his arms crossed, his scowl deeper than ever, as though even he knows what she has done. He must know that she is looking for Atlas, he must have heard her shouting, but instead of pointing in any direction, he simply turns his back on her and walks inside his shop.

At a literal crossroads, and with no idea which way to go, Gem starts to cry. Only a complete lack of energy stops her from screaming.

It takes her a few moments to realise that her phone is ringing. She looks down at it, just in case it's Atlas. She would happily hear him yell at her, tell her how awful she is, anything, just to hear his voice. Just to know that he is still invested, in some way, *any* way, in their relationship. But it isn't Atlas, of course. It's her mum. Almost as if she knows Gem needs her.

She picks up, ready to blurt the whole thing out. 'Mum. I've really messed up.'

But it isn't her mum's voice she hears. Instead, she can hear the background noise of a hospital. She would know that sound anywhere. The bleeps of the machines. The typing of someone in the background updating patient notes. A doctor being called. The whoosh of a trolley being pushed down the wide corridor.

'Oh hello. Is that ... Gemima?'

If the background noise isn't enough to tell her what she already knows, the official, professional tone of the voice is. And for once, Gem doesn't care that they have used the wrong name. She only cares about what's happened, and why someone she doesn't know is calling her from her mum's phone.

'Yes, it is,' she hears herself say. 'What's happened? Is my mum OK?'

Chapter 42

When Gem first walked into the hospital room, it took her a while to recognise her mum. She was usually always bright and moving. Like a pinball in an arcade, constantly flitting between one thing and the next, making everything she touched light up. But the only person in that hospital room had been so still. Her hair was limp, her skin was grey, and her arms weren't moving. Her legs looked oddly small under the knitted blue blanket, and she wasn't smiling. So even though she was the only person in the room – a sign that in retrospect should have alerted Gem to the seriousness of her mum's injury – she still couldn't recognise the person as being her mother.

Gem was only eight when the accident happened. She knew that something was wrong as soon as she saw Uncle Mike walk through the door. Apart from the fact he was late and hated picking up Gem from school – he always complained that the mums hit on him even though Gem had never seen anyone even talk to him – his face was pale and pinched with worry. He's never been very good at hiding his emotions. He's also never been very good at lying. Especially to Gem. So, when she asked him what happened, he told her the truth.

'Your mum's been in a car accident. And not a small one,

Gemmy. She's hurt pretty bad. She was on her way to pick you up from dance class, and a lorry clipped the back of her car, flipping her over. She's paralysed from the lower back down.'

Even though she didn't fully know what the word 'paralysed' meant, she knew from Uncle Mike's serious face that it wasn't good. And she knew that from that day on, her mum was going to need help, even if she didn't know quite what that help was, or how to do it.

Back then, when Gem finally recognised her mum – when her mum finally opened her eyes after sensing someone else in the room – she ran out of Uncle Mike's grip and practically leapt on her mum in bed. This, of course, was something she should not have done. She still worries that this moment of selfish stupidity worsened her mum's injury. Maybe if she hadn't leapt on her, her mum's back might have unbroken itself and the nerves might have glued themselves back together?

Her mum spent a total of nine weeks in various hospitals and recovery units, leaving Gem in the care of Uncle Mike. She could have been out in six, but they kept her in there longer because of Gem. Gem knows this for a fact. On one visit, she arrived a little earlier than usual, walking down the blue corridors that had become so very familiar to her. But something – the slightly shut door and the hushed voices – made her pause before she pushed her way into her mum's room. While she might not have been able to understand all of the nuances of her mother's care, she could understand the words.

'We'd like to keep you in for another few weeks. You are healing well, but with it being only you and your daughter at home, we're concerned that there will be a lack of care available for you.'

*

Gem can still hear the words as clearly as if they had just been spoken. And she is just as determined to prove them wrong now, as she was then. She can look after her mother just fine.

Luckily, this time Gem's mum only had to be in hospital for a couple of nights, meaning they are now free of the sterile blue hospital walls and are back in Mum's happy, bright blue lounge. From her position – leaning over her mum as she lies on the sofa – Gem can see her pupils moving about behind her closed eyes.

'Gem, stop hovering.'

'I'm not hovering, I'm just making sure you're OK.'

Her mum's eyes open, but Gem doesn't move away. While she's here, she might as well pull the blanket up a little higher. It's still warm and sunny outside, but her mum feels the cold more than most and she isn't moving, so she'll feel it even more. Plus, your body temperature usually drops when you sleep, Gem reasons. Her mum hits her hands away and pulls the blanket further down than it was before.

'Gem, I'm fine. You heard the doctor. I will be sore for a little while, but the thing I need more than anything else is rest, and I can't rest if you keep coming in here, waking me up.' Her mum's tone had started off nicely but took a turn towards pissed off at the end.

'Well then, don't sleep so quietly.' Gem would never have thought it, but she's come to realise that snoring has its benefits. It lets everyone know you're alive, which is something Gem might not be for much longer if the look her mum's giving her is anything to go by.

'OK, fine. I'll be in the kitchen.'

She backs into the kitchen, refusing to take her eyes off her mum, but as soon as she's there, risking a quick look around, she knows it won't work. At least not in its current configuration. She's going to need to move the table. Unfortunately for her mum's sleep goals, the table is surprisingly heavy and makes quite a loud noise as she drags it across the floor.

'Gem, what on earth are you doing?'

Gem peeks her head around the corner, her hands still on the table, her butt sticking out. Her mum's eyes haven't lost any of their fire. 'I'm just moving the table a bit. Sorry. I'm almost done.' She heads to the other side of the table, deciding to push, instead of pull it the final foot, in the hopes the noise is slightly less aggravating.

It isn't.

'Tell me you're not moving it to the doorway so you can watch me sleep?'

With one final shove, the table is where Gem wants in. Right in the doorway.

She smiles at her mum, who she can now see perfectly, no walls in the way.

'Fine. I won't tell you that's exactly what I'm doing.'

'Gem.' Her mum's tone is a combination of exhaustion, frustration and stubbornness.

'Mum.' Today, Gem is a more potent version of her mother.

Finally, her mum looks away. 'Fine. But you're going back to work tomorrow.'

'I'm already back at work.' After all, despite giving everyone a soporific hit, the tax world never sleeps. 'Martin said I can work from home for the next two weeks.'

When she called Martin to explain the situation – that her mum, who is in a wheelchair, fell and sprained her wrist while trying to reach for something – he had absolutely no idea what to say, and therefore agreed to everything Gem asked for. Which is good: if he hadn't, she probably would've quit on the spot.

And she needs her job now more than ever before. Gem is pretty sure that Shanti is going to have to take her out of the study, meaning she isn't going to get paid the final instalment, and maybe not even the second, which still hasn't hit her bank account. It is too late to cancel the order for her mum's chair, but even if she could, there is no way she would, especially after what's just happened.

Her mum couldn't – or wouldn't – tell Gem exactly how she fell, but she knows that it must have been down to her clunky chair. Gem shouldn't have bought it for her. The guy even told her it could occasionally get stuck. She should have realised that his admission was less of a friendly warning and more of a way to assuage his own guilt. He was getting rid of it for a reason. Gem should've known better than to buy it.

The new chair is getting delivered in a week, however, and Gem can't wait. Not only is it smaller and easier to manoeuvre, but it is also lighter and comes with a guarantee. Her mum will be back on her feet – so to speak – more quickly.

The table now in the perfect place, Gem opens up her laptop, peeking over the screen to make sure her mum is still breathing. Maybe she could put a feather or a piece of paper next to her nose to make sure?

'Gem, I can feel you watching me.'

Gem continues to look at her mum – just for a moment longer. Her eyes are closed, but if anyone believes in the power of a sixth sense, it's Gem.

'OK, fine. Sorry.'

She looks away, but her eyes keep flicking back.

She won't make the same mistake twice. Or should that be thrice, seeing as she has already let her mum down twice? Some twenty years ago, and again just a couple of days ago. She's never going to let her mum out of her sight. Not again. She should have picked up her phone. She should have realised that something was wrong when her mum called. She should have been listening to her intuition instead of turning it off and fooling herself that everything was going to be OK. But she was distracted.

Atlas isn't around any more to distract her though.

She should have run the very first moment she felt the ick. If she had, none of this would have happened.

If she hadn't been with Atlas, she would have picked up the phone to her mum. Or maybe she would've even been at home to reach the stupid bowl that her mum had wanted from the top shelf. Without Atlas, she will now have much more free time on her hands, free time that will be much better spent by being here, where she can concentrate on what matters the most. Her mum.

Gem takes a quick glimpse at her once more.

So many people complain about all of the wrong things when they talk about growing up. They complain about ageing skin and greying hair. Tired eyes and stiff backs. But none of these things are important.

The worst thing about growing up is all of the realisations.

Working hard doesn't necessarily mean you'll be successful.

The news isn't necessarily the truth.

A midlife crisis might not be a crisis at all, but instead the point in life at which you finally know what you want and can finally afford to do it.

Summer holidays have to be paid for. Worse than that – essentials have to be paid for.

The movie *Free Willy* is about freeing a captive orca while using a captive orca to play the orca they were pretending to free.

All of these realisations ruin the magic of life, little by little.

They group together until gravity is no longer the thing that is keeping you on earth; instead, you're kept grounded by the weight of knowledge, and the creeping realisation that nothing is as it seems and that, most of the time, everything is a little bit worse.

But the worst realisation for Gem is that her mum is human, and she is getting older. Again, the ageing thing doesn't matter. Gem couldn't care less that her mum's hair is now significantly more grey and her taste in music seems to be getting progressively worse. Growing old in itself isn't bad. Heated blankets are a great invention. And retinol really does help with wrinkles. But growing old – and the realisation that her mum is growing old – means that she isn't all-powerful and all-knowledgeable and indestructible. One day she won't be here any more. And Gem is determined to make sure that that day happens as far away in the future as possible.

Gem can see her mum's chest gently rise just in time. Another three seconds and she was going to have to wake her up.

Slowly, she draws her eyes back to her computer screen, but on their journey back, they snag on the dining table, and specifically Atlas's seat.

She has an overwhelming urge to go over to it and smell the chair, just to see if there is any trace of him left. She would do too, if her mum didn't finally look to be getting some sleep.

It's probably for the best. Sniffing furniture isn't exactly normal behaviour. It's the kind of behaviour that leads to people asking if you're OK, or if you need to go to therapy. Sure, therapy and talking about your feelings has become popular recently, but just last week Gem also saw something about baggy cargo pants coming back into fashion, which is proof that being fashionable is not necessarily all that good of an idea.

So no, Gem will not be fashionable. She will not be talking about her feelings.

Instead, she moves the table a little bit back into the kitchen, not so much that she can no longer see her mum, but enough that she can no longer see Atlas's chair.

Chapter 43

'Gem.'

At the sound of her mum's voice, Gem looks up. It takes her eyes a moment to adjust. The same spreadsheet has been open on her computer screen all day, and not because it's too interesting to look away from or because she has been working hard on it. It's a painfully boring spreadsheet detailing cost margins and she hasn't managed to do any work. Her mind keeps wandering, just as often as her eyes wander over to Atlas's chair, and the conclusion she has quietly been coming to over the last few days.

'You OK? Do you need anything? Cup of tea?' Gem has been trying to keep her tone of voice neutral, but she can't help a hint of panic sneaking in. She is still on tenterhooks in case something goes wrong. Again.

She's still working from home – her mum's home. Luckily, they don't specify whose home you need to be in. It's been a week since her mum's accident, and six days, fourteen hours and approximately thirty-nine minutes since she last saw Atlas.

Her mum is now very obviously totally fine, but Gem has made no move to return back home. Aside from needing to make sure her mum is OK, it's been nice to step back from everything.

From her responsibilities.

From the rush of working in the city.

Even from dance.

But especially from Atlas.

And Shanti asking her about Atlas.

And not knowing what's happening with Atlas, either in terms of what is going on between them – which is absolutely nothing, as it should be because she treated him like an absolute dick – or what is going on in his day-to-day life, which she is desperate to know.

She wants to know if he's playing football.

If he's laughing with Shauna.

What he's eating.

If anything has made him smile.

If he is as broken as she is feeling.

So, essentially, yes, she is still here because she is hiding.

It would be working so much better if only she could stop thinking about all of the things she is hiding from.

'I do need something actually.'

At the call to arms, Gem's back instantly straightens and her whole body stands to attention, first figuratively and then literally. *Something* is exactly what she needs to be doing. The only thing that is helping to take her mind off Atlas is doing many *things*. The more physical the *thing*, the better. Anything that involves thinking is proving difficult, hence her lack of progress with the spreadsheet. So keen is she not to think, she jumps up, a little too quickly. Her chair makes an awful sound as it scrapes against the floor, but she's in too much of a rush to push it back quietly.

She's over at her mum's side before she has even had time to put down her book.

'What is it?'

Gem sits down next to her mum, careful not to get too close. She's been snapped at a few more times for hovering.

She carries out a complete – and subtle – inventory as she sits down. From the looks of things her mum is OK. There are no obvious signs of illness or weakness.

Her pallor is healthy. Her breathing seems fine.

Her eyes have lost that slight yellow tinge they had for a while when she was clearly still in pain from her fall, and then worn down further by a few nights of fitful sleep.

Her drink is still half full, and her snacks haven't completely dwindled. Obviously, the apple is still there, but that doesn't really mean much. Nobody eats an apple. Plus, there's still some peanut butter left in the jar, and a fairly generous amount of hummus in the bowl. You only need to worry when the dips dwindle.

'What's wrong?'

Her mum's eyes level at her.

'You.'

'Me?' Gem draws back.

'Yes. There's something wrong with you.'

Gem squints at her mum.

'Has anyone ever told you that you have a great way with words?'

Unfortunately, Gem's mum isn't even close to getting distracted, especially not by a playful tone of voice and some gentle joking.

'What's going on?'

Having failed before, Gem tries a different tactic. She lies.

'Nothing's wrong. I'm fine. Don't I seem fine?' She smiles, as wide as possible, but it has absolutely no effect.

'No, you're not, and no, you don't. At first, I thought you were just worried about me. It was annoying but I could handle all the fussing. I understood it. But now. All this.'

She waves her hand in front of Gem's face, gesturing at everything and nothing in particular. 'There's something going on, and I want to know what it is.'

'I still don't know what you mean.'

Her mum's eyes narrow on the lie.

'You know exactly what I mean. It's Thursday evening. You should be going to dance, but instead you're still here.'

Gem opens her mouth to object, but her mum doesn't let her. Her strength really has returned. 'Plus, there's the fact you haven't left the flat in over a week, you've got a stye which you only ever get when you're stressed, you have bags under your eyes and you've barely spoken to any of your friends.'

Her mum looks at Gem again, studying her. 'Plus, your hair—'

'What is wrong with my hair?'

'Well, for starters you haven't even bothered to brush it for a week. I can see it breaking from here. Now don't change the subject.' The bite to her voice confirms that she's definitely feeling better, a fact which Gem is trying her hardest to find solace in.

'You're the one who brought up my hair.'

'You're the one who's avoiding people. Tell me why?'

For a few beats, Gem contemplates her next move.

Three options spring to mind.

She could continue to lie; eventually her mum would have to give up and admit defeat.

She could simply tell her mum the truth and be done with it.

Or she could pretend that she's having one of those rare strokes that makes you wake up fluent in a completely different language.

Unfortunately, only one option is actually viable, although she will forever regret giving up French.

Her shoulders, which have been in a perpetual state of flex for a week, go in the opposite direction, and finally slump.

'It's pretty bad, Mum.'

'OK. Just to recap so I can make sure I'm not going completely insane...'

Gem watches as her mum's eyes dart backwards and forwards. Gem's dumped a lot on her in the last half-hour. Not all of it, but the key parts. Somehow the story seemed to take both much, much more and much, much less time to get through than Gem thought it would.

'So for years, any time you've been slightly put off by someone, you've put it down to getting *the ick*, which you essentially think is your intuition telling you that you are incompatible with that person?'

Her mum goes silent for a moment, looking at Gem for confirmation.

Gem nods. 'Yes.'

Her mum nods back, not in agreement, because the idea is insane, but in confirmation of the facts. 'OK.'

Her eyes narrow as she remembers more of what Gem has just told her. Or possibly searching for the logic in what has just been said.

'And so Shanti, who is studying to be a clinical psychologist, suggested you be one of her subjects for her final dissertation, which is all about studying intuition and whether or not it is a real thing?'

Gem nods again. 'Yes.'

'OK.' Once again, her mum's eyes resume searching, trying to find some sense in all of this.

'And so you started dating Atlas, a lovely boy who not only I, but your uncle Mike, think is wonderful and smart and kind and thoughtful, just to prove that the ick is real and that the ick you felt for him – caused by a *backpack that was a bit big and made him look like a bad imitation of a snail, and his decision to eat soup for lunch* – is the source of some more serious issue?'

This time Gem doesn't nod but she does still agree. Atlas is wonderful and smart and kind and thoughtful. 'Yes.'

'And at no point did you think it would be a good idea to tell him what was going on?'

At this, Gem only just manages to shake her head.

'And at no point – since him accidentally learning of this ridiculous story – have you tried to apologise or explain yourself?'

She shakes her head again. 'Not really.'

At this, her mum also falls silent. Although she doesn't stay that way for long.

'Well, the good news is, I'm not insane. I did hear all of that correctly.' She looks at Gem. 'The bad news is, I think you might be.'

Gem's face squirms all of its own volition. There's no disappointment quite so heavy as that of a parent.

Finally, her mum reaches out a hand. 'I know you haven't explained to Atlas why you did this, but can you explain it to me?'

'Why I did what part specifically?'

'Well, all of it, but I guess the two big things that come to mind are why you would agree to take part in this ridiculous study in the first place, and then why you didn't tell Atlas, or at least apologise to him for not telling him about the whole thing.'

Her mum's eyes widen for a moment. 'Don't tell Shanti I said the study was ridiculous. The intuition bit I get, but the ick bit is still a little ... hard for me to understand. But then I was born in the sixties.'

Gem should have known that her mum would zero in on the two areas she doesn't want to talk about. She exhales for as long as the inhale that follows it, even so neither breath reaches the bottom of her lungs. Far from giving her the calm release and healing powers that yoga instructors lead you to believe, it just leaves Gem feeling even more anxious.

But it's hard to breathe when your body is crumbling under anxiety. It's difficult to know which answer she should start with. Neither comes easily.

'Atlas isn't going to forgive me.' She looks at her mum, pleadingly. 'He's the first person I've been out with for – maybe ever – that I actually want to see again. He's funny and kind and makes me feel loved.'

'Gemmy.' Her mum hugs her, smooshing her so close that she can hardly breathe. She can feel her mum's tears on the top of her head. Her mum kisses her, smoothing down her frizzy, unkempt hair. She has let her conditioning regime go a little lax since coming home.

'But Gem, you don't know that he's not going to forgive you. He might do, if you explain it to him.' Her mum pauses. She can feel a shrug through their hug. 'You might need to explain it better than you've explained it to me, but we can work on that.'

At this, Gem sits up and wipes her own tears away. 'No.' This is the only part of the whole story that Gem has total and complete faith in. 'He won't. He has a history of people lying to him.'

She doesn't want to tell her mum the details. Not because she thinks it's unforgiveable – she has done enough thinking over the last few days to know that Atlas's history isn't what her intuition was warning her against – but because it isn't her history to tell.

'Trust me on this. There's no point in trying. I don't think he'll ever want to see me again.' He certainly ran away fast enough to give that impression.

'Maybe not, love. But I can tell how much you like him. I haven't seen you that happy and comfortable around someone, maybe ever. I think it's worth a try. Isn't it?'

This question, Gem can't answer. Her heart won't let her.

'If not for yourself, then for him. He deserves to know why you did what you did.'

Their conversation has been so intense that neither Gem nor her mum have noticed the door opening, nor Uncle Mike coming in. At least not until he appears in the doorway, hands on his hips, feet wide apart as though he is looking at a burst water main.

'What's happening here then?'

The three of them glance at each other, all unsure how to answer that question. But as soon as he sees Gem and her tears, his face changes from one of an open question to East End Neanderthal.

'Tell me who I need to go sort out.'

'Right.'

The story doesn't get better the more times it's told. Instead, Uncle Mike appears to be just as confused about the situation as Gem's mum, and now Gem herself. Far from helping her make sense of what she's done, repeating the story is having the opposite effect. And now, Gem feels increasingly less confident that her logic makes any sense at all. So much so, in fact, that Gem has come to the conclusion that the only person Uncle Mike might need to go sort out is Gem herself.

'Kids these days.' From the looks of things, Uncle Mike is going to be shaking his head for a long time. 'I still don't get why you would do something like this.' All trace of Neanderthal is now extinct. 'You must've had a good reason.'

His tone is pleading. It's difficult to watch someone like Uncle Mike – who Gem wants to make proud – look at her like he's disappointed.

'I needed the money.'

Admitting the reason is almost – but not quite – as difficult as watching Uncle Mike's belief in her falter.

'What for?' This question comes from her mum.

Gem freezes. If Mike is the good cop, her mum is definitely the bad one. She should look into a career as an interrogator. As Gem contemplates yet another difficult answer, the only noise that escapes is an unintelligible mix of all the vowels. This time, her reason to keep quiet has nothing to do with a feeling of guilt or shame. Once again, her mum is about to ruin a surprise.

'I don't want to tell you.' The sentence comes out, but not easily.

There is a beat of silence.

'Gem.' Her mum's tone makes Gem sit up straight. 'Are you doing drugs?'

'Mum, no!' The strongest drug Gem has ever taken is Diet Coke. 'I've bought you a really cool chair. It's super lightweight and manoeuvrable so you can try out wheelchair dancing. I thought you could dance again. Maybe even teach. I thought it would be fun. I don't think I can afford the final payment on it now though. Not without Tee paying me.'

But as soon as the confession is out, Gem realises her mistake. Her mum knows she isn't doing drugs. This was just another interrogation tactic. Accuse the prisoner of something bigger, so they confess to the smaller crime.

'Gem—'

'It's really cool, Mum.'

'I don't care about not having a really cool chair, Gem. I care about how you got yourself into this ridiculous situation in the first place, and then dragged Atlas into it too.'

'I know, OK. I know it was ridiculous.'

Gem's confusion morphs into something else. Desperation? Anger? A desire to save as much face as possible in a truly ridiculous situation?

'But when I agreed, I didn't know what was going to happen. Do I regret what's happened? Yes, of course I do. I never wanted to hurt Atlas.' Gem pauses before confessing. She might not have been doing much work over the last few days, but she has been doing a lot of thinking. 'But if I had listened to my intuition and not dated him, I wouldn't have hurt him, and you wouldn't have been hurt either because I would have picked up my phone. So, it isn't all that ridiculous in the end, is it?'

'What does that mean?'

'If I hadn't been with Atlas, I would have picked up my phone on that first ring. I could have gotten here quicker to help you. I might've even been here to reach for that stupid bowl in the first place. We were so lucky that all you did was sprain your wrist, that you didn't hit your head that hard. It could have been so much worse. I would never be able to live with myself if something really bad had happened. Not again. And not when I could have easily prevented it. I should never have been with Atlas in the first place, and your accident just proves my point.'

Gem had played ignorant when her mum pointed out her hair and the bags under her eyes. But she knows better than anyone that she hasn't been sleeping. For the last week, her sleep has been plagued by the same nightmare, over and over again. The one where she's walking into her mum's hospital room for the first time after her car accident, Uncle Mike behind her, his presence doing nothing to stop her feeling scared. The dream has the same effect now as the real scene did at the time. As young as she was, she knew that their lives had just shifted violently off-piste.

In that moment, she remembers making a promise to always protect her mum. And it's that promise – thanks to her feelings for Atlas – that she's broken.

'Gem.' Her mum reaches out a hand and places it over one of Gem's. 'I love you. More than anything. But don't use me as an excuse.'

Gem glances up.

Her mum looks as though she is swimming, the lower half of her body all distorted. It takes Gem a moment to realise that her mum is still completely dry and that Gem is the one that has started crying.

'They were both accidents. The second one was particularly stupid and had absolutely nothing to do with you or who you were with or what you were doing. It isn't up to you to look after me, and you have to stop protecting me. Apart from the fact I don't need you to, I don't want you to either. For your sake, or for mine. In protecting me, you are hurting yourself, Gem.'

Her mum gives her hand the lightest of squeezes. 'I know you worry, and I know that it helps you to know that I'm OK, but I am capable of looking after myself. I'm an independent person, Gem. Don't take that away from me.'

Gem's mum reaches out a hand to wipe away her tears. 'I didn't have a child because I wanted someone to look after me. I had a child because I wanted someone else to experience the magic of life, with all of its ups and downs.'

She brushes another tear away with her thumb.

'I wouldn't be much of a mum if I didn't encourage you to go out and live that life, now would I?'

Chapter 44

Gem has barely opened the door to their flat when she hears her name being called.

'*Gem?*'

She's not even inside when Shanti tackles her into a hug that has the two of them falling against the door for support.

'You're back!'

Shanti mumbles this into Gem's hair, as Gem mumbles back into hers. She feels bedraggled from lugging her stuff across town. She knows her hair is falling out of her bun, and not in a sexy way, but in more of a crazy scientist way, and her sweatpants are so bent out of shape that they make her look like she is sitting even when she's not. But still, she is glad she made the journey. It feels right to be here. Home.

'I'm back.'

Shanti pulls back a bit to look at Gem, as if she's making sure that her friend is really here. Her grip on Gem's shoulders is so strong that she wouldn't be surprised if she's bruised.

'How are you? How is your mum? How are things with Atlas?'

Gem knew all of these questions would come, but she had hoped they would come a little later or at least a little further into the flat. Having cocooned herself at her mum's, the outside world doesn't feel real to her. It feels a little post-apocalyptic.

'Can I come all the way in and maybe sit down?'

Apart from anything, Gem is still wearing her jacket, and no casual conversation has ever been had while wearing outdoor clothing. It's too crinkly to be conducive to emotions.

'Oh, God! Yes.'

Shanti finally lets go, but as Gem puts down her bag and takes off her jacket, she feels like she's being tracked. Not in a hunted way, but in the way of someone who doesn't want their friend to disappear again. Shanti isn't wrong to worry.

'Lounge?' She asks the question, but she doesn't wait for an answer.

As soon as she walks into the room, she realises that maybe she should have waited for an answer. The lounge – all except for Gem's sofa, which is untouched, almost like a shrine – is totally destroyed.

She stops to take it in before turning to Shanti.

'Is there any fabric left in London?'

Shanti's smile makes her look like she's just been caught with her hand in a cookie jar.

'What can I say? I had so much nervous energy worrying about you, I had to do something.'

Gem looks back at the room. She can see cut-offs of fabric, dresses, skirts, jackets, shirts, embroidered dragons, sequins and what looks like a fabric-dyeing station. 'I can see that. What is all this?'

'No, you first.'

This isn't a request that Gem can deny, especially as Shanti drags her over to Gem's sofa, pulling her to sit down with her. Their lounge is about to witness yet another formative moment.

Her mum's words are still ringing in her ear, but so are her latest theories.

'The ick is real. And I'm gonna tell you why.'

*

No matter how many times she tells the story, it doesn't get any easier or sound any better or make any more sense. In fact, Gem's aware that it is getting more difficult to explain, sounds progressively worse and makes even less sense.

'So basically, my ick was telling me the truth all along. I should have stayed away from him.'

Shanti is looking so confused that she looks constipated.

'If I had, I would have been with my mum, or at least I would have been able to get to her quicker.'

Shanti squirms, but it does nothing to shift the look off her face. 'Are you sure that this is, well, the right conclusion to have come to?'

'What do you mean?' Gem has been so passionately defending her position that she hasn't noticed that the only person in the room even vaguely convinced is herself.

'Well,' Shanti goes into full-on therapy mode, her voice deepening and her movements becoming slower and more thoughtful, 'I think you are almost there in revealing the true reason for you getting the ick, but I think you need to follow the thought process through. I don't think you're quite at the end of the story. Is the ick telling you to stay away, or are you using the ick as a scapegoat for staying away?'

Gem's brain starts to hurt, right by the temple. 'What do you mean?'

Shanti has obviously reached the end of her patience, waiting for Gem to wake up and face reality. 'Don't you think that you have some serious commitment issues because you're worried about not being there for your mum? And maybe you're also worried about inviting someone else into your family, just in case they don't fit? Or in case they see your mum in a way you don't want her to be seen? You've protected her for a long time. It's understandable. It's essentially you two against the world. You've been through a lot together, and you love her. She is your mum. But you shouldn't protect her by hurting yourself.'

Gem inhales in preparation to reply, but instead her breath catches, a frown forming. There is a good minute of silence before she speaks again.

'Shit.' She looks up at Shanti, only now realising that while she's been thinking, she has also been doing her best to dig a hole into the arm of the sofa. Her hands immediately still. It takes a surprisingly short amount of time for her world to come crashing down around her.

'The ick is total bollocks.'

At Gem's admission, the whole room seems to get bigger.

'I'm afraid I think it is, my friend.'

'Shit.'

'So ... are you gonna try to get Atlas back?'

Despite her personal growth, Gem is as resolute as ever. 'No.'

From the way that Shanti smarts, Gem can tell that her answer is not what her friend expected.

'Don't you at least want to try? I thought you liked him?'

'Not trying to get him back has absolutely nothing to do with me not liking him, and whether the ick is real or not doesn't affect anything. All it does is make me feel even more stupid.'

'You are not stupid.' But Shanti doesn't exactly sound convinced.

'I am,' Gem insists. 'And of course I like Atlas. I love Atlas.'

Shanti smarts again. 'But there's no point. He isn't going to forgive me, and quite frankly I think he's probably better off without me.'

'Gem, babe.' Shanti has been unusually quiet throughout the whole of Gem's explanation. 'You need to speak to him. Try to explain.'

'I just don't think there's any point.'

'There absolutely is. Especially if you love him.' She leans her head closer, forcing Gem to meet her gaze. 'Do you love him? Really?'

'Yes.'

Shanti smiles at her reply, but before it can grow too big, Gem stops her with a dose of reality. 'But he's not going to forgive me. And he shouldn't. There are some things that are just too big to forgive.'

Shanti's look is assessing. 'Well, even if he doesn't forgive you, he deserves an explanation.'

'That's exactly what my mum said.'

'Well, she's a very wise woman.'

This time it's Gem who squirms. They're right – Atlas does deserve an explanation. Her reason for not trying lies somewhere else.

'I just don't know if I can face him again. He was so hurt.'

At the memory, Shanti inhales as though someone has just rubbed alcohol over a cut. 'He was.'

Gem levels at her friend. 'You're not exactly making me feel better, ya know?'

Shanti shrugs it off. 'I'm not trying to make you feel better. I'm trying to make you do the right thing.'

A heavy weight settles in Gem's stomach. She doesn't say anything more, but the look on her face tells Shanti all she needs to know.

Her goal now complete, Shanti visibly relaxes. 'Let me know if you need me to help.'

'I will.'

'Good. Speaking of which ...' Shanti's voice turns from being resolute to being softer than Gem normally hears it. 'Gem, if you needed the money for a chair, I would've given it to you. Apart from the fact I love you, I love your mum too.'

'I know, but I'm not going to ask you to do that.' She is, after all, as independent as her mother and Shanti knows that. 'Speaking of which, I'm really sorry but I'm gonna have to stop coming to dance.'

A look of utter devastation crosses Shanti's face. 'What? Why? But your hips are finally moving like they need to! And your hands!' Shanti grabs one of Gem's hands and splays it out. 'They are finally looking alive, and less like dead, dried fish!' The sadness in her eyes is so powerful that Gem immediately tries to placate her.

'It'll just be for a few months. Maybe a year. I need to pay off the rest of the chair, and now that I won't be getting paid the final two instalments for taking part in your dissertation, I need to save money somehow.'

For as far back as her memory goes, Gem has always taken dance lessons. It will be an adjustment to miss out on them. But she can still dance. Maybe not in the lounge, unless Shanti moves all of her stuff, but there is always her bedroom. And its five square feet of unused floor space.

'What do you mean you won't get paid the last two instalments?'

'I assume you're going to have to remove me from the study. Apart from the fact I broke the last condition by telling Atlas, I really fucked everything up.'

Shanti sighs. 'You have two good points there. But,' she pauses almost as soon as she starts talking, 'well, I've kept you in the study anyway.'

Gem freezes, not letting herself believe the words that she just heard. 'You what?'

Shanti shrugs, as though what she is about to say doesn't completely alter Gem's outlook on life. For the better. 'I've kept you in the study. If you haven't received the second instalment, let me know and I'll chase them. And then I guess the last should be coming in another week. Ish.'

Gem is still defrosting. 'Is that, like, allowed? If you get found out, won't you be, like, disbarred or something?' She really needs to brush up on her knowledge of exactly what it is that Shanti is doing.

'Well, it won't matter, because I don't plan on using my degree anyway. At least not in the long term.' A frown forms on Shanti's forehead. 'Or maybe even in the short term. Besides, technically you didn't really tell him. He overheard.'

'Wait.'

When Gem decided to come back to the flat, she knew that she would have a lot to update Shanti on, but she didn't know that her friend would have a lot to tell her, too. She looks around the room, her eyes landing on the half-dressed mannequin now wearing an outfit that Gem has never seen before. Patterned Lycra shorts and a top that looks like it might fall off, if not for an embroidered flower over one shoulder. The mannequin looks ready for the eighties.

'Does this mean what I think it means?'

The two friends look at each other, eyes wide, both slowly sitting up straighter, looking like they're ready to jump. Or scream. Maybe both.

'That I'm really gonna give the clothes thing a go?'

Gem nods.

So does Shanti.

The screams that follow are so loud that they can only just hear the knocking on the wall from their neighbours.

'Tee, this is great news.' Gem gives her friend a hug. Her new vantage point lets her see the room, and the mess, from a whole new angle. 'Is that the kitchen table halfway through the hatch?' Gem pulls away and looks at Shanti. 'Are we expecting visitors?'

Shanti once again inhales a bit too sharply to be natural.

'Yes. My parents are coming over. They'll be here in about an hour.'

This time, when Gem looks at the mess, she does so not with hope, but fear.

'OK. Right. Well, if we work together, we can get most of this put away. We can just shove it all in my room.' She starts to move, ready to spring into action, but a hand on her arm stops her.

'No, leave it. I'm gonna tell them.'

'Holy shit.'

Shanti just nods, completely in agreement.

'You want me to stay this time?'

Again Shanti nods. 'That would be ideal. You couldn't have come back at a better time.'

Exactly fifty-six minutes later, there is a knock on the door, swiftly followed by the sound of a key being turned. Shanti's parents have the same attitude as Uncle Mike when it comes to letting themselves into the flat. In fact, they are so efficient with the dodgy lock that Gem doesn't have time to reach the door, let alone open it before they come inside.

Gem, with a silently mouthed, *'Thank you. I owe you,'* from

Shanti, greets her parents just as they walk in. They have always liked Gem, and although her role in Shanti's plan is likely to slightly damage her reputation, it's a price she is very willing to pay.

'Georgina! Such a beautiful girl. Come here.' Shanti's mum, dressed in a bright purple sari, greets her with a huge smile on her face and a hug, all while managing to pass over a massive vat of food. 'Put that on a low heat. It's a simple Nihari. It needs twenty minutes.'

Gem heads through to the kitchen, giving a quick nod to Shanti's dad who is dressed in his usual outfit of pressed chinos, a shirt and a burgundy jumper. Shanti's mum walks straight to the lounge, her dad following a respectable distance behind.

Shanti's mum and Gem's own have always gotten on really well together. Gem has always thought it's because they both have that innate *motherness* about them. It's this that makes them both very skilled at homing in on exactly where the action is. It's this motherness, Gem knows, that has called Shanti's mum straight to the lounge, where Shanti is waiting, among the mess.

While Gem doesn't want to miss out on the action, or leave her friend abandoned, she also needs to follow instructions or risk making the situation worse. She puts the pan on the front right burner on the cooker and turns it on to a low heat, just as instructed. But as soon as that's done, she heads back into the lounge.

Luckily, or perhaps not, it looks like Gem hasn't missed a thing. Shanti is still standing exactly where Gem last saw her, and her mum, despite being very capable of slipping through small gaps and avoiding mess, is standing on the outskirts of everything. Assessing.

'What is all this?' Shanti's mum doesn't specify what *this* means, but then, she doesn't need to.

Shanti's dad is standing next to his wife. He is a man of fewer words than his wife, but that is not difficult.

'Mum. Dad. I've decided that I'm going to start a clothes up-cycling business.'

A silence fills the room. Not that it was particularly loud before.

Of course there is a lot more behind Shanti's declaration. The fact they are still at the early stages of looking into exactly what they need to do, and how on earth to run a business. They have a lot to decide on the split of responsibilities, the financials, price points, selling avenues, marketing plans, to list a few issues. But Shanti decided a simple, top-line approach would be best when speaking to her parents. Apart from sounding punchier, it also means there would be fewer holes for her mum and dad to pick at.

As the silence stretches on, and with twenty minutes until the food is ready, Shanti pushes for a response. 'Would you like to say anything?'

The silence continues. But then, Shanti's mum rotates, slowly, to face her father, a finger poised for action.

'I *told* you. I told you that we were tempting fate calling her Shanti. "Peace!"' Her arms throw themselves into the air. 'The irony!'

Her pointer finger is still out, and she appears and sounds quite angry.

And yet Gem and Shanti share a look, because although her voice is raised, Shanti's mum hasn't said no.

Chapter 45

'Is everything ready?'

Gem looks up from her most recent spreadsheet.

'Yes.' At least for the meeting that Martin is concerned about. 'The report's done. I sent it to you about an hour ago.' From memory, he was eating a croissant at the time. Blowing onto his keyboard between every bite to get rid of the flaky pastry.

'Great.' Gem can hear his clicks and track his eye movements as he minimises whatever was taking up his attention – using the entirety of its limited span – and opens up his email. Gem already has the report ready to resend, knowing he won't be able or bothered to look that hard to find it. He squints at his screen.

If only the other aspects of her life were as predictable as Martin.

'Gemima, would you mind resending that report, please? I can't find it.'

Already prepared, Gem sends the email before his request is even complete.

She can hear it as it wooshes into his inbox and unmuted computer.

'Ah, yes. Here it is, thank you.'

She tracks his eyes as he reads through the report, clicking through the usual slides. She started perfecting this little trick as a way to pre-empt questions about the report itself. She wanted to be as ready as possible if Martin was going to ask her to change something, or to explain how she came up with a particular figure. That was way back when she thought being good at your job would be enough of a reason to get a promotion.

But today, she's tracking his movements so she can answer his questions as quickly as possible so she can leave the office as quickly as possible.

She doesn't know quite how her evening is going to play out, but she's going to be prepared in the hope that it turns out the way she would like it to.

Finally, she can see the last slide reflected in Martin's glasses. She made sure to add in a distinctive blue box. It's a bit of a clunkier look than she would normally go with, but she wanted to make sure the ending was as easy to spot as possible. Gem's computer takes quite a while to shut down these days, but knowing he's reached the end of the report without asking any questions means she is in the clear. Martin isn't known for holding back when he spots a mistake or has an idea for how to make something better. Gem assumes it's because both types of thought occur to him so infrequently that he has to capitalise on them whenever they do.

'Looks great; thanks, Gemima.'

'My full name is actually Georgina, but no problem.' Martin's eyes widen at being corrected, but Gem just smiles. Hopefully he will mistake the happiness in her voice for job satisfaction, instead of relief that she will be able to leave early, and pride in herself for finally setting him straight.

*

Once again, she takes the stairs to leave the office. She slips past two people who definitely look like they are having an illicit affair, and one other person who looks even dodgier. He looks like he is actually *enjoying* walking up the stairs.

Today, the mundanity of her job has definitely come in handy. It means she was able to concentrate on other more important things.

Namely, her plan to Explain Everything To Atlas.

Unlike her job, which used approximately five of her brain cells so far this week, this plan has required a lot of thought, preparation and bribery. It also contains a second, secret plan to Get Atlas Back.

Of course, this second part is only known to Gem, and only deep in the subconscious parts of her mind. Every now and then, a hopeful thought slips through into reality, but Gem is careful to bury it as quickly as possible. She can't let herself think that maybe he could forgive her enough to go out with her again. The pain caused by the disappointment if this didn't happen would be impossible to recover from. Gem would probably just disappear on the spot. And not in a magical way. She'd slowly melt. Like a sad ice cream.

All of the big pieces of the plan are already in place or have at least been put into action. She only has one small errand to run – to pick up the special order cake she has bought – but she's left work in plenty of time to collect it and to get it home safely on a relatively empty tube.

As she reaches the bottom of the stairwell, just before she pushes out of the fire door, she checks her phone, both to double-check where she is going, and to triple-check that she hasn't missed any messages. There's still nothing from Shanti. They stayed awake all Sunday night coming up with a plan, the Nihari fuelling their study session instead of their usual snacks. But Gem isn't worried at the silence. At least, not *overly* worried. She has faith in her friend.

If anyone can convince Shauna to get on board, it's Shanti.

And if anyone can convince Atlas to let Shanti take over the football coaching session, leaving him free to make his way over to their flat, it's Shauna.

She even made him an invite. One of the ones where you just have to write in the details, little ellipses left blank for your awful handwriting.

Gem pushes out of the door, and turns left, blinking her eyes as she walks into the midday sun. She keeps walking until she meets the alley that she is looking for, where her phone is directing her down, and then keeps walking some more.

Maybe when Shauna is old enough, they can employ her in their clothes business. She would make an excellent debt collector. Gem pushes away that thought. She has a few things to get sorted, and she doesn't need any more distractions.

She strides a few more feet, but then she stops, abruptly, even though the bakery is still about fifty feet further ahead.

She hadn't realised, but it is down the same alley as Madame Sybil, the fortune teller who warned her that nothing good would come of her date with Atlas. Which, as it turns out, was a good call. It was going OK there for a while, but not so much any more.

She checks her watch. Gem has half an hour before the bakery closes, giving her plenty of time to have a second reading. Before she can change her mind, she looks around for the shrouded entrance.

But it isn't there.

She checks her phone, and double-checks where she is.

Without realising, she's stopped right in front of where Madame Sybil's shop *used* to be, but it has been totally transformed. Long gone are the dark purple curtains, and instead, in their place is a very open, very bright-looking stationery shop.

Unable to resist, Gem makes her way inside. The bell is still hanging in the doorway and is still unnaturally loud. But this time, instead of alerting Sybil, a tattooed, bespectacled person looks at her from behind the counter, offering her a quiet smile that Gem tries to reciprocate. Being London, that is as far as the conversation goes, and so Gem is free to look around, if not exactly feeling welcome to do so.

Everything is neatly displayed, organised firstly by colour. She makes her way over to the red table. It's just the kind of shop where she would have spent all of her money as a child. She has a huge urge to try all of the pens, but because she is an adult, she only tries one of them – a purple-ink, faux fountain pen – smiling when it glides smoothly over the tester paper. She puts it back, but as she does so her eye alights on something else.

The shop is pin-droppingly quiet, so Gem tries to walk as silently as possible. Unfortunately, her trousers are definitely not a natural material, and so she makes a slight hissing noise with every step, stopping when she reaches the display and the item that has caught her eye.

She picks the item up. It has a nice, comforting weight to it, feeling solid in her hands. She opens it up, just to see what it's like inside, and runs her fingers over it, enjoying its smoothness.

She doesn't need it, but the subconscious part of her mind tells her that someone else might. Maybe. One day.

Before she can think too much about it, or even before looking at the price, she takes it over to the counter.

The smile she gets from the person behind the desk is the same as before.

Breaking with tradition, Gem speaks.

'Didn't this space used to be a fortune teller?'

'Yep.' The person behind the counter simply nods and points towards a notice.

> Due to unforeseen circumstances, I have
> had to relocate my services.
>
> MADAME SYBIL

'You should have seen the stuff we had to clean out of here. Weird stuff. Tiny bags full of those animal erasers. Sold them all on, but it was weird.'

Gem, wisely, just nods back, appreciating the safety that silence can sometimes give you.

'That'll be £24.99.'

At the extortionate cost of one item, even more than her original fortune telling, Gem stays silent. Her subconscious, getting louder and louder, simply tells her that maybe it will be worth it. She gives a final smile at the clerk before leaving, the bell once again ringing her out.

Outside, Gem heads back to the bakery, and not a moment too soon.

Her phone pings with the message she's been hoping to see all day. It's from Shanti.

The party's on.x

Her subconscious does a happy, if nervous, little dance all the way home.

Chapter 46

Gem has stage fright.

It's the first time she's ever experienced the feeling while standing in her own home, but it's there. Her palms are sweaty. Her heart is pumping way too fast, and her breaths are too shallow to sustain her body for much longer.

Shanti has confirmed that the handmade invitation was delivered to Atlas and that he'd left football practice before it began, but she still doesn't know if he is going to turn up.

A party at her own flat seems a little retro, but apart from the fact it's been impossible to find a private room on such short notice, the idea of an audience watching her get her heart broken isn't very appealing.

Gem's pacing the room, completing the same circuit she's been doing for the last hour. She looks at the clock on the wall. OK. It's only been ten minutes of pacing. But it feels like longer. He's half an hour later than he should be if he was coming straight to her flat from the park.

When setting up the lounge – which is now acting as a party room – she contemplated music, or no music. In the end, she decided to get the music ready, but not actually press play. This way, similar to how she likes to keep an eye on Martin's moves by watching his reflection in his glasses, she will be able to hear if Atlas is coming.

She wants time to both race forward – she won't be able to function fully as a human without knowing how this is going to end – and stand still. At least now, in this awful moment, there is still an ember of hope that Atlas is going to show up and forgive her.

Her phone rings. It's her mum.

This time she picks up.

'Hey, Mum. You OK?'

'I'm fine. Has he showed up yet?'

'No.'

There is a beat of silence.

'OK. Well. Let me know how it goes. I won't call again. Sorry, I just ... wanted to check in.'

Gem can hear a noise in the background. It sounds suspiciously like Uncle Mike issuing another empty promise that nobody wants him to fulfil.

'Thanks, Mum.'

But before she can hang up, another noise comes through.

'Mum, it sounds like someone's at your door.'

There is another beat of silence.

'That's not my door, Gem.'

Gem freezes, and the knock comes again. It's a lot closer than she thought it was.

'I gotta go.'

Her mum's 'good luck' is barely out before Gem hangs up.

On the way to the door, in an effort to calm her heartbeat, Gem thinks the only thought that will make her heart beat a little more slowly.

It can't be him.

There is no way he would come.

It's probably their landlord. Or maybe a local politician. Or someone to read their electricity meter.

Anybody but who she really hopes it is.

But when she opens the door, her efforts are instantly wasted.

Because standing in her doorway is a man with a very, very large backpack and very, very blue eyes.

'Atlas.'

At once he looks like someone very familiar, and someone Gem has never met before. It's only been a couple of weeks since she has last seen him, but the memory of them in bed together contrasts starkly with the distance that is between them now.

He stays standing in the doorway. Despite the distance – both literal and figurative – Gem is itching to get close to him. All of her limbs are drawn to him, like a magnet, but she stops herself. He might have shown up, but he doesn't look happy about it. There is no hint of smile. No hint of dimple.

Despite the big bag, he looks smaller than he did two weeks ago.

He is still wearing his coaching outfit – shorts and a lightweight, long-sleeve sports top – which means he must have come straight from the park. Which means he's late, not because he had an extra stop to make, but because he didn't know if he was going to come.

He looks a little tired, like his eyes can't quite open fully, but apart from that everything about him looks controlled. Even distant. Only a single lock of hair is out of place, threatening to poke him in the eye. It's the same piece of hair that was trying to escape the first night she met him.

The hope that initially swelled when Gem saw Atlas lands heavily somewhere near her kidneys.

'Do you want to come in?' Usually when people ask this question, it's a formality. But not this time.

He still doesn't say anything, but thankfully he does nod, and after a few false starts, his body follows.

Gem's whole body reacts in turn as he walks past. Every pore is reaching out to get closer to him, like he has his own magnetic pull. Her fingers twitch, wanting to touch him. She had forgotten how good he smells, the mix of spice and fresh mint filling her lungs. How good it feels to have him so close by. She hadn't realised how quickly she had gotten used to him being in her space, but now that he is here, the loneliness she has been feeling really hits home.

Having him so close and yet not being able to touch him is a unique kind of pain. Her body is yearning to touch his, but he looks so hurt. All she wants to do is make him feel better, but seeing as she is the one who's made him feel this way, the best thing she can do is stay away. She should push him back out the way he came. And this time when he leaves, she should let him go.

But she can't.

Especially not with him so near.

She isn't strong enough. Or maybe she is too selfish. Either way, instead of pushing him away, she shuts the door behind him, making it a bit more difficult for him to leave, taking a little longer than necessary over such a simple task.

When she's done, her eyes follow Atlas as he walks down the hallway. He pauses as he passes the kitchen, as though he too is remembering what happened last time he was here.

That night had been the best night of her life. Images of her hands on him flash in front of her eyes. But the morning that followed was the worst. The pain in his eyes is a memory she is unlikely to ever forget.

Maybe having this conversation here is a terrible idea. A pub might be public, but at least that way her home wouldn't be forever tainted by more bad memories. She doesn't need to add an extremely unsuccessful apology to the memory of his leaving.

Resigned, and knowing she can't exactly stay in the hallway the whole night, she follows him into the lounge. Or at least, to the doorway of the lounge. He hasn't moved more than a step inside.

There are some ideas that should forever remain ideas, and it's only when Gem looks into the room with Atlas by her side that she realises throwing a party as an apology is one of those ideas. She realises that this whole idea is ridiculous. Even more ridiculous than the idea of being paid to date someone and thinking she would get away with it and that nobody would get hurt.

'I am *so* sorry.'

How on earth did she ever think this would be a good idea? She's cleared the centre of the room for Twister, and even hung a string of bunting. Who hangs bunting? Inside? Under the age of forty? And over the age of eight?

In contrast to the decorations, Atlas's mood is serious. They have serious things to discuss. The garish decorations sit uncomfortably against the feeling in the room. Why did Gem think it would be a good idea to *throw a party*?

'I ... This was meant to ... I thought it would be ... ' The irony of being unable to explain yet another situation isn't lost on her, but it doesn't make her laugh.

She moves forward, trying to block Atlas's view of the room. When she realises that this isn't going to work, she instead tries to figure out how to undo about four hours' work (not including any of the planning or sourcing time) in precisely ten seconds. Nothing comes to mind, so she turns back to Atlas, eyes firmly closed. She can't bear to look at him. She doesn't want to see the total disbelief on his face, alongside the hurt.

'I am so sorry,' she says again.

Eventually, she opens her eyes. She can't keep them closed forever. Especially not when Atlas has stayed silent, making the sight of him the only thing she has to go on to tell what he's thinking.

And when she does, she is met with an unexpected sight, and all the breath in her lungs leaves.

There is a very small hint of a smile playing on Atlas's lips. It's only on the one side of his mouth – the left – but Gem has seen him smile enough to know that this is how his best smiles start.

'What is all of this?'

Gem looks behind her, as though she's already forgotten about the ridiculous scene she spent hours meticulously setting up, and the last two minutes wishing she could forget.

'It's a party.' She shrugs helplessly. 'It was meant to be thoughtful and funny and show you how much I care about you.'

Gem watches as he takes in every inch of the scene behind her. She would look, but apart from the fact she already knows exactly how ridiculous it is, she also can't face the awkwardness.

'I can see now that a simple apology would've been better.'

Although Gem wants everything behind her to disappear, Atlas appears to be unable to look away. She watches, transfixed, as his eyes roam the room. She can't tell if she wishes it into being, but she swears that she can see the outer edge of one of his eyes start to crinkle. He even starts to walk forward, as though he wants a closer look.

Gem follows him as he goes. At first, he looks up towards the ceiling. She's created a – fairly impressive – balloon arch made out of white balloons that she's coloured in to look like footballs.

Then he looks at the table. She went back to the awful pub and bought three bottles of the terrible wine they shared on their second date. She also went to see Jay and bought all of the horrible fish-flavoured crisps he had left in stock.

She's propped up a whiteboard that she stole from work and has drawn up some football plays. She put the football pitch cake – the one she bought from the bakery near work – on white bowls that she turned upside down and also coloured in to look like footballs.

She even added little figurines to the cake.

She used the one that looks most like Atlas to score a goal, and the one that looks most like her to cheer on the sidelines. There is even one that looks serendipitously like Shauna.

'I tried to throw you an Atlas-themed birthday party.'

He picks up one of the presents from the pile, and then looks at her.

'Can I open it?'

Traditionally, her mum makes her wait until after the cake has been cut before she can open presents, but traditionally birthday parties are also thrown to celebrate birthdays instead of being used as apologies.

'Sure. Yes. Go ahead, they're your presents.' She wouldn't say no to anything he asked for. Especially now that some colour has returned to his cheeks.

When Gem sees which present he is reaching for, she nearly tells him to open a different one, but he's ripped the paper before she can say anything. It's the one she bought from the stationery shop this afternoon. A last-ditch attempt to make everything OK.

'A diary?'

But despite her worries, his glimmer of a smile hasn't faded. It emboldens her. She steps towards him.

'Yeah. I thought that way you could write down our dates, and your football practices and stuff. To avoid double-booking again.'

While Atlas appears to be rationing his words, they are flying out of Gem.

'Not that I didn't love going to watch you play. Far from it. I really loved it. I mean I still don't really get what was going on.' She swallows. 'With regards to the football. Or anything else, now that you mention it. But I'd love to watch you play again. If you'd let me.'

He still doesn't say anything, instead turning back to peruse the table.

The next thing he picks up makes Gem instantly regret all of her life decisions up until this point.

'Why is there a T-rex?'

He pivots to face her, the little figure pinched between his thumb and forefinger. It was one of Gem's more rogue ideas.

'I thought he was cute? And he kinda reminded me of you.' She won't lie to him. Not again. But on this occasion, she can see how the full truth might not be helpful.

Luckily, he puts the dinosaur back down without asking her any more about it.

'Nobody's ever thrown me a party before.'

The tone in his voice gives Gem even more hope.

'I'm so sorry.' She has more to say, but so far, this is all that comes out.

'You shouldn't be.'

He pokes a finger into the icing, tasting it. It's another brave move that Gem would never normally allow, but the sight also brings other, badly timed but not-unwelcome images into Gem's mind. 'This is delicious.'

'No. I mean, yes. I'm glad. Also, I'm sorry about the party. But I'm particularly sorry about the whole "dating you for money" thing and not telling you about the study.' She takes another step towards him, her body needing to close the distance. Her heart skips a beat when he doesn't move away. 'If you could just let me explain ...'

He shakes his head and closes his beautiful eyes. 'You don't need to.'

Gem shakes her head back. 'No, I do. Please let me.' She doesn't love the pleading note in her voice, but it's there anyway.

'No.' He closes his eyes. 'You really don't need to because Shanti told me everything.'

'She did?'

'Well,' he shrugs, 'the top line anyway. Enough to convince me to come here.'

Meaning he wouldn't have come otherwise.

'Plus,' his smile starts to widen, and this time there is no denying its existence, 'there was no way Shauna was going to give me that invite without some kind of hint. I think she might need an apology party more than I do. It's why I'm a bit late. Shanti had to work hard before Shauna would let me leave. I would have been earlier if it wasn't for her.'

Gem really owes her best friend. But then his smile fades once more, his face growing serious.

'I have some questions.'

'I will answer them all.' After the last few days, she has become really good at answering questions.

'Why didn't you just tell me? I would have understood.'

She should have known that Atlas would start strong. It's a question that Gem has been asking herself on repeat for the last two weeks.

'At first, I didn't really care. I mean sure, I felt guilty. I am human, but all I really thought about was my mum, and I genuinely thought that the ick was real. I've come to realise that everything I do, I do for her.' At this point, Gem does have to pause. 'Well. I mean, there are *a lot* of exceptions to this. My toastie innards are solely down to me. But my job I do for her. I kinda hate being an accountant but it means that I will one day hopefully earn enough money to help pay for her care. I know she's going to need it and I don't know where else the money is gonna come from. I kinda even dance for her. I love dancing, but part of the reason why I keep going is because I know that seeing me dance keeps her connected to it. And the study. I did it for her. Her chair broke, and I needed to buy her a new one.'

She looks at Atlas, taking a beat to see if he is still following. Unlike Gem's eyes that can't keep still, his appear to be glued to her.

'And *the ick*. I keep people away because I don't want anyone to take me away from my mum. I never want to let her down again, and I did, or at least I thought I did, when I was younger. It was a real struggle to look after her when she first got back from hospital after her accident, but if I had been better at caring for her, she could have been home quicker. She could have healed faster. Plus, I'm scared.'

This part of her confession comes out quietly. 'My mum, myself and Uncle Mike are all we have, and I am scared to break us. I don't trust people to see past her chair. And I never, ever want to put her in a situation again where she's uncomfortable about it.' Gem shrugs, unsure where to go next.

'But I'm sorry because I didn't give you enough credit. I didn't trust you. Nobody has ever hugged my mum the way you hugged her.'

This admission makes Gem's voice break. 'It made me think that maybe humans aren't all that bad.'

She licks away a tear that has broken free, travelling quickly down to her lip. 'But then I started caring about you – and it was too late. I couldn't see a way out that didn't lead to me losing you, and I didn't want to risk losing you. Which I realise is exactly what I did anyway.'

Finally, exhausted, Gem shrugs again, all of her main points covered, if a little messily. When the silence stretches, and Atlas doesn't say anything, she contemplates jumping through the hatch to disappear.

Only Atlas's continued presence is keeping her here. She won't leave unless he does.

'What was my ick?'

At his question, Gem's eyes flick to all available exits.

'Oh no. You don't need to ... It's ridiculous. It's not even a thing.'

Unfortunately, although her words don't answer, her eyes betray her, and they glance towards the hallway, Atlas's eyes following.

'My bag?'

Gem grimaces. 'I told you it was ridiculous.'

'What's wrong with my bag?' The tone he uses suggests Atlas is taking this very personally.

'It's just so ... *big*.'

The confession hangs in the air. But eventually Atlas's slightly lopsided face smiles, dimple and all.

'It does get pretty heavy.'

'Oh, I don't care about that, I just think it makes you look like a snail.'

As soon as she says them, Gem regrets her words almost as much as the party idea. She tries to save herself. 'But if it makes it any better, I actually now have a soft spot for it.'

'Just for the bag?'

Atlas's question makes Gem pause. Could he really be forgiving her?

Her heart is yelling at her to jump in, with both feet. To tell him exactly how she feels and to risk it all. Her head is telling her to be cautious.

Her heart wins out.

'No.'

It's time for Gem to be brave. 'I've really missed spending time with you. And I am *really* sorry. I am so sorry that I hurt you. I really did start this whole thing with good – if really naive – intentions. But I didn't know that I would end up loving you.'

The silence stretches out for longer than ideal for Gem's nerves. But then Atlas steps towards her and she notes some of the rigid formality of his stance has disappeared.

'Luckily, it turns out I'm a sucker for a party.'

Gem is finally able to breath, exhaling deeply.

'I understand why you did it. I probably would've done the same for my mum. Or my dad. But next time – not that I want you dating anyone apart from me, even if you're pretending – just let me in on the details.'

'That I can do.'

Atlas closes the distance between them, and like two pieces of a perfectly fitting puzzle, she reaches up just as he leans down, not quite touching. He is close enough that she can feel his breath on her skin, and although it's impossible, she swears she can feel his heart pounding. They are so close that when she looks up and into Atlas's eyes, Gem can see that they aren't just blue. There are also flecks of gold in them. She never wants this moment to end, but at the same time, her body yearns to touch him.

Before she can, Atlas stops her with a question.

'Can I open another present now?'

Having never thought he would be this close again, Gem doesn't want to step away. But she does, dying a little inside at the continued lack of physical contact. 'Of course you can.'

She moves towards the table and the rest of the presents. But she doesn't get the chance to move far.

For the first time in what feels like forever, she feels Atlas's hands on her. He touches her lightly, his fingertips at her elbow, but it is enough to make Gem stop. And when she feels a slight increase in pressure, a request, finally, she turns towards him.

It feels amazing to be touching him again, and now that her body has remembered what he feels like, she can't stop. She reaches her hands out, finding their place on either side of his hips, holding on to him as tightly as possible. A natural reaction designed to make it impossible for him to get away.

But luckily, she and Atlas are on exactly the same page.

He winks at her. It's a move that used to make her squirm, but now she's so glad to see it. Then he leans down, planting a soft kiss right in the middle of her forehead before whispering in her ear.

'I had a different type of present in mind.'

Epilogue

'So, when do we get to eat the cake?' Atlas whispers in her ear. Even now, after a week of practically continual contact, it still sends shivers down Gem's spine, which is a huge shame as she can't currently do anything about it. Not when her mum, Uncle Mike and Shanti are all in the same room. Atlas's party last week had been an *intimate* party for two, but today, Gem's party feels much more traditional. At least for Gem. Atlas, though, still has no idea how to act at a party.

Uncle Mike is playing DJ with his phone while her mum and Shanti are huddled in the corner, no doubt discussing her mum's return to dancing, and Shanti's next designs. Her parents might not be fully on board, but her mum did come by the apartment yesterday to drop off all of her old thread that she said she no longer needed. Overall, it's a much better version of Gem's tenth birthday party, even though there is no special background to dance in front of.

'After the presents.'

She tries to tell him this on the sly, through a smile. A birthday party newbie, Atlas has been asking her all morning what the proper etiquette is. The party she threw for him wasn't exactly a good run-through. They had an *excellent* time, but it wasn't an event that Gem would be comfortable inviting anyone else to. A shiver travels down her spine and straight to her core. The memory of Atlas licking icing off her will remain one of her all-time favourite presents.

As the family albums suggest, Gem has had a lot of good parties in her time, but her Atlas-themed party will remain one of her favourites, mainly because it helped convince him to forgive her. The only thing she still feels a bit guilty about is that, despite all of her personal growth and all of Shanti's very sensible explanations, Gem is actually more convinced than ever that the ick exists. Not that she is about to confess this to anyone. After all, it did keep her away from everyone until she met Atlas.

'But you've already opened all of them.'

She turns to him a little bit more. 'There is one more.'

He looks towards the table. 'I can't see any more.'

'There's a hidden present.'

At this news, Atlas's eyes light up. He's going to absolutely love Easter.

'Do we get to find it?'

Gem shakes her head. 'No. We don't find it, although I know exactly where it is. Uncle Mike is sitting on it.'

Atlas looks over at Mike. 'How do you know? He looks the same as he always does.'

Gem glances over at him. He does look exactly the same as usual, although Gem knows he's made more of an effort. He is wearing his favourite T-shirt for the occasion. It's dark blue, and a slightly thicker cotton than normal. Shanti has promised to upcycle it as and when it gets too worn in its current condition.

'Because he's always the one to hide the present, and he always hides it by sitting on it.'

'So let's go get it.' Atlas starts to stand, but a quick hand on his thigh is enough to stop him.

'No, I don't go get it. I get given it—'

'But you got given all of the other presents.'

'Yes.' Gem loves Atlas, and all of his questions are valid, but she does also currently wish that he would stop asking them. Hopefully he will get the hang of it quickly. She hopes that they will have many more birthday parties in his future.

'This is different. It's more like a forgotten present, rather than a hidden present. After an unspecified amount of time, just long enough for everyone to relax, but not long enough for everyone to get bored, I have to suggest getting cake. At that point, and not before, I get given the present.'

Atlas falls quiet and Gem's relieved the questions have stopped. Then, he adds, 'Birthday parties are weird.'

Although this isn't a question, Gem does answer. 'Yes. They are.'

'I absolutely love them.' For the first time, Gem risks a look at Atlas. She still can't believe that he's all hers. 'And I love you too.'

His words make her smile from the inside out.

'What are you two lovebirds talking about over there?' Uncle Mike seemed even more relieved than normal to hear that everything has worked out between Gem and Atlas and that no 'sorting out' is going to be required.

'Actually,' Atlas finally looks away from her, releasing her from his spell, 'we were talking about you.'

At Atlas's answer, Gem freezes. The biggest thing about the hidden present is that everyone has to pretend that nobody knows anything about it. She really hopes Atlas doesn't risk his first family birthday. She doesn't want to have to pick sides. She doesn't know if she could.

'I was just saying to Gem that maybe I'll take you to Charlton's next game.'

At this, Uncle Mike looks so chuffed with himself, like he was the one to introduce Gem and Atlas. 'I could be open to that idea. They're shit, but it's always good to be charitable.'

'Great.'

'Good save.' This is whispered, but the squeeze Atlas gives her knee tells Gem that he heard.

Although Gem knows the *unspecified* amount of time hasn't yet passed, she fears that Atlas won't last too much longer before he goes hunting for the present himself.

'Shall we have some cake?'

Her question cuts through the rest of the party and everyone turns to her and stops what they're doing. A scowl forms on Uncle Mike's face. He hates it when he doesn't get to play his role for as long as he wants to. It might be Gem's birthday, but it is everyone's party.

Fully committed, Gem stands up to play her part. She even starts to walk over to the cake.

She is less than halfway across the room when a cry of pain – heavily exaggerated and completely fake – comes from Uncle Mike's corner. Right on cue. He winces, grabbing his side, as though he is in actual pain.

The only one who reacts is Atlas. He jumps up from his seat, rushing over to Uncle Mike, totally unaware that it's an act.

'Are you OK?' Atlas kneels down, one hand swiftly going to the pulse point on Uncle Mike's wrist, his other hand reaching up, and forcing Uncle Mike's face up so he can look in his eyes, making sure they are clear and focused.

It takes him a moment, but Atlas finally realises that nobody else has moved.

Suddenly, but subtly, his body shifts. He goes from looking in total control of the situation, to a little bit embarrassed. A flush blooms on his cheeks when he realises that everything is fine.

'What's all this about then?' Uncle Mike looks down at Atlas's hand, his fingers still gently pressing against his wrist.

'Sorry, every year I have to go through first-aid training, and I guess it just kicks in.' Gem smiles, as she vaguely remembers him saying that he was good in an emergency. It's inappropriate, but she has a huge urge to get him naked. For the second time today. 'I got carried away and forgot about the hidden present.'

Uncle Mike scowls again, but this time it's directed solely at Gem. 'You *told* him?'

Gem shrugs. 'He's never been to a party before. I had to tell him what was going on.'

Luckily, her betrayal is quickly forgotten when Uncle Mike's frown is replaced by the smooth glow of dawning realisation. 'So, you knew about the present, and you *still* thought I was in actual pain.' He grins at everyone in the room, but only Shanti laughs. Gem's mum rolls her eyes, knowing that this anecdote is going to be inaugurated into the Hall of Fame.

Slowly, Gem walks over to Atlas, touching him gently on the shoulder. As he stands, Uncle Mike shifts a little more to the side, reaching behind him for Gem's final, hidden present.

'Thank you.' She takes it from him, and he nods, smiling to himself in a way that lets everyone know he's still coming off a high.

Once again, Gem takes her place next to Atlas. Although he has no idea what's going on, it feels completely right that he is here.

But before she opens the last present, she stops and looks around. She really is surrounded by everyone she loves, just as she requested. Of course, they've had all the minimal requirements for a party – cake, music, presents and a tablecloth. But there have been no baby tigers.

Her mum is by the table.

Shanti is sitting on one of the dining chairs.

Uncle Mike is making mischief in the corner.

And Atlas is right next to her.

'Thank you, guys, for being here. This is all I wanted to do.'

Her mum smiles at her. A smile reserved just for Gem. Uncle Mike might have hidden the present, but Gem knows that this final gift is always one her mum has chosen. It's always a present that Gem never knows she needs, but it's always one that she cherishes.

Not wanting to cry, she turns her attention to the gift, which has been wrapped in football-themed paper, in honour of Atlas. It is fairly thin, but relatively strong. About the size of her laptop, but significantly lighter. As light as paper. Unlike all of her other presents, which she's ripped open, this one she takes her time with.

She runs her finger along one crisp fold and then another, until it is open. There is a layer of bubble wrap, which she quickly unfolds, and then she turns it over so it's face up.

It's a mounted map of the world.

She looks up at her mum, searching for an explanation.

'It's one of those maps that you can scratch out every time you go somewhere. So you know where you've been, and where you've got left to go.'

Her mum's eyes flick between Gem and Atlas. Gem makes the mistake of looking at him too. Atlas's eyes are swimming, and as soon as she sees them, Gem's own tears start.

'I thought maybe the two of you could use it. I think it's about time you both go on some adventures.'

The feel of Atlas's hand encircling Gem's makes the weight on her chest lift enough so she can breathe.

'Thank you, Mum.'

It's a small present, but to Gem it feels like a pretty big step. One that she is ready to take with Atlas by her side.

She turns to him, and he looks just as ready for the adventure as she is.

A Note from the Author

Rom-coms (which this book is, according to marketing and publicity and the publishing world as a whole) are often seen as being full of fun and humour and romance. And hopefully, you will find these elements within *The Ick*. However, I think that rom-coms (especially those that are emerging now in the 2020s) are also often the fiction books that are closest to resembling real life. As such, they contain more than just fun and humour and romance. They contain life, in all of its messy, complicated and nuanced ways.

And *The Ick* is no different.

There are bigger themes than just humour and romance in here. There is disability, money worries, race and GBH, to name a few. As a white woman with no disabilities, the stories captured here are obviously not my own. But as much as I love to write, I also love to listen. I am lucky to have friends from many different backgrounds, and friends who have experienced different lives to the one I have lived. I want to include all of my friends in my stories because they are an important part of my life.

Every one of the characters in this book deserves their own story, but as much as I want to include all of them in my books – as they are included in my life – I don't think it is my place to write their stories in full. I worry I wouldn't do the job justice. But if you read this book and feel that I haven't portrayed a topic in the way it needs to be portrayed, I am sorry, and I hope that if this is the case, you are spurred on to write the story yourself. We need stories from as many people and as many backgrounds as possible. Otherwise, how do we learn?

Acknowledgements

The biggest, and first thank you has to go to Christina. I simultaneously want to tell everyone what a great editor you are and how wonderful it has been to work with you, and also pretend to everyone that you don't exist, so I can keep you to myself. I had an absolute blast writing this book, and your support has been the main reason for this. Since day one, you have believed in me and my writing, you have given me boosts when I needed them, guidance when I steered off course, and support all the way through. You have also skilfully navigated the very tricky task of telling me when my jokes don't land. This isn't something I take very well, and yet, from you, I don't mind! Working with you has been an absolute dream. Thank you. A million times over!

BUT, Christina, as brilliant as she is, doesn't work alone. The whole team at Renegade Books has been amazing. Thank you in particular to: Eleanor, for working so wonderfully to make sure *The Ick* (and its writer) stayed on schedule, Millie Seaward, Izzy Warner and Hope Ndaba in Publicity, Emily Moran and Mia Oakley in Marketing, Caitriona Row and Ginny Mašinović in Sales, Charlotte Stroomer in Design – and the gods that be, Production.

Thank you also to Mallory for designing an absolutely flair

cover. I love it so much! When it came through, I was sitting in a Dunkin' Donuts car park, and almost threw my breakfast out of the window. Gem's expression is absolutely amazing. Thank you!

Huge thanks also go to Agent Becky and Agent Florence (who are both as cool as their titles suggest). Florence – thank you so much for looking after me while Becky was away growing an actual human! You took me and my quirks in your stride and handled it seamlessly when I dropped this nugget into your lap. As for you, Becky (*BECKY!*), I feel so lucky to have you on my side! Thank you. You bring such peace and support and happiness and that warm squishy glow you get when you go on a summer holiday to somewhere actually sunny! I don't know how you do it, but I am eternally grateful that you do! Also, big thanks to Harmony, who I know is a big support to both Florence and Becky. It was so, so lovely to meet you in person! Also thank you to Gosia, whose emails are (usually) my favourites. Without you all I would be totally lost!

I also need to send a special thank you to Mitali, who heavily influenced the character of Shanti with both her dancing and entrepreneurial skills. My memory is terrible, but I still vividly remember seeing you in the bathrooms at work, saying you were 'going to dance class'. At the time I had been picturing my own version of 'going to dance class', and have since learnt that you are a *much* better dancer than I am. Although this isn't difficult (I am a terrible dancer), the difference is really quite stark. I would suggest you write Shanti's book yourself, if you weren't already busy being the main character in your own story! If you are interested in hearing more about what Mitali has to say, she records an amazing podcast, *Brown Game Strong*, where she advocates for and skilfully showcases a range of South Asian creatives.

They can't read, but I'd be remiss if I left out a thank you to our Ozzie Bear and my little Ted. They are shit at reading (to be fair, they are dogs), but they are great supporters, even though they have absolutely no idea what they are doing, both of them living the blessed life of the completely naive.

This book – my third to be published – has been a while in coming, but throughout the silence, I have been so lucky to experience the warm support of a bunch of readers and book bloggers. Thank you so much to anyone who has taken a chance on me and the words I have muddled together! There are more of you out there than I can thank individually, but special thanks have to go to Ashleigh and Eleanor, who keep me entertained either via memes or reading suggestions. I hope very much that you enjoy Gem's story!

Thanks also to my writing community, in particular Mary, Abi, Nicola, Sophie and Amanda. Thank you for listening to me waffle on and occasionally lose my mind! This journey would be a lot more lonely without you.

A special thank you to Mrs Knott, one of my two beloved Mountain Mommas, who was kind enough to let me use her internet so I could email this book across. (Please kindly note that I owe you thanks for more than this!)

But the very, very biggest of thanks go to Mum and Drew Bear (the latter of whom will never, ever read this book despite not having the excuse of being a dog). Without you both, I wouldn't be me. Thank you for the hugs, the food, the clean bed sheets, the distractions and the buying of my books!

Bringing a book from manuscript to what you are reading is a team effort.

Renegade Books would like to thank everyone who helped to publish *The Ick* in the UK.

Editorial
Christina Demosthenous
Eleanor Gaffney

Contracts
Anniina Vuori
Imogen Plouviez
Amy Patrick
Jemima Coley

Sales
Caitriona Row
Dominic Smith
Frances Doyle
Ginny Mašinović
Rachael Jones
Georgina Cutler-Ross
Bukola Ladega

Design
Charlotte Stroomer

Production
Narges Nojoumi

Publicity
Izzy Warner
Hope Ndaba

Marketing
Mia Oakley

Operations
Kellie Barnfield
Millie Gibson
Sameera Patel
Sanjeev Braich

Finance
Andrew Smith
Ellie Barry

Copy-Editor
Aruna Vasudevan

Proofreader
Jill Cole